THE HALF-KNOWN LIFE

BY THE SAME AUTHOR

The Sunlit Stage

To my mother, Ornella

For as this appalling ocean surrounds the
verdant land, so in the soul of man there lies
one insular Tahiti, full of peace and joy,
but encompassed by all the horrors of the
half-known life . . . Push not off from
that isle, thou canst never return.

Moby Dick, Herman Melville

How mild, how equable, are sun and sea.
The lean, lithe body of my child at play
Is not distinct from its desire, and I
Acknowledge and inhabit no desire.

Woman on a Beach, Dick Davis

Athens, 1975

One

Interestingly, the girls met Theo on the day of the penis in the National Gardens.

It was midday, and they had stopped to examine the inscription on a bust when they heard 'psst psst psst' coming from the direction of the flower beds. At first only Lorna turned to listen: this sound had more or less accompanied them since their arrival in Athens, groups of men hissing on street corners and from pavement cafés; they were getting used to it by now, and besides Celia was too absorbed trying to make out the inscription on the marble plinth to take much notice.

'What's the upside-down V letter, Lorn?' she muttered distractedly as she searched for the glossary in her Frommer's guide. The Christian name she thought she'd cracked; Aris-to-te-lis, it looked like, which meant the upside-down V in the middle of the surname had to be an L, whereas the first letter, the one that looked like a B, she seemed to recall you pronounced like a V. How confusing to have an alphabet that only half resembled the English one, she thought, yawning.

A little apart, Lorna stared into the statue's sad eyes; a pigeon was sitting on his head and a chalky trickle of dropping streaked down his nose on to his stony moustache. Who was this man in a bow-tie? And why should

Celia want to find out his name? She felt disconnected from this day – from her whole life, come to that. Only those last few months at Newfield seemed vivid enough to break through. Though Celia, it turned out, wasn't too keen on reminiscing about school.

'Time to move on, Lorn, we didn't come all this way just to yak about Newfie girls,' she said as the coach bumped along the rutted highway. 'Come on, you haven't had a thing to eat since Vienna.'

She passed over the box of Ritz crackers they'd bought at Victoria coach station.

'At least have one,' she wheedled.

Obediently, Lorna took out a cracker and rolled it between her fingers like a puffy golden coin. The edge felt pleasantly bumpy, the surface dimpled and grainy with salt, but it was about the last thing she felt like putting in her mouth; she would just as soon chew the cardboard box. She took a bite; instantly it turned to a slimy paste which slithered down the back of her throat. The inside of her mouth felt as though it had been blasted dry with a hair-dryer, and something strange was going on with her swallowing reflex; that must be the Xanax.

They'd driven all night without stopping. Past Novi Sad, in a grey dawn, the bus broke down beside a gypsy encampment surrounded by the cooling towers of an industrial plant. As the driver got out to change a tyre, Lorna looked out of the window. The site was littered with rubbish: car parts, broken-up furniture, bicycle wheels, a pile of wooden crates. Women in headscarfs and plaits, and long, brightly coloured skirts, drifted like wraiths around the sleeping camp, squatting down on the ground as they boiled up pans of water on an open fire. Blankets and sheets were strung on lines between the sagging tumbledown huts; and in a pall of smoke, scarcely visible from the bus window, crouched some kind of shaggy, mythological creature, tethered to a tree. The creature raised its head and Lorna started back in terror. It was a bear, with a leather muzzle strapped around its nose; then the smoke cleared and she saw the chain was attached to a ring in its nose. The ground around the tree had been churned up into a kind of moat, and the fur of its loose-fitting coat stood up in muddy peaks. Lorna stared into its sentient, close-set eyes as though she were gazing into the darkness of her own soul. There could be no joy in this trip for her; she finally understood that.

'Psst, psst, psst.' This time they both heard it.

'What was that?' asked Celia, looking up from her book. It was siesta time, and in the midday heat the gardens were deserted, with only the rumble of traffic, sirens, hooting and the drone of scooters, encircling the park like a buzzy electric garland. A Greek flag fluttered above the parliament building, while a man pushing a wheelbarrow walked slowly across the tiled roof. From nowhere, it seemed, a tortoise had appeared and was shuffling dully across the white gravel path towards the shade of some bushes. Fascinated, the girls stopped to watch its progress; and that was when they saw the man.

Only his legs were visible in the grove of dwarf pine trees, his face and upper body screened by the branches. His trousers were bunched around his ankles, and in one fist he held an erect dark purple penis.

After staring at it for perhaps longer than was strictly necessary, the girls looked at each other – faces crimson, eyes wild with shock. Celia dropped her Frommer's guide at the foot of the statue (where it would remain until it was picked up later by a Greek-American seminarian who would donate it to his college back in Astoria); then, gathering up her knitted wool shoulder bag, she grabbed Lorna by the hand and pulled her down the silent avenue.

Without stopping, they ran, past the Botanical Museum with its red-tiled roof, and a white-haired old lady rocking a muslin-covered pram, past two lovers sitting opposite each other on the marble bench, their conjoined limbs forming a diamond of negative space, until they reached a little wooden bridge at the edge of a lake. Flocks of tame geese swarmed around their ankles, pecking at each other with their flubbery orange beaks. Shrieking with surprise, the girls ran stamping up the bridge and, panting, they held on to the wooden parapet. Down below, a woman in a head-scarf, wearing clogs and white ankle socks, was picking around the pale green mud at the water's edge; and at the sight of her straight-backed, big-bottomed waddle, the trail of obedient geese following in her wake as though playing Grandmother's Footsteps, the girls hooted even louder.

A sudden rent in the fug of Xanax, and Lorna thought she might die from the vividness of it. She looked at Celia and saw that the worried crease between her eyes (the same crease that hovered, unseen, over all her letters to the hostel, *Come on, Lornie, you can't let them beat you*, shadowing her face with doom the instant they laid eyes on each other at Victoria, and never letting up once throughout the four-day journey, not even for a second, so that on the bus she'd awake, time and time again, to find those troubled eyes upon her) had finally disappeared. They grinned at each other, newly friends.

'I'm starving,' said Lorna.

Later they sat in the park *kafeneion* beneath an arbour of vine leaves, listening to the trickle of a fountain as they ate their lunch. Celia too was ravenous; worrying about Lorna had taken her appetite away, and on some unconscious level she'd found it embarrassing to eat on her own.

The café was pleasantly tranquil; wood pigeons cooed throatily from the treetops, while in a corner a dog lay sleeping in the sun with its head between its paws. At the table beside them two men, one in a suit, the other bearded, in jeans and sandals, sat engaged in earnest discussion, while, a little apart, beneath the green painted shutters, a young man with a foamy, copper-tinted Afro and rows of wooden lovebeads wound around his neck sat reading a Penguin translation of Aristophanes's plays. Celia had noticed him the day before in the Plaka; black faces, she was coming to realise, were a rarity in this city.

They ordered Greek salads, cheese and ham toasties, and glasses of freshly squeezed orange juice.

'What the hell is *zabon*, anyway?' mused Celia as she scrutinised the menu. She was going to die if they didn't hurry up with the food.

'It means ham,' said an English voice behind them. Both girls turned around; and through a tumbling curtain of vine leaves, they caught their first glimpse of Theo.

He was sitting on a Vespa by a broken-down marble column; unusually, for 1975, he was wearing a linen suit and tie, though, as Lorna was the first to notice, the bottom half rather eccentrically consisted of Bermuda shorts instead of trousers. A worn leather satchel hung from one shoulder (later they would learn that his nickname among his all-male Syntagma café set was *Tahidromos*: 'Postman') and on his feet he wore expensive-looking penny loafers with no socks. He looked around thirty years old, thirty-five maybe, though it turned out he was over forty, with foppish dark hair, greying at the temples, and horn-rimmed spectacles, one of whose arms was held together with Elastoplast.

The girls would have differing recollections of this encounter. Lorna would mostly remember his legs, coming so soon, as they did, after those shocking legs in the bushes; while Celia's eye was mysteriously drawn to the headline of his week-old English newspaper, which happened to be 'Missing Earl Guilty of Murder', thus establishing a permanent, though unconscious, link in her mind between

Theo, Lord Lucan and home, which until now she had not even realised she was missing.

'Allow me to join you. My name is Theo.'

Without waiting for an answer, he got up from the Vespa and walked past the sleeping dog to their table. Pulling out a chair, he sat between them, just as the elderly waiter was bringing their food on a tray. '*Ena metrio, parakalo,*' he said in rapid Greek to the man, who with one hand was deftly tucking a paper sheet into the elastic cord hidden beneath the table top, and with the other thumping their plates down on to the cloth.

Right from the start, Theo seemed to understand that the girls came as a package, treating them as though they were merely two aspects of the same person (which to some extent they were). Intuiting Celia's peculiarly English hunger for all things unEnglish, he patiently translated the bits of the menu she did not understand ('*zabon*, you see, comes from the French *jambon*; we don't actually have a "j" sound of our own'), explaining, too, that his name was pronounced the Greek way. 'Tay-yo,' murmured Celia thoughtfully, as she rifled through her shoulder bag for a scrap of paper on which to make a note of this, whilst simultaneously discovering that her Frommer's guide was missing. (In the years to come she would look upon this as the seminal moment she ceased to be a tourist.)

For a while, Lorna was too busy eating to contribute much to the conversation. This, too, Theo seemed to understand, signalling twice for more bread when the basket was empty, and ordering a whole lot of other dishes besides, which they would never have thought of asking for themselves: mashed-up broad beans with garlic, tiny spinach pies and a bright pink fishy paste that he told them was made from cod's roe. (On hearing this, Lorna paused for an instant, looked up from her plate frowning, then doggedly resumed eating.)

When they had finished, and the elderly waiter had taken it all away, Theo ordered another round of *metrios*. (Celia was so thrilled to be finally tasting Greek coffee that she gulped hers down too quickly and came a cropper with the sludge at the bottom. Didn't they have strainers in this country? Coughing, and surreptitiously wiping the grounds off her tongue with her napkin, she made a mental note always to leave the last third undrunk.)

That evening, as they were packing their cases on the roof of the hotel in Omonia (which unbeknownst to them was a brothel, and where years later, in leaner, darker times, Lorna and Alexander would one day rent a room), they both agreed that it felt like they had known Theo for ever. Perhaps it was because he was half-English.

'At least if he tries to get jiggy in the new flat, we can tell him where to stick it,' giggled Lorna.

Celia didn't answer, so overcome was she at the double good fortune of having the old Lorna back once more, plus having encountered a proper home-grown Greek person, or at least a half-Greek one, *in their very first week*! She also felt retroactively worn out by the responsibilities of the last few days – running away from Newfield in the middle of the night, the reverse-charge battles over the phone with her father before he finally agreed to telex over some money; and for a while there she honestly thought she'd lost Lorna. Now at least they would have somewhere to live while they decided how they were going to survive in this city. To think that this time last week her most pressing worry had been how to smuggle in ciggies from the village when she'd been grounded!

Just then Theo came up to the roof to get their bags, rapping on the asbestos fire door, and politely waiting for an answer, before entering the sweltering corrugated-iron hut where they had been sleeping. He carried their cases down the stairs and left them in the lobby while he went to settle up with the woman behind the desk. The girls watched, transfixed, as the warty old hag shuffled off to unlock her cashbox and handed over their passports, all gold-toothed smiles and whiskery effusions; she even agreed they could leave their bags at the hotel until Theo sent someone round later to collect them. (Though until just a few minutes before she had been threatening to hand their documents on to the tourist police unless they paid up until the end of the month, having quickly cottoned on to the fact that they were both underage.)

Theo, too, became another person in Greek, gesticulating and exchanging pleasantries and jokes in the same wheedling, expansive singsong as the woman, as though they were long-lost relatives, or at the very least acquainted.

'The classes must be more integrated here,' hissed Celia as they watched him slide a hundred-drachma bill between the pages of the guests' register.

Outside the hotel Theo kickstarted the Vespa and the two-stroke engine stuttered to life. Awkwardly, the girls climbed on to the saddle behind him, Lorna in the middle, Celia at the back holding on to her waist.

They would do it this way for the next year.

Two

'You know, we could make our own way to Sounion,' suggested Celia thoughtfully, in the manner of someone to whom it had only just occurred.

'My treat,' she added somewhat unnecessarily, as in almost seven months Lorna had never yet been known to pay for anything.

But just then they heard the unmistakable putter of Theo's Vespa coasting around the bend into Propilleon Street, and Celia knew she'd missed her chance. Too late. She should have suggested it earlier, before Lorna flopped down on the divan for her siesta.

On the way to Cape Sounion, Lorna seemed to liven up a bit, and even did her favourite trick of pretending to be a fly. Holding still her many bangles, she trailed the plaited cord of her cheesecloth blouse along Theo's ear, creasing up with laughter each time he let go of the handlebars to irritatedly swipe it off.

Celia felt her heart quicken with joy; she adored it when the two of them ganged up on Theo. He could be so cocky at times, a real know-it-all, and to be perfectly honest, Lorna often seemed to forget where her true loyalties lay. Or ought to lie. Sure enough, Celia's joy was short-lived; for on a sharp bend past Lagonissi, Lorna leaned forward and draped an arm casually over Theo's shoulder – even though both girls were quite competitive about never holding on, no matter how bumpy the ride – where, infuriatingly, it would remain until they reached Cape Sounion.

The sun was setting as they climbed the slippery cobblestones up to the ruined temple. Down by the tourist kiosk, a group of hippies squatted on the ground, plucking softly at guitars. One of the girls had a baby tied on to her back in a ragged cloth papoose. Celia's heart lurched as she watched Lorna stare at the baby; for a moment it looked like she was going to stop, until from nowhere, it seemed, Theo appeared and clasped her firmly by the elbow. Obediently, Lorna allowed herself to be steered barefooted up the steep path to the ruined temple. For once Celia was glad of Theo's proprietorial hand on the small of her back.

'So as the story goes, Aegeus anxiously waited at Cape Sounion for his son Theseus to return from Crete, where he planned to dispatch the monster Minotaur or die trying. A signal had been prearranged: white sails upon return would indicate victory; black sails, defeat and mourning.'

'Professor Higgins to the rescue,' murmured Celia to no one in particular, hoping to rekindle her and Lorna's earlier complicity on the Vespa. Though in truth Theo's ancient history lectures were fascinating; if they'd been alone, she'd have been bombarding him with questions. Instead, as usual, she trailed behind them like a maiden aunt or chaperone. Why did it have to be this way, *why*? Celia asked herself for the hundredth time; though in her heart she knew the answer lay firmly with her. A triangle needed three sides to exist . . .

'Were the sails of the boat white or black?'

Theo stopped and turned around, beaming at Lorna's unexpected question. In the brilliant evening sun, the lenses of his glasses glowed like two orange discs.

'For various reasons, Theseus forgot to change the sails to white, and at first sight of the ship, grief-stricken Aegeus plunged into the sea which bears his name. This does appear to be the most likely spot for a fatal plunge,' he added thoughtfully, gazing down at the waters of the Aegean roiling and spuming on the rocks beneath them.

'I need a drink,' muttered Lorna, steadying herself on a sun-warmed marble pillar.

'I think we could all do with a nice cuppa,' said Celia brightly. She didn't like the expression on Lorna's face. Not one bit. Hopefully the hippies would have gone by the time they climbed down to the road. Slipping her arm around Lorna's waist, whilst resisting the urge to throw Theo a triumphant look behind her, she led her down towards the waiting Vespa.

At the seafront café in Glyfada, Lorna insisted on ordering a quarter-litre bottle of ouzo.

'It's made of grape skins,' she said stubbornly, folding her arms across her chest. 'Vitamin C.'

'Ouzo before supper? At least have a cocktail, or a gin and tonic.' Theo's tone was more irritated than disapproving; he had a surprisingly conventional side, Celia was coming to realise, and she could tell the elderly waiter's complicit gaze was making him uncomfortable. Still, it made a change from her being the one to nag Lorna about her drinking. Which happened to be getting worse by the day.

'Yum yum,' said Lorna, raising the glass of cloudy white liquid. 'Tastes just like Liquorice Allsorts.'

'*Stin yassou*,' replied Celia sourly. She suddenly felt exhausted.

Everything was a game to Theo.

He was obsessed with sports – fencing, squash, backgammon, but most of all ping-pong, which apparently he had once played on a national level. In every other aspect of his life, however, he was a kind of professional amateur – if that wasn't a contradiction in terms. (Which of course it was, but there was no other way of describing someone who was that serious about being frivolous.)

The only person he appeared the remotest bit devoted to was his mother, Maro, an intelligent, white-haired old woman who lived in a beautiful *belle époque* villa in the northern suburb of Kiffissia.

One afternoon he drove them to his mother's house for tea. At five o'clock a manservant brought toast and Gentleman's Relish and a plate of sponge fingers out on to the terrace, and poured them cups of Earl Grey from a silver pot with legs. Theo was extraordinarily attentive to his mother, fetching an extra cushion for her bamboo chair, then a Chinese shawl, embroidered with dragons and orchids, which he insisted on wrapping around her shoulders. The air was heavy with the scent of orange blossom and jasmine, which grew in a thick curtain down the garden wall.

His mother appeared amused by Theo's almost comical fussiness, smiling conspiratorially at the girls as he disappeared yet again into the house in search of the manservant for more hot water, but they could tell that in some way Theo was a disappointment to her.

'My son is a butterfly,' she murmured in her faintly accented English, as she accompanied them to the door. 'He has no talent for conclusions.'

'God knows what she thinks we're up to,' muttered Lorna as they watched Theo wheel the Vespa out on to the pavement. 'A bit of the old *Jules et Jim*, if you ask me . . .'

Celia was certainly under no illusions as to why Theo had befriended them; it was obvious he was just biding his time. Well, for that matter, so was she: two could play at that game . . . *We'll just have to see who blinks first . . .*

And while it was very nice – well, all right, more than very nice, downright amazing – that he had found them the flat in Filoppapou – *don't worry about rent, a cousin of my mother's owns the building* – and had set up a network of private-lesson students for her (Lorna was still too up and down to work), Celia sometimes wished they could have had a go at sorting things out for themselves in Athens.

That generosity of his was a golden cage. Surely she hadn't come all this way to exchange one man's tyranny for that of another?

At times, when she heard the putter of his moped on the pavement, ready to collect them for the evening's entertainment, her heart would flood with bitterness and she would look through the barred windows of the flat and wish they had never laid eyes on him that day in the National Gardens.

'So why don't you leave then?' Lorna asked Theo one afternoon at the lake.

She sat up on her striped sunlounger, the straps of her white crocheted bikini top bunched up in her hand, the other arm lying across her naked breasts. Her stomach was so flat that the taut crease of her belly button resembled the linked C's of the Chanel logo.

Celia flushed; like Theo, she'd been caught red-handed, staring at the sublime contours of Lorna's body. She turned away, refusing to meet Theo's smirk.

For a moment Theo appeared uncertain how to answer; then behind his horn-rimmed spectacles, his eyes flickered like a con man's.

'I mean it,' continued Lorna. 'If you think life here is so crap, why don't you leave? No one's forcing you to stay. Why don't you go and live in England?'

'I couldn't possibly leave you two girls to fend for yourselves,' blustered Theo. 'Anyway, I've got my research at the museum, and the ping-pong tournament season starts soon. Plus Maro's not exactly getting any younger, is she?'

'You're such a bullshitter, Theodore Montgomery,' Lorna said, before flopping back lazily on to the sunbed. 'The only reason you stay in Greece is because you enjoy feeling superior to everyone else here.'

But Lorna had got it all wrong; she didn't have a clue. Only Celia knew why Theo couldn't leave Athens.

Like her, he was a prisoner of love.

'*Ethó, eimaste,*' *we're here,* said Celia in halting Greek, as they turned the corner into Tsami Karatasou Street.

She knew Thalia, her student, would have preferred to converse in English during their walk to the flat (no doubt the real reason she had been so keen to accompany her teacher in the first place to collect the Proficiency past papers) but, selfishly, Celia felt her need was greater than her pupil's. Theo rarely lasted longer than a few minutes in the role of Greek teacher before losing patience with her mistakes, and at the end of the day, who else was there to practise with?

Searching in her bag for the keys to the flat, Celia rehearsed a rueful apology.

'*Signomi, tora tha milame Angliká,*' *now we'll speak English* – but, mid-sentence, her thoughts broke off into nothingness. Leering with shock, she stood on the pavement, unable to take another step. For there stood Theo's Vespa, parked on the pavement!

Bright, annihilating despair bleached through her veins. The shutters of the flat were ajar; Celia heard the clink of plates and cutlery, and the low hum of the radio in the background. The two of them were having lunch – except that Theo was at a ping-pong tournament in the Peloponnese. And he wasn't due back until the weekend.

Then, from nowhere, a capable stranger sidled into the foreground and took charge.

'*Signomi, Thalia, then echo ta klithiá,*' said the stranger apologetically. She even had the presence of mind to root around in her knitted shoulder bag in a pantomime of searching for the keys, and continued to converse in eerily fluent Greek all the way back to the Frontistirion in Pangrati.

But all that afternoon, it would rise to the surface in sickening waves. The sound of tinkling laughter, the image of the two of them lying on Lorna's divan bed, limbs entwined, in the cool underwater dusk of the basement flat. *But Lorna despises Theo, how could she be sleeping with him?* Because she's Lorna, that's how . . . Celia stood in the dusty classroom, piece of chalk in her hand. It was her they were laughing at, of course it was: *Oh Celia, she's such an old booby!*

When the lesson was over, she took the long way home, walking slowly through Zappeion and the National Gardens where they had first met Theo. The thing was to behave as normally as possible with Lorna; there was no point attacking her before she had all the facts. It was quite possible that there was an innocent explanation for Theo's presence at the flat.

Then, just as Celia entered the Plaka, a small firework of joy exploded in her breast. *It wasn't Theo's Vespa!* Of course – their neighbour Kyria Effi's son was home on leave from the navy, he too had a red Vespa. She really was an old booby! Unable to contain her delight, Celia stopped off at the *zaharoplastio* in Veikou Street to buy a box of Lorna's favourite pastries: fried *loukoumades*, *baklavá* and squares of eggy *bougatsa*. They would celebrate the misunderstanding with a feast!

Lorna was out on the balcony watering the pots of geraniums; she glanced up and gave a laconic wave of her cigarette as Celia turned the corner into Tsami Karatasou Street. Unlocking the metal front door, she entered the room and put the box of pastries down on the table. For once the flat was tidy; Lorna's sheets were folded up on a chair, and the elasticated tartan cover was stretched tight over her divan bed.

Slipping off her shoes, Celia switched on the gas bottle behind the stove and put the copper *briki* to boil on the hotplate. They would have the pastries out on the terrace with a nice pot of Lipton's tea.

'How was your day?' she called out to Lorna, as she punctured the tin of Nou Nou evaporated milk.

'The usual. Had a nap, went down to the shop for ciggies. Planted Maro's cuttings into pots. Oh, and I finished off that Castaneda book Theo keeps banging on about.'

'Talking of which, when *is* our ping-pong champ back?' asked Celia carefully.

She heard Lorna take a long whistling drag of her cigarette. 'Dunno . . . he didn't say. The weekend, I guess.'

Celia shivered. The power of the human imagination was awesome sometimes. This afternoon with Thalia her mind had tricked her into seeing what she most feared; she had to learn from this experience to be more trusting. Things were slowly but surely turning a corner; Greece was healing Lorna, she could feel it in her bones. Today she'd come back to find her dressed *and* the flat tidy – a first!

Pouring the water into the teapot, Celia reached up into the cupboard for a plate.

And that was when she saw them: Theo's horn-rimmed glasses on the floor beneath Lorna's divan.

Three

'Come on, Lorna, I haven't got all day!'

Lying in the dark, Lorna trailed her fingers through the coarse tufts of the sheepskin rug until she came to a knot. Through a gap in the shutters, she could make out Theo's sturdy calves flexing impatiently on the pavement above the window.

'I know you're in there!'

Naked, she got up off the divan and, slipping on Celia's towelling bath robe, walked barefoot along the cold stone floor to the lobby. Pulling back the catch, she opened the metal front door and, without greeting Theo, drew the robe tighter about her body as she walked back along the corridor to the bedroom. She stood in the dark by the window, listening to Kyria Effi beating the carpets on the balcony above her. How energetic that woman was! Her life a non-stop round of cooking and cleaning and going to market.

'Oh, and hello to you, too,' said Theo humorously, switching on the wine-bottle table lamp in its raffia basket. Sitting down heavily on Celia's neatly made bed, he stretched out his legs.

'How about a spot of lunch? If you put on a nice frock, I'll take you to Zonar's.'

Distractedly, Lorna shook her head, hunting around the

untidy flat for cigarettes. The desire for nicotine burnt her throat like a thirst.

'Or we could even go to Aegina for the day.' He looked at his watch. 'There's a hydrofoil leaving from Piraeus in about an hour.' She heard the sound of one leather-soled loafer drumming on the stone floor.

'I don't want to go anywhere, Theo,' said Lorna. The first words of the morning, and her voice sounded strange and croaky; she should never have got up to answer the door. Left alone, she would have taken another sleeping pill; effectively this day might never have happened.

In the end, she found a single bent Rothmans at the bottom of her bag. She held it up against the shutters to check for rips in the paper, while behind her she heard the scrape of Theo's lighter. He patted the bed and she sat down obediently beside him on Celia's stripy counterpane, leaning forward until her cigarette leeched itself to the flame. She inhaled deeply as the delicious smoke whispered and curled through her lungs.

'I guess we'll have to play indoors again then,' said Theo, cupping her breast in his hand.

Lorna shrugged, letting the robe fall open over one shoulder.

Four

'So, to what do I owe the honour?'

Celia just couldn't stop a cheesy tone from creeping into her voice when she spoke to Lorna. It drove Lorna mad, she could tell, but she couldn't help it. On some level, she still believed that if only Lorna could somehow *engage* with her surroundings a little more – not even fully, just enough to bring her out of herself – then Greece would work its magic on her too. 'I love Greece,' she murmured to herself, '*agapao tin Ellada* . . .' Even Theo said her accent was finally improving.

'I couldn't sleep. Those arsehole builders have been drilling since six.'

It was true; but Lorna usually managed to sleep through it anyway – if sleep was really what she did all day in the flat. *Don't start thinking about Theo's glasses under the bed . . .*

'Fancy a coffee?' She was at it again; why did Lorna always manage to make her feel sleazy?

'Yes, no . . . I need some water first.'

Celia peered closely at Lorna and gave a start; she looked dehydrated, her lips were puffy and pale, gummed together with dried saliva, and there were little green seeds of sleeping sand in the corners of her eyes. It was her fault; she had forgotten to leave a bottle of Loutraki by the bed before she went out in the morning. Lorna would never have found the multi-pack beneath the table out on the terrace.

'Quick, let's get you to a *periptero*.' Narrowing her eyes against the sunlight, Celia peered across the road. The nearest *periptero* was in the middle of the square, but she knew from experience that those lights didn't last long enough to make it even halfway across the road, and she wasn't sure if she was up to attempting the second half, freestyle, with a dopey Lorna in tow.

'Why don't you wait here. I'll bring you a bottle in a sec.'

'For God's sake, stop treating me like I'm a baby.'

Well, stop acting like one then, Celia felt like retorting, but of course she didn't. *You can't knock someone when they're down*, she said reprovingly to herself. *Wait till she's sorted herself out, then you can tell her a few home truths.*

She scanned the street, looking for a safe place to cross. *Stop, look, listen*, the lollipop lady used to teach them at school. Ha! Fat use the Green Cross Code would be in this jungle . . . *look right, look left, look ahead, look behind, and while you're at it check the pavement behind you for mopeds . . .*

They were called *papakia*, little ducks, after the squawking noise made by their two-stroke engines. Celia was in love with the Greek language; even the medallion men who spent their time hissing and leering at tourist women had a cute name – *kamakia*, harpoonists – after the nature of their occupation. (For some of them, spearing rich foreigners literally was an occupation; their sole source of income.)

'OK, quick – *now*!' Hand in hand, taking their cue from the pack of other pedestrians, Lorna and Celia stepped over the kerb. All around them, the waiting cars snarled impatiently like Formula One engines behind the starting line; they could feel the hot breath of the exhausts on their bare legs as they picked their way between vehicles. They didn't even make it a third of the way across before the lights changed; for a second it looked as though they would be swallowed up by the hungry Athenian traffic beast – a sudden howl of klaxons, men's faces leaning out of their cars, gesticulating to each other in mock indignation through rolled-down windows, skinny dogs snapping at the heels of moped riders – but, as Theo said, it was all for show: no one really wanted to end up in a police cell for knocking down a pair of tourist girls. *It's all for show, it's all for show*, panted Celia under her breath as she dragged Lorna on to the pavement. There – they had done it!

The *periptero* in the square sold everything: cigarettes, newspapers, combs, toothpaste, worrybeads, pens, lighters, nuts, nail clippers, soft drinks, condoms, dusty sunglasses, scuffed green lenses bleached by the sun, even imitation Casio wristwatches hanging from the roof like the hooked pieces of a Barrel of Monkeys game.

While they waited for the *periptero* man to finish his telephone conversation, Lorna tried on a pair of huge Jackie O sunglasses with white plastic frames. They suited her (everything did), drawing attention to her high, surprisingly intellectual-looking brow – Celia had to remind herself that Lorna had been something of a maths prodigy at school, she'd been on a full academic bursary at Newfield Hall – and the blunt, almost Asiatic hollows of her cheekbones.

'*Poli oreo!*' murmured the stallholder appreciatively, peering though a tiny gap in the row of rude magazines as he handed Celia her change. '*Efharisto,*' replied Celia, pocketing the drachmas and opening the bottle of Loutraki before passing it to Lorna. 'It's easy to remember the Greek for thank you,' Theo had told her that afternoon at Sounion. 'F. Harry Stowe – get it? – sounds like *efharisto . . .*'

Pouring some water into her cupped hand, Lorna threw back her head and splashed it over her face, then turned towards Celia. She was smiling – at least the corners of her mouth were turning upwards – but there was no fooling anyone with the expression in those light, blank eyes. Something was definitely brewing, but if Celia refused to acknowledge it, and instead made a big deal of the fact that Lorna was up and about, maybe she could coax her back into a more positive frame of mind.

'I thought we were going for a coffee?'

Celia looked at her watch. It was one o'clock; she had forty-five minutes before she was due to teach a Proficiency class at a *frontisterion* in Omonia Square. (That job too was thanks to Theo; the language-school owner was an old university friend, part of his Syntagma Square backgammon-playing set, and no one seemed to care she didn't even have an English A level, let alone a teaching qualification.)

'OK, a quick one then.'

'Actually, I don't want a coffee . . . I'll walk you to your next lesson.'

'What, you, walk? With your own feet?' Already she could imagine telling Theo about it that evening, turning Lorna's unexpected appearance at the bank into a joke. It was quite pathetic, actually, the amount of time and energy they spent discussing Lorna, as though they had nothing else to talk about. (Which in a sense they didn't, apart from Greek language and politics, which Theo professed to be heartily bored of. *'It's punishment enough being condemned to live in this Third World country, without being constantly reminded of it.'*)

Typically, it would never cross Lorna's mind now to ask whether Celia wanted anything to eat or drink before going on to her next job; she hadn't even offered her what remained in the water bottle after she'd washed her face. Never mind that she'd been teaching for two hours solid, and had another two hours ahead of her. Never mind that she was supporting both of them while Lorna got her act together. *Like – hello? It's been nearly ten months now . . . and you still think it'll happen any time soon?*

Tears of self-pity pricked her eyes. 'People only do what you let them get away with, Celia, don't you forget it,' her grandmother used to tell her when she was a little girl. She was right; if Lorna treated her the way she did, she herself was partly – no, wholly – to blame. What could you expect after everything she'd been through? It was a miracle they'd even made it to Athens.

'Are you sure you're up to walking? It's quite a long way to the college.' She looked down at Lorna's bare feet; they would be taking a short cut through the meat market in Athinas Street.

'The only thing that makes me feel tired is you asking me if I'm tired. Let's just go.'

In offended silence, they walked down Stadiou Street. If Lorna wanted to get offal and sawdust between her toes, then that was her business. She wasn't going to change her route on a whim. *You've got to start sticking up for yourself, girl . . .* Besides, she was starving and wanted to get some nuts from the dried-goods stalls near the Agora. Maybe there she could persuade Lorna to buy a jar of that sickly pink mastic she liked so much, something to get her blood sugar up, or even a cube of pistachio *halva*. Theo's mother said it was made of sesame paste and was terribly nourishing, packed full of essential minerals and nutrients. How that girl survived was a mystery; these days she seemed to be getting most of her calories from alcohol.

They had just passed the old parliament building when Lorna abruptly stopped outside a tiny shop selling religious artefacts: candles, censers, oil burners, vestments, little tin plaques depicting parts of the body in relief: arms, eyes, legs, feet, a puffy bleeding heart. The churches here in Athens were full of these plaques; Theo said they were votives people bought in times of need: the most terse kind of communication with God.

Lorna pressed one cheek against the shop window. 'You go on,' she said. 'I'm not coming.'

A single tear was streaking heartbreakingly down one cheek. At the sight of it, Celia felt her bowels twist in panic; Lorna never cried, *never* – not even when she was seven years old and her parents left her sitting on the bed in the dormitory at Newfield Hall. Dots of sweat broke out on Celia's upper lip and beneath her hairline. 'What d'you mean you're not coming? I was looking forward to showing you the pig with a flag in its bottom. And some skinned rabbits, and this kind of big woolly mammoth thing –'

'You go . . . I'll make my own way back to the flat.'

'Lorna, what is it? Tell me what's wrong?'

Lorna turned around to face her; her grief laid bare. That flat, Asiatic face of hers was a mask of pain. She was racked, ghastly with sorrow. Take something, Celia thought treacherously, take one of your pills, make it go away . . . This was one thing she couldn't cope with, not now, not after all this time . . . *Better a shadow Lorna than this* . . . Unheeded, the tears continued to trickle down Lorna's cheeks, spurting out of her eyes like a cartoon of someone weeping. She rested her face against the glass while all around them the noise and bustle of traffic on Stadiou Street subsided.

'It's been a year, Celia . . .'

'Stop it, Lorna, you're only making it worse for yourself . . .'

'. . . One whole year . . .'

The glass was wet, smeared with tears and dust; Lorna's cheek was blackened like a gypsy child's. For a moment even the icons appeared to be weeping in sympathy, while all around them hundreds of little candles shivered in their blood-red glass holders. They were alone, trapped inside the airless cave of her grief. An old woman dressed in black, a twig broom in her hand, stared at them from the shop doorway.

'Please, Lorna, *please* don't –' She was so pale, Celia thought she might faint. Then, abruptly, she pressed both hands to her chest, as though staunching a wound, or performing CPR on her own heart. Her gums were bared like those of an animal, while her breath issued raggedly from what sounded like a keyhole on her neck.

'It's Tatiana's birthday . . . Today's my little baby's birthday.'

Five

Celia awoke a few seconds before the alarm went off.

As she lay in her bed, a kind of dread, some leftover unhappiness from the night before, insinuated itself into her bones. It was to do with Lorna, of that much she was certain. Then it came to her. Lorna was missing. Gone since lunchtime of the day before. Even in the dark she knew the tartan-covered divan by the window was empty; her absence in the room, the negative non-Lorna, was as strong as her presence.

She would have to ring Theo; there was no avoiding it. Either that, or else call Lorna's parents in Hastings. Theo would ask about yesterday afternoon, the last time she saw Lorna . . . and –

Celia got out of bed and opened the shutters. *It's your fault.* She should never have walked away, leaving her in tears outside that shop. Yet there was nothing accidental about it; she did it to punish Lorna.

'And why?' she asked her reflection in the bathroom mirror as she stood at the sink brushing her teeth. 'Why did you need to punish her?'

It wasn't just the humiliation of finding Theo's glasses under the sofa; something inside her had snapped when she saw Lorna selfishly splashing all that mineral water over her face; the downtrodden little worm inside her finally lifted its head and turned. *Yet admit it, you would never have dared to kick her if she hadn't been so down . . .*

She would walk to the Plaka before ringing Theo; there was a slim chance she might find Lorna there. She would also have to call the Frontistirion to let them know she wouldn't be coming in. She'd promised to do some last-minute revision with her First Certificate students, but it would have to wait until tomorrow.

There were some German hippies squatting in the court-yard of an abandoned Ottoman villa where she knew Lorna sometimes bought drugs; it was just possible she had spent the night with them in their camper van. The moment she found her, she would bring her home, cook them both a nice meal and apologise, sincerely, from the bottom of her heart. Hopefully Lorna would have it in her to forgive her . . .

Celia was just lighting the gas burner to boil the water for coffee when a truly dreadful thought occurred to her. Dropping the open matchbox on to the floor, she pulled out a chair from under the Formica-topped kitchen table, and, panting, carried it into the bedroom. Standing on the chair, she reached up to the top of the wardrobe and pulled down a tin of Quality Street. But even before opening the box, she knew it was gone. Lorna's passport, and the last £60 of their travellers' cheques.

Shock made her lucid. She had to ring Theo straight away, see if they were in time to stop Lorna from boarding a plane. She was absolutely in no fit state to travel. Slipping on a pair of clogs, Celia grabbed her key, her address book and change for the phone.

Unlocking the door of the flat, she saw Theo standing on the front step.

'Lorna's missing! I was on my way to ring you!' she gasped, her voice cracking with relief.

'She's not missing. I've taken her to the airport.'

'What do you mean?' she faltered. A dull flush crept up her neck.

'She caught the early-morning flight to Heathrow.' Theo's face was ashen, and dirty grey stubble covered his jaw. He looked as though he'd slept in his clothes.

'I don't know why she had to be so secretive,' said Celia in a trembling voice. 'She could at least have said goodbye.' The two of them must have planned this weeks ago in one of their secret meetings. *But she was my friend first . . .*

Theo paused, as though considering whether or not to reply. He walked towards the Vespa and switched on the engine. 'If it makes you feel any better, I offered to go with her to London. She refused.'

Six

It was gone four when Theo and Celia left the bouzouki club in Omonia; and the night felt either too young or too old – Celia couldn't decide which – to contemplate going home to bed.

'How about some *patsas*?' she said hopefully, as they walked past the covered market.

To her surprise, Theo agreed, and they entered the tiled, neon-lit building, which looked strangely demure with all the stalls boarded up and the floor hosed down. Usually the market resembled a horror film, with ripped-out lungs and hearts and other unidentified body parts hanging from hooks, together with carcasses of lamb and flanks of beef, in a way that was so much more full on than England.

There were a few people sitting at tables outside the all-night canteen: a gaunt old man with a long white beard, and a battered straw panama hat on his head, who must have been an artist, judging by the paint stains on his shirt; a middle-aged blonde woman, dressed in a long flowery dress, seated beside a young, smooth-faced gigolo type; a shabby, grey-faced old man who looked like one of those job-for-life civil servants working in a ministry; and a little gypsy boy with a bucket of gardenias, whom the elderly waiter was pretending to cuff round the head.

The first few mouthfuls of tripe were worse than anything she'd had at Newfield: a kind of watery gruel, tasting like the smell of men's urinals, with unidentified wrinkly grey bits floating on top. Theo's pigs'-knuckle soup was much thicker, with gelatinous chunks of meat floating inside it that were soft enough to cut with a spoon. It was so oily that it left a film on her mouth like lipgloss; and actually glued a scrap of napkin on to her finger like the découpage they learnt in Art.

Yet it was strangely restorative, too, and gradually Celia could feel herself beginning to sober up. Under the harsh neon lights, she noticed Theo looked drawn, and *really, really* old – you could see the grey streaks in his hair and the crow's-feet at the corner of his eyes. Lorna's departure had aged him; four whole months had passed, and still no one had heard a word from her.

'I think we should get married,' he said abruptly.

'What did you just say?'

'I said I think we should get married.'

Oh, right. Theo's a world-class joker.

'I'm honoured, Theo, let's do it right now,' replied Celia lightly.

'Not right now, you'll have to convert first. I've discussed it with Maro; she knows a priest who can do it *taka-taka*. Sometime in early spring, we were thinking.'

'Oh, yes, any time will suit. And of course I'd love to convert to the Orthodox faith.'

Then Theo asked for the bill, and when he'd paid they walked back through the market which was beginning to come to life: stallholders were hosing down their marble slabs and opening the shutters on the lock-ups. Out on the street, the dry-goods stores were bringing out baskets of nuts, raisins and figs, and great big hunks of *halva*, together with jars of the fluorescent-pink mastic Lorna used to like so much.

They climbed on to the Vespa just as dawn was breaking

over the Acropolis. It was a gorgeous sight, Celia's first Athenian sunrise, and she mentally promised to climb up to the Parthenon early one morning on her own. Driving back through the Plaka, she honestly didn't give Theo's joke back at the taverna a second thought, so busy was she absorbing the unfamiliar sights and sounds of the early-morning city.

By the time they reached the flat it was gone six and, being the well-brought-up girl that she was, Celia thanked Theo for a lovely evening.

'Aren't you going to invite me back in?' he said, switching off the engine.

'I'm teaching tomorrow – sorry, today, I mean,' she said, suddenly feeling exhausted.

Then . . . . . . then . . . Theo took hold of her hand and said, 'I wasn't joking, Celia, I really think we should get married.'

At once it stopped being funny; but maybe the most unfunny thing of all was a little voice in her head going, *well, why not?*

'Why not?' said Theo, as though he'd become psychic.

'Why not? I'll tell you why not. One, you don't fancy me, and I don't fancy you. Two, you're in love with Lorna, and so am I. And three . . .'

'Yes?'

'Three, I'm a lesbian.'

At which Theo burst into peals of laughter.

'What the hell is so funny?'

'You, that's what.'

The first time the 'L' word had crossed her lips – at least in relation to herself (and out of the pages of her journal) – and Theo *laughed*.

'I'm sorry, but I don't get it,' she said stiffly.

'Look, Celia, every convent-school girl worth her salt thinks she's a lesbian. Once they try the real thing, they never look back.'

'Yes, well, I'm not every convent girl. And for your information, just the thought of the "real thing" is making me feel sick.'

'Don't knock it till you've tried it.'

'I'm telling you I'd rather die!'

'Just once. Let me make love to you –'

'*Theo!*'

'Look, we're basically compatible, aren't we? We've been on holiday together, hung out for all these months? We must have something in common!'

'Yes, but that's not the same as . . .' She honestly couldn't say it, she could not bring herself to use the word 'sex' in relation to Theo. And yet, he was also right. They *did* get on well together . . . *go on, admit it* . . . once Lorna was out of the picture.

'Anyway, at least let me come in so that we can discuss it. I can't exactly seduce you out here on the pavement, can I?'

So Celia let him in. She could try and justify what happened next by saying she was drunk or stoned (Theo turned out to have a pre-prepared reefer from Patmos handily stashed in the pocket of his blazer), but if she did, it wouldn't be the truth, at least not the whole truth.

They lay on the *flokati* sheepskin rug, smoking the reefer and listening to the Voice of America on the transistor radio, the shutters closed, so it still felt like the middle of the night when Theo rolled over and, taking off his glasses, started kissing her. The coarse stubble on his chin instantly made her come up in a rash, and she did *not* enjoy discovering tufts of hair growing in unexpected places, like in his ears and between his shoulder blades, obviously never having properly observed him in his swimming trunks.

There were plenty of awkward moments as they kissed, clashing of teeth, and a sudden impasse between their two noses, but it was all strangely tender and affectionate.

And Lorna? Well, Lorna's ghost was the third person in that room; they were two lonesome people left out in the cold, clinging to each other for warmth.

Then, almost too freaky for words, the Joan Baez song, 'Diamonds and Rust', came on:

> *Well, I'll be damned*
> *Here comes your ghost again*
> *But that's not unusual*
> *It's just that the moon is full*
> *And you happened to call . . .*

By this stage, they were down to their vests and pants (Celia didn't do bras, especially in the summer) and she'd more or less guessed what was about to follow, trying to avert her eyes from the astonishing Action Man's tent which had sprung up in his Y-fronts.

'It's got to happen some day, and it might as well be me,' he said, sliding her pants expertly down her legs.

And how was it? Well, it hurt, she couldn't pretend it didn't, especially as she wasn't exactly 'up for it' in a physical sense; and she thought his 'it' was quite a big 'it', though she'd nothing to compare it with. There were a few minutes of Theo grinding in and out, propped up on his elbows, during which she lay in the dark and listened to Joan Baez singing the words of her heart:

> *The original vagabond*
> *You strayed into my arms*
> *And there you stayed*
> *Temporarily lost at sea . . .*

'Right, now that's out of the way, we can discuss the wedding,' said Theo as he rolled off. Then, wiping the blood off his 'thing' with a pair of Celia's old Newfield trackie bottoms, he opened the shutters and, without a hint of shame, walked around collecting his clothes which were strewn about the room. (He happened to be wearing the three-piece suit with Bermudas he'd had on when she and Lorna first met him in the National Gardens, only this time with a purple silk kerchief knotted around his neck, which he had kept on throughout their sesh – not a look she could imagine catching on.)

Celia got up, too, and walked into the bathroom to wash 'down there'. Admittedly, she felt rather pleased with herself, as she balanced with one foot on the edge of the sink to rinse away the blood and you-know-what smeared inside her thighs. She'd done it – it was a rite of passage, just like getting her period – and she was now officially a woman!

Back in the room, Theo was already dressed. 'Come on, hurry up, I'll take you to the Plaka for breakfast.'

As luck would have it, Kyria Effi was outside, hosing down the balcony. It wasn't that big a deal walking out of the flat first thing in the morning with Theo (she must have witnessed no end of comings and goings when Lorna was still here), but nevertheless Celia was *desperately* embarrassed at the bright red stubble rash all over her chin and neck.

'Hmmm, next time I'll shave,' said Theo, as they sat at a pretty outdoor café on the slopes of the Acropolis.

'What makes you think there'll be a next time?' replied Celia archly as the waiter brought yoghurt and honey, and glasses of freshly squeezed orange juice.

'Of course there'll be a next time, we're about to be married,' said Theo without skipping a beat.

'Theo, think about it for a moment. I'm not exactly wife-material, am I? Wouldn't you rather marry a nice Greek girl?'

'No, they're way too venal. Money's the only thing that gets their juices going. And they're frightful masturbators.'

'Look, Theo, last night was fun, I won't deny it, but come on, tell the truth – the earth didn't exactly move for either of us, did it?'

At which Theo took off his glasses and Celia saw the warmth shining in his little brown eyes.

'Listen to me, Celia. I'll be forty-one next birthday –'

'I thought it was forty-four?'

'Whatever, same difference – it's just a number. The point is, I'm no spring chicken. I've been round the block a few times, had my fair share of experiences . . . call them what you will . . . and I feel I'm ready to settle down now.'

'With me?'

'With you.'

Celia shifted in her seat, feeling a dull, bruise-like ache in her vagina. He had penetrated the most intimate part of her, staking his claim on her truest self. It was crazy – she was starting to sound like one of those boy-mad Newfie girls!

'I mean it, Theo, why me?'

'Hmmm, let me see . . .' Theo paused, pretending to think. Then he began to tick the reasons off on his fingers: 'One, you're young and healthy, and you come from solid English stock. Two, you're quite a decent human being. Three, you're a virgin – oops, we'll skip that one . . . Four, Maro likes you –'

'Maro likes me?' It was ridiculous, but the thought that Maro liked her filled her with elation.

'She does, she thinks you're a "clean soul", whatever that's supposed to mean. Come on, Celia, you love this country. Wouldn't you like to be Kyria Montgomery, a proper Greek *nifi* going to market and learning to make *pastitsio*? Maro says we can have the house in Filoppapou as soon as we're married.'

When he put it like that, it did sound tempting. To shed her skin, that awkward English skin of hers, and become a real Greek person! Put down roots in the country she loved so much . . . Apart from the tiny problem of her sexuality.

'I know you think it's a phase, Theo, and who knows, maybe it is. But I doubt it – I honestly don't think I could have a relationship with a man . . . in that way.'

'All right, spit it out. You're still hung up on Lorna, aren't you?'

'I'm not, as it happens, I'm over Lorna.' And as those words left her mouth, they crystallised, finally, into the truth, and she felt a kind of contentment settle deep into her bones. 'Even if it's not Lorna, who's to say it won't be some other woman next time?'

'I'm broad-minded. We'll cross that bridge when we come to it. Now finish your breakfast and I'll drop you back at the flat. I've got an appointment with Professor Themistocleous at eleven.'

England, 1974

Seven

They nicknamed him the Dapper Gent.

He owned some kind of insurance company with smart premises on the high street; they would pass it on the way to the off-licence on the corner of Market Street. There was a big double-fronted bay window in the front, with dimpled panes of glass like in a cottage parlour. All day long, he sat at a desk beside a large cheese plant; he would raise his hand in salute as they sauntered down towards the seafront with their bottles. 'There goes the Dapper Gent again,' they would giggle, swinging their unmarked carrier bags in anticipation. Once they bumped into him coming out of Sainsbury's with a jar of Coffee-mate in his hand; he smiled at them and held open the door. Then, one day, when the woman in the off-licence refused to sell them a bottle of cider, he came out and stood beside them on the pavement.

'No luck this time?' he enquired sympathetically. He had a long, boozy face, with a domed bald head, and tinted oversized glasses. His voice was fruity, and surprisingly deep. Big balls, thought Lorna automatically. Heather Winters swore it was a medical fact the two went together; she'd read it in one of her uncle's science journals.

Lorna stared at him; he was dressed in a smart navy-blue blazer, with a Rotary Club crest on the pocket, and a patterned silk cravat around his neck. He smelled of some kind of woody man's aftershave; later she found out it was called Aqua Velva.

'Nope, no luck.' She was aware of Celia digging her elbow into her ribs, but she ignored her; you couldn't go around assuming every Tom, Dick or Harry was one of Matron's spies. She liked his face, anyway; he didn't look like he would go back into his office and snitch on them to the school. He was probably around her father's age, fifty or thereabouts, but in spite of the formal clothes, he seemed like someone who still knew how to enjoy himself, who was open to life's possibilities in a way that neither of her parents had ever been. And yet there was also something a bit tragic-looking about him, a kind of soul-sadness which felt like the mirror image of her own. (Don't ask how, she just knew he drank too much; there was an overheated, purplish tinge to his cheeks, he had what appeared to be a shaving cut under one ear, and the ends of his straggling walrus moustache looked as though they'd been tipped in alcohol.) Beneath the tinted specs, he had beautiful gentle brown eyes with long feminine lashes. I really, really like you, she remembered thinking, surprised at the swooping and soaring in her breast. None of the Napier boys had ever made her feel that way – as though she could tell him everything that troubled her heart, the whole sorry mess, and know that he would understand . . . She glanced down at her Timex; it was three-thirty, they weren't due back in school for another three hours. The most they could hope for now was a milky coffee at Pam's Tea Shoppe and a ciggie down on the beach by the sea wall. If they were lucky, one of the French kitchen boys from school would show up with a joint.

'So, what do you suggest we do?' For a moment, Lorna was appalled at her own temerity; what did she think she was playing at? Celia, too, was exaggeratedly clearing her throat, like there was something stuck in it. Ignoring her, the man straightened his cravat with a flash of his gold signet ring.

'I suggest I lock up the office and the three of us go out for a drive to Peacehaven. I know a nice little pub there where we can get a drink.'

'We can't, we're due back at school,' replied Celia promptly.

'Not yet, man, lighten up,' pleaded Lorna.

Celia glared at her. She hated to be contradicted, loathed and detested it. Lorna sometimes felt that without a friend like her, Celia would have been a prefect by now. Maybe even a future head girl; her school reports certainly hinted at it. But there was no chance of that now; she was marked by association with 'disruptive elements' . . . Even so, Celia's inner prefect occasionally refused to be silenced.

'I think it's time we got going. We've got prep to do by Monday. Nice meeting you . . .'

'Roy. Roy Strong.'

He held out his hand to Celia, then to Lorna; it felt dry and warm, and surprisingly strong. Black hairs glinted around his knuckles and on his thick fingers; she couldn't see if he was wearing a wedding ring on the other hand. She suddenly desperately hoped he wasn't . . . *please let him not be married* . . . Beneath the contrasting white cuff of his striped shirt, she caught a glimpse of a chunky identity bracelet; what a lot of gold he wore for an English man!

'See you around, Roy. Are you coming, Lorn?'

Lorna stared down the high street: J. Bolt, Quality Fruiterers, Marsden and Son, Butchers, Snowe's Family Bakery, Treasure Trove Souvenirs and Curios, Pam's Tea Shoppe and, on the horizon, a band of dark grey sea: the dreary vista of her own soul . . .

'I'll catch you up at school. Bye, Celia.'

She turned to watch Celia walk huffily across the road towards the library, swinging her knitted wool shoulder bag, arms folded defiantly across her chest. She would be in a stinking mood all weekend, there'd been hell to pay for weeks after she'd got off with that Napier boy on the Downs, but she'd deal with that later.

'So?'

Roy glanced rapidly across the street. 'Give me five minutes to lock up the office. I'll meet you on the esplanade, by the bandstand. Best no one sees you getting into my car . . . you know what busybodies people can be.'

Lorna grinned; the fun was about to begin.

They fucked everywhere.

The first time was in the front seat of his car, which he parked in a Lovers' Lane on the outskirts of Peacehaven. The plumpy cream leather of the seats was the exact colour of Campbell's chicken soup; Lorna felt it squeak beneath her bare knees as she lifted her skirt and, pulling back the gusset of her knickers, lowered herself on to his penis. She knew what to do without being shown; you would never have guessed in a million years she was a virgin.

When she climbed off his lap, he was surprised to see the tails of his shirt, and her dark-green school knickers, smeared with blood. She took the knickers back to school and, without washing them, hid them at the bottom of her locker; he said not to worry about the shirt, he kept a spare one at the office.

All through that autumn and winter he would wait for her on the seafront beside the deserted bandstand. Wrapped in her embroidered Afghan coat, sheepskin hood pulled tight about her head, she would look out for his wine-coloured Jaguar gliding cautiously down the wave-streaked esplanade. The moment she saw him, her heart would flip with joy; she would run towards the car, he would open the passenger door, and before she had time to kiss him, he had already driven off.

He was married, of course he would be; she was stupid to have hoped otherwise. He even had children, two of them, Cynthia and Roger, both older than her; Roger was an accountant somewhere in the Midlands, Cynthia was engaged to be married to an Australian and would be moving out to Melbourne after the wedding. One less person to mind about, thought Lorna as she rested her head on his withered old-man's breast. The wife, Gloria, she never dared ask about. Long white hairs grew all over his chest, right up to his bony shoulders; around his neck he wore a gold chain with a St Christopher's medal. His skin smelled of aftershave with a surprising vinegary tang of sweat. The ghost of the virile young man she had never known.

She loved and adored him; she didn't dare tell him how much. *He'll leave you if he ever finds out . . .* She took down all her posters in her cubicle at school – Alice Cooper, Marc Bolan, David Bowie, dressed in stripy leg warmers and hotpants, exposing a sexy rope of tendon between his thighs – and replaced them with souvenirs from their outings together. A menu from a hotel restaurant in Worthing (they ate potted shrimps with warm French bread, steak Béarnaise and flambéed crêpes), a beer mat from the pub in Peacehaven where they were supposed to have gone with Celia for that first drink, the label from a half-drunk bottle of 'Le Piat d'Or' he brought one day from the office which they drank on the cliffs of Beachy Head.

'It's disgusting, Lornie, he's just a dirty old man, a *goat*! How can you possibly say you love him?'

Celia's face was hot with fury as she shuffled her history notes. Lorna stared down at the top page: 'Cavaliers and Roundheads; the Principal Causes of the English Civil

War.' Exams began in ten days' time, and she had scarcely opened a book. *Anyway, I won't need A levels when I'm married to Roy . . .*

'Because I do love him. Read my lips: I . . . love . . . Roy –'

'Nee-na-na-na, nee-na-na-na, I'm not listening to a word you say.' Celia stuck a finger into both ears and twisted her head from side to side whilst looking towards the window. It was growing dark; the tennis courts were floodlit, and the *puk* of lacrosse sticks could be heard from the pitch, followed by the sharp trill of the coach's whistle. Lorna used to be on the team, until she got kicked out for missing too many practice sessions. Celia stopped waggling her head, peered at Lorna and cautiously removed her fingers from her ears –

'IloveRoyStrong,' gabbled Lorna before she had time to replace her fingers.

'Stop it, or else get off my bed,' said Celia. 'Some of us have mocks to revise for.'

'You were the one that asked, in case you'd forgotten.' Celia was in a foul mood, she had been for weeks, but Lorna could put up with it; she could put up with anything as long as she was given the chance to talk about Roy.

'OK, tell me one thing you like about him –'

'*Love*, Celia, not like.'

An expression of distaste crossed Celia's freckled face and, theatrically, she pretended to shudder. 'All right . . . love –'

'Actually, not love, *adore*.'

'If you don't stop it right now, I'll be sick, I'm warning you.' She wasn't putting it on; her face did look a bit pasty.

'OK, man, chill . . . So, why do I love Roy? Do you want the truth?'

'Only if it's not too disgusting.'

Actually, it was quite disgusting, or at least bits of it were. He had huge swinging testicles (Heather Winters's uncle's journals were right about men with deep voices) which, after making love, would nestle lopsidedly inside her thigh like two dusky purple fruits. Just before he came, his beautiful brown eyes would swim with tears; then he would close them, and she knew his moment had arrived. She felt his orgasm more deeply than her own . . .

'He makes me feel beautiful,' she said lamely.

Celia snorted. 'Lorna Gillespie, I've never heard such tosh in my whole life! Like you of all people really need someone to tell you you're beautiful! Half the fucking Napier boys are in love with you, not to mention the village yobbos who follow you every time you go into town, not to mention the caretaker and the bursar and that creep Mr Beardwood, and most of the Frog kitchen boys. Do me a fucking favour! *Because he makes me feel beautiful.*'

'Well, let me tell you that none of that attention makes me feel beautiful. It actually makes me feel like . . . running a mile, if you must know.'

Leave me alone, she felt like telling them; besides, they'd run a mile of their own accord if they ever got even half an inkling of how damaged she was . . . Roy, on the other hand, was like a magnet, one of those great big industrial magnets that sent any metal object clanking and rolling irresistibly along the ground towards it. When Lorna was with him, she felt uniquely whole; no one had ever made her feel like that, not even when she was a child. On the contrary, her childhood was mostly an exercise in fragmentation.

She remembered a glorious day, the start of the summer holidays. Everything she needed was laid out neatly in front of her on the lawn: Coppertone Sun Milk, her flip-flops, a sunhat and a tall beaker of orange squash with ice cubes; the idea being that she wouldn't have to go back in the house all afternoon. If she managed to keep right out of her mother's way, she might even forget she was home. Lorna closed her eyes, congratulating herself on her far-sighted-ness, basking in the orange glow behind her eyelids, and the surprising moistness of the grass between her toes.

Then, without warning, the air grew chill, and she sensed, rather than saw, a shadow looming over her. She opened her eyes just in time to see her mother raise her arm and slap her hard across the cheek. From the window of an upstairs room, she had caught their neighbour, Mr Down-ing, spying on her with his binoculars through the french windows of his house. 'It's your fault for provoking him, you're too old to be playing outside in your bathing suit,' she hissed, as she dragged her into the house, pulling on the nylon straps of her costume like they were the reins of a donkey.

Her father watched sadly from the doorway of his study, as barefoot and sobbing, clutching the towel in shame, she ran past him into the cold shadowy hallway and up the stairs to her room. From the window, she watched him walk out on to the lawn and stoop to pick up her suntan cream and hat; how stupid she had been to set herself up like that, as though all that paraphernalia could bring happiness . . . The glass of orange squash he left on a tray outside her door.

It was always her fault; every natural impulse that ever throbbed through her body had been her fault. Roy saw all of that, the whole lot; every sorry layer peeled away so that all that was left when she stood before him was her true self. His soulmate. That hot place between her legs which had caused her so much shame seemed made to accommodate his gentle fingers.

Similarly, when they sat opposite each other in one of those dark little country pubs, she ignored the knowing smiles of the regulars seated at the bar; she could genuinely find nothing strange about their being together. *Are you idiots blind or something, can't you tell we're soulmates?* He'd had a thirty-year head start on her, that was all. Thirty more years of wrong turnings: marrying the wrong woman, joining the Rotary Club, wearing those silly cravats. Thirty wasted years of their not being together. But so what? They were only outward appearances, at the end of the day they were meaningless. *My folks were dirt poor; I needed these status symbols, my darling, at least I thought I did . . . How was I to know one day I'd fall in love with a funny little beatnik schoolgirl . . .?* Gloria was the daughter of a town councillor; her family had been bitterly opposed to the wedding.

One day he showed her a photograph of himself as a little boy. They had driven to Brighton, where they had lunch in an Italian bistro in the Lanes. Throughout the journey, Roy scarcely uttered a word; he appeared preoccupied, and anxiously Lorna wondered if she had done something to offend him. Perhaps he was worried about business, or maybe he disapproved of the tiny suede miniskirt she had borrowed from Heather. As they entered the bistro, she caught the waiter signalling and grinning to the kitchen boy through the hatch; pulling her sheepskin coat tighter about her, she vowed never to wear such a short skirt again.

During the meal, he allowed his Fettuccine Alfredo to congeal on his plate; the saucer of grated Parmesan beside her smelled like dried vomit. She should have been in the library studying for her mocks; on Monday they had Biology multiple choice.

As the waiter poured her a glass of fizzy red Lambrusco, she watched Roy picking at the gnarled needles of wax sprouting like stalactites out of the neck of the Chianti bottle which served as a candle holder. They needed to talk about their future; it was hardly worth her while staying on at Newfield simply to fail her exams. Her parents and

Gloria would just have to get used to the idea; and she was certain, given time, that Cynthia and Roger would come round too. Once they saw how happy she had made their father . . . *He's like a different person with you, Lorna . . . you barely notice the age gap . . . of course you have our blessing . . . don't worry, we'll square things with Mother . . .*

After lunch they went for a walk on the pier; when the wind grew too cold, they took shelter in the tearooms overlooking the bulging grey swell of the ocean. The sight of the waves was making her feel queasy. As they entered the café, the Terry Jacks song, 'Seasons in the Sun', was playing on the jukebox: 'We had joy, we had fun, we had seasons in the sun . . .' So far, nobody at school knew what the singer looked like; every week Pan's People moodily danced to it on *Top of the Pops*. A rumour was going around that the lyrics were really about him, Terry Jacks; he was dying, too weak to appear on television. A few girls would always cry when the song came on, just in case.

The waitress brought them their tea in a stainless-steel pot, and a plate of rock cakes studded with tiny blackened currants. Lorna poured them both a cup, remembering to add three lumps of sugar to Roy's. She adored performing these small homely tasks for him; when they lived together, she would do a cordon bleu cookery course and have a gourmet meal waiting for him every evening when he got back from the office.

She saw him reach inside the breast pocket of his blazer and for one delirious moment thought he was going to pull out a ring. *I knew it! That's why he went all quiet in the restaurant . . .* But there was no ring; and she tried to hide her crushing disappointment when she saw what appeared to be a square of yellowing card in his hand. 'Look, this is me, sweetheart, the real Roy Strong,' he said, placing a photograph on the Formica table. 'It was taken in Wales by some army photographer from the base near where I was sent as an evacuee.'

Lorna picked it up from the edges, careful not to touch the image with her fingers. It was a black and white picture of a scruffy little boy dressed in a shirt buttoned up to the neck and a tight V-neck jumper. A thatch of coarse-looking unbrushed hair grew in strange whorls and waves about his head; he was smiling, his whole expression shone with mischief and energy, even though a war was on, and he must have been a long way from his parents, and home.

'Were your brothers and sisters evacuated with you in Wales?' asked Lorna, taking a sip of her tea and lowering her eyes to hide the tears that were threatening to well up inside them. When you looked closer, the yellow Formica was overlaid by a grid of tiny white squares like graph paper . . . It wasn't just the absence of a ring, *you can't rush these things*, it was that song, the angry waves lashing against the pier . . . the passing of time itself.

What had the years done to that optimistic little boy in the picture? *Goodbye, Papa, please pray for me, I was the black sheep of the family* . . . And her poor father, what had he done to deserve a daughter like her? All her life they'd hovered on the brink of a friendship that had never had the chance to blossom. Her mother's rages never permitted it . . .

But the wine and the song, like the seasons have all gone . . . She brushed a speck of sugar off the curling edge of the photo, trying to compose herself before meeting his gaze.

As though he could read her thoughts, Roy took off his tinted glasses and held them in his hands. His long jowly face quivered above his cravat; the broken veins on his cheeks looked livid in the harsh sea light.

'It's over, sweetheart. Gloria found the shirt. She knows everything.'

Eight

The girls at the hostel jeered when they found her green tunic with its lacrosse captain's badge folded up in the bottom of her locker.

'Jolly hockey sticks', Kim and Jackie and that mental girl, Hazel, called her, as they imitated her accent over tea.

'Would you be so *awfully* kind as to pass the marge, old slag?'

'Why, certainly, old slag, tuck in.'

They stared at her across the table, murder in their eyes; and soon Lorna stopped coming down at mealtimes. She bought a pound of own-brand strawberry jam from the Co-op which she would eat straight from the jar with a spoon, and little bags of sunflower seeds from the health-food shop in the village. Anything else just made her feel more sick. The hippie in the shop swore they were a miracle food: 'We lived on these for a whole month in Afghanistan,' he droned each time she went in to stock up.

Jackie and Kim steamed open her letters from home, and stole the postal orders her father sent. They helped themselves to her toiletries, smearing Silvikrin shampoo over the balding candlewick bedspread, and one night, as she slept, they even cut off a chunk of her hair.

Lorna awoke to discover the kitchen scissors speared into the end of the mattress; and for weeks she would find clumps of her hair blowing around the garden of the hostel, draped in strands over the wintry rose bushes.

Lorna searched inside the drawer for a blanket.

She could have sworn there was a warm shawl in there somewhere, she remembered handwashing it herself with Dreft the last time she was on laundry duty, but now it was nowhere to be seen. The girls were like that; the moment anything half-decent got donated, there'd be a scrum to scavenge it for their own babies. Like kids fighting over the dressing-up box. She didn't dare risk bringing one of the hostel's big metal prams to her appointment with Roy; they were like tanks, she'd stick out like a sore thumb if any of the staff happened to be passing by. Best thing was to wrap her up tightly and carry her under her coat.

She glanced down at the bed; Tatiana lay asleep on the yellow candlewick bedspread, arms raised trustingly above her head. The milk spots had cleared, the skin on her cheeks was now the colour and texture of a magnolia petal. Over her terry Babygro she was wearing the lemon-yellow matinée jacket with matching bonnet and booties that Gillian Aspell's mother knitted; Gillian was one of the lucky ones: in the end her parents softened up and agreed to let her keep her baby, Cheryl, providing she let her mum pass off Cheryl as her own. That made Gillian the big sister of her own child, but it was better than nothing: 'At least that way I get to see her every day . . . when she's eighteen I'll tell her the truth . . .' Her parents were coming to collect her at the end of the week.

Each time Lorna looked at her daughter, her heart cracked with joy and pain, like someone splitting open a peach with a hammer . . . she could never have imagined she would love her baby so much. She hadn't counted on loving her at all; she had watched her thickening waistline with something like disgust and at night she would lie in bed, listening to the snoring and groaning of the other girls, Hazel in the bed by the window, grinding her teeth down to stumps, fists clenched by her sides to prevent herself from punching her own belly. When she could bear it no longer, she would roll her knuckles up and down over the bump, not hard enough to bruise, but enough to make the baby writhe about like an eel inside her . . . Twice, as the date of her confinement drew near, she had considered walking to the railway bridge on the edge of town and throwing herself under a train. It was only the thought of the driver forced to live the rest of his life with the knowledge that he had killed a young girl that prevented her; enough people had already paid for her actions, no need to spread the stain wider.

She looked at her watch: two forty-five, another half an hour before she had to set out to meet Roy. The room was deserted; the other four girls she shared with were in the sun lounge putting the babies down for their naps. It was a crisp autumn day, and sunlight was pouring through the window, illuminating Tatiana's high forehead. She'd got that from the Gillespie side of the family – Lorna's father came from a long line of intellectuals – but the rest of her was pure Roy: her eyes were getting browner by the day. Most of the other babies were bald, but she was born with a head of hair which reminded Lorna of Roy in that snapshot he showed her in Brighton; she remembered touching the damp shock between her legs as the head crowned.

Such a long, cruel labour; she thought she would die before pushing her out. 'Should've thought of that, shouldn't you, before you grabbed your two minutes of fun behind the bike shed . . .' The ginger-haired midwife hated her; she could tell from the way she pinned her shoulders back down on to the pillow each time she tried to spring up on the bed. Her forearms were doughy and freckled, strong as a man's. 'Keep still, won't you, you want this baby to be born alive, I take it?' No, she remembered thinking, I don't . . . I want us both to die, here, now, in this ugly room.

She was beautiful from the start, even the midwife had to admit it, without a single mark or blemish on her face. 'They'll be queuing round the block for this one,' she said grudgingly, as she placed the tightly wrapped bundle into her arms. 'Here, make the most of her while you can . . . she won't be yours for long.'

'You're wrong,' whispered Lorna, as she gazed down at the calm, bright face. 'She's mine . . . she's not going anywhere.' She thought she had never seen anything so clean and new in her life; how could this radiant creature have emerged from her body? It was like looking at an image of her own soul, the ghost of the child she must have once been.

'*Tatiana . . . Tatiana . . . Tatiana . . .*' Lorna whispered her name out loud as she bathed her in one of the vinyl folding baths in the nursery; after her bath, she hung the rubber draining tube over the edge of the sink and pulled up the padded flap so it became a changing table. She laid Tatiana face down over a towel she had warmed first on the radiator; Tatiana had a raised strawberry mark on her left ankle, which Matron said would fade as she grew older: '*Her Forever Mum will be the one to see it go . . .*' Lorna had turned her face away so as not to let her see the hot tears which sprang into her eyes.

As Lorna rubbed baby lotion on to her body, Tatiana arched her strong back like a cat, lifting up her head and pecking hungrily at the edge of the towel. Gripping on to the slippery body, Lorna turned her on to her back and picked up a folded terry nappy from the pile on the shelf. Tatiana smiled lopsidedly at her and sucked her fist loudly like a baby in a cartoon. She was breastfed; whatever happened they could never take this pleasure away from her. Instinctively, she knew this was the right thing to do, no matter what the midwife suggested: 'I'm giving her the best start in life, there's no way the powder can be better than my own milk . . .'

Sometimes, in the common room, she would be sitting in the feeding chair by the window, staring out across the street at the neighbouring gardens, a gardener clipping a hedge, a woman in a headscarf going out to post a letter, a child kneeling down drawing a hopscotch on the pavement with a biscuit tin of coloured chalks, everybody in Chudleigh Avenue going about their normal business, when she would become aware that Tatiana had stopped sucking. She would look down and see her daughter gazing up at her with a flushed dreamy face, pure soul, nothing mediating, in her eyes . . . It was like catching a glimpse of the other world she had so recently left behind . . .

She had a beautiful, calm nature; Lorna had understood that from the moment she was born. Even when she was hungry or in pain, she would purse her lips downwards between cries, as though to stifle the next whimper until she was really sure whatever it was still hurt. Her fingers were still tightly closed, and whenever Lorna managed to prise them open she would find a little ball of blue lint – it was always blue, no matter what clothes she was wearing – which she would place in an empty jar of Pond's Cold Cream, together with her nail clippings and the blackened stump of the cord.

She would spend hours strolling around the grounds of the hostel with Tatiana asleep in the pram, learning to angle the fringed canopy so that she would not have the sun directly in her eyes. Sometimes she would pretend that she was in a real park: an ordinary young mother out for the morning with her baby. There were times when she really believed her fantasy; the rooming-in period at the hostel could last for weeks, months even, until the adoption society found a suitable family. During this time, the girls lived with their babies for twenty-four hours a day, five to a room. They were taught by the midwives how to care for the infants, who slept in metal cots by their bedsides. They learned how to place a liner inside the terry nappies, then a layer of zinc and castor-oil cream on their bottoms, to prevent a rash; they learned how to mix up bottles of Cow and Gate half-cream and wind the babies over their shoulders halfway through a feed; the correct solution of Milton's for the sterilisers. Because Tatiana was breastfed, the contents of her nappy looked, and even smelled, like the butterscotch Angel Delight they used to eat at Newfield Hall. Nothing about her daughter disgusted her; she would scrape the slops into the toilet pan, then leave the nappies to soak in the industrial-sized vats of Napisan in the laundry room. Tatiana's nappies she would rinse by hand; the hostel's twin tub always left a residue of soap which gave her a rash.

Walking up and down the straight paths between the lawns, lined by rose bushes with their tight little buds, Lorna would turn everything over in her mind. She'd always been a drifter; all her life she'd never planned, or fought, for anything she desired: the idea that happiness might in some way be worth striving for had been stamped out in her early on by her mother's rages. The scholarship to Newfield Hall which made her father so proud, and gave her mother such status amongst the neighbours, had almost landed in her lap; the exam was so easy, for a moment she thought it had to be a joke.

Even leaving home to board at seven years old was merely a change of circumstances, a new kind of unhappiness. This passivity no doubt came some way to explaining why she found herself in the situation she was in today; she had accepted Roy's decision, the ending of their love affair, without a fight.

Yet this was different; somehow she had to find a way of keeping Tatiana. The love she felt for her daughter was a primitive magnetic force dredging up the incomplete personality she had settled for over the years, bringing in its wake a fierce and unexpected desire for perfection; she was literally incapable of settling for less. She could not rest at night knowing that Tatiana might have soiled her nappy; most of the other girls let them stew in their mess rather than get up to change them, but, no matter the time, Lorna would take her off to the nursery for a top and tail after her feed; how could a few more minutes' sleep compare to the pleasure of knowing that she was putting her down with a full belly and clean nappy, that there was literally nothing in the world she could do to make her daughter more comfortable?

No matter which way she looked at it, in the end it boiled down to her parents; if she could just persuade them to come and visit, in particular her mother, surely they couldn't find it in their hearts to force her to hand away their only grandchild; putting aside their feelings about her, their disappointment of a daughter, some sense of kinship would be bound to kick in . . . When their letters arrived, together, in one of those mean-looking brown envelopes her father used for correspondence with tradesmen, she had no choice but to contact Roy. *I do not, repeat do NOT, consider her to be a grandchild of mine* . . . Her mother had even returned the snapshot of Tatiana.

She hadn't seen Roy since the day she told him about the baby. They had parted one winter's evening in the cricket pavilion at the edge of the village; the ground was frozen, white needles of grass that stretched all the way down to the sea, crackling like broken glass beneath their feet. He gave her a cheque for £200 and the address of a doctor in Pimlico. 'Tell the hotel I'll settle the bill when I'm next in town.'

He slipped the cheque into the pocket of her sheepskin coat, and in silence she watched him shuffle cautiously across the field like an old man learning to ice skate. Alone, she walked down to the esplanade; there, she drank half a bottle of Southern Comfort in the deserted bandstand, listening to the waves battering the sea wall. It had grown dark; she might have sat there till morning, frozen to death, maybe, if Celia hadn't come looking for her after supper.

'You're better off without him, Lorn. What kind of creep goes sniffing around schoolgirls' skirts?'

They managed to walk back through the silent, snow-filled village, Lorna clinging on to her shoulder for support, and climb back up the fire escape of the main building without being discovered. Celia put her to bed in the clothes she was wearing, opening the cubicle window to sober her up; when Lorna awoke the next morning, her sheepskin coat was powdered with a fine dusting of snow.

She never went to the doctor in Pimlico. At the time, she couldn't have isolated which rogue thread in that crushing blanket of despair, which enveloped her morning, noon, and night (stifling her even as she slept, so that she would awake in her cubicle, gasping for air), prevented her in the end from having an abortion. It wasn't the thought of killing their child – she was beyond caring about that – and nor was she holding out for Roy to change his mind. Not really, anyway. The way his face turned to stone as he drove past her one Saturday on the high street said it all. Actually, the reason was straightforward: she wasn't pregnant any more. Simple as that. Nobody knew about it, anyway, apart from Roy; she hadn't breathed a word to a soul, not even Celia. She'd got it wrong, that's all. A false alarm. Besides, there were any number of reasons why her periods should have stopped so suddenly. All that winter, she swam lengths in the icy-cold outdoor pool, got herself back on to the lacrosse team, and went on punishing cross-country runs across the Downs. She couldn't be pregnant, surely, could she, if at five months she could still fit into her Speedo swimming costume without a shadow of a bump?

It was Matron who forced her to have a blood test; she'd noticed Lorna hadn't visited the surgery for a while now to collect her monthly supplies of Dr White's; and one morning, while the whole school was at breakfast, she searched her cubicle. Under her mattress she discovered the glass test tube of the home pregnancy kit she'd bought on her last trip to London, still in its original packaging; the coloured ring at the bottom of the test tube was more faded but there was no mistaking the result. She was holding it in her hand when Lorna returned to the dorm to collect her pencil case before Double R.E. At the sight of it, Lorna felt her body slump, her entire centre of gravity forced downwards towards her belly; in an instant she looked, and felt, five months pregnant.

As though her condition were contagious, she was immediately placed in isolation in a dusty attic room above the sick bay, filled with trunks, bales of rolled-up carpets and old sporting trophies, some of them dating back from between the wars. Her few possessions were hastily crammed into cardboard boxes while the rest of the school was at morning lessons. No one knew she was up there; the word went around she had been sent home with glandular fever.

A chamber pot was left in the corner of the room; three times a day, it would be collected and emptied when Matron came up with her meals on a tray, locking the door hastily behind her. Lorna allowed the school doctor to take a blood sample, obediently rolling up her sleeve as he crouched beside her on the mattress, but she refused to utter a word throughout her entire confinement. 'We'll call in the police if you won't tell me his name,' but Lorna knew Matron was bluffing; she was still underage (for all Matron knew, so, too, was the father), and the last thing the school wanted was a scandal on their hands. By the end of that week, her father came to collect her and drive her to the hostel; halfway through the journey, in a motorway service station, she told him Roy's name.

Lorna looked at her watch: three twenty; Roy would be waiting on the corner of Chudleigh Avenue. Removing the cot sheet from her daughter's mattress, she folded it into a triangle and laid it out on the bedspread. She'd been practising for days, ever since Roy's note arrived, and she knew it could be done. She got the idea from pictures of the Kalahari bushmen in the *National Geographic*. Careful not to wake Tatiana, she sat down beside her on the bed and, scooping her up with one hand, held her against her breast, while with the other she wrapped the sheet around her body. Placing her own feet on to the edge of the mattress, the baby wedged between her knees, she managed to tie the ends of the sheet into a double knot behind her back. As she supported the bundle with one hand, she slipped on her sheepskin coat which was folded over the back of a chair. She had lost so much weight since Tatiana's birth that there was plenty of room to fasten the buttons around the sling; indeed it was such a snug fit that she scarcely needed to support the bundle as she walked.

At the corner of Chudleigh Avenue, she saw Roy's maroon Jaguar parked by the postbox. He opened the door, and she climbed inside.

It was the smartest children's outfitters in Hunstanton: Little Nippers, on the high street. The window was lined with sheets of wrinkled yellow Cellophane to prevent the clothes from fading in the Norfolk sun which rarely seemed to shine.

This was the first time she had been inside the shop, though she had often stopped to admire the outfits in the window. Two child-sized mannequins, a girl and a boy, dressed in Brownies and Cubs uniforms, stood on a carpeted platform in the centre of the shop, while the walls were lined with shallow wooden trays, each one with a handwritten label in black ink: Tights, Pants, Knickers, Socks, Vests, Aertex, Ties, Blouses, Cardigans, Gloves, Scarves, Caps.

The woman stared at Lorna, taking in her sheepskin coat, her ringless hand, the old-fashioned Silver Cross pram. *Oh. A Dunstan's girl . . .*

'Did you have anything particular in mind?'

'Something smart. For special occasions,' replied Lorna steadily.

'Any price range?' Her face was sceptical, preparing to be amused.

'The price doesn't matter,' said Lorna, fingering the envelope in her pocket which contained the last of Roy's abortion money.

There was a pause, then abruptly the woman turned towards her assistant and said: 'Wanda, fetch the merino jacket from the storeroom.'

'Yes, Miss Aldiss . . . *She's gorgeous,*' whispered Wanda conspiratorially to Lorna as she lingered over the pram.

She returned from the storeroom a few moments later with a flat cardboard box, which the woman opened up on the counter. Folding back a sheet of tissue paper, she took out a cream knitted double-breasted coat with mother-of-pearl buttons, and laid it out on the glass.

'Hand-finished and fully lined, with a matching bonnet and mittens. How old did you say your baby was?'

'I'm sorry?'

'Your little girl. How old is she?'

Lorna swallowed and stared out of the window. *You said no crying. Not today.* 'Oh. She's nearly four months.'

'Is she big or small for her age?'

'I think she's about average,' she said hoarsely.

'Shall I pick her up and we'll see?' asked Wanda eagerly.

Blinking, Lorna nodded; while leaning over the pram, the girl took her in her arms, making a great show of supporting the back of the baby's head with one hand. One of her booties had fallen off under the covers. Matron was right: the strawberry mark on her ankle hadn't faded, though the blood spots were no longer joined together. *Her Forever Mum will be the one to see it go . . .*

'I'd recommend aged six to twelve months. Allow for some growing room.'

'It has to fit now,' said Lorna sharply. 'Today, I mean.'

The woman stared at her curiously. 'Are you sure? For three pounds fifty you want to get a bit of wear out of it.' She gave a brittle laugh, as though to apologise for her earlier coolness.

As she watched the woman fold the coat back into the box, Lorna took the envelope out of her pocket and began to count out the money on the counter, aware all the while of the assistant, Wanda, playing with Tatiana. *Round and round the garden, like a teddy bear.* Somewhere it would say on her records what her baby was wearing; this new outfit had to mean everything.

'May I ask what's the special occasion?' asked Wanda guilelessly.

One step, two step – tickly under there –

And, for the first time in her short life, Tatiana laughed: a deep, silvery chuckle, which flew through the air like a comet of fairy dust.

She bit her lip to stop it trembling. *You said no crying.* 'Her new parents are collecting her this afternoon. I want her to look nice.'

Wanda's hand flew to her mouth.

'I'm dreadfully sorry,' she gasped.

Greece, 1986

Nine

One night, Sappho overheard her parents talking in Theo's study.

'I know he's very clued-up for his age, but how d'you think I'd feel if anything happened to him just because his mother was too drunk to look after him?'

Theo murmured something inaudible, then Celia went on: 'Do you know that child not only gets himself to school in the morning, but he cooks and cleans for Lorna half the time?'

Sappho heard her father get up to switch off the record-player; for days, now, he'd been listening to his *rembetika* records late into the night; the end of summer always filled him with melancholy. 'Cloudy Sunday, you are like my heart . . .'

When he spoke, his voice sounded tired.

'Look, Celia, Lorna will keep drinking with or without Kyria Maria's retsina . . . at least this way you know she's not getting the hard stuff from the chemist's . . . Anyway, left pocket, right pocket, it comes to the same thing . . .'

Left pocket, right pocket . . . so was Lorna a thief now, stealing money from Theo's wallet?

It was the afternoon siesta, and her parents were asleep.

Sappho was sitting on her bed sticking cards into her

Mona the Vampire album with a tub of craft glue, when she heard the buzzer shrill downstairs. The second she opened the door, Lorna grabbed her by the wrist and yanked her out on to the pavement.

'You've got to come with me. *Now!*'

'Where?' Sappho blinked; after the cool of the hallway, the sunlight out on the street was blinding.

'To Kyria Maria's. That spastic won't serve me.'

'It's her husband, Vassily, he had a stroke. Let *go*, Lorna, you're hurting me!'

'Stroke, my *cahoonas*! I'll only let go if you come with me right *now*.'

Sappho had never seen her lit up with such ugly fury, those red bony fingers of hers gripping her wrist like Magwitch kidnapping Pip in the cemetery in the film of *Great Expectations* Theo took her to see at the British Council.

Lorna stood there, panting, with this scary kind of grin on her face, as though on some level she was conscious her behaviour was ridiculous but couldn't help herself.

'At least let me get dressed,' said Sappho craftily. She would make a run for it, wake up her parents, tell them Lorna had gone crazy.

Instead, inexplicably, she allowed herself to be dragged barefoot across the burning pavements in her T-shirt and pants to Kyria Maria's shop. Refusing to meet Kyrios Vassily's sleepy eye, Sappho watched in silence as Lorna lined up the bottles of Kourtaki retsina with their red and yellow labels on the counter.

'Six little soldiers,' she slurred contentedly, as she dropped them one by one into her rucksack.

'*Tha sas plironei i mitera mou, avrio*,' mumbled Sappho, *my mother will pay you tomorrow*.

Afterwards, as she stood at the rough marble sink, scrubbing her wrist with Kemal's block of laundry soap, she vowed to tell no one about it, not even her parents. She would pay Kyria Maria back out of her own money rather than have to think about her shameful spinelessness. *How could you let her do that to you?*

Sappho never forgave her even though a few days later Lorna did apologise, slipping a hundred drachmas through the letterbox with one of her funny drawings of herself standing on the Acropolis looking dishevelled with spinning, saucer-like eyes, a bottle in one hand and a placard in the other which read 'Hic! (and sorry!)'.

Sappho cut up the card into strips which she fed one by one down a crack in the floorboards. The hundred-drachma note she wrapped into a ball and flushed down the guest toilet.

She would find him lying across her bed, his head nestled blindly into the small of her back, a prehistoric tail which sprouted in the night. The soles of his feet were black, there was dirt under his nails, yet his skin smelt of milk and musk and warm sweet earth.

One morning, Alexander shook her awake.

'Saff!'

'What?'

'Can I have a bubble bath?'

Sappho switched on the lamp and looked at her Snoopy clock.

'Alexander, d'you have any idea what the time is?'

He sat up and shook his head. He looked like a gypsy boy with his shaved head and droopy man's vest riding down below the nipples.

'It's half past *five*!'

'Is that early or late?'

'It's early. *Very* early.'

'But can I still have a bath?'

'Why don't we go back to sleep and wait until the grown-ups wake up?' she coaxed.

'But then *they'll* all want the bathroom,' he said logically.

Sappho sighed. 'Come on then, but don't make any noise.'

Barefoot, they tiptoed across the parquet floor to the bathroom. Sappho turned on the hot tap and reached up into the cabinet for the bottle of Matey bubble bath her grandparents had sent over for Christmas, which was inky blue yet smelled mysteriously of bananas. Whenever Alexander stayed the night, he always had a bath; Celia said the *garconiera* in Omonia rarely had hot water.

Unselfconsciously, Alexander took off his man's vest and sat down naked on the edge of the bath, while Sappho cleaned her teeth at the old-fashioned marble sink.

'Have you got any scissors?'

'What d'you need scissors for?'

'I need to cut my nails.'

Sappho splashed her face with cold water and reached into the medicine cupboard. 'We've only got clippers. D'you want me to do them for you?'

Alexander shook his head. He had an almost fastidious sense of personal hygiene, and it was he who would take himself off to the barber in Omonia every few weeks to have his head shaved.

Sappho pulled down the lid of the toilet and watched as he perched on the edge of the bath like a monkey, feet clasped in his hands, frowning with concentration as he collected a little pile of black clippings, his scrotum squashed and gleaming between his thighs like the skin of a newly hatched bird.

'That's better,' he said gravely, as he threw the clippings into the basket under the sink.

While he was having his bath, Sappho went to prepare breakfast. Across the hallway, she noticed the door of the spare room was ajar; Lorna must have forgotten to close it.

In the kitchen, Sappho cleared a space on the stained tablecloth, sliding all the bottles and glasses down to one end, and brushing away crumbs and ash, and shiny green seeds, which she later discovered were from Celia's marijuana plants that she grew at the house on Patmos.

She poured them both a bowl of Golden Nuggets, which happened to be Alexander's favourite cereal, and which in those days, at least, you could only get as a special treat from the Marinopoulos supermarket on Kiffissias Avenue.

When he'd finished his bath, Alexander came to the table and sat down opposite Sappho, dressed in the faded black BMX T-shirt he was wearing when he arrived. His hair was wet, and beads of water glistened on the tips of his ridiculously long eyelashes.

'Are you my sister, Saff?'

Startled, Sappho looked up. 'Of course I'm not, dummy, I'm your friend.'

Alexander's eyes brimmed with emotion; but he had his features under control, his lips pressed firmly together making him look pinched, wizened, older than his years.

'But if I had a brother I'd want him to be just like you,' added Sappho lightly, noticing how quickly his face had grown blank and bored, as though he'd been anticipating disappointment, and had a new expression ready for it.

There was a pause as Alexander lined up the remaining soggy Golden Nuggets on the edge of his bowl.

'Well, will you be my sister when I'm a man?'

Sappho never answered, for the door of the spare room opened, and she saw a figure gliding across the hallway towards the bathroom. Only later did it come to her, like the image on a slowly developing photograph, that it was Celia she'd glimpsed that morning leaving the spare room.

It had to be, though her being there made no sense at all.

*   *   *

71

Sappho must have been four years old, maybe five, when Alexander was born.

They were over on a trip from Athens, staying with Celia's parents in Pinner. She remembered catching a taxi from Hastings station to the rectory, a big cold house at the end of a gravel driveway. They were shown to the sitting room, which overlooked the front garden, with flowery curtains at the bay windows, and a sofa hemmed with a drooping fringe of silky golden loops which shivered as she slid her fingers along them.

It was freezing cold in the room, the air smoked when you talked, and Lorna was wearing a man's jacket over her dressing-gown. The baby was asleep in a Moses basket on a stand; Sappho stared down at him and asked if she could hold him.

'I wouldn't, my dear, he's too heavy,' said Lorna's mother who was standing by the door; but Lorna picked him up anyway and placed him gently in Sappho's arms. He really was heavy, he felt at least as big as she was; and Sappho thought she would burst with the strain of keeping that lolling head upright against her shoulder, aware all the while of the disapproving figure by the door.

Later she found out that Lorna's mother never wanted her daughter to come back home for the birth; she'd tried to make her have the baby in Athens, but there had been complications with the pregnancy, and Theo and Celia had taken her back to her parents' house.

Lorna cried when they left; she stubbed out her cigarette on the gravel path and hugged Celia as though she couldn't bear to see her go, wiping her eyes with the cuff of her jacket sleeve as she watched them walk down the driveway towards the waiting taxi.

Sappho remembered she cried too on the way to the station; she felt it was wrong to leave the baby in that unfriendly house, and she hated to see Lorna sad.

'Where's Lorna's daddy, Mummy?'

'You saw her daddy: he was the man in the cardigan who brought you your squash.'

'Not him, Mummy! Where's the real daddy . . . where's the baby's daddy?'

'He's gone, my darling . . . he can't be their daddy any more.'

'You know you could leave Alexander here,' Celia had offered more than once, but each time Lorna had refused.

'It's the least those fuckers owe me, wouldn't you say?' Sappho overheard her tell Celia out on the terrace.

Then, one summer, just before he was due to leave for England, Alexander disappeared. The first Sappho knew of anything was when she returned from an all-day tennis camp at Theo's club to find the house empty.

'Where *is* everyone?' she asked Kemal, who was in the kitchen stuffing courgettes.

'Little bastard gone. Run away,' muttered Kemal, elliptically.

'Who's gone?'

'Alexander. Mrs Lorna no see him for too many hours. Or maybe it's take her that much time to notice,' he added under his breath.

In the event, it was Theo who tracked him down. While Lorna and Celia searched the alleyways of the Plaka, Theo drove to Piraeus and went around all the shipping-line kiosks asking if anyone had seen him. One of the clerks had got suspicious, and remembered a small boy boarding a ferry to Aegina; he'd told them he was joining the rest of his family there for a name-day celebration.

'Why don't you want to go to your grandparents' anyway?' asked Sappho later on, after they'd all driven out in a taxi and, reunited with the fugitive, were sitting in one of the dingy tavernas along the seafront in Piraeus.

Alexander took a long sip of his Coke. He looked far too self-possessed for someone who had just run away to sea.

'I don't like it there,' he mumbled, playing with his straw.

'What don't you like about it?'

He swirled the straw around the bottom of the glass, then, blocking the top end with his thumb, lifted it out. 'Look, Saff, it's full of Coke!'

'Oh yeah, cool. Anyway, why don't you want to go to Hastings?'

Alexander lifted his thumb off the tip of the straw and allowed a drop to fall into the glass.

'Because it's too cold,' he replied, without raising his eyes from the table.

'And?'

Another drop.

'It rains too much.'

'And?'

Drop. Drop.

'I don't like my granny's food.'

'*And?*' said Sappho, gently, for she saw his face had grown pale.

'Lorna might forget to collect me this time.'

Ten

'And in the left-hand corner, we have the unseeded Lorna Gillespie, about to pick up a nine-year-old child with her bare hands, a young English girl by the name of Sappho Montgomery . . . ladies and gentlemen, can we please hear it for Lorna Gillespie, the undisputed child-lifting champion of Patmos!'

The moment Sappho began to kick her arms and legs, Lorna would surreptitiously remove her hands, one finger at a time, until before Sappho knew it, she was swimming on her own. Or rather just up to the moment she realised she was doing it; for as soon as she saw Lorna grinning at her triumphantly, empty hands on hips, Sappho would sink to the bottom like a stone.

Every evening just after sundown, they climbed down the twisting narrow path to the stony beach beneath the house, towels rolled up under their arms, while Alexander ran on ahead like a sturdy little mountain goat, barefoot and naked, oblivious to the thorns and broken glass which littered the ground.

As she and Lorna glided in the mirror-like shallows from one gnarled finger of rock to another, Alexander crouched beneath the overhanging branches of a pine tree, penis tucked neatly between his thighs, hunting for pine nuts in their mimetic charcoal cases. He could only have been four or five years old at the time, but he was extraordinarily skilled both at finding the nuts and cracking them open between two stones; by the time the lesson was over, he would have a little pile of buttery kernels waiting for them on a sun-warmed boulder.

The evening Sappho managed to swim by herself from the green and white painted rowing boat to the first finger of rock was when Lorna finally declared herself satisfied.

'*See*, Saffy, told you you could do it,' she said, holding out a towel as she emerged from the water.

It had grown dark; the beach was deserted, and Alexander was almost invisible behind his curtain of pine needles. Recently he had taken to painting his body with lumps of charcoal he would wet in the sea then rub over his skin like a loofah: an eerie little savage in his lair. It took Lorna hours to hose him off in the garden before Celia would allow him into the house. Even so, his sheets were invariably covered in black streaks, which, grumbling loudly, Kyria Vasso would have to soak in bleach in a tin bucket outside the kitchen door.

That evening, Sappho sat on the beach wrapped in a coarse white towel, watching Lorna as she rolled one of her funny-smelling cigarettes. She was wearing a beautiful, sugar-pink kaftan over her bikini, which was the exact shade of the bougainvillaea that grew outside the house. Her cats' eyes were the colour of sea-glass, light green with a ring of yellow around the pupil, and tiny freckles, like brown inkspots, dotted the bridge of her nose. Alexander was lucky to have such a pretty mother, Sappho thought disloyally; Celia looked nice sometimes, too, but recently she'd had all her hair cut off at the barber's in Skala, and she looked a bit like a man.

'I wouldn't care to run into you in a dark alley,' was Theo's dry comment as he watched her wheel the Piaggio back into the courtyard.

One afternoon the three of them walked across the island to the beach at Lambi, where they collected a bag of coloured stones: purple, green, pink, even a strange vivid dark blue, which was the colour of the sea at night. Back at the house, they made fairy cakes with wings, filled with a sugary paste called buttercream, which made Alexander sick, and sheets of hand-drawn Magic Marker tattoos – hearts and aeroplanes and flowers – which you cut out and licked on to your skin.

On the last night, before Theo and Celia returned from Athens, they ate supper at the fish taverna down on the beach in Kampos. Summer was nearly over, most of the tourists had left and theirs was the only table outside; the waiter had carried it out specially for them. The sun umbrellas, grim as sentinels in their rows, were fastened shut with metal clips, and the deckchairs had been folded up and stacked on one side, ready to be hosed down before being stored away until next season.

A group of Greek men around a neon-lit indoor table were playing the accordion and the lyre, the music drifting out in snatches on to the windy beach. It was Lorna who had insisted on eating outside: 'Come on, Saff, just put a jersey on if you're cold.'

Sappho recognised some of the *rembetika* songs the men were singing from Theo's collection; more than anything else, this music signified the end of summer to her. The men inside the taverna kept sending Lorna out glasses of ouzo and Metaxa, some of which she sent back, but others she drank. Five at least, Sappho reckoned, not including a half-litre jug of retsina.

To be fair, Lorna didn't look or sound drunk, but Sappho knew from experience this didn't mean a thing; you rarely got a warning with Lorna, from one moment to the next she would begin slurring her words, overcompensating by talking in an exaggeratedly loud voice. The trick was to get her home before her mood turned ugly.

'Alexander's tired, how about we ask for the bill?'

It was true, he was slumped over the tablecloth, head resting on his folded arms, the way they were made to sit during Quiet Time at school.

At Sappho's words, he sat bolt upright. 'You promised, Saff, you promised we could build a volcano,' he said indignantly.

It was true; ever since Lorna had told them about the volcanoes she used to build with her father when she was a little girl in Hastings, Alexander had been desperate to build one himself. The beach at Vagia was too stony, but here on Kampos it was ideal: a perfect crescent of sand. Actually, it wasn't such a bad idea, thought Sappho; it could be a diversion, and at least it would get Lorna away from the table full of drinks, maybe even sober her up.

The three of them walked barefoot down to the edge of the water, Lorna, swaying slightly, with a half-drunk glass of retsina in one hand. Alexander, wide awake now, began digging away two-handedly, like a little beaver, and pretty soon they had enough sand piled up to build the volcano. They patted the domed walls until Lorna said that was enough; then picking up a twig, she began to roll it around on the point of the cone to dig out the chimney. She can't be that drunk, Sappho thought, though the smell of her breath – *skordalia*, a puréed garlic dip they had eaten with the fish, pickled in her gut by the sour retsina – was making her feel ill.

While Alexander foraged for leaves and dried seaweed, Lorna excavated an opening at the mouth of the volcano, feeling with her fingers for the end of the twig. 'Got you, you bugger!' she grinned, giving one more roll of the twig to make sure the flue was clear. Trousers rolled up around his ankles, the elderly waiter from the taverna joined them with a pile of old newspapers, crouching down beside them as he helped them stuff the mouth of the volcano with scrunched-up balls. Pulling his lighter out of his pocket with a flourish, he lit a corner of the nearest sheet, which happened to be a photograph of Karamalis. They all cheered when the leaves caught, and flames began to lick up the sides of the compacted sand walls, and a column of smoke blew out of the hole at the top.

On the way back to the house at Vagia, Alexander was so tired they had to pull him up the hill. He didn't complain, Alexander never fussed about anything, but his head was slumped forward on to the breast of his unironed Aertex shirt, his eyes were closed, and he appeared to be literally sleepwalking, sandalled feet slap-slapping on the dusty white road. Sappho stared straight ahead, refusing to talk to Lorna. A priggish rage burned inside her – she was furious with Lorna for ruining it all, breaking the spell of the last few days by getting drunk. *I hate her, I hate her, I hate her . . .*

In some ways it was worse that Lorna hadn't made a scene back at the taverna; she didn't even have that to reproach her with. No, it was the understanding between them that Lorna had betrayed; all those girlie hours they spent eating *passatempo* under the canopy of the swing, Alexander lying naked and asleep between them (throughout that summer he would only wear clothes if they were going down to the village), while Lorna let her style her hair, or they took it in turns to read *Marianne Dreams* out loud. She'd led her on to believe that she'd changed her ways, that she wasn't the same drunken Lorna who dragged her out in the middle of the day to buy retsina from Kyria Maria's.

Back at the house, they discovered a bag of figs left outside the gate by Michali, the farmer who owned the field which bordered on to their land. Sappho picked the bag up and brought it into the kitchen, while Lorna carried Alexander to bed. As she emptied it, the figs scattered and rolled across the marble worktop; they were hard and green, they needed to ripen in the sun. Sappho walked across the kitchen towards the noisy Izola fridge with its fake wood veneer which had been in the house since Yia-Yia and Grandfather Charles's day; she was looking for an egg box in which to put the figs to ripen. She had seen Celia doing this before, with tomatoes, too, even though she knew it was slightly ludicrous to treat fruit like cotton wool, surrounded as they were by the casual plenty of the island.

Theo certainly thought so. 'You can take the girl out of Pinner, but you can't take Pinner out of the girl' was his comment each time he caught her doing anything he called 'suburban': namely, not rinsing the washing-up properly, using a flannel, or being stingy with the olive oil.

Out of the corner of her eye, Sappho was aware of Lorna pouring herself a tumbler of wine from the demijohn under the sink; she heard the fat glug of liquid from the wide-necked bottle. Without turning round – *you weren't brave enough to look her in the eye, were you?* – Sappho said, 'I think you've had enough to drink, Lorna.'

Lorna didn't answer, but her words must have stung; Sappho heard the splash of the wine being emptied out in the sink, and the sound of running water as she rinsed the glass.

Lorna pulled out a chair, dragging it across the stone floor, and began rolling a cigarette on the table. Sappho was aware of Lorna sitting down at the table, watching her as she placed the bullet-like fruits one by one into the empty egg box.

'My mummy says this way they don't get bruised,' Sappho said in a tight little voice. Celia might not be as pretty as Lorna, but at least she wasn't a drunk. Or a scrounger.

Lorna looked up at her, the half-rolled cigarette suspended by her mouth, ready to lick.

'Your mummy's a very clever lady,' she said wistfully.

For the remainder of that week, Sappho did everything she could to make Lorna and Alexander feel unwelcome. She made a point of siding with Kyria Vasso when she complained about the house being a pigsty in her parents' absence, and when Celia bought her a box of Caran d'Ache pencils from Skala, she refused to let Alexander try them even once.

'You'll just ruin them, use your crayons.'

Which was not only unfair, but untrue: Alexander was an unusually careful and tidy little boy; every slummy room he had shared over the years with his mother – the brothel in Omonia Square, the disused Fixx beer factory, the basement in Tavros – invariably contained a little shrine-like corner where he kept his possessions: his collection of Smurfs, the miniature hurdy-gurdy which played the tune of 'Strangers in the Night', his Knight Rider car.

But the worst, worst thing Sappho did that week was to deny Lorna the satisfaction of showing her parents she had learned to swim.

'I can't do it,' she said sullenly, sitting in the shallows, looking down at the outline of her thighs shifting and dappling in the current. No normal adult would put up with such a barefaced lie, and she was prepared to give an ungracious demonstration (around seventy per cent of her true swimming power) after a little more persuasion. But Lorna just smiled sadly and said nothing, and after a while her parents gave up trying to convince her.

'Stick to the belly dancing, Lorn,' Celia said finally.

The day Lorna and Alexander were due to catch the ferry back to Piraeus, Sappho made sure to be out of the house so she wouldn't have to say goodbye to them. It was their favourite time of day, those few rosy minutes after sunset, before it grew properly dark, the water shimmering greyly beneath a bare, sun-warmed sky.

She hid beneath the branches of Alexander's lair, watching Theo back the Peugeot out of the gate. The pebbles on the beach were littered with lumps of charcoal and hundreds of stripy pine-nut shells. She heard the car doors slam, and the sound of wheels skidding drily down the slope. As the car rounded the first bend, Sappho walked into the water and swam to the fishing boat; she sat on the painted wooden seat, hugging her resentment, until it grew dark and chill, and her swimming costume clung clammily to her body like the skin of her guilt itself.

Eleven

Celia was the only one who hadn't wanted to leave Athens.

She hadn't lived in England since she was a schoolgirl of sixteen, and always made a great show of kissing Greek soil each time they landed at Athens airport.

For years, she had been battling with various ministries to obtain Greek citizenship, even though Theo pronounced himself perplexed as to why anyone should wish to acquire the most useless passport in the world.

'You know, Celia, the word overkill does rather spring to mind. You don't need a Greek passport to prove to the world you're a card-carrying *Ellinida*.'

But if anything, Theo's mockery made Celia even more determined to shed her British identity once and for all.

The only son of an English doctor and a Greek mother, Theo was an expatriate by inclination as well as by birth, invariably choosing the disengaged life of a foreigner over that of the citizen; thus in Athens he read the *Spectator* and *The Times*, gleefully following the misfortunes of the Tory Party from a distance, while after the move to London, he only took in Greek newspapers and the *Athenian* magazine, not even caring to watch the news on television.

With the kind of grim pleasure he once devoted to what he called Margaret Thatcher's infatuation with Cecil Parkinson ('That woman could never resist a cad'), he now followed the love life of Andreas Papandreou, with whom he had studied at Athens University Law School, and who had just taken up with an Olympic Airlines hostess called Mimi.

'She must have snared Andreas with her prodigious intellect,' he would comment drily each time Mimi's round face, with its inscrutable, rather pig-like, features, appeared in the paper.

The weekend before Sappho's tenth birthday, Theo flew to London, to oversee repairs at the house in East Sheen where his father, Grandfather Charles, had lived as a boy. The tenants, impoverished friends of his parents, who had been living there at a peppercorn rent since the fifties, had just moved into a nursing home, and the house was to be put into the hands of a letting agency.

The evening he returned from London, Sappho was playing in her room, when she heard a scream from the other side of the house.

'You can't make me!'

Puzzled, she put down the brown-faced Sasha doll that Theo had brought her from London. What could Theo have said to make Celia so angry? For a moment, she considered getting up to go and investigate, but there was still Sasha's delicious outfit to unpack from its box: jeans, a dark blue fisherman's sweater, and a pair of darling little gladiator sandals.

Picking up a pair of scissors from her desk, Sappho began unpicking the stitches affixing the outfit to the card; she had just cut away the second sandal when Celia burst into the room.

'Here, take a look at this!' she spat, thrusting a brochure into Sappho's hand. Red-faced and panting, she sat down on the swivel chair beside the desk.

'Welcome to the community of St Cecilia's,' it said in swirling gold letters on the dark blue cover, beneath a photograph of two smiling girls in blazers.

'What is it?' asked Sappho slowly.

'According to your father, it's where you'll be going to school next term. He's already paid a year's fees in advance.'

'I don't get it. It says here that St Cecilia's is in . . . Richmond.' In spite of herself, Sappho's heart quickened.

'If Theo has his way, we'll be leaving Athens by the end of August. The whole thing was a pack of lies from start to finish. The real reason he went to London was to get the house ready for us. And it turns out there's precious little I can do about it,' she muttered bitterly, as she stood by the window looking out towards the floodlit Acropolis.

When she turned around, Sappho saw her mother's cheek was wet with tears.

She tried to mind; for Celia's sake Sappho felt she should contain her joy at the move, or at least try to hide it. But in secret she would spend hours in her room poring over the glossy school prospectus with its photos of cheery, uncomplicated-looking girls in their dark blue St Cecilia's capes, their tasselled corduroy caps which she now knew were called tam-o'-shanters, the summer uniform which consisted of a striped dress, worn with a straw boater and white gloves. Nothing, she thought, could ever go wrong in a school like that. And maybe even Celia would start acting more like a normal mother once they went to live in England, far away from her old bad habits and haunts.

On some deep level, Sappho blamed Lorna for everything that was erratic and untidy in their lives – she always had.

The fact neither of her parents had what you'd call a proper job (even though Theo would disappear for hours in his study preparing his monographs on the Punic Wars), the twenty-five-year age gap between them, Celia being too distracted – *with what, though, exactly?* – to join the parents' committee at Hellenic College – even the exterior of the house needing a coat of paint was somehow attributable to Lorna's influence.

(In Sappho's mind, nobody caring about the Pasok slogan sprayed outside her bedroom window was directly, if obscurely, linked to Theo, Celia and Lorna having once shared a flat in Kolonaki with no curtains, and some yellowing photographs she once found of the three of them nude sunbathing on Patmos.)

Lorna and Alexander were a kind of messy adjunct to their family, which prevented them from presenting a tidy front to the world. Admittedly, theirs wasn't a constant presence; they would disappear for months – once Lorna got a job dancing on a cruise-ship, leaving Alexander with her parents; another time they spent the winter on Samos, house-sitting for a wealthy American – but the possibility of their return was always there, like the certainty of disaster, made all the worse by never knowing when it might strike.

Now, for once, they would be the ones leaving and, by some celestial twist of fate, Lorna had vanished. There had been some talk the last time she came round, about spending the summer fruit-picking on the islands, she and Alexander sleeping rough in barns, but nothing definite. Once or twice, in that month before they left for London, almost as though she couldn't bring herself to leave without saying goodbye (even though Sappho knew that for years the friendship had caused her nothing but anguish), Celia had gone looking for them in the tiny room she and Alexander shared on the roof of a brothel in Omonia Square, but each time she had found the terrace door padlocked. That didn't mean anything, though; sudden reappearances were Lorna's speciality.

It wasn't until she was actually standing between her parents in the queue at the Olympic Airlines desk, her new My Little Pony zip-up colouring case under one arm, her

Sasha doll in the other, that Sappho allowed herself to believe they had done it: they had finally broken free.

As the plane took off, skimming above the evening crowds on the beaches of Glyfada, Sappho pictured Lorna outside on the pavement ringing the bell, the electric buzzer sounding harshly through the rooms of the empty house. She would bang hard on the metal door with the flat of her hand, then stepping back on to the corner of Thiramenous and Propilleon Streets, she would look up at the empty balconies with their pots of withered geraniums, dark green shutters closed to the world. From there, she would walk down Propilleon Street to Kyria Maria's, stopping perhaps to look up at the sky and admire the silvery vapour trail which, unbeknown to her, was pointing like an arrow to their new life.

In her terrible Greek, she would demand to know where the family had gone. '*Pou eine i Kyria Celia? O Kyrios Theo? POU EIENE?*'

And Kyria Maria, awoken from her siesta, which she took behind the till, perfectly erect on a wooden stool, head occasionally tipping forward like one of those long-necked ornamental glass birds dipping their beaks into a container of coloured water, would open her eyes and stare sightlessly at Lorna, frowning at some invisible spot behind her shoulder as though she had only just noticed a gap on the shelves. And even after she had blinked a few times, and straightened her auburn wig, uncricking her neck from side to side, like a ball in a socket, Kyria Maria still wouldn't be able to say where they had gone – no one would. *Then xero pou figane . . .* I don't know where they went. No one would know; that was the beauty of it.

Sappho leaned back in her seat and shut her eyes. She would never find them now.

London, 1987

Twelve

The terror of it shook her awake. *She'd overslept again.*

There was no need to check her Snoopy clock; the needle of light between the curtains said it all. Sappho sat up in bed and looked at her brown serge apron folded over a chair. Of course, it was Thursday – Home Economics. They were meant to be making syllabub; and she had forgotten to ask Theo to buy cream and sherry. At least, she thought, miserably, she'd miss out on the humiliation of not having brought her ingredients.

Downstairs, Theo was eating his breakfast in the kitchen. He looked up from the imported Papadopoulos rusk he was spreading with honey.

'I was wondering when you'd surface,' he said mildly. His hair was wet, and he had a small shaving cut behind one ear.

Sappho glanced at the cooker clock: it was only nine fifteen; the whole school would still be in Assembly. If they dashed, she'd make it for the second half of Double Geography.

She plumped herself down heavily opposite Theo and poured herself a bowl of cereal. She couldn't bear it, she really couldn't. This was already the second day she'd missed since Celia had left for Athens.

'So what's it to be this time? Ears? Bowels? Throat? Or shall we go for another iatrogenic complaint?'

'No, not that. No one knew what it meant,' muttered Sappho sullenly.

'That's rather the point,' replied Theo. 'Blind the poor creatures with science.'

Doggedly, Sappho bent over her cereal, lining up broken filaments of Shreddies on the edge of the bowl. It was just so *mean*. Theo could easily have woken her up on time; he must have been up for ages if he'd already had his bath and shaved. He just didn't get it that St Cecilia's was much stricter about missing school than they were at Hellenic College. Sometimes she wondered whether he did it on purpose just to avoid having to drive through the rush-hour traffic to Richmond. Though at the end of the day, it was still mostly Celia's fault for going off to Greece. Again.

Sometimes, Theo would just murmur to the secretary, Mrs Finkel, that his daughter was indisposed; the next day, she would present a letter outlining her 'pathology' in unusually precise terms.

A look would pass between whoever happened to be in the office that day; unable to bear it, Sappho would turn away, pretending to study the photographs on the board of Monty Bear, the travelling school mascot you could take on holiday with you. There he was in Orlando, Florida, with Sherril Carter and her mean-looking mother, while in another he was perched on the bonnet of a dusty Mercedes between the Adebayo twins in Lagos.

One thing was certain: over her dead body would she ever take Monty Bear on holiday with her back to Greece; the last thing she wanted was anyone at her new school making comments about their rather shabby villa in Athens, which in any case had been let to an archaeologist from the Swedish Institute in Mitseon Street, and was therefore thankfully out of bounds. Besides, that summer Ghisela had offered to take her on holiday to Vienna to stay with her mother. (If Monty Bear wasn't already bagged, this sounded like a place she might actually agree to being photographed in, providing Ghisela remained strictly out of the frame.)

'So how about Mavrodaphne's for lunch? Run and get dressed, while I call the school.'

Her father was trying to make it up to her, Sappho could tell. She could carry on sulking, at least for a bit longer, but this was risky. What you couldn't tell was when he would suddenly tire of being conciliatory; you never got any warning with Theo, and after his mood changed, there was no going back.

When she was dressed, they sauntered up Sheen Lane to Mortlake station, stopping off at the newsagent's to buy *Kathemerini* which Mr Higgins ordered in specially, doing this kind of hi-diddly-dee, 'look at us' comedy walk, arms linked as though they hadn't a care in the world, while Sappho tried to match his gigantic stride.

And yet it wasn't what you'd call relaxing, at least not properly; on the one hand, she had his undivided attention, that was true, inasmuch as he ever gave anything or anybody his undivided attention, but the thought of having to present her letter at the office the next morning lay over the day like a pall. The worry of it gnawed at her, *gnawed at her*, and, aware that she had grown silent, she tried to crank up her mood, forcing herself not to turn lumpish on him. (Nothing would be more guaranteed to dim the hot flare of his gaze.)

On the train to Waterloo, he sat opposite her on the shiny velvet seats, so bald and worn that the edges had become soft as kid, and she watched him read his newspaper, trying to make out the headlines. But she had never learned to read Greek properly: at Hellenic College you only started Greek in the Upper School, and they had moved to England in her last year in the Juniors.

As though he sensed her stare, Theo looked up, frowning over his green-tinted Onassis glasses. Then his gaze swivelled over to the passenger seated beside him, and, looking perplexed, he raised a single eyebrow. Automatically, Sappho followed his stare: a teenager with a floppy orange fringe dressed in black drainpipe jeans and, on his feet, those thick, crêpe-soled shoes that looked like dodgem cars. Covertly, she studied him. He was reading *Smash Hits* and listening to his Walkman; she recognised the song: 'With or Without You' by U2. That didn't mean anything, though – of course school inspectors didn't go around dressed like school inspectors, they'd stick out too much. Anyway, the teenager was probably older than he appeared; it was obvious they'd choose the young-looking ones for undercover work.

Urgently, Sappho scanned Theo's face for a clue as to what they should do. Perhaps they could change carriages at Clapham Junction, or else get off and wait for the next train? Mustering up all her psychic energies, she willed her father to look up from his paper, urgently popping her eyes over in the direction of the inspector, whilst at the same time folding her arms and sidling down into her seat in an attempt to disappear into her surroundings. Unperturbed, Theo continued reading his paper, fastidiously snapping back the spine before turning each page, until just as she was on the verge of breaking her cover, begging him to take action, *do something, please*, he gave a kind of comical, abstract wink, and she realised he'd been teasing her.

It seemed incredible that she could have fallen for such a trick more than once – as an adult, she would ask herself how she could have been so gullible, or, for that matter, Theo so cruel – but such was the tinderbox of her anxieties in those days that anything could set it off. Tears of relief pricked her eyes, and she turned her face towards the window, staring out towards the Peek Freans biscuit factory which filled the carriage with a sickly vanilla sweetness, as though it were being piped in through the air vents.

Mavrodaphne's was a basement taverna in a little cobbled mews off Moscow Road; sitting opposite Theo, Sappho watched her father's hands on the brilliantly white starched tablecloth as he poured the wine from a tiny pink copper jug, just half a glass for her mixed with Amita, the carved sealstone of his Minoan ring the exact amber of the dark retsina. Learning back on the vinyl banquette, she breathed in the homely smells from the kitchen – mutton, tomato sauce, bleach – while a kind of contentment settled deep inside her bones.

It wasn't Theo's fault they'd overslept. Tomorrow she would set the alarm.

Thirteen

Her parents stood by the french windows, watching Sappho pierce the newly mowed lawn with her stilts. She was acting up for them, pretending to lose her balance, arms Catherine-wheeling through the dusky air as she grabbed on to the trunk of the pear tree for support, even though she and Gail were now circus-perfect on their stilts.

Celia was wearing a flame-coloured raw silk shawl, which lay across her shoulders in hot, metallic-looking folds. She'd spent the afternoon sunbathing in the hammock, and from where she stood, Sappho could make out the blurred outline of her bikini straps against her tanned skin. She looked young and pretty, and there was an unusually engaged expression on her face as she stood there fiddling with the knotted threads of the shawl. Mostly, her vital self appeared to dwell elsewhere – more noticeably so since the move last year to London.

None of her friends' mothers had that faraway look; even though Gail's mother wore high-waisted jeans which sliced upwards, right through the crack of her buttocks, creating a spare set of bottoms underneath, and putty-coloured sandals with towelling socks, at least there was something reliably set and grim in her features, as though she had accepted her life and didn't wake up every morning hoping her destiny might still be blowing on the wind. Even Sappho could see how unrealistic that was.

Nor, for that matter, did she keep making unscheduled trips abroad, which whilst no big deal within the context of her own unusual family, Sappho was finding increasingly difficult to shrug off to her friends. Sherril Carter at school had started a rumour that Celia had walked out; soon after, her teacher, Mrs Richmond, came to look for her in the lunch queue and, putting an arm around her shoulder, invited her to eat her sandwiches in the classroom with her, 'in case you feel like a chat'.

She was so close that Sappho could make out dark red veins spidering around each nostril, and even smell the greasy old-ladies' smell of her face powder. Black silky down, invisible from a distance, grew sideways over her face, flattened down over her cheekbones as though at night she wore a burglar's stocking on her head. Everything was made even more embarrassing by the fact that the tartan lining of Sappho's satchel happened to be coated that day with a crusty purple slick of yesterday's split blackcurrant yoghurt; and worse, her sandwich, prepared by her, con- sisted of a squashed, turd-like *bifteki* between two slices of dry bread.

Oh, and at home time last week a dinner-lady mistook their neighbour, Ghisela, for her mother when two evenings in a row she turned up to collect her in her red Lufthansa uniform.

Not ideal, but all right, so long as at any given time at least one of her parents' heart appeared to be in the job. Which, to be fair, it mostly was. (Though sometimes it wasn't.)

That summer's evening on the lawn, Sappho knew why she was showing off: on a very deep level, something was wrong. For starters, the gardener had been that day – the sprinklers were on, sashaying arched needles of water on to the flower beds – and yet no one was telling her off for ruining the lawn with her stilts. At the heart of her unease, though, was the sight of her parents, framed like a formal portrait by the french windows, as though posing for a photograph. Recently, it was rare to see them in the same country, let alone in the same room. Her relationship with her parents was entirely dependent on their never present-ing anything resembling a united front; all the clowning around now was a battering ram, an attempt to drive that familiar wedge back between them.

She had no recollection of anything particularly heated ever taking place between Theo and Celia, none of the arguments or, for that matter, the disgusting displays of affection some of her friends complained of. Christine Samuels, whose chubby little mother wore Laura Ashley skirts with matching waistcoats, and a pair of half-moon reading glasses on a chain around her neck, famously once came home early from school and discovered her parents lying naked in a corner of the playroom floor, sandwiched between her Sylvanian Families doll's house and her broth-er Adam's space hopper; Christine would conduct visitors to the spot, rolling her eyes and gagging.

And yet her own parents never even held hands, let alone kissed, though once, just before Celia's first trip back to Athens, Sappho walked into the bathroom and discovered them both sitting on the edge of the bath, Theo's arm around her mother's shoulder. She had been crying, and Theo had a balled-up handkerchief in his hand as though he had been drying her tears. But the embrace was more fatherly than soppy; you could tell he was impatient to be out of there, back in his study, and besides the sight of Celia's snotty nose and teary face didn't exactly lend itself to the idea of romance, let alone anything more sexy.

That evening, she remembered Theo, grey-haired and handsome in his open-necked linen shirt, stooping down towards Celia as he leant against the doorframe, and her mother looking up at him with an expression on her face that Sappho had never seen before: her eyes were liquid, and the orange shawl had slipped down her shoulders; she looked wide open, dreamy, expectant.

Her entire pose was an invitation to violence; any idiot could see that. *You should know your husband by now* . . .

Sappho watched them through narrowed eyes, wondering whether to throw herself off her stilts in order to create a diversion.

Snap out of it, she wanted to shout, *pull yourself together!*

Instead, there was a cringingly pregnant pause, then Theo spoke.

'Your scent smells . . . suffusive,' he said, his words drifting harmlessly in the evening air.

She saw her mother flinch as though to ward off a physical blow; there were tears in her eyes, which she wiped hurriedly with the heel of one hand before fumbling on the window ledge for her sunglasses.

Sappho didn't know what suffusive meant – even when she looked it up in the dictionary, it still made no sense – but from the sardonic look on her father's face, she knew it was an insult. He was *suffused* by Celia's very presence, by the surrendering of her guard, by some kind of truce which had been agreed then unilaterally broken by her.

You don't love her, she remembered thinking, that's what all this means; and at once the fragility of their family life was made solid.

Fourteen

The knocking began around midnight, firstly in a dream.

In the dream, Sappho and her friend Gail were at school, on lunchtime door duty, sitting on the bench eating their sandwiches, when they heard someone knocking. They peered through the little grille, yet there was no one to be seen out on the pavement. And instead of the Green, they found themselves looking out on to a field where some kind of raggedy gypsy procession was going on, with drums and violins, and half-naked children dancing with muddy goats. It was a hateful, familiar scene, and Sappho kept turning around to Gail, as though to apologise for its strangeness. After that, she and Gail were running down the forbidden passage which led to the High School, chased all the while by this massive stone boulder which kept striking the brick walls as it rumbled after them; until protean and cunning, the dream then transposed itself to the courtyard of her grandmother's house, where a dwarf with a stick was beating the branches of an olive tree with what looked like Yia-Yia's silver-topped cane –

She opened her eyes and felt for the switch on the bedside light. As her eyes took in her surroundings, she felt the terror of the dream scrolling away in waves. Everything was as it should be: her copy of *The Railway Children* lay neatly on the desk beside her Snoopy clock, Celia's postcard of

Cape Sounion slipped among the pages for a bookmark. Ghisela must have picked it up off the floor when she brought in her hot-water bottle.

The knocking was getting louder and more insistent: she shut her eyes, hoping to slide back into sleep. Whoever it was was now striking the glass door panels with what sounded like a ring or a key. There was something savage and crazy in that sound which made her catch her breath: surely it couldn't be Celia back early from Athens? Or Theo locked out? And where was Ghisela to open the door?

Then it came to her: *she's gone back next door and left me on my own.* Her eyes widened in horror, and she felt the whites prickle drily. 'Ghisela,' she whispered. 'Oh, Ghisela, there's someone at the door.'

Then, abruptly, the knocking ceased. Hesitating a moment, Sappho swung her feet over the bed and felt for her pom-pom slippers. Her legs felt heavy and weak, as though she'd just emerged from a fever. She crept out of her room on to the landing and peered down the stairs. There, right by the door in her stockinged feet, stood Ghisela – she hadn't gone anywhere!

Hysterical with relief, Sappho ran down the stairs and flung herself into her arms. Ghisela hugged her, making *tskk, tskk* noises between her sticking-out teeth. 'So those crazies woke *meine* Sappho,' she said, smoothing her hair behind her ears. 'Don't worry, *liebe*, they've returned to their beds now.'

Sappho stared up at her. It was the first time she'd seen Ghisela without her glasses: her eyes were puffed-up and watery, her cheek all quilty as though she'd been asleep. She looked hilarious.

'I'd thought you'd gone back next door and left me.' She giggled, suppressing a sob.

Ghisela patted her on the shoulder, straightening the collar of her pyjama jacket.

'You think your Ghisela would leave you alone before Daddy came home?'

A little sappily, they linked arms, and she rested her head on Ghisela's flat bosom. She was wearing a lemon-yellow sweater with a silver locket pendant on a chain which felt cool against her cheek. A gigantic yawn shook Sappho, making them both laugh. With watery eyes, she looked down at the black and white floor tiles: her slippers were on the wrong feet.

Then, without warning, a dirty hand flapped through the letterbox.

'Sappho, it's me, open the door.'

She knew that voice. It belonged to another life, to the field with the dancing gypsies.

'Who is this, please?' Ghisela was saying. 'I cannot open the door unless you tell me who you are.'

Grotesquely, the hand began to wave about; and Sappho saw the palm was quite black, as though its owner had been doing handstands on the pavement.

'Just open the fucking door, will you! I'm a friend of Celia and Theo's. From Athens.'

Ghisela wavered; then motioning to Sappho to remain silent, she slid the chain into the lock. Sappho leant against the wall, panting; her heart was beating in a kind of dry drumroll, and a spasm of pain twisted her bowels. *How did she find me?*

She opened her eyes; slowly, Ghisela's finger was drawing back the trigger of the doorcatch. *Stop*, she wanted to say, *please don't let that devil into my house*. Yet a kind of lassitude lay over her like a fog: she literally couldn't dredge up a voice to protest, her jaw locked in a rictus grin which made her cheeks ache. She stood against the wall, picking at a flap of loose wallpaper, as Ghisela turned the mortice lock, one two three times; then, bouncing back slightly on its chain, the door swung open.

In the harsh glare of the porch light, Lorna stood on the doorstep. She was wearing a sleeveless brown T-shirt over some kind of checked man's jacket, and cut-off leggings which barely reached her knees. It was November, yet her legs were bare, and a toe poked out of one worn plimsoll. The nail was ridged and yellow, grown right over on to itself. She reeked of drink, and some kind of gamey women's smell. Sappho stared down at the bag at her feet: a Waitrose shopper, bound with a canvas belt. Her calves were mottled with cold. She slipped her hand into Ghisela's, marking out time. Her future position.

'Saffy, aren't you going to open the door properly?'

Only then did Sappho look up at Lorna's face. Her hair was matted, and one of her cheeks was grazed as though she'd been scraped along a brick wall. Her complexion looked raw and inflamed, and a kind of tic kept drawing her eyebrows together in a frown, as though she was on the brink of recalling something. Sappho stared at her, feeling the night air on her cheeks, flash-freezing that treacherous grin on to her face.

'Come on, Saff.' Lorna's face broke into a pleading smile, and for a moment she looked like the old Lorna.

Sappho's heart twisted. She'd painted stones for them on the beach: pebble-girls, turtles – a ladybird with five spots. The next day, she cycled down to the village and bought a can of Elnett hair lacquer to fix the paint; grinning, they closed their eyes and breathed in the delicious fumes, until sternly Lorna said that was enough and threw the remainder of the can into the bin. One night, they all climbed down to the rocks and swam naked in the sea; later, back in the kitchen, she'd boiled up *salep* on the stove, which was made of powdered orchids and glimmered thickly in her glass like pearls.

Sappho fought the connection: it was a putrid wave out there, vomiting through the windows of her house . . . the wretched stink of her old life – the tug of the past almost too much to resist. Almost. She stared up into Lorna's beautiful grey eyes.

'I'm sorry,' she said, 'I don't know who you are.'

London, 2003

Fifteen

Laleh never took her eyes off the child, not for one minute.

The swimming teacher, in a stiff black body suit which came down to her knees, was crouched over the edge of the pool, in her hand a pile of weighted rubber hoops which she was throwing one by one into the water. Fearlessly, Maro would dive to the bottom of the shallow end, shrieking with delight each time she surfaced with one of the rings in her hand, looping them on to her wrist like giant bracelets. Laleh smiled at her and waved; it was a joy to watch her play so freely in the water, her strong little white body so quick and light, but the pleasure was mixed with terror: she must watch her always, make sure also that the young teacher never lost her concentration. She couldn't understand why she was not in the water with her pupil; surely the body suit was worn for this reason, it was her job to be beside her all the time, 'one on one' Sappho called it, but perhaps, thought Laleh, tartly, the teacher wished to be free to communicate with the handsome, curly-haired pool attendant sitting on the lifeguard's chair.

Beside her, Reza slept in his new buggy; she wasn't certain if she was allowed to bring a pram into the spectators' area – nobody else had a baby with them – but so far none of the attendants had said anything to her. It was the wheels she worried about; she knew outdoor shoes must be covered with elasticated plastic socks – she had remembered to take a pair from the dispenser – but there was nothing to stop her bringing in the dirt from the street on the wheels. She just hoped that if one of the attendants did come over and ask her to move, she would understand where it was she must take Reza, and, more importantly, that wherever this place was, she would still be able to watch Maro in the water.

It was the first time she had taken Maro for her swimming lesson on her own, and so far everything was as Sappho had told her it would be. Once or twice, she had accompanied them to the pool, so she already knew how to find the street where it was situated, but for Maro's sake she wanted to make sure that everything else to do with her lesson was as regular as it could be. She was a good girl; she showed her how to put the ten pence into the locker (the money went in before, not after, you shut the door) then gave her the key on a green plastic bracelet to put around her wrist. So many things to learn . . . The number, which corresponded to the number on the locker door, had faded, so she made sure to memorise its position in the changing room. There was nothing of value in it, apart from Maro's beautiful pink wool coat which came from a new children's shop in Queen's Park (Sappho told her she was too ashamed to say how much it cost, even though Laleh would never have dreamt of asking) and her new shoes with the button strap which Tom had taken her to buy one Saturday afternoon. Maro's hooded bath robe she kept with her on the bench, together with the orange rubber sandals which she herself had bought as a gift from the one-pound shop on the Harrow Road. Everything in that shop cost exactly one pound, no matter what its true value was.

In England, objects did not appear to have a fixed worth like they did in her country; the prices changed from store to store, and sometimes you would get one item without even paying for it. 'Two for the price of one', it was called, or 'buy one, get one free'. She had wept when she saw those sandals on the pavement rack, identical to the ones she and her sister had worn as little girls back home – same colour, same cartoon duck on the front. Even the factory where they were made, the name of it stamped on the sole, was just a few kilometres from the city where she had grown up. The shock of memory made her stop on the pavement, the shoes pressed against her heart.

A summer's morning, soon after sunrise. She was nine years old; she and her sister were helping her mother hose down the courtyard floor. Madar had covered her and Ladan in black plastic sacks with holes cut out for the head and arms. Ladan was still tiny, younger even than little Maro was now, and she remembered the plastic bag dragging along the wet cement, until Madar tied it up with a knot at the back. The soles of their rubber sandals filled with water as they sprayed the courtyard walls; she could feel it puffing and squelching beneath her toes as she walked. When they had finished washing the floor, Madar took off their shoes and pressed both hands down on the soles so that all the water and air could escape, then she left them standing up against the step to dry. The sun was already high in the sky, bleaching dry the courtyard walls. Soon it would be too hot to play outdoors.

Before entering the water, she remembered Maro must shower; it said so on a notice on the wall. There was nothing separating the female changing rooms from the pool area, just an open tiled doorway, on the other side of which sat the lifeguard in his chair. At home this could never have happened; the guard would have been unable to perform his job, knowing that naked women stood showering a few feet from his back: all he had to do was peer around the wall to see them. And the women would have been beaten for their shamelessness in provoking the men.

One of the women was bending down to pick up her shampoo bottle, her pale, almost hairless sex exposed for all to see. It looked like a wound between her legs, something dangling, unfinished; with a shock, Laleh thought, I have never seen how I am made inside . . . It was better like this, surely this was how God preferred human beings to live, but Laleh wondered if she would ever get used to it.

Many times Sappho had offered to lend her a bathing suit so she could use the pool – she even offered to pay for lessons with the excuse that she could then accompany Maro in the water. 'If not for Maro, then for Reza's sake do it', she would say. 'Do it for your son.' She already owed Sappho and Tom so much; how could she now accept swimming lessons from them? Besides, her soul was so heavy she was sure that if she ever got into the water she would sink to the bottom of the pool like one of the teacher's rubber hoops . . .

Over in the swimming lanes, a man and woman were having a conversation: he was in 'Keep it Slow', she, on the other side of the rope, in 'Getting Faster'. On the signs a circle of arrows denoted the direction the swimmers must take: clockwise; this made sense if they did not want to bump against each other as they swam. The woman was leaning with her elbows against the edge of the pool, shoulders back, breasts thrust outwards and up. Two almost naked strangers, face to face in public, and nobody was giving them a second glance! Sometimes Laleh thought she would go mad with the strain of not reacting to her surroundings. It wasn't as though she disapproved – all her life she'd hated the way women in her country were made to feel dirty, as if their very presence contaminated the higher nature of men – but it was the suddenness with which she'd had to put these untested beliefs into practice.

The curly-haired lifeguard had finished his shift and was being replaced by a young girl. She looked scarcely more than a child with her high ponytail, and yet already she must be an expert enough swimmer for such a responsible position. She had a pretty, cheeky face, with heavily kholed eyes, and large gold earrings like many of the black girls in London wore. They were called Creole hoops; she had seen them in the jewellery shop windows on Kilburn High Road. The girl was wearing sports shoes on her feet, surely for indoor use only, and loose exercise trousers with one leg rolled up to the knee. Many of the young people favoured this fashion; although to Laleh it merely looked like they had not finished getting dressed. Trousers should be long or short – not one leg each.

She and the curly-haired guard exchanged places, and he stood by the steps of the lifeguard's chair chatting to her as he zipped up his fleece. He was wearing black flip-flops on his feet with an invisible thong; and was that a toe ring she could see? On a man? Tom, Sappho's husband, had a brown pair of those sandals; they were from a Japanese shop in Whiteley's Mall called Muji.

Laleh looked at her watch: another ten minutes before the end of the lesson. She wondered whether Reza would continue to sleep while she gave Maro her shower. The little girl loved to play with him; it would be difficult to get her dressed if Reza was awake. She would put her face right into the pram, and Reza would pull her ears and laugh. Sappho told her that Maro sometimes said she wished Reza could be her brother instead of the new baby in her tummy.

'We don't need your baby any more, we have Reza now,' she would tell her mother.

Laleh felt bad about this, it was all wrong that she should feel this way before the baby was born, but Sappho just laughed and said it was good that she got used to having a new baby in the house. A practice . . . a practice . . . something, she called it. A practice *run*, that was it. She must write this expression down when they got home so she wouldn't forget it. How many times had she told herself she must carry her notebook with her at all times?

The man and woman had got out of the water and were walking with their towels towards the steam rooms at the other end of the pool. They wore yellow paper bands on their wrists; Sappho told her this permitted them to use the spa. For years, once a week, she and Ladan would visit the bath house together, lying side by side on the bellystone, whispering secrets in the vapoury twilight, as the woman scrubbed their bodies with a straw glove, until one day he found out, and this too was forbidden.

Laleh looked up; the curly-haired lifeguard was walking towards her. No, please, it couldn't be . . . She felt her face burn; he was going to ask her to move the pram. How could she explain to him that she needed to be near Maro in the water?

'Is your baby?'

Laleh nodded. He had a kind face, with olive skin and unusual light-coloured eyes. Green, perhaps, with bronze reflections, like some of the Afghan people's. His brown hair, long as a girl's, puffed out around his head like a cloud, the tips of the curls a light yellow as though they had been bleached by the sun.

'Boy or girl?'

'Is boy.' Perhaps if she pointed to the clock to show that the lesson would soon be finished he would allow her to remain for the last few minutes.

'How old?'

'He . . . five months.' *You must say he is five months – you should know that by now* . . . She could feel the eyes of both the young girl lifeguard and the swimming teacher upon her. Even Maro was looking at her questioningly, her wet little face peering out of the water.

'May I sit?' he asked, pointing to the tiled bench. Laleh nodded, picking up Maro's bath robe and her orange rubber clogs. She held them protectively to her chest; she thought she would die of shame; never again would she take Maro swimming. It was her fault; she should have learned to put Reza in the sling. None of this would be happening if she hadn't been so stubborn about learning to use the sling. It was the long straps that confused her . . . She pointed to her sleeping baby in the pram.

'I must take out of pool area?'

The lifeguard laughed and a dimple appeared on his left cheek. 'Pram is no problem. I want to say you about Aquababies. You know what is Aquababies?'

She would never learn this language, not even if she lived here a hundred years. What was Aquababies now? Then she thought, But he isn't English either. She couldn't explain why she knew, but suddenly she was certain of it; and mysteriously, this knowledge made her feel better.

'What is this Aquababies?' To her surprise, she realised she was smiling; an insolent bud of a smile had cracked right through her armour. She lowered her eyes, ashamed. Where had that come from?

He smiled back, picking up her expression, mirroring back to her with added joy. 'Is mother–baby swimming lessons. You know to swim?'

Once, before the earthquake, she and Ladan had travelled to the Caspian Sea. Hand in hand they walked into the lake, their black manteaus flapping in the wind . . .

'I do not swim.'

'But you *must* to swim! Is dangerous for all mother to no swim!'

That was what Sappho had said: *for Reza's sake you should learn* . . . But what was the point of learning how to swim, what was the point of anything, when she didn't even know how long she would be allowed to remain in this country?

'I teach you.'

'Excuse me?'

'I will teach you swim.'

Laleh looked up at his face. A new dimple had appeared beside his chin, and his long-lashed green eyes were sparkling with fun. This was a game; she was sport for him. She should never have spoken to him; she had nothing to say to such a man. What a fool she was to have let him sit beside her on the bench, making a spectacle of herself in front of all these people!

Laleh felt her face harden, and her blood throbbed with anger. Let him flash his dimples to all the other girls in this place . . . She looked towards the water, where the swimming teacher was leading Maro up the steps towards the edge of the pool. Her teeth were chattering, and her lips looked blueish beneath the neon lights. Haste was essential; the child must not catch cold.

Quickly, Laleh got up from the bench, holding out the robe and sandals. She knelt beside her, slipping the hood over Maro's head, chafing dry her back and arms. 'Who is that man, Laleh?' asked Maro, sliding her frozen little fingers beneath the collar of Laleh's blouse. Out of the corner of her eye, she saw the lifeguard had got up from the bench and was peering into Reza's pram. Now he would wake the baby, she would have to feed him, and they would never get out of this place.

'Is one teacher, Maro. Come, we must to shower.'

'So when we begin our swimming lessons?'

Was this person stupid *and* big-headed? Without looking up at him, Laleh slipped a sandal on to Maro's foot. 'Thank you, but I am *never* like to swim,' she said icily.

'What's your name?' asked Maro, balancing on one foot as she held on to Laleh's shoulders.

Was there no escaping this humiliation? Now Maro was talking to a strange man in public, and it was her fault. It was unbearably hot in the pool, she was sweating beneath her coat, perhaps she even smelled. She would have to tell Sappho when they got back, *Sorry, I bring Maro every place you like, but no more swimming pool . . .*

'Come, my dearest, we take Reza for changing area,' said Laleh, tying the belt of Maro's bath robe firmly around her waist. *Just let him try, just let him dare ask my name . . .*

Without consulting her, the man had picked up the pram and was carrying it down the steps. Then he crouched opposite her on the pool-side, the two of them squatting on the floor like a pair of circus midgets, and he shook Maro's hand beneath her sleeve. His face was serious now, no sign of the dimples.

'My name is Enzo,' he said, looking at Laleh. 'I am so happy I meet you here today.'

One day there were bruises on her legs.

She first noticed them at the bath house as she was combing Ladan's hair: five black fingers between her sister's thighs. 'What is this, *jan?*' asked Laleh, but she already knew; there was no need to ask.

Putting her arm around Ladan's shoulders, Laleh slumped back against the baked stone wall, letting the comb drop to the floor. She would roast him alive, press his piggy buttocks on to the edge of the bath-house furnace so that the flesh of his privates squeaked and hissed like chops on a grill. Tears burned her eyes, instantly drying to salt on her cheeks. He had dirtied her beautiful white skin with his hands.

She felt Ladan's fingers searching her own. 'Don't cry, big sister, all will soon pass.'

Sixteen

They met in Queen's Park on a summer's afternoon, one of those razor-like, sunless days which after all those years still filled Sappho with despair.

She would look out of the window at the contracted skies, and no matter how hard she tried to buck herself up, it still felt like the end of the world. She ought to have been used to it by now – she had a kind of honourable pact with herself never to complain about the weather, just as during that year at St Cecilia's she would force herself not to dwell upon any remotely pleasurable aspect of her previous life in Athens – but nevertheless it would still catch her unawares.

Part of it was never having anything suitable to wear. All her warm clothes were packed away in camphor – 'I don't know why you bother, it's not like you won't be needing them,' Tom would warn her year after year – but the change-of-season habit was too deeply ingrained to resist. In Athens, regardless of the weather, you could mark the official start of winter simply by the smell of mothballs on the trolley bus; everybody unpacked their woollens on exactly the same day. But the thought of wearing socks or tights in summer was so depressing that she would rather freeze, and so freeze she invariably did.

On the way home from nursery Maro asked to go to the park.

'It's been raining, my darling, the toys will be all wet,' replied Sappho, shivering in her low-cut cardigan; hopefully at least the baby was warm in there.

She knelt down to fasten the poppers of Maro's pink spotty raincoat.

'How about we go home and have a nice bowl of *avgolemono* soup for lunch?' *So that in the shortest time possible we can both be snuggled under my quilt for a nap.*

(At least she'd finally learned not to pack away the winter blankets.)

'Remember Granny and Roo are coming to take you to the puppet show this afternoon,' she wheedled.

'Mummy, I want to try the new tyre swings. Please.'

Sappho glanced across the railings at the park; the weather was so vile that even the hearty English children, with their frostbitten cheeks, their dripping noses and raw little gloveless fingers, were no doubt all snuggled indoors in front of their Pingu and Maisie videos.

The main playground was deserted; only a group of Asian schoolboys in the black blazers of the local comprehensive were smoking cigarettes beneath the miniature bandstand. She would die if she had to spend another minute in this cold.

'You never take me to the park any more, Mummy.'

It wasn't true, but it might as well have been. She stung with remorse: if Maro felt hard done by now, how on earth was she going to react when the baby was born?

'All right, we'll go, but only for ten minutes. Look at my watch, see the big hand?' Maro peered at it, then looked back up at her, frowning; beads of rainwater sparkled on the tips of her lashes and, in spite of feeling so cold, a needle of pleasure pierced Sappho's heart. How had she and Tom made such a beautiful child? 'Well, when the big hand is on the number twelve –'

'Which one is number twelve?'

'Here. Look, it's here on top, the one and two together.'

'Where, Mummy?' she asked, shifting impatiently from one wellington boot to the other.

Of all the idiotic moments to begin teaching Maro the time . . . 'Never mind, darling, I'll show you when we get home. Go and play now.'

Without waiting to be asked twice, Maro ran through the green painted gate towards the swings. Sappho looked around her, trying to decide where would be the most sheltered place to sit. She could sense the schoolboys in the bandstand staring at her defensively; and as a peaty cloud of skunk drifted towards her, she realised why. No wonder they were looking so shifty.

Then, to her surprise, she saw a figure seated on the bench by the plastic dolphin waste bin. It was a woman, carrying a baby wrapped up in one of those synthetic mink blankets which the gypsies used to sell in Monastiraki.

Automatically, Sappho glanced around to see where her older child could be playing, but the playground was empty. There was something about the way the baby was swaddled so tightly that made Sappho think it must be newborn; what on earth was the mother doing out on a day like this?

Maybe if she hadn't been pregnant herself, and felt that very morning the sweet shock of recognition at her baby's first rippling movements as she lay in the bath – *There you are! At last!* – she might never have been drawn to sit beside the woman on the bench; it wasn't as though she was planning to stay long in the park.

'How old is your baby?'

'Excuse me?'

'Your baby, how many months?'

The woman stared at her; she had an unusual, almost disconcertingly symmetrical face: wide-set dark eyes, a high forehead and pale full lips whose bow looked as though it had been drawn in with a calligraphy brush. Sappho was suddenly reminded of the portraiture classes she had taken at Goldsmiths; they were told to draw the model's head as an oval, and divide it up into alignment lines: a vertical one straight down the middle, then horizontally to mark the eye height, nose and mouth. After that came a whole series of complex calculations based around the size of an average eye (forehead equals three eyes, head equals seven, nose equals one and a half. And what was it? One eye-width between eyes, plus one more on either side . . .).

Rarely, however, did the models' faces match up to these idealistic parameters, but there was one girl, a music student called Dolly, who like this woman had a perfect, almost freakishly proportioned face; it had been almost too easy to draw her. Often Sappho had wondered what it must be like to go through life with a face like that.

'Four. Is four month.' She pronounced it 'munt'.

'Boy or girl?'

Automatically, Sappho had slipped into talking pidgin English back to her.

'Is boy.'

There was a weary, almost hostile, edge to the woman's voice. Perhaps she resented being interrogated by a total stranger. Fair enough, not everyone subscribed to the notion of instant camaraderie between mothers. Though what she was doing sitting with a baby in a windswept playground was anyone's guess.

Sappho glanced at her watch; another five minutes and she would tell Maro it was time for lunch. She tried to remember if she'd had a decent breakfast; Tom had got her up before leaving to catch his train – where was it again he was going? He did say, on his way out of the door, but it hadn't registered – later she'd text him to find out – and she'd come downstairs at eight to discover that Maro had dressed herself in an eccentric combination of clothes: a checked sleeveless summer dress over a pair of silk Chinese pyjama bottoms, with a back to front ballet cardigan worn over the top.

She seemed to recall seeing toast crusts on a plate when she came downstairs, though they could easily have been Tom's, and a half-eaten bowl of muesli, which she herself had finished before they set off for Maro's nursery. Mysteriously, she was now starving again.

'Is your girl?'

Sappho looked at the stranger; her expression had softened, making her appear less offputtingly patrician. 'Yes, she's mine. I have another one in here.' She patted her stomach beneath her cashmere cardigan.

'I think is boy?'

Unwittingly, Sappho felt herself flush with pleasure. 'Why do you say that?'

'In my country, say baby girl destroy mother beauty. Baby boy, how say . . . baby boy is make beauty stronger.' She pronounced 'stronger' as though it had three syllables: *seh-tron-ger*.

Sappho hadn't even admitted to herself that she might want a boy, at least not properly. Tom was so smitten with Maro that he would be delighted with another girl – in fact he actively wanted one – whereas on some primitive level she subscribed to that Greek thing where a man with a son and six daughters would declare he had one child – *child*, not even *son*, it being implicit that male offspring were the only ones that truly counted.

Sappho wondered where the woman could be from; somewhere in the Middle East, she reckoned, though she didn't exactly look Arabic. Turkish, maybe, or one of the eastern ex-Soviet states. That kind of platonic beauty tended to subsume racial characteristics.

'Do you live in this area?'

Once again, an expression of hostility shadowed the woman's face, instantly making Sappho feel wrong-footed, as though she'd asked a far more personal question. Though she herself had cleared the way for it by paying her that extravagant compliment about her looks.

'I live Stonebridge, near Harlesden.' Again she broke the names up into three syllables: *Seh-tone-bridge, Har-les-den.* She spoke slowly, as though winkling the information out of herself.

'So quite a way from Queen's Park, then?' replied Sappho, encouragingly.

'I like come here, is better. Sometimes, when raining, I go all day Whiteley's shopping centre. Is warm, safe. Come back Harlesden in night.'

There was something about her manner, the way the words came tumbling out in disconnected blocks, that made Sappho think she had been living mostly in her own head. Then there was that stilted English which, instead of making her appear vulnerable, seemed to denote a kind of inner steeliness, capable of bouncing even the most innocuous question back to the interlocutor as though it were an impertinence.

She glanced around the playground: no sign of a pram or buggy. Could she really have walked all the way from Harlesden carrying a four-month baby in her arms, or did she take the 18 bus along the Harrow Road? Even with a sling, that would be hard-going.

Sappho hadn't seen the child yet; it was swaddled so tightly that, from the back, all that was visible was the tip of the blanket pointing stiffly upwards like a splint. For all she knew, there could be a doll in there. She smiled, remembering how, as a little girl in Athens, she would take her Tiny Tears doll, Koukla-mou, to Kyria Maria's shop on Erechthiou Street, pretending to the other customers that Koukla-mou was a real baby, and that she had popped out to buy a tin of evaporated milk for her bottle. The funny thing was that on some level she really believed it.

Why would anyone actually choose to spend the day in a shopping centre? *Is warm, safe.* Was the woman in some kind of physical danger, perhaps? Sappho looked across the playground towards her house, just visible through the gaps in the railings. In a few moments, she would call Maro, and together they would walk out of the park gates towards home. Elsa, the Colombian cleaning woman, was coming in later, so the house would be just as she left it: breakfast things on the table, towels on the bathroom floor, yesterday's supper dishes in the sink.

Secretly, she liked the house in the mornings, even the smell: a mixture of coffee, toast, unaired rooms, thick with used oxygen, Tom's Penhaligon's English Fern, and the sour odour of empty wine bottles left in the recycling basket in the kitchen: a complex distillation of their lives.

'Do you have family in this country?'

'I am nobody. Asylum seeker.'

I am nobody . . . Did she really say that? It had to be a slip of the tongue, thought Sappho. *I have* nobody, surely she meant . . . So she was an asylum seeker; that explained the prickliness.

Sappho felt an exhilarating kinship with Laleh's silence: this woman's past, like her own, was inviolable; on some deep level, she felt she already knew all there was to know about the stranger. Later, Tom, Andrea, Bridget, and several of their friends, would find the gaps in Laleh's story proof of a kind of moral unreliabilty – *half of them are bogus, everyone knows that* . . . *you can't just take in somebody off the streets* . . . *she'd tell you her story herself if she had nothing to hide* . . .

She felt a hand on her shoulder, and started; it was Maro, she had completely forgotten about her daughter's presence. For all she knew, Maro could have walked out of the park gates with a stranger.

'Look, darling, look at the sweet baby,' Sappho trilled, even though, as it happened, she had not yet laid eyes on it.

Maro stared at the woman; and instinctively, as though the child's curiosity was the most natural thing in the world, Laleh turned the baby around, shifting the bundle into her other arm so that its face was finally visible. *Strange she never did it before . . .*

'This my son, Reza,' she said, smoothing back the corner of the blanket, so that Maro could peer inside.

So it *was* a real baby, thought Sappho.

He was dressed in what looked like several layers of hand-knitted clothes – bonnet, mittens, jacket, waistcoat – all in garish shades of purl-stitched acrylic: mustard, violet, maroon and Germolene pink, the kind of leftover wool old ladies used to knit jumpers for jumble sales. The bonnet, in particular, reminded Sappho of the dolls' clothes she would buy for her Tiny Tears at the Anglican Church summer fête in Athens.

She glanced over towards Maro, willing her not to comment on the baby's strange apparel: *Why is he dressed like a girl, Mummy?* Her daughter was usually acutely fine-tuned to what people were wearing. Maro, however, seemed to understand there was something unusual about the situation, and merely stood there staring raptly at the sleeping infant.

He stirred as the woman settled him more comfortably into the crook of her arm, drawing the folds of the blanket once more around his head. He had a broad, sallow face, with black hair growing low on his forehead, and long, silky eyelashes.

'What *your* name, dear?' The woman held out her hand to Maro, no trace of her previously surly manner; even the timbre of her voice was softer, more melodic.

Maro took her hand and settled comfortably on to the bench beside her. 'My name is Maro, with an o at the end. M-A-R-O. What's your name?'

'I, Laleh – like yellow Teletubby.' So she did have a sense of humour, thought Sappho, surprised. *Then why was she so offhand to me, just now?* Strange how animated she became around children, she was like a different person; then, with a pang: *That's how Lorna used to be . . .*

Any minute now, Maro would remember she was hungry and would demand to go home for lunch. She herself would get up from the bench and shake the woman's hand – 'Nice meeting you' – then utter that dreadful, dreadful phrase: 'Take care. You take care, now' . . . She shuddered; but what else was there to say? 'Good luck with being an asylum seeker, and I hope the Home Office let you stay . . .' Or 'Do you really not own a buggy? What will you do when your baby gets too heavy to carry?'

A fierce impulse was welling up from somewhere deep inside her: *invite her to lunch, invite her to share your soup* . . . Her legs felt weak; her heart was pounding furiously, and she could hear the words floating around in her head, untethered, useless. That woman's life had its own course to run; meeting her and Maro in the park wouldn't change that destiny, she was too disengaged for that. No, she was the hungry one . . . *For God's sake, just ask her* . . .

In the end it was Maro who took charge. 'Do you want to taste my mummy's soup, Laleh?'

'Tank you, I eat.'

Sappho sensed the woman's body stiffen in something like horror; there was a hunted, almost wild, look in her eyes, and you could see her shoulders collapsing down into the collar of her ugly maroon windcheater. She held her baby closer, clasping the bundle to her breast like a shield.

Oblivious to her unease, Maro went on: 'It's a really nice soup, you'll like it. It's got chicken and rice, and then my mummy puts some eggs and lemon in it at the end.'

She paused, and looked up at her expectantly.

'We don't live far, you know, just across the park. Look, Laleh, that's our house.' She got up from the bench, tugging earnestly at Laleh's sleeve. Pointing, she said: 'See, that's it, the one with the green door and the red flowers on the window.'

Sappho could tell by Laleh's face that she was desperate to get away, she was electric with discomfort, but, amazingly, the desire to please Maro appeared to be stronger than her distress. 'Yes, dearest, I see red flowers,' she murmured weakly.

At that moment, Sappho knew for certain that she would come, and that by the end of the day she would have asked Laleh to live with them; this knowledge gave her the courage to find her voice.

'I think Maro won't let you go, Laleh,' she said easily. 'You're going to have to come back and try my soup.'

They looked at each other – game over, all the awkwardness gone.

'Tank you,' said Laleh, 'I come.'

'How many times have I told you girls not to stare?' scolded Madar as she rinsed the rice in the sink.

The sisters were fascinated by the woman's wart; it was a little powerhouse of energy that appeared to keep her nose in a state of perpetual motion. Ladan even bet it must glow in the dark. They tried not to stare, but they found it impossible to address their remarks to any other part of her face; besides which, she had rather sly, close-set eyes which did not invite confidences. Her name was Atifeh, and she was married to a wealthy relative on their father's side, a colonel in the army.

'This time we won't stare,' promised Laleh, as she prepared glasses of orange soda and pomegranate juice to take to the guests in the next room.

As she set the tray down on the plastic oil cloth covering the carpet, Laleh motioned for Atifeh to join them. But as usual, she refused; nodding her head upwards, she pulled her chador closer about her face, sidling further against the wall in the corner of the room.

Not even when Madar and Ladan came in with steaming dishes of food would she agree to join the other guests on the carpet. Instead, she foraged shamelessly for the choicest morsels – crispy squares of *tadig* from the bottom of the rice pan, saffron chicken, and spinach stew with prunes – which she piled up on a plate for her husband.

'He never even says thank you to her,' said Ladan indignantly, later that evening when they were washing the dishes in the kitchen. 'If I had a husband like that, I'd make him get his own supper.'

It was true; in all the years of visiting the house, Atifeh's husband never once addressed a word to her, though he was extravagantly cordial to the sisters.

Their father smiled and stroked his youngest daughter's cheek. 'Your uncle is a private man, *jan*. Perhaps he thanks his wife later, when they are alone.'

Their relative would enquire about the sisters' lessons, and bring boxes of sweetmeats from the best confectioners in the city: threads of rose-flavoured fairy floss, sour cherry nougat, and Ladan's favourite, citron Turkish delight. From the corner of the carpet, his wife would observe his every movement, her tiny eyes darting from side to side as her gaze followed him around the room; she would understand it was time to go home the moment he picked up his keys from the table.

The years passed. The girls' father encouraged them to attend the university; he was a liberal man who, unusually for their rather traditional circle, wished to widen, not narrow, his daughters' horizons. Many of their acquaintances disapproved; they said the sisters would be too old to

126

marry by the time they finished their studies. But their father always replied: A woman is more than a womb; the brain too is a vessel . . .'

From when they were children, they would read the great poets together in the evenings, and over the years he taught them the rudiments of algebra, physics and astronomy. On moonless nights, they learned to ride their father's bicycle in the courtyard, clinging on to the vine-covered walls for support. Laleh dreamed of unlocking the gate and cycling down the tree-lined boulevard to the outskirts of their city; they could be arrested for indecency if it was ever known they had even mounted a bicycle.

Then, one day, news reached them that the woman's husband had cast her out because she was barren; three times, before a witness, he uttered the words: 'I divorce you, I divorce you, I divorce you.'

On hearing this, the sisters regretted thinking that her wart was an object of amusement; they remembered the greed with which she would pile up her husband's plate, her refusal to take even a glass of water for herself, the long hours she spent sitting in the corner of the room. It was rumoured among their circle that, after the divorce, her own family in the north of the country refused to take her back; some even hinted she'd ended up on the streets of the capital.

In time, the man became even more powerful; he had a new hungry look in his eyes and the girls grew to dread his visits. The moment he left, his boxes of sweetmeats would be taken around to a neighbour's.

Seventeen

Andrea called on a dark Monday morning as Tom was sitting in his shed listening to the pleasant sound of the rain thudding on to the felt roof above his head. It was autumn, almost two months since Laleh had moved into the upstairs flat, and through the window he could see the leaves of the passion flower trembling in the wind.

At first he didn't answer, in the hope that Laleh or Sappho or Elsa, the cleaning woman, would pick up the phone . . . two rings, three rings . . . *come on, you slackers, one of you must be in* . . . five, six, seven . . . *you can't all be out* . . . eight, nine – *oh, I give up* . . .

'Hello?'

'Hello, darling, is this a bad moment?'

'Not especially.' *As in: yes, but no worse than any other.* 'How are things with you, Mother?'

'Not too bad . . . I've been rushed off my feet driving my grannies to the surgery for their flu jabs . . . Daddy's knee has been playing him up a bit, he had to rest it for a couple of days, but he's better now, he's down in his shed too as it happens.'

Like father, like son . . .

'Apart from that, we're not complaining. Now, I won't keep you, I know you're a busy man. I'm ringing to find out about Maro's birthday party . . .'

'Mother, you know I'm the wrong person to ask about that kind of thing.' *Don't tell me Sappho's gone and invited them to the party . . . they only came up last week for the inauguration of the lofts . . . Then before that there was all that fuss about going to Peter Jones to choose a double buggy . . .* He looked out of the window on to the lawn; was it possible for a mother to be stalking her own son? It was Sappho's fault; she was the one who'd given Andrea that first inch.

'Yes, well, as it happens I did ring the other day to discuss the birthday party with Sappho, only Laa-Laa answered the telephone –'

'For the hundredth time, Mother, her name is Lah-*leh*, not Laa-Laa. Laa-Laa's a Teletubby.'

'And she informed me that Sappho was out,' continued Andrea, smoothly. 'That was it, she just mumbled "Sappho go", or something which sounded like that, without saying where it was that Sappho had gone, or when she might be back. She could have been in the early stages of labour for all I knew . . . She knew perfectly well who I was, it's not as though we'd never met, the least she could have done is ask if I wanted to leave a message . . . which makes one think telephone manners must rather leave something to be desired in her country. Still, I imagine you and Sappho must be getting used to her gruff ways by now.'

'Mother, Laleh's a very warm and friendly person once you get to know her.' She wasn't, actually, she was a sphinx woman, and a disturbingly good-looking one, though fortunately not his type.

'Anyway, let's hope she'll be a help for Sappho once the baby's born, though how much of a help she can realistically be when she's got her own baby to take care of is another matter. Of course when it comes to the crunch she'll put her child first . . . blood is thicker than water, any mother will tell you that. How many times did I end up sticking my neck out when you got into one of your scrapes?'

None that I recall. However we'll let that pass.

'Still, under the circumstances, I'd say giving a hand to Sappho is the very least she can do in return for the luxury flat –'

'I wouldn't exactly call it a luxury flat, Mother, two rooms and a kitchenette.' It was unbelievable: he was doing it again. Justifying his life to his mother, as though he cared even the slightest bit what she thought.

'Still, if Sappho hadn't offered the flat out of the blue to . . . *Lah-lay* – there, is that dashing enough for you? – if she hadn't offered the flat to . . . *this person* and her baby, you would have still had your office upstairs, instead of having to traipse down to the bottom of the garden in all weathers.'

'I like it here, as it happens. I like my shed, I actually like having to traipse down to the bottom of the garden in all weathers.' Enough now, this was getting silly, and he could hear his smart-alec voice coming on. Next she'd be telling them they should move to a bigger house.

'You need a bigger house, Tom, it's plain for anyone to see –'

He cleared his throat and looked out of the window. 'Mother, there's a couple of things on my desk that need dealing with; I'll get Sappho to ring you about –'

'Of course, darling, you've got the business to take care of.' Her voice was suddenly brisk and understanding: the model tycoon's mother. It never failed: any mention of work instantly shrank her back down to size, turned her into a rational human being, a pussy cat.

Truth was, she adored him being a millionaire.

At least on paper, and if his accountants were to be believed.

Either way, Tom was increasingly starting to think of himself as the victim of his own good fortune. It was ridiculous, he knew it; he was about the last person on earth who had any right to feel sorry for himself: *Get a grip, minger!* But the gnawing discontent wouldn't go away. He actually despised his life; there was no other way of putting it. On the one hand he had Sappho and Maro, and the new baby, about to be born – they were the good bits, if you like, his success stories. While on the other hand, well – where to begin?

Where, indeed? He tried to pin down when this unease with his wealth had begun. Not in the beginning, that was for sure. Four million pounds, at six per cent per annum. 'Do the maths,' he would declaim to the silence of his office, 'do the maths . . .'

The unease was somehow connected to Laleh, of that much he was now certain. Nothing to do with having a stranger *per se* in the flat upstairs; they'd agreed they'd need a live-in somebody after the baby was born, in principle, at least, and Reza was a great little kid, no trouble at all, so that wasn't the problem either. No, it was more the manner of her coming. The manner of her coming? *You pompous prick!*

One afternoon he'd let himself into the house, back from a big investors' shindig in Newcastle, and she was just *there*, in his kitchen, sitting on the couch with Sappho.

'This is Laleh, darling, we met this afternoon in the park,' Sappho said, as he placed his laptop down on the floor beside the rocking chair. 'Laleh, my husband, Tom.'

Smoke from next door's bonfire was drifting over the wall and seeping invisibly through gaps in the french windows. The room had grown dim, they had forgotten to switch on the light, like two very old friends who had been talking for so long that they had lost track of time.

She was extraordinarily good-looking, with a lithe,

almost athletic body, and the most wonderful ripe breasts, which even in the half-light no amount of baggy clothes could disguise. If anything, the fact that her charms were hidden under frankly rather unattractive clothes – waffle-knit jumper, grey jeans, dodgy-looking granny trainers – just seemed to heighten them. And then to really throw you, this severe nun's face, pale skin, no make-up, with a long dark plait twisted over one shoulder.

Her manner was stiff, surly almost, as she held out her hand; and Tom had the sensation of something in the air left hanging, a confidence perhaps that had been interrupted by his arrival. She doesn't like me, he thought, surprised at how certain he was of this knowledge. It was unusual for strangers to react strongly to him, especially women. *Bland Man, that's me . . .*

Sappho leaned back to switch on the Anglepoise lamp on the dresser; and as Tom went over to kiss her, he noticed a tiny baby asleep on a blanket between them.

'This is Reza, Laleh's little boy. He was born at St Mary's.' Instinctively, Sappho placed a hand on her bump, though it was still barely noticeable beneath her low-cut, cashmere cardigan. That green suited her, thought Tom, then: Christ, you'd never have guessed what's-her-face there had just had a baby . . .

Sappho looked different; there was a kind of spark in her, something pleading, almost wizened-looking, in her expression that he hadn't seen for a long time. Her eyes appeared to be brimming, and her cheeks were flushed and hollow. At times, he felt that everything happened in reverse between them: she had ripped out the stops all in one go, bruised his heart with her heart so that he loved her at once, he had no choice; then the moment they got back to England, the slow, invisible march inwards. Or perhaps that was just marriage for you. Maybe it happened to everyone in the end.

'Is there any tea left?' He was being exigent, childish; he wanted someone to notice him. Break the spell between the two women. Sappho got up from the sofa and poured him a cup from her grandmother's silver teapot. The outside of the pot had grown tarnished; Andrea was itching to polish it for her, but Sappho wouldn't let her. She claimed it magically transformed any old tea you put in it; she was worried polishing it might disturb its powers.

'Where's Maro?' He had brought her a new colouring set and artist's pad from the John Lewis in Newcastle.

'She's with your parents. Don't you remember they were taking her to that puppet show on the barge in Little Venice? They're catching the train back tonight.'

That was all right then, as long as they weren't planning on spending the night . . . Sappho's voice sounded bright, false, as though she was acting. She wasn't what you'd call a loner, but nor was she one for close friendships; she had her circle of mums – Bridget, Nick's wife; some women from NCT classes; other mothers from Maro's nursery – but nobody she was really intimate with. Certainly no one like this Laleh person, whoever she was.

He looked towards the sofa; Laleh had got up and was zipping up her coat, some sort of maroon windcheater affair with an elasticated waist, a garment he could easily imagine his mother wearing. She had narrow, Barbie-doll hips, with supple-looking legs, *easy, tiger*, and those unforgettable breasts which somehow managed to draw attention to themselves even beneath the stiff fabric of her jacket.

It was obvious his presence was making her uncomfortable. None of the other mums would have dreamt of shifting just because he walked into the room. There would always be a bit of chit-chat, the mildest type of flirtation (*so mild, you're probably the only one doing it*), he would make an effort to remember the children's names – seemed to be a glut of Freyas and Olivers recently – perhaps even sit down with them for a cup of tea or glass of wine, depending on the hour.

As he watched Sappho accompany Laleh to the door, he had a sudden memory of the kitchen at his parents' house in Rye: lying as a small boy on the floor beside the Rayburn, playing with his Fisher-Price garage, endlessly cranking a lift full of cars up to the numbered parking bays on the roof, for the sole purpose of sending them one by one back down the blue spiral ramp. The dry biscuity smell of burning coke embedded between the flagstones, glittering beads of it, which he would pick up with a wet finger and drag along the floor.

His mother and her friend, Helen, would be drinking tea at the table, when there would be the sound of his father's key in the lock. The two women would look at each other and sigh, and a kind of rueful smile would pass between them. *Well, I'd best be off then . . .*

It had taken surprisingly little to convert his office into a flat for Laleh. Such was Sappho's urgency that by the end of the month a bespoke red cedar shed had been ordered from a company called Urban Sanctuaries, and erected on a poured-concrete base at the bottom of the garden where the wisteria bush used to be.

Larry, the Irish doorman at Iskander, had come in for three weekends in a row with his wife's nephew to hang shelves and help move Tom's stuff into the shed. As he stood by the kitchen window, watching them carry his computer monitor down the garden path, Tom had a sudden, almost comical vision of himself as a dog slinking off to its kennel, banished in disgrace from the family home . . . *Come back, Fido, all is forgiven . . .*

On Sappho's instructions, they painted the two rooms of the flat in some kind of neutral-coloured, organic nonleaded paint, and fixed the broken sash-window which for years had been jammed quite satisfactorily with an old cork sliced lengthways. On the second weekend, a van from John Lewis delivered a nursery suite for the baby, together with a wardrobe and double bed for Laleh.

'Where's she living at the moment, anyway?' asked Tom, watching Larry and his nephew assembling the flat-packed changing table. The instructions were spread out over the newly sanded floorboards, propped up against a tin of varnish. Not to be petty or anything, he hoped their visitor would appreciate the magnificent welcome that was being rolled out for her.

'In an asylum seekers' B&B in Stonebridge or Wembley, somewhere like that,' replied Sappho absently, unpacking the foam, vinyl-covered changing mat and propping it up against the wall. It had a pattern of blue and white checks with a red sailing boat in the middle to match the cot-bumpers and curtains which were still in their packaging. She had never been this manic about her own nest-building, thought Tom, not even when she was expecting Maro, her firstborn. In fact, she'd been so superstitious about bringing any baby equipment into the house that most of it had to be ordered online from the hospital.

'So what's her legal status?'

'I just told you, Tom, she's an asylum seeker.'

'A refugee?'

'Kind of, only she doesn't know whether she'll be allowed to remain in this country.'

Holding on to the ladder for support, Sappho pulled herself up from the floor. Since her twenty-week scan, more or less overnight, it seemed, she had swelled into her pregnancy. It suited her; her lips were engorged, bruised-looking, and there were erotic shadows beneath her eyes.

'I'm just wondering whether perhaps we should have waited a bit . . .'

'Waited for what?' asked Sappho sharply. Her cheeks had that flushed, sunken look again, and he could see a muscle in her jaw working.

'You know, to see whether it works out with . . .'

'Laleh, Tom – her name is Laleh. Not so difficult, really.'

You mean even for a thicko like me, thought Tom.

'You know, we could have had a trial period or something, see whether it worked out, before she and the baby moved in. No point in getting everyone's hopes up for nothing.'

And how the hell were they going to get rid of her if it all went pear-shaped? They couldn't exactly throw her out on to the streets with a small baby. Turned out she didn't even own a pram – or so she claimed.

Out of the corner of his eye, he was aware of Larry making a great show of being immersed in the assembling of the cot, scratching his head and jabbing at the instruction leaflet with a nicotine-stained forefinger whilst trying to look oblivious of the spat going on between the boss and his wife. Come Monday morning, everyone at Iskander would know that they were getting a dodgy nanny on the cheap. *What a true bohemian you are, Tom!*

'I mean, have you even talked about the job? Hours, duties, that kind of thing? And there's Maro to think about; it won't be easy for her having someone looking after her who barely speaks English.' *Now you really sound like Andrea and her bloody Daily Mail-reading cronies.* 'Plus the small detail that Laleh's already got a baby of her own. Hardly fair when Maro's about to have a new brother or sister herself to deal with.'

That was below the belt – he knew how worried Sappho was about the effect the new baby would have on Maro – but he was on a roll now, a negative roll, firing out objections for the sake of it. He used to love, *still loved*, the dottiness of Sappho's background, the fact that neither of her parents had ever had a job whilst she was growing up, even though after the divorce Celia did end up by opening quite a successful gallery in Athens.

Now, however, he was irritated by the fact that Sappho had obviously acted on a whim with this Laleh woman, without giving the practicalities even a second thought. References, work permits, the dynamics of sharing their house with another family. The possibility of the baby's father, whoever he was, one day showing up. *But then that's my role, being boring, thinking things through . . .*

'Maro loves her, actually.' Her voice sounded defeated.

'How do you know Maro loves her?' asked Tom.

'She met her too; we were together that day, on our way back from nursery. You were in Leeds.'

'It was Newcastle, but never mind.' *She could at least pretend to be interested in the job I no longer have . . .* 'So what, Maro was there too?' His heart lurched with something like fear, and a picture came into his mind of the two women sitting in the dusk-filled kitchen, the sleeping baby, the sense of an invisible circle having been closed.

'For some of the time, then she went off with your parents. Look, Tom, let's just forget the whole thing. It's obvious it's not going to work.'

He couldn't see her face – she was standing by the window with her back to him – but her voice was trembling, as though he'd invaded, defiled, some basic human right of hers. It had got out of hand; they'd ended up in a darker place than he'd meant to lead them to, a dank and tangled grove. *Turn back, Tom, before it's too late . . .* If Sappho felt so strongly about having this woman in the house, then he should trust her instincts, those same instincts which had first drawn her into his arms, to his bed in that Athens hotel.

'I'm sorry, darling, I'm being an arse.' Thankfully Larry and nephew had got the hint and finally left the room. He stood behind her and slid an arm around her waist, slipping his fingers beneath the thin elastic of her skirt. The flesh had thickened; it was dense and warm beneath his hands. *She was swollen with child . . . his child . . .* Gently, he drew Sappho's face towards his and their eyes met; she was smiling, but inwardly, distantly, and her cheeks were wet. At the sight of her tears Tom's heart ached with desire, and something like rage. They kissed, and he pressed his penis beneath the swell of her belly.

One false step, and you're back out where you belong . . .

Eighteen

'Why does my name end with "o", like a *boy*?' asked Maro
one day in the bath. She was playing a game with a linen
hand towel: dragging it along the surface of the water, then
poking it up from underneath until the cloth billowed up
like a parachute.

Sappho leaned forward and tucked a stray lock of her
daughter's hair into her bath cap.

'Because it's a Greek name, like my name. You see:
Sapph-o ... Mar-o,' as though that somehow made it
more normal, more desirable. 'Anyway, my Greek yia-
yia was called Maro, and I loved my granny even more
than I loved my own mummy. Well, about the same as I
loved my mummy,' she corrected herself quickly.

Maro pursed her lips and said nothing; sometimes you could
watch a thought surface from somewhere deep in her daughter's soul – see it take form, grow steady, in those brimming
eyes. Then her expression grew skittish and, snatching up the
wet hand towel, she plastered it on to her chest and giggled.

'Look, Mummy, a boob tube!'

'A *what* tube?'

'A *boob* tube. For your boobies. Eden's mummy wears
one. *And* Eden does.'

Well, no surprises there, thought Sappho primly as she
went to get Maro's bath robe from the bedroom. Eden had

also recently been sporting what looked suspiciously like black nail varnish on her toes, while her ponytail appeared to have been straightened with electric irons.

Later, as Sappho was drying her, Maro put her arms about her neck and said, 'I don't love Granny Celia more than you. I don't love her even the same as you.'

Sappho turned her face to hide the molten pleasure coursing through her veins; that would teach Celia, she thought.

'You know you're a *bit* hard on her,' said Tom, on the way back from Stansted.

'Hard on who?' asked Sappho, looking out of the window as they drove through Whitechapel market. The stalls were covered in sheets of tarpaulin so it was impossible to see what they were selling.

'Come on, Saff. At the end of the day, you're her daughter. Her *only* daughter. It's natural for her to want to come over for the birth. You didn't have to be quite so snippy when she offered.'

Here we go, she thought. As usual, the end of Celia's visit had left her feeling ragged. All she could think about was getting home and into a hot oily bath. She didn't feel like discussing Celia now; the visit was over, and the last thing she needed was a post-mortem from Tom.

'Anyway, you're a fine one to talk. You're hardly the world's most devoted son,' she said lightly, hoping to turn the subject around.

'That's different. For a start, Andrea's not on her own; she's got Dad to keep her company, not to mention Miles and Christine. Also, unlike my mother, you can actually have a decent conversation with Celia. You know, she's not as . . . as *full on* about everything as Andrea is.'

Celia and Tom had bonded during this visit, she could tell. The further she retreated, the thicker they seemed to get – the earlier she went up to bed, the later they would sit around the kitchen table drinking duty-free Metaxa. It was almost as though Tom had taken on the mantle of son to Celia. Sappho shuddered: *I don't know how long I can keep doing this . . .*

'Saff, you know just because she was a bit scatty when you were a kid –'

'You call a bit scatty fucking off for weeks on end without saying when she was coming back. If it hadn't been for Ghisela –'

'I would have been delighted if Andrea had fucked off a bit more when I was a boy. You try having a mother who's on first-name terms with your teachers!'

'Look, Tom, at the time Celia made her choices, and now I'm making mine. Being a mother, I actually find the choices she made back then harder, and not easier, to understand. I either cut ties with Celia, full stop, which I don't want to do, partly, as it happens, for Maro's sake, or else we carry on bumbling along like this until the day I wake up and find I'm grown-up enough to forgive her. Anyway, it's cool; Celia and I understand each other.'

Which was a lie, and they both knew it.

Over time, the hurt in her mother's eyes never diminished; nor did the confusion. Each time she walked through Arrivals, it would take a few moments for her to remember the deal, for her eagerness to subside, for the olive branch in her hand to be set aside. She was cautious in her dealings with Sappho, and developed the alert, apologetic manner of someone whose family pet had turned ugly. The end of her visit invariably came as a relief to both.

At Stansted, Tom always took her into the terminal while Sappho waited in the car.

*   *   *

141

Their favourite book was called *No Matter What*.

Small says to Large:

> 'I'm a grim and grumpy
> Little Small
> And nobody
> Loves me at all.'

To which Large replies:

> '. . . Grumpy or not,
> I'll always love you no matter what.'

So then the little fox comes up with a series of improbable worst-behaviour scenarios: what if he turned into a grizzly bear or a bug or a crocodile? But Large remains unfazed by his questions, serenely continuing with the evening bath-time ritual.

Not until the two foxes are lying tucked up in bed with a book do Small's questions turn dangerous:

> '. . . But what about
> When we're dead and gone?
> Would you love me then?
> Does love go on?'

Unspeakable, voluptuous sadness washed over Sappho each time she read those words to Maro. The knowledge that their years together on this earth were limited. That the cosmos was indifferent to the unique love she felt for her daughter.

In reply to the question, Large picks up Small and carries him to the window, pointing up to the starry sky.

'Small, look at the stars –
How they shine and glow
But some of those stars died
A long time ago.
Still they shine in the evening skies –
Love, like starlight, never dies.'

Nineteen

The parcel arrived a week before Maro's birthday.

When Sappho saw the East Sheen postmark, she realised at once it was from her stepmother, Ghisela. What
over-the-top gift had she sent this time? wondered Sappho
with a stab of irritation as she signed the postman's
electronic pad. The sight of her digitally altered signature
made her smile; it looked like ghost writing on Maro's
magnetic Megasketcher.

The box was so huge that she hesitated before picking it
up; she was over the tricky first stage of her pregnancy, but
even so, she didn't want to risk putting her back out before
the birth.

'I carry,' murmured Laleh from the stairs.

Sappho started – she hadn't heard her coming down.
Effortlessly, so it seemed, Laleh picked up the box and
padded barefoot into the breakfast room. In spite of being
so thin, she was extraordinarily strong; only the other day
she turned over the futon in Sappho and Tom's room,
single-handedly, and when once they had discussed moving
Maro's heavy bateau-lit bed away from the window (the
light was waking her up in the early hours) Sappho came
back from a pregnancy yoga class at the Iyengar Institute to
discover that Laleh had moved not only the bed, but the
wardrobe and a heavy marble-topped chest of drawers, as

well as choosing the most pleasing way of rearranging the furniture, which had the unlikely effect of making the room appear simultaneously cosier and more spacious.

'Would you like some tea?' asked Sappho as she followed Laleh into the kitchen.

'I already make.' Laleh handed Sappho a cup of tea in her favourite Onkar Singh Kular mug.

The mugs came in the one hundred and twenty-eight hues of brown of a Pantone chart, each one corresponding to a strength of tea; she and Tom had first seen them exhibited at the Design Museum, and they now owned ten of the more popular shades, including her own, which was a kind of rosy fawn colour.

Laleh had got the tea spot on; it looked like a cupful of paint in a mimetic container – even Sappho herself rarely got such a perfect match. Before Tom tracked the mugs down, she had tried different ways of explaining to him how she liked her tea. 'First you need two teabags, left in for no more than thirty seconds.'

'Why two teabags? Why not just put one in for twice the time?'

'This way it doesn't stew; you get the first infusion, with no bitterness.'

'Who taught you that?'

'My Granny Maro; she had to learn how to make a decent cup of tea, didn't she, when she married an Englishman. Greek people only drink tea when they're ill; if you order tea in a café the waiter will ask what's wrong with you!'

'Is this all right for you, my Greek princess?' he would ask, handing her a cup, at the same time humming the tune of Pulp's 'Common People'. This was their song, their anthem – a perpetually delightful joke:

'She came from Greece, she had a thirst for knowledge, she studied sculpture at St Martin's College' – though in fact Sappho had begun a Fine Arts course at Goldsmiths before falling pregnant with Maro. It was the chorus, though, that really cracked them up:

> I *want to live like common people*
> I *want to do whatever common people do*
> I *want to sleep with common people*
> I *want to sleep with common people like you.*

How much slack they'd cut themselves in that first year, thought Sappho as she looked through the window towards Tom's shed; they were wholly charming in each other's eyes . . . No wonder they called it a state of grace . . . Making love, too, was a kind of open-ended conversation which had to be urgently resumed whenever the mood took them, a delightfully unresolvable conundrum. Where had all that hunger come from?

She'd been so raw after Theo's death; it was as though a horse had just stamped on her heart: she felt literally winded by grief. Plus the events of that terrible, terrible afternoon on Patmos, *all water under the bridge now*, meant that somehow the usual corners had been cut. Anyone could have had their way with her in those days; it was just luck that it happened to be Tom . . . *My sweet beloved husband, who brought me on to dry land* . . . Within forty-eight hours of first setting eyes on each other, they had travelled together from Patmos to Athens to London; and one rainy Monday evening he led her out of a taxi to the flat in Ladbroke Grove –

'I go finish my homework.'

'What was that, Laleh?'

'Reza sleeping now, I must complete Use of English test.'

'You don't want any tea?' She enjoyed the companionship of drinking tea with Laleh; before she and Reza moved in, she would always bring Tom up a cup in the attic, she thought guiltily. Now he had his own kettle in the shed.

'Tank you,' and Laleh did that funny upwards, raised-eyebrows nod, which also meant 'no' in Greece.

The similarities between the two cultures never ceased to amaze her, thought Sappho, as she listened to Laleh's footsteps on the stairs. It wasn't just the food, which was broadly comparable, though every meal seemed to be consumed with quantities of raw herbs – tarragon, parsley, coriander, as well as some obscure ones she had never tasted which Laleh found in a grocer's on Kilburn High Road – but even simple things like the way she looked after her child or cleaned the house were somehow redolent of home.

She would wash every available surface – walls, skirting boards, light switches, even the upholstery and carpets – as though she were battling with the ferocious, endlessly self-renewing dust of the Middle East, not the sluggish, slow-moving London dust you could more or less ignore from one week to the next, though how she had all that energy, with a small baby to look after, was a mystery to Sappho. And she still found time to study English during Reza's nap.

The obvious answer was to get the cleaner in for more hours; Laleh's main job was to look after Maro and the new baby, when it was born, not to be a domestic skivvy.

Or was it? It was two months since she had moved in, and in some ways Sappho was still no clearer in her own mind about why exactly Laleh was living with them. A bored housewife's caprice? Tom certainly thought so, not that he actually came out with it; and though she herself couldn't bear to think of it in those terms, there was undoubtedly an element of showiness, a kind of wilful eccentricity, in the way she had invited this stranger into her house.

On some more or less conscious level, it had to be a protest against the comfortable monotony of their lives.

Twenty

The invitation was pure Bridget.

Dear . . .

Please come to Maro and Freddie's joint fifth and sixth birthday party, at the café in Paddington Recreation Grounds.

Theme: What I want to be when I grow up. (Mums and Dads, think outside the box! Costumes and gifts don't have to be gender-restricted! Adults welcome to participate!)

Any parents wishing to remain for the duration of the party, please bring a suitable book or quiet activity (eg, puzzle, game, quiz) to be shared amongst small groups of children during 'winding down' time between 4.10 and 4.30 p.m. (We will assign a group of children to all adults at the start of the party; this will be on a strict 'names out of a hat' basis in order to break down any pre-existing cliques.)

Please let us know if your child has any allergies regarding food or latex balloons etc. A copy of the menu can be provided upon request.

A fully referenced (including police-checked) entertainer, Mr Majika, will be performing at 3.45 *sharp*. If you do not wish your child to participate, please inform me or Sappho before the show commences, and ensure she or he is not seated in the audience. Out of respect to Mr Majika, please keep 'littlies' under control! (You may find quiet activities come into their own here!)

If you have any concerns regarding your child's ability to integrate into the dynamics of a mixed group, you are welcome to ring me or Sappho for a chat between now and the party. I will be happy to take any 'wallflowers' under my wing!

Please bear in mind that all 'games' will be on a strictly non-competitive basis.

'Christ, Nick's a saint,' was Tom's comment, as he replaced the invitation on the dresser.

This was not entirely true – at least Sappho privately had her doubts about Nick (he was a bit too fond of making money, he worked ridiculously long hours in the City, and Bridget was forever dragging him off to weekend couple workshops with titles such as 'The Power of Two' or 'Getting the Love You Deserve' which suggested that he needed to be kept on message, at least as far as their marriage was concerned) – but there was no denying that being married to Bridget must be trying for any man.

Her family – Nick, and their two children Freddie and Martha – was Bridget's work in progress – literally. Her bookshelves groaned with titles such as *Toddler Taming*, *The Seven Golden Rules for Happy Families* and *Don't Sweat the Small Stuff*, as though the experience of family life, of all life, could only make sense refracted through the schema of received wisdom.

Reading between the lines, Sappho guessed that Bridget was overcompensating; her own childhood had been un-happy, her parents had divorced, and for years she had been a latchkey kid in charge of two unruly siblings with whom she was now barely on speaking terms. Her family was her second chance; for this, Sappho felt a secret bond with Bridget, not that she herself would have ever been aware of it. *My past is truly another country . . .*

Beneath it all hummed a constant anxiety; Bridget's hair was crispy with cortisol, more so on certain days, when it appeared literally to stand on end. There was also some kind of unhappiness in her life which Sappho could only guess at.

She adored Nick, a rather inscrutable, blank-faced man with whom in all these years Sappho had never once had anything resembling a meaningful conversation. He was younger than Bridget, by four or five years at least, with a smooth, unlined face, and a pelt of surprisingly thick dark hair; even in a suit he tended to look like a sixth-former on Speech Day. David Miliband, Sappho privately nicknamed him.

Bridget, on the other hand, was a big-boned, chaotic-looking woman, with a high-pitched, nasal voice, which sounded as though it were emanating from an empty chamber behind her slightly collapsed nose. She also had a knack of wearing the wrong clothes for her type; literally nothing she put on ever looked right, even outfits that strictly speaking should have suited her. Her school-run outfits were frumpy: fleeces, ill-fitting jeans, the occasional slightly infantile foray into high-street fashion: shaggy mock-sheepskin waistcoats, peasant tops or, worst of all, leather trousers over kitten-heeled mules. She was a walking, talking advertisement for a makeover programme: 'Improve Me' her whole look screamed.

What Sappho really would have preferred for Maro was an old-fashioned birthday tea at home, but she had been feeling so tired recently that the thought of organising a party for even six or seven children was enough to keep her awake at night. On some level she was still humble enough to feel remorseful about her so-called exhaustion; she had two people, Elsa and Laleh – three, if you included Tom, when he wasn't travelling – whose main remit, in spite of whatever else was going on in their own lives, was to make her life easier.

Put baldly, at least as far as Laleh and Elsa were concerned, that was their job.

Careful not to disturb Tom, Sappho rolled over on to her side and hoisted her legs over the edge of the bed like a very fat old lady climbing out of the bath. She sat there for a while, staring down at her belly, which perched on her lap like some massive bundle of washing; until, naked, she walked barefoot across the bedroom floor towards their en-suite bathroom, where she peed in the dark so as not to activate the fan light.

The baby was asleep now, worn out by the night's stunts. She stood up and looked out of the window; the streetlights were switched off, but dawn seemed an age away. The witching hour, she thought, gazing out at the starless sky. *Two souls, one body* . . . Only a thin membrane separated her child from this world, the womb its watery *haramlek*. Across the street, a row of spiky black railings pierced the bushes at the edge of the park, while a silver helium balloon sagged from the branches of a tree.

The birthday was only days away, and she still hadn't made up her mind. Maybe they could forget about a party altogether, and take Maro to the Tricycle with a few friends; or even the indoor adventure park on Bramley Road, she thought, as she searched on the shelves for her Weleda calendula cream.

The centre of her palms felt rough, with little cobweb-shaped stigmata of dry skin, even though she wasn't exactly killing herself with housework. She found the tube and rubbed a small amount on to her hands; the wheaty antiseptic smell reminded her of when Maro was a baby.

With a pang, Sappho realised those days were gone; she would never reclaim them . . . She looked at her reflection in the mirror; her face had filled out, she looked dopey and a little coarse. *I am with child* . . . What was it Laleh had said to her in the park? 'Baby boy is make beauty stronger . . .' Well, you're not very beautiful now, she thought to herself, grinning, though if she was truthful, she loved the way she looked when she was pregnant. Fortunately, so did Tom, though this pregnancy didn't have quite the same erotic charge as the last.

From the bedroom, she heard him stir and switch on the bedside light; then the sound of his footsteps on the wooden floorboards. He was flying to Stockholm that morning to meet some architects; perhaps he was due up anyway, she thought guiltily.

'Let me guess, you've been party planning again,' he said, embracing her from behind, his thick forearm lying diagonally between her breasts. They were really quite astonishingly enormous, though this time round not quite such a novelty for either of them. He too was naked apart from an old white Fruit of the Loom T-shirt. She stared at their reflection in the mirror; unlike her, he really did look like someone who had been woken up from a deep sleep. He yawned, rubbing his eyes with one fist, his fair hair sticking up sideways. Recently, it had begun to go grey around the temples; he rarely discussed it with her, but she knew the Iskander Lofts had been causing him problems.

'What about Disneyland Paris?' he suggested, leaning on to the tiles as he peed in the unflushed toilet, his brow resting sleepily on one outstretched arm. The wide band of his wedding ring caught the light from the bedroom reading lamp. His urine was dark and smelled of last night's wine.

He flushed the toilet, then, putting down the cover, settled on to the seat and pulled Sappho on to his lap. 'We could go over to France for the day, maybe even spend the night in one of those themed hotels. Maro would love it.'

'Oh, and what if I go into labour on the Eurostar, or right in the middle of Disneyland?' she said, shifting awkwardly on to his knees. There was no way he could possibly be comfortable with her gigantic weight resting on him. She placed her feet on his, trying to match up their ten toes. He had solid, hikers' calves, covered in long fair hair; he was the first blond man she had ever slept with.

'It's all very well for you, flying off all over the place. You're not the one who might be stuck having a baby all on their own.' She felt close to tears, but safe; the utter text-book unreasonableness of her behaviour was so predictable that she might just as well have been acting out a part. Which she sort of was.

'All right, all right, keep your shirt on . . . oops – I forgot you're not wearing one,' he said, sliding one arm around her belly and up between her breasts. She felt his penis stir beneath her thighs, and a slow thickening of her clitoris in response. He turned her around to face him, neatly sliding himself inside her.

'Good morning,' said Sappho, as she took his face between her hands.

They smiled at each other, instantly refreshed.

Twenty-one

Sometimes Sappho thought that Andrea must have a scrap-book at home where she pasted in her horror stories about asylum seekers from the *Daily Mail*, saving them up for her visits to London.

One afternoon, a few days before the party, she had just embarked on a new tale about a Peruvian nanny when Laleh walked into the kitchen carrying a pile of ironed tea towels. Sappho smiled at her feebly, praying that her mother-in-law's stentorian tones had not carried to the top floor of the house. If she'd known Laleh was in, she would have shut Andrea up long before. The moment Laleh left the kitchen, Sappho took down a pottery mug from the dresser.

'I forgot, Andrea, Maro made this for you in nursery. See, the children drew a picture on to a piece of card, then the drawings were sent off to this company to be laminated on to mugs. We ordered a couple of spares as presents.'

Andrea's face softened. Putting on her glasses, which hung on a thong around her neck, she inspected the mug.

'How *lovely*, what a clever little poppet she is. I suppose that must be you with the big tummy –'

'Actually, it's Tom.' It was true: Tom was developing quite a competitive paunch as her pregnancy progressed.

'Oh, yes, of course, silly me, you're wearing a skirt,' said

Andrea hurriedly. 'Oh – and how sweet, there's Maro holding her new brother or sister.'

'No, actually that's Reza in her arms,' said Sappho evenly. Too late, she'd forgotten about Reza being in the drawing. Now there really would be no steering Andrea off the subject.

'Are you *sure* it's Reza?'

'Positive. Maro's very fond of him, you know. Of both of them, as it happens.'

For a moment, Andrea's face looked actually pained as she tried to digest this unappetising information; until, collecting herself, she took a sip of tea and, placing the cup back on its saucer, smiled brightly at Sappho.

'Anyway, I never finished my story. So Mother gets home from work, looks around the house: no baby, no nanny. Turns out the girl had kidnapped the baby boy and taken him off to some village pension' (Andrea pronounced it like the old people's fund). 'Four months she'd been with the family, good as gold, butter wouldn't melt in her mouth, just like your Laa-Laa. You didn't read about it? It was a shocking case, all over the Italian newspapers when we were staying at Lake Garda . . .'

Sappho tried not to react, but a dull fist of dread clenched her heart.

'What happened, did they find the baby in the end?'

'Oh yes, they found him all right . . . Some woman at the station, I forget where exactly, noticed he looked very upset, thought there was something strange about a foreign woman travelling with a baby on a train so late at night, put two and two together and phoned the *carabinieri*. Thanks to her, the police tracked them down to this godforsaken village up in the mountains . . . and listen to this, Sappho, this is the most shocking bit of all – *they'd pierced the poor mite's ears to make him look like a girl . . .*'

She paused expectantly, and an unpleasant silence fell over the room.

155

'So what you're saying is that Laleh could also be a kidnapper.'

Sappho tried to sound light-hearted, but in spite of herself, a hideous image flashed into her mind of Maro being bundled into a car –

'These people are desperate, Sappho. You and I can't begin to imagine what life must be like in their country . . . it stands to reason they resort to desperate measures when they finally make it to the West. Why don't you get yourself a nice Australian or Kiwi girl from a reputable agency? There's a young mother in the next village, she swears by them, says they're wonderful with children, and at least they speak the same language . . .'

You're wrong, thought Sappho. If anyone here speaks my language, it's Laleh, but I can't tell you that, Andrea. You'd never understand.

For weeks before, Maro endlessly discussed the party with Laleh, explaining in detail the rules of the games they would be playing ('Then they take one of the chairs away, and the one that doesn't have somewhere to sit when the music stops is out') as well as the mystifying concept of party bags.

'Children bring present, then take back same present?'

'*No*, Laleh! My friends bring *me* a present, then we give *them* a bag of different presents to take back at the end of the party.'

'Leave party with whole bag presents? Is too much tings!'

'Not big presents, Laleh, little things like rubbers –'

'Robbers? Like man who steal from bank?' and picking up a pair of Maro's pants from the floor, she stuck them on her head, scowling comically while holding out both arms like a gun.

Sappho watched Laleh from the landing; Laleh was so playful around Maro, no wonder she adored her; whereas even after all these months she rarely got more than a polite smile from her – the very smallest of small talk – and she doubted whether Laleh had addressed more than two sentences to Tom in the whole time she had been living with them.

Actually, she happened to agree with Laleh's point about 'too much tings'; the excesses of English children's birthday parties still made her uncomfortable. Name days were what you celebrated when she was growing up in Athens, though admittedly some of the American children at her international school tended to have big birthday parties as they did over here. But even these often merely consisted of a picnic in the forest, or a day at the beach for those fortunate to have summer birthdays – a world apart from the competitive, themed events English parents organised for their offspring. Maro was not yet even five, and so far she had been to a party on a double-decker bus, to the Science Museum, London Zoo, the kitchens of Pizza Express in Bayswater, and, most memorably of all, to Cadbury's World in Birmingham. (The parents laid on a minibus for that one.)

She couldn't help but view the preparations for Maro's birthday through Laleh's eyes, as indeed she was beginning to view every aspect of their lives. She never got any feeling from Laleh that she disapproved of the way they lived – Maro's complex social life, the triple-figure amounts they spent at the supermarket, the crates of wine and oil regularly delivered to the house – it was more Sappho who felt uncomfortable about these extravagances.

Every day, Laleh tidied Maro's toys, folded her Rachel Riley pinafores, ironed her round-collared shirts, and made up her beautiful bateau-lit bed with its Frette linen sheets, as though it was right and fitting that a four-year-old child should have a room, a life, such as this. *Anyway, at least she's not spoilt*, Sappho would say to herself. And it was true; Maro was an unusually unmaterialistic and kind-hearted little girl.

Now the day of the party had arrived, and Sappho was decorating the room behind the café while Tom and Maro went to collect the cake from the baker on Kensington Church Street.

'Try not to leave the invoice lying around,' she muttered to Tom as they set off in the car.

'Oh, stop being such an old puritan,' he said, kissing her goodbye through the rolled-down window.

'What's a puritan, Daddy?' she heard Maro ask from the back seat as they drove off.

Unpacking the string of fairy lights, which spelled the words 'Happy Birthday' on multi-coloured globes that she had bought from a shop on Golborne Road, Sappho searched around the room for a socket. Discovering one behind the trestle table, she lowered herself carefully on to all fours and plugged them in. She felt ridiculously elated as she saw them lit up: Maro would be thrilled.

Picking up the illuminated string, she climbed up gingerly on to a chair to hang them above the doorway, and it was then that she got the sensation that someone was watching her. She glanced around her; perhaps it was Bridget, back from the carpark where she had gone to collect the party bags, or Tom and Maro with the cake, but the room was empty.

Then, looking towards the courtyard, she saw two little girls standing behind the high-barred gate which separated the café from the private party area. They looked around eight and ten years old, both dressed in the height of pre-teen fashion: one wore a miniskirt over patent-leather pink cowboy boots, and a long knitted cardiagan with a faux fur collar, while the other was all in black, with a silver puffy gilet on top. Clutching the bars of the gate, they were both staring hungrily at the food laid out across the table: jellies, sandwiches, drumsticks with thyme, hand-made crisps, iced biscuits, powdery *kourabiedes* dusted with icing sugar, and miniature cheese pies from the Greek baker's in Green Lanes. (For which Bridget had seriously expected her to get a list of ingredients, and which, to her endless shame, she did actually ask the baker's assistant for, knowing full well in advance what the answer would be. *Then ton echoume*, we don't have it, with a sleepy blink and that bored levantine upwards nod.)

The children's stare was making Sappho uncomfortable; they reminded her of Victorian orphans outside a pastry-shop window, or the gypsy children in Athens who would go from table to table in the tavernas, with their buckets of roses, their money-bags around their waists. Mostly the taverna owners would shoo them away, especially from the more touristy establishments in the Plaka; but here and there you would come across a kind-hearted one who would bring them a slice of watermelon, or some fried *saganaki* cheese in a napkin.

Like those gypsy children, there was something knowing, feral about these girls. Their clothes were catalogue new, and they both wore elaborate hairstyles, corn rows, decorated with dozens of minature butterfly clips. But they were unhealthy-looking with dark circles under their eyes. They resembled children who didn't go to school, who spent their days excluded from those comforting routines. Like you at St Cecilia's, thought Sappho with a pang. That's who they really remind you of – you and Theo wandering the Charing Cross Road instead of going to school . . .

But surely I never had the look of those girls, thought Sappho, unwrapping the paper party tablecoth from its cellophane packaging – the kind of 'At Risk' look that had teachers' fingers itching to ring Social Services.

Fair enough, in an ideal world her parents should probably never have had children, but they weren't as bad as, say . . . Lorna was . . . *Oh, and how have we ended up down that particular Memory Lane? On your daughter's birthday, of all days* . . . She knew what it was: since Laleh had moved in, the edges of her life had grown frayed; things weren't all of a piece any more.

Something told her Lorna was living in Britain again; Celia claimed not to have heard from her for years, but Sappho didn't believe her. It was just a question of time before she and Alexander would turn up one night at the house . . .

Unable to ignore the children any longer, Sappho put down the tablecloth and walked towards the gate.

'Do you girls want something to eat?' she asked them through the bars. The younger one nodded and looked up hesitantly at her sister.

They looked Eastern European, Polish or Albanian maybe, with their pale complexions and mayonnaise-blonde hair. Unlocking the gate, Sappho let them into the room and handed them each an Angelina Ballerina plate. (The boys' tableware had an all-purpose 'Under the Sea' motif, even though, not very hopefully, Freddie had asked his mother for Power Rangers or Spiderman. 'Sexist and violent, the pair of them' was Bridget's verdict, though she did offer him Winnie the Pooh as an alternative; he refused.)

The girls stared impassively at Sappho as she filled their plates with food: a drumstick and sandwich each, a cheese pie and a handful of crisps. 'Say thank you,' the elder one said, nudging her sister. 'Thank you,' she said in a voice which played adults at their own game: mocking, cynical. Sappho looked at her watch: in fifteen minutes the other children were arriving; she didn't really want the pair of them hanging around for the remainder of the party.

'Why don't you two take your food into the park, you can have a picnic there? Are you here with your mummy?'

The elder one shrugged her shoulders vaguely. 'Coming later.' Sappho still couldn't make out from their accents whether they were English or not; all she could think about was getting rid of them before the party began.

Their presence was starting to make her uncomfortable; it felt like an omen. *That's right, chuck them out, even though you know there's no one to look after them in the park . . .* But that was no concern of hers, surely? Tom was right: 'You're not the Salvation Army, Sappho, you can't keep wading into people's problems like that.'

The girls picked up their plates, but instead of taking them towards the gate, they settled down on the plastic chairs lined up against the wall. 'We wait for Mum come,' said the elder one easily, gnawing delicately at a chicken leg.

She wore a silver charm bracelet around one wrist; one of the charms was a Nike swoosh, another a glass evil eye. Sappho knew they weren't English. It was uncanny: like two little animals, they had sensed her reluctance to let them out into the park on their own. There was something almost menacing in the way they sat there like a pair of squatters who knew their rights, daring her to throw them out.

Just then, in walked Bridget carrying a cardboard box full of party bags. '– was on the point of giving me a ticket, literally as I was standing by the machine looking for some change – Oh,' she paused abruptly, catching sight of the girls with their plates of food.

Unsubtly, she raised an enquiring eyebrow at Sappho, who breathed a sigh of relief. Let her deal with them. Bridget looked more peculiar than ever, dressed in a tartan shirt and OshKosh dungarees tucked into boots, with a yellow plastic Bob the Builder hat over her frizzy hair; of course, she'd forgotten: the adults too had been invited to come in costume. Had Bridget really dreamt of being a lumberjack when she was a little girl?

'These two are waiting for their mum to collect them. I said they could have a snack . . . but they're going now. Aren't you, girls?'

Sappho could sense them weighing up the situation: it was obvious that Bridget's arrival had upset things for them; she was plainly not such a soft touch . . . Placing her box of party bags on the table, Bridget knelt before them so that their faces were almost level (*Good communication means never talking down to your child . . .*), though she had rather misjudged the height of the girls, so that, bizarrely, they were talking down to the top of her yellow-helmeted head.

'Now,' she said, in her high nasal voice, 'would you like me to telephone Mum, or another adult, and tell them you'll be waiting outside the café?'

'We got a phone,' said the younger girl sullenly, pulling out a tiny Nokia camera phone from the sequined pouch she wore around her waist. Sappho and Bridget exchanged wry glances; neither they, nor their husbands for that matter, owned such a sophisticated mobile.

'Well, why don't you call her and tell her to come and get you. I can speak to her if you like.'

Without warning, both girls stood up, forcing Bridget to rock back on the heels of her boots. There was something vicious in the way they had synchronised their move, staring at Bridget contemptuously through narrowed eyes as she scrambled to her feet, straightening her plastic helmet.

What was it about Bridget that invited physical violence like that? She wouldn't put it past Nick to be an occasional wife-beater, though Tom had known him for twenty years: surely he would have guessed by now if it were true . . . Sappho felt a twist of remorse as she watched the girls pick up their plates from the seats, as though in spite of everything, they couldn't quite bring themselves to leave the food behind. In silence, they walked towards the gate, high-heeled boots clacking on the laminate floor; and slamming it behind them, they disappeared into the park.

'Quite extraordinary,' murmured Bridget. 'Makes you see the case for compulsory parenting classes . . . leaving two girls alone like that in a public place. Anyway, to work. Now, as you know, you'll be in charge of handing out the stickers –'

'What stickers?'

'The name tags, Saff, remember we discussed it over the phone last week? I've got a list here of all the RSVPs; you tick them off as they arrive, and you write their name in blue on the top, and what they've come dressed as in red at the bottom.'

'Oh yes, now I remember.' She hadn't a clue what Bridget was talking about.

Just then, Tom and Maro arrived with the cake in a huge box from Patisserie Valerie. Sappho peered inside: it was a 'Macedonia' topped with kiwis, passion fruit, strawberries, cherries and pineapple, with 'Happy Birthday Freddie and Maro' piped in black chocolate Letters.

Beneath her coat, Maro was dressed in a beautiful Ariel mermaid costume, made by Laleh entirely out of orange and turquoise crêpe paper. It was truly a work of art; Laleh was a genius to have thought of it. The top half consisted of a shell-shaped bikini made of hundreds of tiny paper pleats, and below it a long layered fish-tail skirt came to the ground. The back was fastened with a shell; and when Sappho looked closer, she saw Laleh had even embroidered a button hole. How on earth had she managed to sew through paper without making it rip?

The next question was where to put Maro's name tag without ruining the costume. 'You can stick it here on my tummy,' giggled Maro. 'Maro: mermaid' wrote Sappho, placing the sticker carefully on her daughter's hot, taut flesh.

Where had those two sisters gone? wondered Sappho; why had it seemed so important to get rid of them before the other guests arrived? For a moment she considered slipping out into the park and inviting them back for the party . . . they'd think she was bonkers; she could imagine the expression of scorn on their faces as they saw her puffing across the playground towards them.

'What time's Eden coming, Mummy?' said Maro, anxiously fiddling with the crossover ties of Sappho's linen maternity shirt. Eden was the most popular girl in the nursery; everyone wanted to be her friend, even the boys.

Sappho wasn't keen on Eden; she was a little too knowing for a four-year-old. She was the one who had first got Maro worrying about her name ending with an o. And she didn't like Maro worshipping at her altar. It had taken a surprising amount of courage to approach Eden's mother: a petite, big-breasted woman with a freckled face and babyish voice. A pocket Venus was probably how she pitched herself. She wore short girlish skirts over Ugg boots; somehow it looked like a con, drew attention to her sun-aged skin. Her name was Amanda; she ran a chi-chi bespoke lunchbox service for schoolchildren: organic sandwiches in little retro tins ('clingfilm is simply loaded with phthalates') and home-made fruit bars wrapped in greaseproof paper, all packed in a fun little cardboard box which looked suspiciously as though it had been cut from the template of a Mcdonald's Happy Meal carton.

Standing beside her, Sappho always felt like a fat giantess. Amanda's thing was physical contact; squeezing past her in the narrow nursery cloakroom, she would make a point of clasping Sappho by the waist as though marvelling that her little arms could stretch that far.

'Don't worry, Eden will be here in a minute, come and say hello to your friends. Look, Marlon and Iris are here.' Actually, there was no guarantee that Eden was coming at all, but Sappho didn't have the heart to tell Maro this. When, until last night, she had still heard nothing, Sappho had swallowed her pride and telephoned Eden's mother. Maro's day would be ruined if Eden didn't come; they might just as well cancel the party.

'Oh hi, Sappho . . . I'm glad you rang, I was going to call you later . . . you won't believe it . . . Eden's been invited to another party in West Hampstead . . . such a shame . . . yes, I thought of that myself, but you know what the traffic's like on Saturdays . . . no, she'll have to choose one party . . . with the best will in the world, we can't be in two places at once . . .'

She'll have to choose one party . . . Amanda knew – or maybe didn't know – how much her annoying daughter's presence would mean to Maro. Sappho would have walked over hot coals to have spared her daughter the unhappiness of Eden not coming – she would have done anything, literally anything: sent a taxi over to West Hampstead to pick the pocket princess up, driven there herself . . .

More and more children were arriving, some of them Freddie's friends she had never seen before. (Toby: astronaut; Jack: footballer; Noah: doctor – bet his parents are pleased, thought Sappho as she stuck a label on to his miniature white coat.) It was the dream of every Greek mother to be able to airily namedrop to the neighbours about *o ios mou, o iatros*, my son, the doctor . . .

Bridget was off; standing on a chair with a clipboard in her hand, yellow helmet askew, she was calling for silence.

'I'd like you all to listen out for your names, and pair off with the child whose name comes after. So if for example I call out "Toby and Iris", that means Toby and Iris are partners.'

'You don't say . . .' muttered one of the fathers sardonically under his breath.

The two children who had been called, one in the knot of preschoolers by the door, the other in the gang of rowdy Reception boys eyeing up the food, stared at each other. So much for breaking down pre-existing cliques, thought Sappho.

Out of the corner of her eye, Sappho noticed Laleh had returned with Reza in the pram; she had wanted to get him off to sleep before the party began. She smiled at her and made their private sign of a cup of tea, pointing to the table where the kettle and the milk stood. Nodding gratefully, Sappho smiled back; most of the children were here, but still no sign of Eden.

Bridget came towards Sappho, accompanied by a beautiful black woman with a shaved head. 'This is Arlette, Jacob's mum. Jacob is the little pirate with dreadlocks,' she said, patting the head of a mixed-race boy wearing a stripy Breton jumper.

Trust Bridget to make a point straight away of mentioning his hair; they weren't locks anyway, more like twists or knots. Sappho would have liked to talk longer to the woman – she had intelligent eyes and an attractive, gap-toothed smile – but she had noticed Maro sitting disconsolately in a corner, surrounded by a protective gaggle of her nursery friends.

'What is it, darling?' asked Sappho, kneeling down by the child-sized chair.

'I don't want to play any games until Eden comes.' She looked close to tears, and Sappho felt her own eyes pricking in sympathy.

'Me neither,' said her friend Ella, staunchly.

'Me neither,' echoed Ruby, a little girl dressed in wellingtons and overalls, with a miniature gardener's belt around her waist. 'We're sad because Eden isn't here,' she added unnecessarily.

Sappho looked around her; in vain, Bridget was trying to calm down Freddie and his friends who were kicking Jack's football around the room. It was mayhem. In all of this she was aware of Laleh's presence: how spoilt and badly behaved these children must appear to her.

And then she caught sight of the two Eastern European girls standing behind the courtyard gate. This was becoming unbearable; was everything going to implode at once? One of the fathers was just about to buzz the girls through, when she saw Bridget lunge towards him.

'Thank you, Mark, I'll deal with this.' They're children, thought Sappho, they're only children . . . A picture came into her mind of that winter's night when Lorna turned up on the doorstep of the house in East Sheen, the sly way she sidled up to Ghisela in her pyjamas to show Lorna just how cosy and perfect her life had become. At eleven years old, there had been that Judas seed of cruelty in her heart . . . She knew she would pay for it; one day she would be made to pay for what she had done: in a sense she had been paying for it ever since . . . She turned to Bridget.

'I think we should let them in.'

For a moment, Sappho caught an expression of panic flitting across Bridget's face, the wounded leer of her inner child.

'They won't know anyone here,' she murmured weakly. 'They're the wrong age-group, they won't interact . . .'

'It won't make the slightest difference, it's bedlam anyway.'

This was her second chance, a way of making amends. Her luck would turn if she let the girls in, if she could find it within herself to coexist with the disorder they trailed in their wake . . . And Eden would come; she had never been more sure of anything in her life.

She was aware of Laleh walking gracefully towards her with a cup of tea; automatically, she saw Bridget's eyes flicker across the room to locate the whereabouts of her husband. Not for the first time, she wondered what kind of merry dance Nick must be leading her on.

'Come on, Bridget, it can't get more chaotic than this.'

'Well, you'd better keep an eye on the presents,' muttered Bridget ungraciously.

Then the miracle occurred. Sappho was walking towards the buzzer to let the two girls in when she heard a blood-curdling shriek coming from the girls in the corner.

'Eden! Mummy! *Eden's* here!' She could hear the catch of raw emotion reverberating in her daughter's voice. The other little girls too were swept up in the hysteria of Eden's arrival, and even the boys paused momentarily in their game of football.

'Do we know Eden?' she heard one of the mothers ask.

'E-den! E-den! E-den!' they shouted, clapping their hands and stamping their feet as though awaiting the arrival of a pop star or an actress on a red carpet. Where on earth could they have learned such behaviour?

The gate buzzed open, and in walked Eden and her mother dressed in matching miniskirts and pink Ugg boots. So relieved was Sappho to see Eden that she forgave the Cheshire cat grin which broke on Amanda's face as her gaze travelled slowly around the room, taking in the glances of the children and the mothers, and especially those of the fathers . . . all eyes upon her and her popular daughter.

It had worked; her bargain with the fates had worked. That was all that mattered. As Sappho watched Eden being led away by her adoring little acolytes, a kind of music struck up in her heart, and she felt an immense warmth creeping up through her belly. She looked towards Tom drinking beer with the other fathers, oblivious to the storm which had been raging in her breast. They were safe; nothing could touch them now.

Later, when they were clearing up, and she discovered her purse was missing from her handbag, she didn't tell Bridget or Tom. There was hardly any cash in it; and besides, she was almost certain she'd dropped it in the park.

Twenty-two

Sappho went into labour on a Friday afternoon.

Laleh was in the playroom, rooting around for Maro's goggles inside the wooden toy washing machine, when she heard the sound of Tom's footsteps clattering down the stairs. Dolls' clothes, crayons, a long bead necklace, an empty box of raisins, but no goggles. She paused, the string of plastic pearls hanging from her fingers, while she waited to hear which way Tom was going. Reza was asleep in his pram in the conservatory; she hoped he wouldn't wake before they set out for the pool. Where had she last seen the goggles? The children were playing with them one day last week when Maro had friends to tea. The footsteps were growing closer now; Tom was approaching the playroom. The moment his head appeared around the door, Laleh understood at once what was happening; she had seen that expression before on the faces of English men at the hospital.

'Sappho . . .?'

'In the car . . . we haven't got long. I just came to collect her bag. Where's Maro?'

'She put on swimming dress upstairs. You want I call her?'

'Yes . . . no, actually, on second thoughts, don't . . . she'll only worry if she sees her mother like this.'

He paused, drumming his fingers nervously on the door lintel. For a moment, he looked like a confused little boy. Then, unexpectedly, he looked up at her with his cold blue eyes. 'What do you think I should do?'

Laleh felt herself flush; was this some kind of test? She knew Tom and his mother didn't like or trust her; she could sense their hostility in every word and glance they directed towards her. Recently, too, Andrea had made a big fuss about coming to London to buy a new pram for the baby, as though to rub her nose in it that Reza was using Maro's old buggy. Even though Sappho assured her time and time again that it was not suitable for newborn babies, and that in any case for the first few weeks she intended to use the sling. *Such are the bitter fruits of charity . . .*

Her first instinct now was to lower her eyes and play safe; no one could accuse her of saying the wrong thing if she remained silent. Let him make his own decisions; he was a grown man. But this would be doing an injustice to Maro; if panic was preventing her father from thinking clearly, it was up to her to take responsibility. She owed as much to Sappho.

'I think is better I bring Maro pool for lesson, like normal.'

If that was the wrong answer, so be it; Sappho told her some mothers allowed their children to be present at the birth of a new baby, but in her country children were taken away to stay with relatives when a woman went into labour. Tom, she knew, intended to be there for the birth – most English fathers were – though in her country this would be considered sacrilegious, a crime against modesty.

Most unusually, her father had managed to be present when she and Ladan were born, though few people outside the family ever learned of this fact. His sister, their aunt, was a midwife, who delivered them both in the matrimonial bed where they were conceived, and she had allowed their father to enter the room during the final stages of labour. Their mother used to say this explained the unusually close bond he shared with both of his daughters.

'All right, you take her for her lesson . . . I'll call you later on from the hospital.'

'If Mrs Andrea telephone?'

This was part malicious, part helpful. She knew how Tom felt about his mother, but on the other hand she didn't want to be caught short again by one of Andrea's irate calls.

'If my mother calls . . . just tell her we're out. Which happens to be the truth,' he added defensively. How did that saying go in her country? *No son is ever a man in the eyes of his mother . . .*

On the way to the swimming pool, they walked through the park.

'Remember, Laleh, this is where me and my mummy met you,' said Maro as they passed the playground. Today it was crowded, filled with children and their nannies, some of whose faces had become familiar over the months. It had been so cold that day; how could she have spent all those afternoons alone with Reza on the bench? *You were desperate, that's how . . .*

'You right, my dear,' replied Laleh, stroking Maro's cheek.

She remembered how at first she had found Sappho's questions invasive, but Maro she loved straight away. She felt the same aching tenderness towards her, the same desire to shelter her from harm, as she did towards Ladan.

She had loved her sister from the moment her father carried her upstairs to meet the new baby in her mother's arms. Whereas Reza . . . *What about Reza? . . . Tell us about your son, your own flesh and blood . . .* Reza she loved because she had to – who else was there to love him? – but without joy . . .

172

'Where did you live before you came to our house, Laleh?'

'I live one hotel.'

'We stayed in a hotel when we went to Greenland to see Father Christmas. And you know what, Laleh?'

Maro stopped by the gate, clutching on to the railings with both hands. Her eyes were shining with excitement. 'The hotel was made . . . of *ice*!'

'Is not possible!'

Actually, Laleh had seen the photographs; Sappho showed them to her one afternoon when Maro was at nursery. Incredible to think human beings could invent such a building.

'Move, dearest, lady need pass.'

They were blocking the entrance to the park with Reza's buggy. Gently, she pulled Maro to one side and, taking her hand, they walked out of the gates, down Harvist Road towards the swimming pool.

'It's really true, Laleh. The walls and the floor were made out of ice, but there was a fire in the bedroom and it didn't feel cold. And on a shelf in the bathroom there was a basket with little tiny bottles of shampoo and bubble bath that *you were allowed to take home*! You were really allowed to, the hotel people said you could!'

'You bring bottles to London?'

'I did, but I haven't got them any more. I used them to make a potion in the garden,' Maro said sadly.

She looked up at Laleh. 'Did they have little bottles in your hotel, Laleh?'

'No, dearest, my hotel no good one.'

At night she would lie in her bed listening to the men in the room next door, gambling and drinking until the early hours. When Reza cried, they would bang on the thin walls; and once they even tried to force open the door. In the morning, when she stepped out of her room, one of the men was passed out in the corridor in a puddle of his own urine.

'Why did you stay there, Laleh?'

'I must stay there . . . Laleh have nowhere else to go.'

When she first arrived in the city, she slept in a telephone box in an alleyway near a theatre, squatting down on the dirty floor, clutching her bag on her lap like a pillow. The walls of the booth were covered in postcards of naked women, their private parts exposed like those of the monkeys she had seen in the zoo. Some of them looked young, scarcely more than girls.

Is this the fate which had befallen the man's first wife after he divorced her? The same fate which awaited her when her money ran out? Yet if she had stayed in her country, she would have been arrested and sent to jail. Then one morning, a young policeman found her and took her to the station, where she was told she could claim asylum. None of the men on the lorry from Dover told her this was what they must do when they reached London.

Strange to be talking of these things now with Maro; for months she had been living entirely in her own head, so much so that she had almost come to believe some of the fictions she wrote in her letters home to Ladan.

The letters were addressed to an old schoolmate who lived near by; Ladan would collect and read them when her husband was out at work: she didn't dare bring the letters back to the house.

Dear Sister, you have no reason to worry about me. Everything we have heard about the hospitality in this country is true. As soon as I arrived in the United Kingdom, the Government allocated me a comfortable apartment filled with all necessary articles for living . . .

They were nearly at the swimming pool. She searched inside her pocket for Maro's swimming pass.

'Laleh?'

'Yes, dearest.'

'Did you like that man?'

Here was the card. She showed it to the girl at the desk, who pressed a button so they could pass with the buggy through the automatic gate.

'Which man?'

'The man who was talking to you in the swimming pool the other time you took me.'

'Ah, this man!' She had forgotten about him . . . well, no, she hadn't exactly forgotten about him, but nor did that mean she had thought about him or had any desire to see him again. On the contrary, she had no need for this kind of annoyance. Thankfully, he appeared to have left the sports centre, or else now he worked different times from Maro's lesson.

In the changing room, she helped Maro take off her clothes and tied the bath robe tightly about her waist. In all the panic and subterfuge about Sappho going into hospital, the goggles never turned up, but Maro said she didn't mind having her lesson without them. 'When Mummy comes back from her going out, she can buy me some new ones.'

She seemed to have no inkling that something unusual was happening. Or perhaps she did, and was choosing not to think about it. Children still had this power; the force of their self-belief was that strong.

Reza was awake now; she could see his solid little arms beating against the plastic shell of the raincover.

'Can I pick him up, Laleh?'

'One minute only. Teacher waiting in pool.'

As she unstrapped him, she wondered what she could do with the buggy. No point bringing it into the pool area – she'd been lucky to get away with it last time without anyone telling her off – but nor did she want to leave it unattended here in the changing room. At home, there might be a new double buggy, still in its carton from the store, but that did not mean she was entitled to abuse this one.

Every so often, she removed the seat covers and scrubbed them by hand in the bath; there were old stains of mashed banana and other unidentifiable food substances worked into the seams of the fabric from when Maro was a baby, which no matter how hard she tried, she was unable to get rid of.

Sappho begged her not to bother, *please, Laleh, you really don't have to*, but to ignore the stains was like saying she did not appreciate the generosity of their gift. Reza was far too heavy now; she would never manage to carry him in her arms any more as she used to when he was smaller. Without the buggy she would be a prisoner of the house.

Laleh looked up, scanning the tops of the lockers; perhaps she could fold the buggy and hide it up there.

'Maro, please you sit with Reza, I put buggy up top?'

Obediently, Maro knelt before Reza on the slatted wooden bench. Reza thumped his fists on her shoulders and grinned; he knew he was being funny. Maro buried her face in his fat tummy and, as he always did, he pulled her hair.

'Naughty Reza, must not hurt Maro,' said Laleh in English, tapping him gently on his hand. The dimples on his fist resembled pinpricks in a lump of dough; sometimes she would stare at them, expecting them to dissolve before her eyes.

Maro looked up. 'Don't smack him, Laleh, it didn't really hurt.'

Maybe she was too hard on him, thought Laleh sadly as she watched the swimming teacher lead Maro down the steps of the pool. Always on the lookout for signs of a deviant nature. As though to further reproach her, Reza began to nuzzle her breasts, looking up at her trustingly through his thick eyelashes. 'My son,' she whispered in her own language, 'my sweet boy . . .' He was her blessing, too; without him she might never have found the will to survive in this country.

Now he was hungry and hot – she had forgotten how overheated the swimming pool was – and worse still, in the rush to get out of the house, she had not thought of packing him anything to eat or drink. He was still mostly breastfed, anyway, but sometimes if they were out he could be persuaded to gnaw at a rice cracker or stick of raw carrot.

Everything she did for her baby had to be an approximation of how she believed things ought to be done; she wished she'd better observed the way mothers did things in her country, she thought as she unbuttoned his snowsuit. *My mother, where are you now?*

She, like her father, had wanted better for their girls; neither had wished them to marry young. Who could have imagined her parents would have been taken away from them so suddenly, so much in their lives left incomplete; though in the light of everything that subsequently befell the two sisters, perhaps this was a blessing . . . But her mother would have loved Reza, she was sure of this, no matter how he came into the world . . . She clasped him fiercely to her breast, pressing his solid chest against hers.

Now the health visitor at the clinic, Jenni, said she must give Reza real food; she said he was a big baby – she used a word that sounded something like bonnet: 'You've a bonnet baby there' – and insisted he was ready for . . . how did she call it? . . . ready for *solid*, that was it.

But surely in her country babies had only milk until the age of one, or was it until the appearance of the first tooth? Sappho recommended breastfeeding as long as possible, and under no circumstances ever giving him powdered milk. She said it was full of hormones, and chemicals which could provoke cancers in later life, and even cause male children to develop female characteristics. Whereas in her country, mothers would go without food themselves in order to buy formula, topping it up with a dried cereal that they dissolved into the milk, then cut a hole in the teat to allow the gruel to pass through. How did that advertisement go? 'Powdered Milk . . . A Mother's Greatest. Gift'.

It was most confusing . . . as was the way English children remained in nappies for up to two years, sometimes even longer. Walking and talking, able to ask for the bathroom themselves, yet obliged to go around with a reeking bundle of waste dangling between their legs; sometimes forced to sit inside their mess for hours on end, if Nanny was too busy doing something else. *No rush, I'll just finish my coffee . . . let him watch the end of his video . . .*

Sappho said it was because some mothers found it hard work to teach baby to use the toilet when they were small, while others believed it caused psychological damage to the child to impose this habit too early. Quite apart from the exorbitant cost of these throwaway nappies . . .

Reza was growing desperate; any moment now, he would begin to scream. Frantically, Laleh bounced him on her knees, swooping him from side to side like an aeroplane, which usually he loved. But it was no use; she had a minute, two at most, before he would begin to howl.

It's nothing to be ashamed of, Laleh, feed him in public . . . if anyone finds it offensive, that's their problem . . .

She looked out towards the water. In the 'Getting Faster' lane, a woman in a purple bathing suit was swimming on her back, sweeping her arms gracefully behind her head, while her legs pumped rapidly up and down in a thick swirl of foam. From where Laleh sat, her face was invisible; all you could see were these round . . . *bonnet* breasts jiggling in their cups.

All her life, she had grown up unable to bare her arms or neck or ankles – even wearing make-up, or an inadequate headscarf, could mean arrest – and yet within the space of a few months she was supposed to be capable of bearing her breasts for all to see in the middle of a crowded swimming pool – essentially the same person she was in her country, but somehow divested of all shame . . .

That was it – time up. Reza clenched his fists, his face grew congested, and a vein stood up on his forehead. A few nerve-racking seconds of silence as he built up a decent reserve of breath; his body grew rigid, then he began to scream.

Her child had the loudest cry she had ever come across, hoarse and powerful, and surprisingly deep; people would turn around in the street when they heard it. The high ceiling and hard surfaces of the pool had the acoustics of an auditorium; it sounded as though his screams were being transmitted through loudspeakers.

'Please stop, my darling, please stop,' whispered Laleh, as she stood up and slid her finger between his gums.

This deception appeared to infuriate him further, and he cried louder still, pumping his legs up and down like a frog in a bucket. The young girl in the lifeguard's chair looked towards her in amazement and something like pity, the backstroke woman flipped over on to her front to see where the noise was coming from, and even the swimming teacher paused in her lesson.

It was the sight of Maro's stricken face, however, looking up at her from the water that decided it. After all, a kind of low wall separated the spectators' area from the pool. If she was careful, no one would see a thing.

Taking off her jacket, Laleh slid a hand beneath her blouse, pulled one breast out of her bra, and shoved it quickly into the screaming baby's face. A howl of rage as he rooted for the nipple, then silence. Blessed holy silence.

Laleh closed her eyes, feeling the adrenalin slowly subsiding. She felt at peace; somehow she had found the courage to feed her child in public. Not such a big thing, compared to everything else she had been through in the last year, *urinating behind a tree in the forest, the men but a few feet away in the lorry, washing your underarms in the toilets of a Mcdonald's restaurant, all those male doctors at the hospital with their faces in your privates*, but maybe it was a sign that one day she would learn to live in this society, assuming of course that the Home Office granted her leave to remain.

Her solicitor had sent all the papers to Croydon months before, but still there was no word from Lunar House. Sappho smiled when she saw the address: Lunar House, the house on the moon . . . Sometimes Laleh believed she had more chance of going up to the moon than ever being granted refugee status . . .

She glanced at her watch; another ten minutes until the end of the lesson. Perhaps when they arrived home there would be a message from the hospital. Sappho had explained to her how to use the 1571 answering service; she must only pay attention not to accidentally press the key for 'delete'.

She hoped Maro would love this new baby as much as she had loved Ladan; what she wouldn't give to have her sister sitting here beside her . . . She was by far the more maternal of the two sisters; how much she would have enjoyed her nephew. *One day, God willing, we will all be together* . . .

Reza was growing restive. She pressed her hand to her bosom; the breast he was latched on to felt flat and empty, while the other throbbed with milk. Her bra was soaked; she had forgotten to place a handkerchief in the cups. Glancing around the pool to check nobody was watching her, she slid a finger into Reza's mouth to break the suction, then quickly attached him to the other nipple before he had a chance to protest. While she didn't exactly feel comfortable doing this, nor was she dying of shame; perhaps in time this really could become a kind of second nature.

And yet something wasn't right; while scanning the pool, her eye had alighted on an object that hadn't registered in her brain, yet was still causing her disquiet. It wasn't Maro, who was leaping gleefully into the water from the edge of the pool, while the teacher, thankfully, appeared to be giving her her full attention . . . No, it was something else . . . And then she saw . . . No, it was not possible! Not him! Why had he suddenly shown up again after all these weeks?

Again he was conversing with the girl in the lifeguard's chair – *was this a full-time job, perhaps, sweet-talking the ladies?* – and for the moment he did not appear to have noticed her. Perhaps after all this time he had forgotten her; she doubted whether he was short of women to importune. His curly hair was longer than ever, growing in a cloud around his head almost like an African person's.

She must look downwards, giving the strongest possible impression that she had no wish to be disturbed. Perhaps if she covered Reza with her jacket, it might give him the idea that he was sleeping. Surely even someone as forward as he was would hesitate before waking a slumbering child?

Reaching on to the seat behind her, she pulled down her jacket and tried to slip it over Reza's legs without interrupting him. This turned out to be a bad move, for in picking up the jacket, she appeared to have dislodged Reza's mouth. Howling with fury, Reza kicked the jacket down on to the ground, rooting blindly for the lost nipple. With one hand, Laleh picked up her breast, trying to guide it back into his mouth, while reaching forward for the jacket with the other hand, at the same time raising one knee to prevent the baby from sliding off her lap.

'I get this for you.'

The lifeguard was standing before her with his elbows resting on the tiled wall. She looked down at the breast in her hand, pointing towards his head like a missile. A single thread of milk pumped upwards into the air, falling in an arc on to Reza's face, while pretty white beads of milk sparkled on his lashes.

She might just as well have opened her thighs and given him a view of her privates; the shame could not have been any greater. In fact so great was the shame that it annihilated itself by its own immensity; there was no frame of reference, no equivalent shame to compare it to.

Calmly, she tucked the breast back into her bra and held Reza over her shoulder. She had done enough public feeding for one day.

They were killed in the earthquake of '97, along with thirty-six other members of their family. That day marked the end of their father's line; not a single relative survived.

Months before, through the whispers of emissaries, it had come to be known that their relative wished Laleh's family to vacate their house. A well-known foreign contractor had made him an offer with the aim of demolishing the entire street and building a complex of new apartments and shops on the site.

Fortunately, the new house in the village would soon be ready; all that remained was to fit the aluminium windows and doors which had already been delivered, and choose tiles for the kitchen and bathroom. Their mother didn't know yet, it was a surprise, but a brand-new washing machine from Turkey had been ordered on the black market, and was there, waiting to be installed.

They were all looking forward to their new life in the village: the knowledge that the man wished them gone lay over their spirits like a pall; the house in the city no longer felt like their home. Besides, there was nothing any longer to keep them there: Laleh had finished her studies and entered a public concourse to obtain a place as a school teacher in the northern provinces; while Ladan, who had two years left at the university, could complete the remainder of her course via correspondence, travelling back to the city only to take her exams.

Over the years, the washing machine had become something of a joke in their family.

'When I married your baba, he promised me all the modern conveniences, but all I got was a plastic tub and a bar of soap.'

That their father had holes in his pocket was a well-known fact; anybody coming to him with a hard-luck story could be sure of his help. If it were not for their mother, every month squirrelling away a portion of his salary from the university, they would never have managed to build the house in the village.

Although Madar complained each time yet another visitor turned up at the door to profit from his generosity, she was proud of his kind nature.

'Every man goes down to his death bearing in his hands only that which he has given away.' Her words turned out to be more prescient than any of them could have imagined.

They were buried in a mass grave, wrapped in blankets donated by the Red Cross. There was no time to wash their bodies; the corpses were sprayed with disinfectant and dropped into the trenches that mechanical diggers had hollowed out towards the outskirts of the village.

Laleh turned her face away as her parents were lowered into the ground; beneath a dark orange sky, swollen with snow and smoke, a line of bonfires dotted the twisting mountain road which led towards the plains.

I am burying myself in this grave, thought Laleh as a mullah wearing a surgical face mask recited prayers for the dead.

When the girls returned to the city, they found a strange car parked in the street outside their house; a man was sitting in the driver's seat reading a newspaper. He stared at them insolently as they walked through the gates. Putting her bags on to the steps, Laleh placed her key in the lock, but to her surprise, she found the front door ajar. Was it possible that in their confusion and haste they had forgotten to lock up?

A light was on in the hall, and at the end of the corridor they discovered their relative sitting in the kitchen with a younger man they had never seen before. Until now, they were not aware that he even possessed keys to the house. A cold fury overcame Laleh at the sight of the two men sitting at her father's table, the half-drunk glasses of tea the girls had abandoned when news of the earthquake reached them standing untouched before them.

Disease was rife in the tent city which had been erected where their village once stood, and Laleh was frightened her sister might have contracted dysentery; she had spent the entire bus journey home retching drily into a pile of newspapers.

Before allowing her to take Ladan upstairs to bed, the man asked both sisters to be seated. His expression was solicitous, yet there was no mistaking the menace in his voice. This was his house, and he wished them to know it. He had not travelled north for the funeral, nor in any way offered his assistance since the disaster; by this omission alone, Laleh understood the true nature of his feelings towards them. *You would not have dared when Baba was alive . . .*

Sick with grief, still in their dusty manteaus, the two sisters crouched together on the low settle. Ladan's legs were trembling so hard with fever, Laleh had to lean on them to keep them still.

Self-importantly, the man cleared his throat and smiled foxily at them. A toothpick was poking out of the corner of his mouth, which he continued to roll around his tongue, frowning perplexedly as though searching in his mind for the right words.

Laleh adjusted her *rusari*, deliberately tucking in a lock of hair which had escaped. She was forcing herself not to betray any sign of impatience; she would not allow the man this satisfaction. How much force, she wondered, would it take to drive the toothpick through the flesh of his cheek? Would it snap before piercing the skin?

Finally he spoke. 'In the light of recent events, I have decided not to proceed with the sale of the house.'

Laleh stared at him. She should find it in her heart to be pleased; at least they would have a roof over their heads in their sorrow.

'I cannot find it in my heart to turn two orphans out of their own home.'

'Thank you,' mumbled Laleh, dazedly. The spirits of her dead parents were watching over them from afar . . . She would apply for a job in the city, find a teaching position while Ladan finished her studies at the university, then, when Ladan was qualified and able to work, they would put money aside each month to rent their own flat. Perhaps one day they would even see some compensation for the house in the village. Somehow they would survive.

'I come instead to collect a debt,'

'A debt?' Laleh flushed in shame. Surely their father had not borrowed money from this man?

His companion, who until now had remained silent, picked up the sheaf of papers from the table.

'My client is referring to monies owed to him by your late father.' He had a high voice with an unpleasant lisp.

'Monies . . . which monies?'

The washing machine, perhaps he lent Baba the money for the washing machine . . .

'Twenty years of unpaid rent, at the favourable rate of twenty-three million tomans per annum, amounting to a total of four hundred and sixty million tomans.'

'Rent for what?'

But she already understood . . . Ice burned her heart, and she flushed with shame at the unworldliness of her father. How could he not have put the terms of their tenancy in writing?

'For this centrally located family residence which in twenty years has not yielded my client one single toman . . .'

Laleh tried to collect herself. It was obvious in a million years they would be unable to pay this money; the man knew their situation . . . he must want something else from them . . . She lowered her eyes modestly, attempting to jolt her dulled wits into action . . . *Think – think what it is he might want from you* . . .

She turned towards the lawyer.

'Might your client consider accepting the contents of his house as an act of goodwill, a first instalment, if you like, of the debt? We are willing to offer all carpets and paintings, together with my father's collection of books and manuscripts, and the few items of jewellery in my mother's possession.'

Their relative laughed indulgently.

'This would comprise but a drop in the ocean. We are all adults here; I think we can safely assume this debt will never be paid in any of our lifetimes.'

He was hinting he might be willing to let them off . . . but at what price?

The lawyer leaned forward; he had a weasely face, with thick purple lips framed by a black beard. There was something shockingly unharmonious in his features: big ears, fleshy nose, close-set eyes, no chin. Everything extruding to the one point like the muzzle of a rodent. Even his mother must have found it hard to love a child so ugly.

'My client is proposing a solution which will benefit all parties. He has a keen sense of familial obligations, and is loath to abandon his relatives, however distant the kinship may be, in their hour of need. He therefore takes this opportunity to offer his hand in marriage to Miss Ladan, whom he has known for years, and whom he has always held in the highest regard.'

A picture came into Laleh's mind of the man's first wife; she had forgotten the woman's name, or perhaps she had never known it . . . She felt Ladan shivering beside her; and she gazed down at her sister's flushed face. Her eyes were glazed, and her breath sounded hoarse and ragged. She wondered how much she could understand of what was going on; she hoped to some extent the fever and shock of their bereavement shielded her from making sense of the man's words.

Ladan had always been the family clown: their mother's funny little baby. There was something irrepressibly comical about her surprised-looking expression, as though she were constantly on the verge of bursting out into laughter. 'They threw away the mould when they made your sister,' her father used to say. And now she was supposed to step into the shoes of the man's first wife, spend the rest of her life reduced to a non-person, an empty pile of clothing huddled in the corner of the room, waiting for her master to pick up his keys from the table. *I remember now, her name was Atifeh . . .*

'. . . And, as a gesture of goodwill, my client is also willing to allow her sister, Miss Laleh, to remain in the house.'

Her relative was such an inadequate person, he needed his lawyer to do his romancing for him. It was almost funny. Contempt made Laleh light-headed with courage.

'My sister and I thank your client for his *kindness*, but we regret we must decline his offer,' she announced clearly.

It was safer to continue communicating through the lawyer; she could feel the saliva rushing up from her gorge and the desire to spit in her relative's face had become almost intolerable.

Ladan's suitor, who had remained silent until now, reached inside his jacket for a piece of paper. *More debts, perhaps? Would you also like our blood?* It was hopeless; their mother had no family; she was an orphan, and not one of Baba's relatives had survived. Yet surely one of those dozens of people her father had helped over the years would be able to do something for them now?

'You will find the situation is not quite as straightforward as it appears,' murmured their relative smoothly.

Self-consciously, he rustled the papers in his hands. Laleh stared out of the window towards the courtyard walls. Her mother's washing still hung on the line; she had wanted to scrub all the heavy blankets and wall hangings before packing them in mothballs for the move. She wouldn't have known about the new washing machine awaiting her as she bent over the bath tub for the very last time with her bar of green soap. '*When I married your baba, he promised me all the modern conveniences.*' Later, after the men had gone, Laleh would have to find it in herself to prise open the clothes pegs one by one, undoing the last few actions of those beloved hands . . . For as long as those sheets and blankets flapped and creaked in the wind, a part of her mother's spirit was still with them . . .

'I have written testimony here from nine independent witnesses, seven of them men, attesting to the immoral behaviour of both Miss Laleh and Miss Ladan . . .'

Article 102 of the Penal Code: Women shall be buried up to their breasts for the purpose of stoning . . .

'All of the above-mentioned witnesses can vouch to having seen Miss Laleh and Miss Ladan on various occasions consorting with male persons known to be outside the family circle, entering a vehicle with unknown male persons, wearing close-fitting, immodest garments, frequenting areas of ill-repute . . .'

Article 104: The stones used shall not be large enough to kill the person by one or two strikes; nor should they be so small they could not be defined as stones . . .

'It's not true,' she whispered. 'None of it is true . . . you know that. You've known us since we were children . . . how can you invent these lies against us?'

She hadn't the measure of the man. In all these years she had never understood the essential ugliness of his nature, at least not properly. Once that hateful document ended up in the hands of the authorities their lives were in danger; they risked arrest with every second they remained in the house. There was not a moment to lose; they would have to leave that very night.

Somehow, she would have to get Ladan into a taxi and drive far away from their old neighbourhood. They would throw themselves on the mercy of friends or colleagues of her father, or else leave the city altogether . . . Yes, that was it! They would journey back north, travelling against the tide of humanity fleeing the earthquake, lose themselves amongst all those thousands of other displaced people . . . She and Ladan would destroy their documents, they would give false names to the workers at the camps . . . perhaps one of the foreign aid agencies there would take them under their wing . . .

Their relative stood up and picked up his papers from the table. He paused for a moment, then looked down at the sisters, crouched together on the settle.

'My driver has been instructed to remain parked outside. I do not advise you to attempt to leave the house.'

Twenty-three

The day began quite promisingly.

The baby slept an unheard-of stretch from midnight till five in the morning; and when he did eventually wake up, Tom lay him down beside Sappho in the bed, unbuttoning her nightshirt in the grainy light and placing Hector at the breast, so that she fed him without ever really coming to.

She was still on a high from all that sleep when they left the house after lunch to catch the Tube to Embankment, greedily savouring those five unbroken hours as though they had been a particularly fine meal. Even her eyelids felt stronger, nourished by all that rest, the muscles snappy and alert.

Tom was wearing one of his padded tartan lumberjack shirts, and a pair of yellow-stitched Doc Martens.

I'm married to the only man in London who still wears Doc Martens, she thought to herself as she watched him play Paper, Scissors, Stone with Maro, who was sitting on his lap, drolly attempting to engulf his boulder-like fist with her tiny fingers.

No matter which object she chose, Tom always seemed to be one step ahead of her, psychically intuiting her call, so that Maro would win. She liked that about Tom: his complete imperviousness to trends or fashions; it kept her free of the London disease, too, by association. That, and the fact she hadn't grown up in the city.

You are the love of my life, Tom . . . I adore you, she thought, surprised at the intensity of emotion that pierced her heart as she remembered his gentle fingers unbuttoning her shirt as she slept.

Poor Tom, she'd been like a zombie in these weeks after the birth . . . As soon as Hector was more settled, they would go out for a meal together, the two of them alone, even if it was just across the road to the Paradise.

Just out of Baker Street, the train stopped in a tunnel. The carriage lights flickered off; and as she sat in the dark, waiting for them to come back on, Sappho practised an imaginary introduction to someone who had never met her family, trying to picture how they would appear to a stranger. 'Yes, the thick-set man with the fair hair is my husband, while the little girl on his lap is our daughter, Maro.'

Gazing through the impersonal eyes of her imaginary stranger, Sappho took in the long hair with the slight curl in it, light brown with a kind of pink aura like a nimbus, her grave eyes, the exact colour of peeled grapes, ringed by bruise-like shadows (she had not been sleeping well since the baby's birth), the lovely erect way she sat on her father's knee, sandalled feet crossed delicately at the ankles.

She never tired of this secret game: waiting to collect Maro from nursery, the invisible stranger at her elbow, she would single out her daughter amongst the other children in their blue gingham smocks, or sitting by the study window waiting for Tom and Maro to return from the park on a winter's evening, she would think *If they weren't my family, I would want them to be*, shivering slightly at so much good fortune.

It had been her idea to see the Weather Project at the Turbine Hall; their first outing as a new family of four. Nothing too taxing and, according to the review in the *Observer*, the indoor sun was popular with children.

'How can a sun be indoors?' asked Maro, as they walked up the steps of the Underground towards the river.

Sappho took her hand, suddenly overwhelmed by the holiday crowds milling around the London Eye: the joggers weaving around the mime artist with his coils of powdery hair, the out-of-town families in their weirdly co-ordinated outfits. It was too full on, after all those weeks at home with the baby.

'I'm not sure, my darling. We'll just have to see when we get there.'

They stopped to watch the Thames lapping about the white iron spikes at the base of the wheel, seagulls bobbing in the choppy brown water, grimly playing at being ducks. Looking up at the grey underbelly of the capsules, you could make out people quite clearly standing in their pods with their video cameras and outspread maps, time travellers in a parallel universe.

A row of little girls sat on the river wall having their photograph taken by their father. They looked out of sorts, hair all ratty, as they glared into the camera with screwed-up eyes, and there was a note of real terror in the voice of the youngest girl: 'Let me *down*, Daddy!' Yet how many times had she been guilty of that herself? thought Sappho. Of shoe-horning the messy present into a Kodak moment?

They walked past a juice kiosk with crates of oranges stacked up on the pavement, a toxic-smelling kebab stall, and a Chinese man sitting cross-legged on the ground beside it, bending wire coathangers into names: Joshua, Jack, Ellie, Elizabeth. Was there anyone in the world still called Elizabeth these days? wondered Sappho.

'Can I have one, Daddy, *please*?' Maro looked up at Tom beseechingly.

'Go on then, Mousie,' replied Tom, pulling out his wallet.

The man handed Sappho a lined exercise book in which to write down the name, and she glanced up into his face: he had ruddy cheeks, more Tibetan-looking than Chinese, and tawny brown eyes which sparkled with intelligence. Beside him on the ground stood a large metal Thermos, decorated with a pattern of orchids on a light green background. M-A-R-O, she wrote, careful to separate the letters. Sappho watched the man's hands as he worked: beautiful virile hands, with long fingers. The letters must look like ciphers to him, she thought, abstract as Chinese calligraphy is to us.

'Maro needs the loo,' said Tom, as they approached the steps of the Royal Festival Hall. 'And actually, you look bushed. Why don't you sit down for a bit, while I take her into the foyer of the National Film Theatre?'

A breeze was ruffling up the water into little choppy waves, while a string of clear bulbs festooned between two lampposts swayed slackly above the parapet. There was one other person on the bench: a plump, white-haired old woman with a folding walking stick laid diagonally across the seat. For a moment Sappho hesitated; the woman obviously had no wish to be disturbed, but all the other benches were taken, and she needed to sit down. Soon. 'Do you mind . . .?' she murmured, placing one hand protectively on the back of the sling.

It was ridiculous, she was already exhausted; whatever happened, she wanted to conserve some strength for Maro, perhaps hand the baby over to Tom while they walked around the Tate.

The woman looked up; she had a puffy face, with a malevolent little cupid's bow of a mouth. Staring for a moment at Sappho, she snapped shut the walking stick and slid heavily up the bench. Sappho settled down beside her, gazing out towards the river; she knew for certain that if she had still been living in Athens she would have said the woman had put the evil eye on her with that look.

Instinctively, she held the baby's foot in her palm, rooting gently through the fabric of his sock for the row of tiny, pea-sized toes. Babies were specially vulnerable to the *mati*: devoted grandmothers in Greece would spit three times, *phtoo, phtoo, phtoo,* to drive away any curse, even an involuntary one born of too much love.

Now, after all these years in London, she would flush with something like rage (against whom, though, and what?) at how she'd let herself be taken in by those superstitions: all that fatalism and ennui . . . something to fill those long hot afternoons . . .

Sappho looked across the river at a pair of tatty, low-flying black ducks skimming across the surface of the water. Though there was something sinister about the ease with which she had cut loose from her past, she'd always known that; the way none of it resonated with her life now. Not a single chord.

Laleh was still the only person she knew in London who reminded her, however obliquely, of different ways of being. Only the other day, she found her sitting in her room sewing a shell into the lining of Reza's fleece. *She sewed sea shells on the seashore* . . . apparently that was how mothers in her country protected their children from the evil eye. Though of course the very fact she'd taken Laleh into her house in the first place meant the apple hadn't fallen so far from the tree.

Like her, Maro was growing up with strangers, a mother and son grafted awkwardly on to the family unit. Reza would be her unlucky little brother in exactly the same way that Alexander had been hers. It was extraordinary that she had never noticed this symmetry before, a purely unconscious re-enactment of her own childhood. Or was it?

Maybe some things were just meant to be. Even before meeting Laleh in the park, she had been fretting about the empty flat at the top of the house. Sometimes she wondered

194

whether her desire to fill those two rooms was a way of declaring to the world that she'd fulfilled her quota of unfortunates, a talisman to keep Lorna from turning up at her door in the middle of the night . . .

The woman on the bench had a theatre programme on her lap, and she was circling events with a ballpoint pen. Sappho stared down at her lap; she was wearing a rust-coloured linen skirt, and expensive-looking black patent-leather Birkenstock's, her toes immaculately painted with coral-coloured nail polish. She had thick calves, with over-spilling ankles: spinster legs, thought Sappho. A smell of perfume hung in the air: something cloying and glandular, disturbingly familiar; it was Opium. Being down by the river, a change of scenery, perhaps, after all those weeks confined to the house, had unlocked a torrent of memories; everything reminded her of something else, a *double-face* reality, so that whatever her eye alighted on was merely a revolving door leading elsewhere.

Unwilling to sit beside the woman, even for a moment longer, Sappho got up from the bench and walked towards the second-hand books spread out over trestle tables under Waterloo Bridge. She began to look through the boxes of prints arranged by subject. Animals, Landscapes, London, Food, Children.

To her delight, in the last box she found a series of charming Kate Greenaway alphabet prints which she thought she could frame and hang up in Maro's room; she needed something for the bare wall above her bed.

And yet she hesitated: for on closer inspection, the illustrations were not exactly what they appeared. She felt cheated: 'R ran for it' showed a little girl in a mob cap, fleeing some unknown terror, while in 'K knelt for it' the child appeared bowed, crushed, by some immeasurable sorrow. Sappho paused, listening to the rumble of trains on the bridge above her. She looked towards the foyer of the NFT; what was taking them so long? Knowing Maro, she had probably persuaded Tom to buy her juice from the café.

Something about those prints had unsettled her; in her naked hunger for cosiness, for everything to be *ideal and nice*, she had sought something in those images that plainly wasn't there. That old woman on the bench, too, with her puffy viperish face had clouded her holiday mood and Maro and Tom's prolonged absence continued to disturb her.

Her fingers brushed the cellophane wrapping around the prints, hovering between the letters F and G. A kind of doom had settled upon her, her shoulders gripped tight by two metal bands of anxiety; she was frightened of what the letter M might depict. She looked down at the sleeping head of her child: *you have everything you ever wished for, and yet you let yourself get rattled by an old picture . . .*

Defiantly, she flicked through the remaining five prints in the box; M was the very last. She looked at it, and a cry escaped her. 'M mourned for it' read the caption, while below huddled a knot of weeping, stricken children. And among them, the most stricken child of all, was her Maro; the same bruised-looking eyes, the cloud of long pinkish hair. A hundred years before, someone had already envisioned the beautiful child who would become her daughter, anticipating a sorrow that would surely one day be hers.

Sappho dropped the print back in its box and hurried away from the bookstall towards the Queen Elizabeth Hall. She was sweating, and the straps of the sling were digging into her shoulders; her heart felt like a boulder in her chest.

Then something caught her eye: a pile of builders' debris in the shadowy gloom between the concrete pillars of the Queen Elizabeth Hall. A flattened bollard, some plaster-board, a heap of broken-up concrete. Part of the area was fenced off, a series of twisted metal cages, one inside the other like a set of Chinese boxes. Everything was a neutral, dusty grey, except for right at the very end, in a shaft of sunlight, something dark orange, metallic-looking.

She stopped, letting her eyes adjust to the semi-darkness. It was a kind of blanket, or sleeping bag, perhaps, and on it, right at the end, a figure sitting cross-legged, with their back against the ribbed concrete wall. Some homeless person had made this cave their own.

The air was dry, and it was surprisingly quiet. She could see better now: it was a man. He was looking away from her into the darker area beneath the building, a kind of stillness radiating out of him like a monk at prayer. His head was shaved, yet there was something about the round-ness of the skull, seen from the side, the sweet, helpless thrust of the neck, that was familiar to her.

It was Alexander.

'Mummy, we've been waiting *ages* for you.'

She found them in the end; they were waiting for her by the bookstall. Maro had a half-drunk bottle of mango smoothie in her hand.

'Taste this, Mummy, it's delicious.'

Sappho took the bottle from her and brought it to her lips; it was thick and cloyingly sweet, with an aftertaste of coconut. The rush of sugar made her feel giddy.

'You still look tired,' said Tom, frowning at her. 'Why don't you let me take the baby?'

For a second she thought he could sense something; her entire being was radioactive with shock. She managed to smile.

'No, it's OK, I don't want to wake him.'

They walked along the river, stopping to watch a fire-eater and a juggler, and a woman in a crinoline skirt spinning around inside a kind of gigantic jewellery box with a cardboard key in her back, arms above her head like a toy ballerina. There was a clingfilm-wrapped sandwich in the leather suitcase at her side together with a banana and a pair of child-sized trainers. She looked hungry, like the children in the prints, the same pinched, little vulpine face. *I just saw Alexander back there . . .* Sappho's cheeks ached; she realised she was still leering. She let her features drop, but instantly the panic became insupportable . . . she felt literally unable to walk another step. *Tell him now, just tell him . . .*

When Tom and Maro had gone on ahead, she returned and dropped two pound coins in the plate at the woman's feet, *this is for you, something to keep the wolf from your door . . .* She stared at her through narrowed eyes, as though she could smell her guilt. *Middle-class bitch.* Always throwing money at the problem, that was her way: *right pocket, left pocket, it's all the same.*

They entered the tunnel beneath Blackfriars Bridge and she heard the creaking and grinding of trains above them. Orange globes of light were mounted along the tunnel walls, illuminating glistening patches of moss which had hardened on to the bricks like varnish. He wasn't safe on that building site, of course he wasn't; someone could creep up on him in the night, knife him as he slept. Her heart lurched, and the horror of it made her clench her fists, digging her nails into her palms.

She remembered his skin, warm and brown, a reservoir of sunlight in those long Balkan winters. As they walked out of the tunnel, she realised she was moaning out loud.

It was a gradual leaching of colours. At the end of the Turbine Hall, an indoor sun, whose sodium rays deadened everything to brown: a giant orange disc, part real, part illusory, reflected in the jaggedly offset ceiling tiles.

She stood on the bridge of the hall, looking down at the people below, shrouded like wraiths in that sickly, numinous gloom: some lying on the ground, scissoring their limbs in the hope of picking out their reflection on the mirrored ceiling, others hugging each other as though for comfort. 'It might not have been him,' she whispered to the sleeping head of her child. 'It might not have been him . . .'

Somewhere down there were Maro and Tom; two of those tiny, hopeful silhouettes belonged to her. My family, she thought, my family, and a wave of such acute anguish washed over her that she had to steady herself on the metal rail.

Alone, she walked through the rooms of the first floor towards an exhibition of artefacts discovered in the Thames at low tide. A giant, double-sided mahogany cabinet stood in the centre of the room, filled with objects, some broken, some intact: clay pipes, shards of Delft pottery, oyster shells, plastic dolls' limbs, credit cards, fridge magnets, animal bones, teeth, claws – detritus from the swamp . . . None of it should have resonated like that, everything so garishly, burningly personal; it was like gazing at the ruins of her own life. A waxy voodoo figure with a sinister hooked arm, a row of bloated leather shoe soles, split heels gaping like jaws, tiny glass phials containing rusting pins and nails.

She looked down at the sling and started in terror: the baby – she'd forgotten all about the baby; what if Hector had picked up some bug in that filthy hole where Alexander was sleeping? He hadn't even had his first shots yet. And what if that bitter old woman on the bench had put the evil eye on him? 'Be healthy, my angel,' she whispered, palpating the slack little thigh muscles through the fabric of the Babygro.

Will you be my sister when I'm a man?

England, 2003

Twenty-four

'So when do I get to visit the famous shed?'

Andrea paused for a moment, the tea towel in her hand. It was useless telling her to wait for the dishwasher to finish its cycle; she was literally incapable of sitting still.

'Maro can give you a guided tour when I'm at Sainsbury's, Mother,' mumbled Tom, trying to concentrate on the list.

They were out of everything: bread, milk, cheese, even Hector's nappies. He opened the cupboard under the sink and glanced inside; no detergent by the look of it either, or bleach. A light had come on on the dishwasher saying it was out of rinse aid; might as well get salt, too, while he was at it.

He drummed his pencil on the kitchen table, trying to conceal his irritation from Andrea. If Sappho wanted to wash her hands of the running of the house, that was her business, but the least she could do was get Elsa and Laleh to pull their weight a bit more. Surely it wasn't asking too much for either one of them to show a little initiative and keep a tab of what they were out of. At least the basics. Oh, hang about, this appeared to be some kind of a list scrawled inside the front cover of the pad: 'Kiddies sand, fram Ajfray, resin.'

Now, that was a lot of help. 'Kiddies sand': what the hell was that supposed to mean? Maro didn't even own a sandpit. As for fram Ajfray, it sounded like one of Sainsbury's more exotic ready meals.

'What d'you think this means, Mother?' asked Tom petulantly, tossing the list before her. He regretted the words the instant they were out of his mouth; the last thing he wanted was Andrea on his case.

Andrea picked up her glasses which were hanging on a neon-coloured thong around her neck and peered at the list.

'Cat litter, fromage frais, raisins,' she said promptly. 'Your Lally's English classes don't seem to be progressing terribly well, if her spelling is anything to go by,' she added blandly.

It could have been Elsa's handwriting, but somehow he doubted it. That backwards-sloping calligraphy was typical of people who were used to writing from right to left.

'So are you sure you want to stay here with Granny while Daddy goes shopping?'

Maro paused for a moment in the rearranging of that ludicrous doll's house Sappho's stepmother, Ghisela, had sent for her birthday. A great big mock-Regency affair, which came with its own dedicated table. 'Buck House', it was called, no less.

Far too pompous for a five-year-old child, full of twee reproduction furniture which was already coming to bits. He'd already had to superglue half the chairs, and a leg was missing from the dining-room table.

'Of course Maro wants to stay with her granny, don't you, poppet?'

'Let her say what she'd rather do,' muttered Tom under his breath.

He was worried about Maro; Sappho was neglecting her these days, there was no getting around it. All that agonising throughout her pregnancy about how she mustn't let Maro suffer, she would hand the baby over to Laleh so the two of them could go on girlie outings, blah blah blah . . .

'Try and see it from her point of view, Tom . . . it's no different from you coming home one day and announcing that you'll be bringing your cute new mistress to live with us . . . All that brainwashing we do to Maro – "you'll soon love the new baby . . . it'll be company for you" – is no different from you expecting me to be friends with your mistress. Assuming of course you have one . . .'

Sitting up in bed, a well-thumbed Penelope Leach baby book lying open on her lap, she'd stared at him challengingly. There was a desperate, slightly unhinged look in her eyes, which he knew too well; one word out of place and she would cry herself to sleep . . . She was due any day now, he had to be absolutely certain of saying the right thing. In the end, he'd settled for: 'Why would I need a cute new mistress, when I've got a cute old wife at home . . .?' which had the added advantage of also being true. He genuinely couldn't think of anyone else he'd rather fuck.

They'd resolved it by making love; in those days, actually pretty much from the start, sex had been a shorthand between them, though by the end of the pregnancy with Hector it had got harder and harder to find a way into his wife. He seemed to remember Sappho lying on the floor, that time, feet resting on the mattress, a cushion under her back, as he knelt between her legs . . . She was so near to her time, he could feel her ripe cervix pulsing against the head of his penis as he came. And a few hours later, she went into labour . . . 'I just hope no one gives me an internal,' she giggled in between contractions as they drove to the hospital.

So far he had managed to excuse Sappho sloping off upstairs after lunch by saying she'd been up all night with the baby. Not true; as it happened, Hector had slept quite well, but Sappho was up wandering around the house in the early hours of the morning; and when Hector did eventually start yelling, loud enough to be heard halfway down the street, he'd found her dozing off in the sitting room with a copy of the Argos catalogue on her lap. What that was all about was anyone's guess.

What could Andrea possibly make now of Sappho with her retinue of staff, yet still unable to get a meal ready on her own when her mother-in-law came to visit? *I thought I'd give my wife a day off for once*; who the hell was he trying to kid with his lame excuses? Paunchy old git in an apron.

Certainly not Andrea; though to his surprise, she didn't comment on the fact that he did all the lunch on his own, and even forbore from interfering too much with the preparation. (He did notice she turned down the temperature on the oven at a certain point; and when she thought he wasn't looking, he saw her add more salt and butter to the mashed potatoes.) From the outside, it must look quite charming, anyway: caring new dad fixes lunch while mum and baby rest upstairs. And if it were a one-off it would be charming.

For now at least, she did still appear to be feeding Maro, though he couldn't swear it wasn't Laleh doing the cooking. The important thing was not to make too much of a big deal about her behaviour; at the end of the day she was a good mother who adored both her children (thank God at least for that). Once upon a time, he would have said she adored him . . . though, like everything else, on her own terms.

It was true Laleh was spending more and more time with Hector (fortunately, under the circumstances, Andrea had been provident enough to get that cumbersome Swedish double buggy with a name like a topless weathergirl – *Emmaljunga*; he couldn't think of it without smirking) but so far there didn't appear to have been all that many mother and daughter outings with Maro.

As a matter of fact, not even one. As far as he could see, Laleh was now lumbered virtually all day with both children, three if you included Reza, while Sappho either rested in bed in between feeds, or else sloped off with Hector in the sling for hours at a time. Weekends, he took over, though to give Laleh credit, she quite often volunteered to take the children up to her flat on Sunday mornings.

Sappho would get over whatever was gnawing at her; she had to. She tended to be fairly grouchy and withdrawn in the weeks building up to Celia's visits, though nothing as bad as this; besides, her mood would invariably lift in the car on the way back from dropping her mother off at Stansted. *Thank God that's over for another year . . .* She would be particularly affectionate to him in the ensuing weeks; and always made a point of inviting his parents for lunch practically the moment Celia was out of the door, almost as though she wanted to show him where her loyalties lay.

The weird thing was that she'd never been at all down in the dumps after Maro's birth – quite the opposite – nor, for that matter, in the first few weeks after coming back from the hospital with Hector. Unless of course it was a kind of delayed reaction, some sort of hormonal thing. Though Hector was now almost two months old . . .

He was tempted to discuss it with Andrea, in the most casual way possible, of course. Just drop it into the conversation, when he got back from Sainsbury's.

Did you find you were a bit low after we kids were born? If so, how long did it last (and for Chrissakes, how the hell do I get Sappho to snap out of it)?

He just couldn't do it, though; pride, and a kind of residual loyalty towards Sappho, prevented him. As far as he knew, Andrea had had no help whatsoever with him and his brother and sister when they were small; money was tight in the first few years of his parents' marriage, and Andrea being Andrea, she would have just got on with it.

He could live with Sappho not wanting to cook for him – he wasn't exactly going to starve; he could even live with her not doing the shopping. No, what really hurt was her refusal to eat even a single meal with him at the table; the moment he entered the kitchen, she would sidle off to another room, almost as though she were scared he would try and start up a conversation –

'We can run up some teeny curtains for the nursery, if you like, darling,' said Andrea, peering into the house while Tom hunted for his keys.

He used to enjoy going to Sainsbury's with Maro; they would get a box of sliced mangos from the salad bar, which she would eat in the front seat of the trolley while he did the shopping. Sometimes, as a special treat, he would buy her a Kinder Egg, or a small bar of Green and Black's chocolate. To be honest, though, today he would be glad of a couple of hours' peace and quiet; it had been a strain getting the meal ready and the downstairs tidied up in time for Andrea's visit, and he could do with some quality time on his own. Was that all he could aspire to these days: two hours alone in the supermarket? *What a glamorous life you lead, Tom . . . Yes, well, someone's got to do it . . .*

'So you'll be all right with Granny?'

'*Yes*, Daddy,' mumbled Maro, without even turning around.

He peered inside the house. Now there was a surprise: Mr Doll's House Family hunched over the butler's sink in the basement, while Mrs Doll's House Family reclined on a chaise-longue in the master bedroom . . . He escaped before Andrea had a chance to comment.

Yet Sappho had been on such a high after the birth; they both had, thought Tom as he reversed the car into his favourite parking bay near the recycling bins. That was the sad and strange thing about it; he would never forget the catch of raw joy in her voice, a sob almost, as she pulled their son up from the bottom of the birthing pool. 'It's a boy! Tom, it's a boy!'

He switched off the engine and took off his seat belt; in the mirror, he caught sight of a woman on a bicycle staring at him as he settled back in his seat. Yes, well, he could be waiting for someone, no need to give him the eye like he was a pervert or something. Though, as it happened, he did have the first stirrings of a boner . . . he and Sappho hadn't so much as held hands since . . . well, since pretty much the birth.

He looked down at his crotch; he could feel his penis throbbing against the stiff fabric of his jeans. He would do it, take his cock out and masturbate in the middle of Sainsbury's carpark; that would teach his wife to ignore him.

He pulled at the buttons of his fly; one by one they pinged open as though they too could bear the strain no longer. He could see the outline of the glans clearly against the white cotton of his underpants, a single wet dot to mark the centre. *The eye of the storm.*

His fingers were moving of their own accord; the desire to liberate his penis had become almost unbearable. The scowling woman on the bicycle had gone; this section of the carpark was deserted. Or perhaps all those cars were full of other desperate husbands pleasuring themselves on a Sunday afternoon . . . There was a time, not so long ago, even after Maro was born, when he would have done it, wanked himself off, then come back home and told Sappho about it; she might even have joined him if she'd been sitting beside him in the front seat.

He heard the steady humping rhythm of a train down on the tracks below; he was just going to have to do it. Glancing quickly around the carpark, he slid back the elastic of his pants and felt his penis thud dully on to his lap. Resigned, he weighed it in his palm, remembering the way Sappho steadied herself on his thighs, wrists together like a gymnast vaulting a horse. As his fist moved up and down, at first slowly, then with a kind of weary urgency, image after image of Sappho – her breasts, the expression on her face as she came, the dimples on the base of her spine – overlaid themselves one by one on to his brain.

He could only masturbate thinking of his wife; it had been that way since the day they met. He was about to come, he had nearly broken through the concentric wisps of cloud to the place of light on the mountain's peak, when he felt his consciousness drift, some kind of alternative erotic image, familiar, yet unresolved, imposing itself like a succubus on to his fantasies: breasts, flanks, willowy thighs, a glimpse of concave stomach as an arm reached up on to a shelf.

With a sickening jolt he realised who it was: it was her – Laleh – as he'd never allowed himself to imagine her . . . Letting his penis drop in disgust on to his lap, he crammed it back into his trousers and slumped forwards on to the steering wheel. *Talk about scraping the barrel, man . . .*

He had a splitting headache; he would buy some Nurofen in Sainsbury's.

He got up and went to look for a trolley.

'We need to talk.'

Sappho gave a start. She hadn't realised Tom was awake. She felt his hand searching for hers under the blanket, closing her fingers around his. The touch of his skin was waxy, inert, that of a stranger.

'What is it, Saff? Tell me what's wrong.'

She lay on her side, listening to Hector's greedy sucking.

'Are you tired? D'you want me to do nights? We could start Hector on a bottle, if you like.'

She shook her head, staring at the Chinese quilt folded over the back of the nursing chair. In the dark, the green satin glimmered like crocodile scales. *Tell him, tell him about Alexander.*

'Is it something I've done? Or said?'

He sat up and switched on the bedside light. Starting, Hector allowed the nipple to fall from his lips, then began to suck with renewed vigour.

She felt Tom's fingers on her cheek, gently turning her gaze to meet his. His eyes searched her face as though trying to recognise a familiar landmark, hoping to ignite something that was no longer there.

'I can't sleep with three of us in this bed.'

Wordlessly he got up and, picking the Chinese quilt off the chair, walked out of the house and into the shed.

Twenty-five

The deck was empty, apart from the couple she'd noticed earlier down on the pier.

Dressed in dark blue, they were both in their early forties, tall, though slightly cushiony and out-of-shape-looking. He could have been head of English at a secondary school, thought Sappho, handsome in a romantic way, with a high forehead, strong jaw and wavy brown hair. She too was the same combination of neglected good looks and frumpiness, but she had a calm, kind face and a pleasantly erect demeanour.

As the boat pulled away from the pier, Sappho settled back in the orange plastic seat, adjusting her coat around the baby's sling. She looked at her watch: almost two hours since his last feed in the Mother and Baby room at Waterloo. The Albanian attendant there had brought her a glass of water, then insisted on holding him while Sappho went to the loo. Before leaving, the woman pulled a picture of her little girl out of her overall pocket; she looked about Maro's age, four years old, five maybe, dressed in a tartan party frock with long plaits wound above her pierced ears and pinned to her head with butterfly clips.

Sappho looked down at Hector's face in profile as he slept, head resting snugly against the padded backrest of the sling, lips parted, his breath coming in steady little gasps.

Both he and Maro before him liked being carried around close to her heart; she liked it too, liked that feeling of the baby being merely an extension of her own body, manageable, portable.

She needed him to sleep now so she could be alone with her thoughts; they were literally bursting out of her skull, little shivers of anxiety crackling along her spine. Not for the first time, she wondered how Hector could find rest against such an unquiet heart.

'But you do sleep, and I love you for it,' she whispered, burying her face in the wispy crown of his head. She was addicted to his smell; she would gulp it down in little huffy draughts, burying her nose behind his ear or under the collar of his vest, hyperventilating with pleasure as the sweet musky scent coursed through her like a drug.

A lumpy woman, alone with her child. Sappho shivered: when had she started talking to herself like that? Like the L'Oréal slogan, only in reverse: because you're *not* worth it . . .

She couldn't face going home, not yet. This time the site under the Festival Hall was empty, but the orange sleeping bag was rolled up in a corner, beside a half-empty holdall. Somewhere she'd read that homeless people were jealously protective of their possessions – she'd heard stories on the news of rough sleepers being knifed for the sake of a blanket – and yet it was somehow typical of Alexander not to think of hiding his belongings. From other . . . from other what? From *other unfortunates like him.*

Tears filled her eyes; Kyria Lena, the monstrously fat madam who owned the brothel in Omonia Square where they rented a room, used to tell Celia that the two of them, Alexander and Lorna, walked through the mire without getting their feet dirty . . . Angels with dirty faces, she used to call them.

Why were their lives so *messy*? thought Sappho angrily; but then an image came into her mind of Lorna's toenail poking out of her holey plimsoll the night she turned up at the house in East Sheen, and her heart smarted. Chances were she was sleeping rough with him . . .

As the boat approached the stumpy red columns by St Paul's railway bridge, she heard crackling and hissing over the loudspeaker, and a man's voice clearing his throat: 'Welcome, ladies and gentlemen, aboard our riverside cruise . . .'

The tinny voice made Sappho start; she hadn't known there would be a commentary. Instinctively, she glanced down at Hector to see whether the sound had woken him; his cheek twitched, and a spasm of worry furrowed his brow, but he slept on. A fine down grew between his eyebrows, reddish in the grey light. Out of the corner of her eye, Sappho watched the couple in blue. There was something so natural and tender about they way they held each other, fingers casually entwined as they gazed out towards a speedboat churning up the yellow, tobacco-stained water, that they could have been anything from brand-new lovers in the early throes of physical passion to a couple of twenty years' standing. Watching them had become a compulsion, a physical ache, and Sappho averted her eyes. When was the last time she and Tom had held one another like that?

She could tell him everything, of course, she'd already thought of that. Explain to him that the day they'd all gone out to the Tate, she might – just *might* – have seen the son of some friends from Athens sleeping rough on the South Bank, friends she'd omitted to mention in all their six years together. And Tom being Tom, how would he react? Well, he'd *deal* with it. He'd want to drive there to Waterloo at once . . . And –

At which point following that train of thought ceased to be an option. How could she involve Tom in all this when their life together was absolutely predicated, at least as far as she was concerned, upon a world which didn't contain Alexander? Especially a homeless Alexander sleeping rough. The thought of the two men – *you realise he's a man now* – in the same city, let alone the same room, was literally unbearable. So instead, Sappho took refuge in silence, hiding behind tiredness, her blameless little baby son.

'We are now approaching the Tate Modern, housed in what was once Bankside Power Station,' said the voice over the loudspeaker; from the mock-jaunty tone, she realised he must be reading from a script.

It hadn't even been two months since their visit to the Turbine Hall, was it possible? She looked up as they sailed towards London Bridge, where three red buses stood in a row like a picture postcard of London.

'We are now approaching Traitors' Gate, what you might call London's first one-way street.' As they scraped along the slimy walls of the Tower, Sappho watched the young man from the ferry company leap nimbly on to the jetty, mooring the boat to a post with a brilliant, synthetic-looking white rope; his was probably the jaunty voice over the loudspeaker. The middle-aged lovers in blue were disembarking, taking that dreamy joy of theirs away with them. *I wonder if you know how cold it is out here, watching the two of you . . .*

She heard the chink of coins, as behind her the barman counted his takings. New passengers had embarked, and an older, gravelly-voiced man had taken over the commentary.

'To those of you who have just joined us, welcome aboard our riverboat cruise – wetter and windier than the Caribbean, but no less scenic. Now, as some of you might know, the Thames has two hours of flood, seven of ebb – and is the only water you can both drink and chew.'

There was a pause while across the aisle an elderly couple

smiled wryly at each other; beside them a harassed-looking middle-aged man in woollen socks and sandals rifled through his zip-up bag for the tickets. Their son, thought Sappho, and unexpectedly a quote she had read recently somewhere came into her mind: *the children of lovers are orphans* . . . And her children . . . what did that make them?

Quickly, she turned towards the water, where a black and red dredger was spurting out water from a hole at its flank like a wound: *Bert Prior, London*, stencilled in yellow letters along the side. Deserted houses, wharves, apartment blocks drifted past, a fading canvas stretched taut along the river.

'We are now approaching the Thames Barrier, site of the world's largest ten movable steel gates.' They looked like shark fins, or hooded aliens, sentinels of the river, tiled in a kind of dull puffy steel like quilted foil. Hector stirred, briefly opening then closing his eyes, as though hoping to gather up the lost fragments of a dream. Past a beach of glistening grey mud, almost indistinguishable from the dark water lapping at its edges, she watched a small plane coming to land at City Airport, threading its way expertly between the tower blocks.

A sudden burst of sun broke through the clouds, saturating the surface of the water with a membrane of wrinkled silver.

Hector was properly awake now; she looked at the time: three-thirty. Maro would have finished nursery by now, her friend Eden was finally coming back to play: Tom was supposed to be collecting, but if he couldn't make it, Laleh would go instead. *Mummy couldn't come today . . . she's out again . . .*

Hector was butting his head between her breasts, tormented by their fullness, by a secret signal only he could pick up. Unstrapping him from the sling, she lifted her shirt and attached him to the nipple; greedily, he stuffed it whole into his mouth, swallowing up even the aureole, as though to devour the breast meat itself. It was so different from the way Maro used to feed, giving delicate, contemplative little licks to the nipple, then pausing to look up at Sappho until their eyes met, like a needy lover in search of reassurance.

On the journey back to Westminster, the sun disappeared behind some clouds; the water looked like a vat of melted silver now, the sky veined with yellow threads of light. Past Greenwich, she saw piles of rubbish compacted on to the banks of the river: powdery, volcanic-looking, like the pictures she had once seen of garbage mountains in India where street children scavenged for a living. The old wharf wall had collapsed, slabs of red bricks, still intact, mingling with the bright green, moss-covered ones at the edge of the water. Beside it was a mesh plant, where cubes of steel wire – some brown, some red, others almost dark blue in colour – were stacked up in tidy-looking blocks. Everywhere she looked, the same pattern of order and decay.

Through the glass, spattered with feathery spots of water, Sappho watched two seagulls cross paths in the sky, the first and perhaps last times their worlds would converge – a fanned frill of tail, then each had gone their separate way, scarcely registering the other's presence . . . A single shoe, a man's trainer, floated on the surface of the water, bobbing confusedly in the trail the boat left in its wake.

Hector had finished his feed; his nappy could do with changing, but it could wait until she was back at Waterloo. Sometimes she felt she was testing herself, finding out quite where the parameters of being a bad mother lay, each act of neglect a small milestone. Perhaps the Albanian attendant would still be there in her glass cubicle; she could do with a friendly face to talk to.

This was the third time she had returned to the river to look for Alexander; she never told Tom where she was going, and he never asked. That was the way things had become; he was spending more and more time in his office at the end of the garden, and recently they'd even given up eating together in the evenings. Conversations had become too difficult; she found it impossible to locate a voice.

There had always been a certain lack of transparency in their relationship in particular with regard to her past life in Athens. A darkness on to which Tom had never felt the need to shine a torch; sometimes she wondered if this low-level secretiveness made her more interesting in his eyes, was a turn-on, even. Apparently, once when he was still a little boy, he had informed his mother he would never marry an English girl, they were too boring; even now, she knew he still got a kick out of telling people that she was half-Greek. (A quarter, as it happened, but it was enough for him that she spoke, and cooked, and sometimes even dreamed, in another language, that his children had been christened into the Orthodox faith.)

Even though they had met in Greece – that was where it had all begun – the deal was that she came to him without a past. It had to be that way; no baggage, literally (she had her belongings shipped over from Athens much later on when they bought the house in Queen's Park), no attachments.

As far as Sappho was concerned, the pay-off for Tom, a reward for living with that lack of candour, if you like, was the passion she dedicated to their shared life in London – her joyous embrace of every aspect of his existence, even his trying mother, Andrea, whom for years he had successfully marginalised, but who was now back in their lives – full time, as Tom sometimes complained.

Six years of busy-bee home-making, establishing roots, networks, hundreds of tiny private routines; then, without warning, retreat. The whole lot of it a sham; these days, she could hardly bring herself to go through the motions of being a mother, let alone a wife. No wonder he chose to shut himself away in the office.

How could it have come to this . . .? Sappho leaned back on her seat and closed her eyes; she felt drained, and there was still the rush-hour Tube journey back to Queen's Park. How many times would she have to make this trip to Waterloo before she found Alexander? *And then, after you've found him? Then what happens?*

Sappho looked at her watch – the girls were probably already home. For weeks Maro had begged her to talk to Eden's mother and arrange a visit. And now that the play-date, booked weeks in advance and cancelled twice, had been entered into Eden's mother's handbag-sized purple Smythson organiser, then cross-referenced against her work diary and her fridge calendar at home ('I'd hate to double book'), 'then run past her personal bloody astrologer, no doubt,' grumbled Tom; now that the day had finally rolled around, and Eden was coming to play, Sappho was halfway up the Thames on a pleasure cruise.

That was the kind of mother she'd become.

Twenty-six

'D'you mind telling me where you've been?'

Tom watched as Sappho finished pouring herself a glass of water at the sink, fingering the edge of the Travelcard he had found in her pocket.

'I've been out,' she said, placing the glass, undrunk, on the table.

'I could have told you that. And so could Maro, who was rather hoping you'd be there when Eden came to play.' A cheap shot, dragging Maro into it, but he was desperate.

She hadn't brushed her hair, it was sticking up in a bush behind her head, and she was still wearing her maternity clothes, even though Hector was almost four months old now. He hadn't a clue what her body looked like these days under her sloppy cardigans and tracksuit bottoms.

Her face was a box of wet matches: strike, strike, no flame.

'Are you ill or something?'

She shook her head. 'I'm fine.'

'You're fine,' he repeated sarcastically. 'You're fine.'

He stared at her for a moment; a split second of dizzying nothingness – *But who am I?* – then histrionically, he picked up his mobile and stormed out of the door. Lately, it would always end like this; he'd turn up the heat, confront her, then leave before things got too hot. *And why is that?* Because . . . because . . .

Disloyally, he felt short-changed; this wasn't the woman he had married. Sorry, but she just wasn't. Sometimes he thought she should wear a badge saying: 'You might not know it, but I'm good-looking.' On some level, it actually offended his sense of pride that he'd been short-changed with Sappho; he knew how to deal with builders and suppliers without getting ripped off, so why had he got it so wrong with his wife?

Tom parked the car in an alleyway by the gym.

It was a rainy autumn evening, and in the residential streets the lights of the swimming pool shimmered like an ocean liner. You used to be able to see people swimming from the pavement, but, according to Maro's teacher, some of the Muslim pool users complained, and a film of adhesive frosting had been stuck on the lower portion of the window to resemble sand-blasted glass. Not that he'd ever noticed a particularly strong female Muslim presence in the pool, unless of course they all came on the Ladies' Evening which was advertised on the board.

Picking up his fleece and bottle of water off the front seat, Tom got out of the car and pressed the button on the remote keyfob device; he heard the muffled chirrup of the alarm, and the four locks thudding down into place. No point taking chances in an area like this; he noticed most of the staff parked their cars in the disused basketball court adjacent to the building, though the West Indian bruiser who seemed to run the joint kept his old-school Beemer right on the pavement. He had never once seen a traffic warden give him a ticket.

Heaven knows, he could have joined a more salubrious gym – the Holmes Place in Notting Hill, just a couple of blocks away from his old flat in Ladbroke Grove, or even the new Carlton Club under the Westway which Nick and his family were members of – but using a municipal pool was part of Sappho's drive to keep Maro's life real. Though, poor Maro, her life had become real enough recently.

Tom walked through the automatic doors and, sliding his pass through a scanner, bumped open the top bar of the turnstile with his paunch like one of those sumo wrestlers in foam bodysuits he'd seen on a children's programme. It was an uncomfortably tight fit in the turnstile, and he glanced over his shoulder to see if the blonde girl at the front desk was watching. But she was too busy chatting to a good-looking Asian boy sitting casually on a ledge behind her, his feet in their white trainers resting on the edge of the sill, to notice his difficulty. *Like she gives a toss about you and your kebab belly . . .*

He walked up the stairs to the gym, nodding to the middle-aged black guy in yellow-tinted wraparound shades, his relaxed salt and pepper hair tied up into a neat ponytail behind his head. His name was written on his badge: Lenny; he'd taken Tom's induction session just two weeks before. Opening the filing cabinet behind him, Tom searched for his exercise plan which they had worked out together on that occasion.

'What are your personal goals, Tom?' Lenny had asked in his pleasant Caribbean accent as they sat by the drinks machine down in the foyer filling in a questionnaire.

To make my wife love me again, Lenny . . . that's all I want . . .

'Oh, the usual middle-aged wish list . . . lose weight, tone up a bit . . . you must be tired of hearing it.'

Lenny looked like a vital man in spite of the greying hair; his posture was perfectly erect, and beneath his yellow polo shirt with the name of the gym embroidered on the chest, you could see the tight bulge of his biceps. Everything about him radiated health and wellbeing. *What's your secret, Lenny, how do you keep the sap flowing at your age . . .?*

In the end they worked out a programme of fifteen minutes each on the rowing machine, the cross-trainer and the treadmill, with one hundred sit-ups and fifty press-ups on the mat. A five-minute practice run on the treadmill had shown him to be severely unfit: '*POOR*' was the unequivocal verdict in red letters on the screen.

'We'll take it slow, Tom, then have a review in six weeks.' Lenny's voice remained courteous as he gazed down impassively at the lardy pancake of flesh clamped in his callipers.

In a mere matter of days Tom became addicted to the gym. Almost at once, it became apparent to him that, providing he managed to keep his post-exercise endorphins topped up to a certain level, he was able to deal with the quotidian despair that had become his home life.

Picking up his exercise card, he walked towards the machines. The gym was not too busy at this time; mornings seemed to be the worst, with a peak around six o'clock when the offices emptied. You could see the stresses and strains of the day etched on people's faces as they pounded out their frustrations on the machines; it was a shame no one had thought of harnessing all that energy to the national grid, thought Tom. *You might not have done anything particularly worthwhile to earn your millions, but at least you've never been a job slave . . .*

The cross-trainer by the window was free; he had become stupidly attached to this particular machine, and would dawdle over another part of his programme until it became free. Placing his bottle in the drinks' container, he slipped his feet into the stirrups, using the arrows on the screen to enter his details into the computer. Age: forty-three; weight: ninety-one kilos; *heart: broken . . .*

Tom's legs felt like lead as he marched on the cross-trainer, back and forth with his arms, ploughing a lonely furrow in the neon-lit gym. Another seven minutes to go; just forty-eight calories burned.

For six years, he had loved her on her own terms, more than he had ever loved anyone – more, it seemed to him sometimes, than he had really been designed to love another human being – then, from one day to the next, as though by a flick of a switch, all communications down.

The timer beeped; his fifteen minutes were up. One hundred and thirty-six calories, probably the equivalent of the cappuccino he'd had that morning at the Golborne Deli.

Taking a swig of his water, he slid his feet out of the stirrups and walked across the floor towards the bottle of disinfectant which hung from a hook on the wall.

'Please show consideration to others and wipe down your machine after use,' said the sign on the wall. Pulling a strip of blue tissue from the dispenser, he sprayed some of the odourless liquid on to the paper and wiped down the handles of the cross-trainer.

Trying not to catch Lenny's eye as he walked past the desk, he stopped by one of the two rowing machines situated back to back along the wall. Usually he preferred the nearer one, but a wiry old man, totally bald apart from a gruesome Chinaman's pigtail hanging halfway down his back, was on it, pumping up and down on the bucket seat like a shuttle on a loom, the long slab of his thigh muscles rippling beneath his tiny satin runners' shorts.

For an instant, Tom imagined yanking at the greasy plait, picturing the look of outrage on the old man's face, the sticky pin-sized blobs of skin on the root of each hair. How many hairs could there be in that miserable plait? Fifty? A hundred?

Climbing heavily on to the seat, Tom leaned forward to set the timer, aware of his pregnant-woman's paunch squatting shamelessly on his lap. Level 10, calories 200, time 15 minutes. The seat felt unpleasantly warm beneath his thighs; he hadn't noticed who was on the machine before him, but he sincerely hoped it wasn't that big-bottomed woman in leggings, each dimple of her thighs visible beneath the stretchy grey fabric, a wet funnel of sweat imprinted down the crack of her buttocks, as she leaned forwards to talk to her friend on the treadmill.

You can talk, Fatso . . .

Adjusting the straps of the stirrups around his trainers, Tom released the chain and pulled hard on the foam-covered handle. He used to like rowing, real rowing, on water; for a while he had been on the university team, though he hadn't kept it up when he moved to London. All those years as a builder meant that he'd kept fit without having to ever really do too much about it; it was the easy life, too many boozy lunches with investors and architects and town-planning mandarins, that had proved his downfall. And now, night after night of solitary ready meals in front of the TV.

Back and forth, knees to chest, as the bucket seat glided along its steel runner, each growl of the chain like the drag and pull of shingle at the water's edge. She never said where she'd been that day, nor had he pressed her. Though the fact that she'd taken Hector with her was comfort of sorts; his baby son, guarantor of his mother's honour.

It was pathetic, he was a pathetic man. Why was he so afraid to push Sappho?

Because you've been a fool, Tom, and you know it . . . When it came down to it there just wasn't enough meat on his marriage to withstand this crisis. And now, as if the breakdown of his home life were not enough, there was the Laleh problem. Which was actually several problems rolled into one.

The other day, Bridget telephoned, ostensibly to talk to Sappho, but he got the feeling that he was the one she was

225

really looking for. There'd always been a kind of unwholesome understanding between them (in spite of his more or less cordial loathing of her) which – on Bridget's part, at least – roughly translated as: *you are as boring and English as I am, Tom, in spite of your foreign wife and the outlandish names you choose to give your children* . . . No matter how hard he tried to disabuse Bridget of this notion, the connection between them remained.

'. . . they're your kids as much as Sappho's, so I might just as well tell you –'

'Tell me what, Bridget?' How the hell did Nick put up with that foghorn voice of hers? *Simple, he just tunes out* . . .

'There's no easy way of saying this, Tom, but I'm worried about Maro and the baby.'

Christ. So even thick Bridget had picked up on Sappho's breakdown. He would have to get her to a doctor; he couldn't cope with it any longer on his own. Not if it was putting his children at risk. Either that, or else phone Celia in Greece. *Oh right – just the thing to tip Sappho over the edge.*

'Really . . . in which way, Bridget?' Patronise the interfering old bat, let her know he didn't take her opinions seriously.

'I think they're in physical danger.'

'What kind of danger, Bridget?'

'Now you know, Tom, I've always had my doubts about Laleh –'

'Have you?' he said lightly.

'You know perfectly well I have. We all have. It was completely irresponsible of Sappho to employ her as a nanny without any references. Not in this day and age, with all the horror stories you hear. As an asylum seeker, she's not even meant to be working, I checked. If the Home Office ever gets to find out, you could be prosecuted.'

'Well, thanks for your concern, but you know . . . you can't always do things by the book . . .' *Though Christ knows, you do your fucking best.*

'Tom, it's obvious you and Sappho are just a meal ticket for that woman . . . she's on the make, you can tell from a mile off. She's got sly eyes.'

She's got sexy nun's eyes, as it happens, but I'm not going to argue the toss . . .

'Listen, Bridget . . . Laleh's actually been a great help since . . . well . . . since the baby. And Maro adores her.' *As for me . . . well, I dream about her most nights, but we'll leave it at that . . .*

'I'm not disputing whether she's been a help with the baby. Frankly, it's the very least she can be, under the circumstances. What I am saying is that Sappho is being taken for a ride. And I happen to have proof.'

Christ.

'What kind of proof?'

'That she's got her own agenda . . . I personally wouldn't trust her as far as I could throw her, but that's me. For a start, she doesn't take Hector where she says she's taking him, which is the absolute cardinal rule for any nanny. *You have to be accountable at all times.*'

'Where does she take him then?' He tried to make his voice sound casual, but his mouth was dry, and he felt his face burn with something akin to shame. *So Andrea was right, all along . . .*

'The other day, it was a Wednesday morning, no, sorry, it was a Thursday . . . and she was meant to be taking Hector and Rizzo –'

'Not Rizzo, Bridget, his name is *Reza*.' What was it with these English women and foreign names? *Shame not everyone's as cosmopolitan as you, Tom . . .*

'Reza, then. Anyway, she was meant to be taking the pair of them to Tumble Tots at the Tricycle; I know that,

227

because Sappho happened to mention it the day before when I bumped into her in the park. Now, just by chance, I happened to be cycling down Kilburn High Road on my way to the reclamation yard in Willesden Lane, when something made me look into the window of a café. Don't ask me what it was, but I turned my head . . . and there was Lalch sitting at a table *taking* to a man –'

'It's not illegal to go to a café, Bridget. And nor is talking to a man. At least not since I last checked.' *Fucking whore . . .*

'Tom, that man was carrying Hector *in his arms.*'

What the hell was happening to his life? How could his sweet baby son have ended up sitting in some café in Kilburn High Road in the arms of a strange man? He would scoop up both children, drive them that very night to his parents' house . . . *That's right, run home to mummy.*

'How can you be so sure it was Laleh?'

'Tom, I had a bird's-eye view into the café. Laleh had her back to me, but I could see the double buggy with her own baby strapped inside.'

'So why d'you think that man was . . . holding Hector?'

Bridget's voice dropped to a whisper. 'Because Laleh's hands were full . . . Tom . . . she was handing him a great big wodge of *greenbacks.*'

Stop trying to sound like a gangster, Bridget. She was a nightmare, a fucking nightmare. 'Well . . . it's Laleh's business what she does with her money,' he said evenly. A thousand pounds a month, as it happened – cheap for a nanny, but a fortune for an asylum seeker with no papers . . .

'Tom, the woman was up to no good. It was obvious from a mile off.'

'Just out of interest, Bridget, how are you so sure Laleh didn't actually go to Tumble Tots that day?'

'I hardly think that's the point, Tom', she blustered.

'Well, it is as it happens. Laleh hasn't been banned from going to cafés, at least not that Sappho has told me, and as I said before, she can do what she likes with the money we pay her.' *Sappho and I haven't actually talked about anything for the last six weeks, but I'm assuming you don't know that . . .*

'Well, I still think Sappho ought to be informed.' The naked disappointment in her voice reassured Tom; he had managed to play it cool. As far as Bridget was concerned, he had taken the whole thing in his stride.

'Leave it to me, Bridget,' he said smoothly. 'I'll run it past Sappho if it'll help put your mind at rest. I'm sure there's nothing to worry about . . . but thanks anyway for your concern.' There was no mistaking the menace in his voice.

The beeper sounded. Twenty minutes, one hundred and thirty calories burned. *Could try harder, Tom . . .* Releasing the handle, he let the chain roll back on to itself. He bent over to unbuckle the straps and eased his trainers out of the stirrups. His legs felt like jelly when he stood up, as though he'd just stepped on to dry land after a storm at sea.

Just fifteen minutes left before closing time. He walked towards the treadmill and, using the arrows, set the machine up on an incline. The deck beneath his feet tilted upwards, then slowly, invisibly, the rubber belt began to loop around on itself, gradually building up speed. Like a demented puppet, his feet began to march of their own accord; if he tried to resist, he would be flung off the back like a cowboy on a bucking bronco. *Running to keep still . . .* Of all dumb concepts, this had to be the dumbest. Uncannily like his life at the moment.

He never told Sappho about his conversation with Bridget. *Why's that, Tom – why didn't you mention it to your wife?*

Well, lots of reasons, actually.

Like . . .?

Like the fact that Sappho was clearly not up to dealing with anything at the moment. Just getting out of bed and brushing her hair seemed to be an achievement of sorts these days. And . . . and . . . the fact that the only thread of normality running through all their lives was Laleh. It was Laleh who remembered to pay the milkman, and wash Maro's gingham nursery overall on a Friday, and make sure that the fridge was stocked. And the cat fed, the plants watered, his son's nappy changed. Who made sure that the recycling was put out on Wednesdays, and knew that Maro needed a packed lunch for her farm trip and that the DVDs were due back at the library.

Who quite literally was keeping the show on the road. And who therefore could not possibly be a low-life criminal planning to kidnap his baby and hold him to ransom. Or whatever else she was up to in that café . . .

Any other reasons for keeping shtum?

Not really . . . well, all right, he had a bit of a crush on Laleh. No, no, it wasn't what it seemed. Totally undeclared and unreciprocated and above board – the usual feeble one-sided flirting which seemed to be his lot as a man, only a bit more intense this time. Well, all right, he fancied the fucking socks off her. Savagely, he pushed the 'Up' button on the monitor, ratcheting up his level, beyond the safe 'ten' which Lenny had recommended.

Eleven . . . twelve . . . thirteen . . . fourteen . . . His feet were thudding heavily on the deck, his heartrate on the monitor was increasing before his eyes. One hundred and thirty . . . one three five . . . one forty. Thump, thump, thump, he could feel the lactic acid flooding his muscles, the sweat was pouring off him, running in rivulets down his forehead into his eyes. He scarcely dared to imagine how ridiculous he looked . . . *Don't be a fool, don't be a fool, don't be a fool . . .*

The only surprising thing was how long it had taken.

Obviously he had noticed she was a stunner – a blind man could have told you that. But then again, he wasn't the one who'd insisted she had to come and live with them. It was Sappho who made the big fuss about wanting Laleh, so now let her deal with the consequences. Inviting a heart-stoppingly gorgeous woman to be their nanny had to denote a complete lack of jealousy on Sappho's part, which in its turn had to signify a kind of deeper indifference. Over his dead body would he employ a male nanny – good-looking or otherwise – to live in their house.

His wife was either unfaithful or insane; he could take his pick. Nothing else made sense. If he could convince himself that she was having some kind of breakdown, then to a certain extent things would be simpler, there was a cure.

Yet maybe he was the one who for years hadn't wanted to see things as they really were. Who was Sappho? *Come on, mate, who is your wife – who is she really?* Why had all that mystery about her past been such a turn-on to him? *You wouldn't choose a supplier like that, on spec, would you? So why a wife? Someone you're planning to spend the rest of your life with, the mother of your children . . .* To some extent the first house in Ladbroke Grove had been a gamble, a gamble that had ultimately paid off. *But people aren't like houses, Tom, they're a wee bit more complicated than that. You can't shore up a marriage like a rickety old building. A lick of paint, a bit of plaster to cover the cracks.*

The point is, meeting Sappho had been the making of him. It made him shine, pulled something out of him which had been on the point of quietly hardening into mediocrity with the onset of middle age. He adored Sappho being foreign, and although she refused to go back to Greece with him, his hope was that one day she would relent, and the four of them could return to Patmos for a holiday.

Actually, what he really wanted to do was move over there for a few years, before Maro got too tied up with school. Let the children experience the beauty of the island . . . Why had she always been so loath to show him the country where she had grown up? Surely the first thing you do when you're in love is share your childhood with your lover? It was a mathematical law. Sappho on her part had certainly never tired of seeing all the places where he grew up: the village church, where they were married, and where every year Sappho and Maro would attend the summer fête, the agricultural suppliers where he had a Saturday job from the age of fifteen – she'd even wanted to visit his grotty comprehensive in Rye.

He'd been dazzled by all that interest in his life; it hurt now to admit it, but the intensity of Sappho's focus had been enough to blind him to her own lack of candour about her past. *The problem is you've never been good at patterns . . .*

Once, years ago, before he met Sappho, he'd seen a documentary about mail-order brides from the Far East. Stunning Thai girls who'd wound up with sad geezers from the UK. Yet to see the couples together you would swear they had been love matches. The blokes obviously looked smitten, that went without saying – who wouldn't with a fit Thai beauty hanging on to your every word? – but the girls too gave a pretty good impression of being in love. 'Richard so handsome . . . English men is good husband for Thai girl . . . Adrian too romantic.'

Where was the line where gratitude ended and love began? Could he point to it with certainty? Perhaps the act of rescue really had transformed those losers into heroes in the eyes of their brides.

What about him? Had he been Sappho's meal ticket out of Greece? OK, not in economic terms; she had a trust fund set up by her grandmother, which meant she had never needed to work, but emotionally – her passport to a new life. *You want jig-jig . . .?*

Some of it was to do with her father's sudden death, of that much he was certain. By all accounts Celia had been a pretty flaky mother, prone to sudden disappearances throughout most of her childhood, and Sappho held it against her that she had been uprooted and forced to return to Athens after the divorce. But was that enough to sever all links to the country of her birth? Of course it wasn't, *dummy*. Something else must have happened . . .

He had to face it. She was having an affair. Nothing else made sense. Perhaps someone new, or one of their friends; or even a figure from her past. Maybe an unhappy romance was the real reason all along she had been so desperate to leave Greece. Just say, for argument's sake – *Go on, say it, Tom . . . your wife is visiting her lover . . .* And yet . . . And yet . . . it still didn't make sense. She had a baby with her, for Chrissakes, surely no one could be that sick? To fuck a woman who had just given birth?

Besides, he thought, disloyally, she looked so rough these days . . . surely no one would go off to an assignation with uncombed hair and milk stains down their sweater? She also had developed some sort of rash on her hands, and would spend hours scratching away at herself like an old tramp . . . *Damaged goods, my wife is damaged goods.*

Without warning, the gym lights dimmed, and he became aware of a figure standing beside him at the treadmill.

'How you doin', Tom?'

'Oh . . . Lenny. Sorry, I was miles away.' He pressed the 'Stop' button on the panel, gripping on to the handles to break his run, as his legs bucked to a halt. He looked around him; the machines were empty, and the blonde girl he had noticed before down at the desk was hoovering under the coffee table. His heart was pounding, and a trickle of sweat was running down his spine. He felt exhausted, empty, uplifted; for a few hours at least, he had beaten back his demons.

'Life treatin' you sweet, Tom?'

Lenny had an unusually sympathetic face; behind the yellow-tinted shades, the expression in his eyes was intelligent, neutral. Tom paused; the desire to confide in him was so great that he could feel the words welling up inside him.

I'm broken-hearted, Lenny, help me . . . For a moment, he almost did it, the connection between them felt so tangible, but when it came to it, he couldn't trust himself to remove the first brick; there was no saying what would happen when his defences came down.

'Not too bad, Lenny . . . can't complain.'

Tom zipped up his fleece, willing the moment of intimacy to be over. Smiling cheerily to himself, he picked up his water bottle and walked down the steps and out of the gym. It was only when he had reached the car that he realised in his haste he had forgotten to wipe down the handles of the treadmill with the anti-bacterial spray.

The thought of it made him burn with shame.

Twenty-seven

It was still dark when Lorna arrived on the beach carrying a plastic bag bearing the name of an ethical boutique on George Street. The bag contained the clothes she had bought the day before, just a few minutes before closing time, with the last of her Giro money. The assistant who served her, a Latvian student called Kasia, recalled Lorna when questioned later that day by the police.

'She never try before buy . . . just take from rails, skirt, jacket, top . . . and painted wood necklace from Mali to match blue colour of jacket . . . At first, I no want to let her in . . . sorry to say this, now poor lady dead, but she look to me like rough sleeper, Hastings have plenty rough sleeper, too much drug in this town . . . But when I let her to come inside shop, I surprised how many items she purchase . . . each clothes made from raw silk, is most expensive range in stock. She pay by cash, from bag she have in pocket.'

She'd left the house early, careful not to wake her father who was asleep in the next room. On the beach, she changed into her new outfit, neatly folding her old trousers and T-shirt which bore the logo of a Dallas croupiers' convention.

Placing her clothes in the plastic bag along with her men's lace-up shoes, and the keys to her father's house, she stood for a moment, looking out towards a single light burning on the pier, then she walked across the cold grey sand to the water's edge.

Earlier on, a jogger out on the promenade had noticed her changing her clothes; it was still dark, but there was no mistaking the outline of a naked woman standing with her back to him on a deserted stretch of beach. Presuming it was one of the town's hundreds of rough sleepers performing her morning ablutions in public, he was appalled at yet another example of the manner in which Hastings was turning into one gigantic al fresco dormitory. The man paused to stare, then continued on his way home, making a mental note to fire off an email to the *Hastings and St Leonards Observer* the second he reached his office.

Out on Hastings Pier, a cleaner was working alone in the Gritti Palace Pub, emptying ashtrays and swabbing the floors in time for the early-morning drinkers; hers was the light Lorna had seen as she stood at the water's edge. The woman's name was Annette; she was a single mother living in a council flat on the outskirts of St Leonards.

She was just settling down for a cup of tea and a cigarette at one of the window tables with a sea view when she saw an object drifting out towards the horizon. By this time, only Lorna's head and shoulders were visible above the water; perhaps if Annette had been wearing prescription glasses that day, instead of over-the-counter ones from Boots, or if she hadn't been so exhausted by the double shift she had just worked, she might have noticed Lorna's once beautiful hair fanning out around her in those last few moments before her head disappeared beneath the water.

Her body was picked up that morning by a police tug-boat patrolling the Sussex coast. At Rye Harbour, it was collected by ambulance, then driven to the morgue in the Royal Infirmary, where, coincidentally, twenty-four years earlier Lorna had given birth to her son, Alexander. Had anyone thought of checking, not that there was any reason why they should have, her medical records were still stored on microfiche deep in the bowels of the building.

Lorna's clothes were removed by the police pathologist and checked for clues that might provide an identity to the corpse. In the pocket of her new skirt, they discovered an empty jar of Pond's Cold Cream, containing thread-like nail clippings and what looked like an atrophied lump of flesh. Under closer examination, it turned out to be the stump of an umbilical cord, miraculously reconstituted by exposure to droplets of seawater – the two veins plaited around the single artery so defined and clean-looking as to suggest a far newer, more recent, cut.

Twenty-eight

Sappho switched on the television and saw Lorna's face on the screen.

She recognised her at once; the same black and white school portrait in her striped Newfield blazer had once stood in a frame on Celia's dressing table in Athens. At the sight of her face, Sappho's heart gave a twist of outrage, then a kind of bleak calm descended upon her. Seeing Alexander that day had already punctured her hermetically sealed world; it was contaminated now, she knew anything could break through.

As the image of Lorna on the screen faded, the camera panned around a room, lingering mawkishly over family photographs, knick-knacks and a copy of the *Daily Telegraph* folded neatly on a canework table, until it came to rest on an old man seated in a chintz-covered armchair staring out of the window towards the sea. After a few moments of silence, the man cleared his throat and spoke.

'As you can see, Lorna was gorgeous, a real looker. Reminded me a bit of that Marianne Faithfull, you know the type – convent school girl, posh, a bit highly strung. Big boobs, blonde, slim – she could've had any man she wanted, just like that.' The old man clicked his fingers, to show how easily.

'But Lorna chose me. A fifty-year-old, balding married man . . . Well, you tell me what all that was about, if you can – certainly never worked it out . . .'

He took off his glasses, and Sappho saw he had surprisingly beautiful eyes, a deep chocolatey brown with long girlish lashes.

'What about the baby . . . how did you feel when you saw your daughter for the first time?' The unseen male interviewer's voice was sympathetic.

'Well, she was beautiful too, like her mother. Lorna thought she looked like me, but I couldn't see it. Too much hair, for a start! We drove around in the car, then after a while we parked in a country lane so Lorna could nurse her. And then . . . then . . . I delivered her back to the hostel.'

'Sorry if this is painful to talk about . . . but did Lorna try to persuade you that you should keep little Tatiana?'

The man was weeping openly now, the tears coursing down his veined purple cheeks. 'Of course she tried, man, that's why she got me up there in the first place, it was obvious.'

'But you didn't consider it an option?'

He smiled mirthlessly, dabbing the tears off his cheeks with a neatly folded handkerchief. 'I was a bit of a cad, d'you know? A lot of us men were in those days. Thought we could have our cake and eat it, and the truth of the matter was we could. Not pretty, but true. At the end of the day, most of us were family men, looking for a bit of fun on the side. I had two children of my own, so I took the long view. I knew that whatever happened, Tatiana would be better off growing up away from all the scandal in a respectable family. Besides, any other scenario was just too risky. Look at it from where I was standing; assuming I helped Lorna out, set her up in a flat somewhere, gave her a bit to live on, and so forth, I was exposing myself to blackmail. At any moment they could just turn up on my doorstep and spill the beans to Gloria. Adoption was the only way to draw a line under the whole sorry business.'

'And how did Lorna react to your stance?'

'Well, at the time, she seemed to agree with me. It was as though in her heart of hearts she'd been expecting me to let her down, just like everyone else had. Occasionally, she'd come out with a suggestion, trying to convince me that it was feasible, that she'd manage, but the truth of the matter was she was on her own, and she knew it. The social workers at the hostel drummed it into the girls that the moment they left St Dunstans, they would be out on the streets, that their babies would be taken away from them anyway and placed into institutions where they would grow up as retards and misfits. Adoption was the only chance of giving them a decent start in life.'

'What about benefits, housing, that kind of thing? Surely social services could have helped out?'

'Maybe the girls would have been entitled to welfare, who knows? But if they were, the adoption society certainly kept it under their hats; I'm pretty certain money changed hands when the babies were placed with a family, so the last thing they wanted was social services muscling in on their cash cows. I remember one of Lorna's plans was to advertise in the *Lady* as a housekeeper or governess, maybe get a job down in London as a hotel receptionist. As if anyone would have employed her with a baby in tow; we both knew she was kidding herself. But she never made a scene, right till the end, she kept her pecker up, even gave me a little kiss as she got out of the car. That was Lorna for you . . . she never gave you grief . . . she was a plucky little thing, kept her sorrows to herself.'

'So Tatiana was adopted?'

'That's correct; I think Lorna signed the papers the very next day. The baby was taken in by a childless couple from Perthshire. Then about a year later, I get a phone call from

Lorna. She's been living in Athens all this time with her pal, Celia. Couldn't stand the girl myself, one of those jolly-hockey-stick types, plain as a post, and surly with it. You know the sort? Can't get a fella herself, so she doesn't want her friend to get one either. Anyway, the long and short of it is Lorna's back in the UK, and she wants me to try and trace Tatiana for her.'

'And what was your reaction to this?'

'Well, I tried to talk her out of it of course . . . any chap would have. The law is quite clear in these cases; she wouldn't have had a leg to stand on. We met up a few times on and off over the years, whenever she was back in the UK, visiting her parents. I still had feelings for Lorna, hardly surprising, after all we'd been through, though the fact she never reproached me about the past made me feel like even more of a heel, if such a thing was possible . . . Things hadn't really worked out for her in Athens. I think she had a bit of a problem with the old bottle, too, hadn't kept her looks all that well, if the truth must be told. Let things slide a bit in the appearance department. Then for about ten years or so, nothing – all quiet on the western front. To be frank, I hoped she'd put it all behind her. Then, out of the blue, when I was already installed here at OAP Towers, she writes me a letter –'

'Sorry for interrupting, but what time frame are we talking about here?'

'Probably about two years ago – two and a half, tops. Yes, that's right, I remember now, my daughter Cynthia and her family were over on a visit from Australia.'

'And what does she say in the letter?'

'She says she's staying with her parents in Hastings, no, sorry, just the father, mother had passed away. And, you've guessed it, she wants me to help her find Tatiana –'

'Who would have been how old by now?'

'At least twenty-five, if not more.'

'And what was your response this time?'

'Well, this time I pulled my finger out; did the right thing by her. Don't think I didn't suffer over the years, young man, because I did. I'll be meeting my Maker soon, and He'll be carrying a fat dossier marked "Roy Strong".'

'And how did you go about tracing Tatiana?'

'Well, it was a long process, didn't exactly happen overnight. St Dunstans had closed down years before, isn't such a demand these days for hush-hush "nursing homes" if you catch my drift . . .'

'So how did you go about making contact?'

'Well, we got in touch with Norcap, a national counselling agency for adoption, who acted as go-betweens, if you like, with the society that ran St Dunstans. All this took time; Lorna had lost vital paperwork, and we had to do a bit of detective work to piece it all back together again. Also she'd been unwell . . . not herself, a touch of the blues, you might say; she was a bit confused sometimes, and the drink didn't help . . .'

'But in the end you succeeded?'

'In the end, we were able to trace the society that handled Tatiana's adoption. Through them, we wrote her a letter that their social workers passed on to Tatiana.'

'And who wrote the letter?'

'We wrote it together . . . Lorna came up here for the afternoon . . . she was the most perky I'd seen her for years . . . quite like the old Lorna, you might say. She'd brushed her hair, and she was wearing a nice skirt and blouse for once, instead of the old gents' togs she would buy in charity shops . . . It was a glorious summer's day, and we sat out on the lawn, and over a cup of tea and a biscuit, we composed the letter.'

'And do you mind if I ask what the letter said?'

'Well, we just introduced ourselves, so to speak . . . told her a little bit about our story, nothing too detailed, didn't want to scare her off at this stage – after all, I don't exactly come out of this whole affair smelling of roses – but at the same time, we wanted her to understand that we let her go only because our hands were tied, that under the circumstances adoption seemed like the only answer. It took us all afternoon, but in the end we were pleased with the result, and Lorna left for Hastings in a very chipper mood.'

'And then?'

'And then nothing. *Nada*. Silence.'

'How do you mean?'

'I mean just that. She never replied.'

'How did Lorna take this rejection?'

'Better than I'd expected, to be honest. She telephoned me when two months had gone by and we still hadn't heard a word, saying we just had to be patient, no point rushing things at this stage of the game. To tell the truth, I was the one who took it badly; by now, all I was living for was the chance to meet Tatiana. I'm no spring chicken, I could pop my clogs at any moment, and I couldn't stand the idea that I might die without the chance of saying sorry to my daughter. I wanted to tell her how much Lorna loved her . . . you've never seen so much love in a mother's eyes. I can't forget the way she held her in the back seat of my car, as I drove them back to the hostel, stroking her cheek, and talking to her about things she could see out of the window, like she could understand what she was saying . . .

'And you know, the funny thing is, I think Tatiana could . . . I've never seen a baby like that – my two were just squalling bundles of piddle and poo, hardly mattered which end up you held them, until they started school. But all through that journey, Tatiana hung on her mother's every word . . . staring up into her eyes as she lay there on her lap . . .'

'Did you make further attempts to contact your daughter?'

'We left things for a few months, then we wrote to her again. This time, separate letters – thought we'd double the odds of her answering. In mine, I tried to get the sympathy vote for Lorna – after all, she was the one who had suffered most. I kept thinking about the way she had loved that baby, and I couldn't accept that none of it had left its mark on Tatiana; something must have touched her heart. I threw all pride to the wind and literally begged Tatiana to get in touch with her mother, at least drop her a line to let her know she had received her letters. By this stage, that was all that either of us could hope for . . .'

'And did Tatiana write?'

'Oh yes, she wrote all right . . . but not to us.'

'Who did she write to?'

'She wrote to the adoption society . . . I have a copy of the letter here in my bureau; you can read it if you like. Here it is: ". . . I have no wish to defile the memory of my real, loving and true parents –" note the "real" is underlined twice – "by allowing my birth parents to intrude into my life after all these years, invading my and my family's privacy and wellbeing. I hereby formally request the society never to forward me any correspondence pertaining to them again, nor to release any information regarding my or my family's whereabouts.'

'And Lorna . . .?'

'She was too fragile to take Tatiana's rejection . . . it was the end of the road for Lorna . . . there was nowhere else for her to go . . .'

I danced on a Friday when the sky turned black,
It's hard to dance with the devil on your back . . .

Switching off the TV, Sappho let the remote fall on to the ground. Lorna was dead; after all these years, she had finally shaken the devil off her back. Never before did she feel so strongly that their lives were the double image on a playing card: one side had to be down for the other to be up.

With Lorna dead, where else was there for Alexander to go but the streets? Any last hope she might have cherished that the figure under the Royal Festival Hall was not him vanished as she listened to Roy Strong's story unfolding.

That night, she never went to bed at all; putting Hector down on his sheepskin in the double buggy in the hall, she lay in her clothes on the sofa, an Indian shawl wrapped tightly around her shoulders. Was there no limit to the number of times Alexander would be betrayed in his life?

Around eight, Maro came downstairs in her pyjamas, carrying her Baby Annabel doll; and without opening the curtains, she switched on the television. *The Rugrats* were on, her favorite cartoon; in this episode, Dee had bought a reproduction mirror from an antiques and ice-cream store called Cold 'n' Oldies, which allowed Tommy and Chucky to visit an imaginary place called Mirrorland *where everything was the same, but different . . .* uncannily how her life had become . . .

On the face of it, nothing had changed; if she were to end her life today – *Selfish bitch! How can you even think these things, with your five-year-old daughter sitting beside you on the sofa?* – no one who knew her would be able to isolate any one incident that had pushed her over the edge. She still hadn't told a soul about seeing Alexander that day. All of them, Tom included, would put it down to a severe case of post-natal depression; it even had a name, she'd read an article about it in the *Observer* recently . . . *puerperal psychosis*, it was called.

Hector hadn't stirred; for the first time in his short life he had slept through the night. With a pang, she realised there was no one to share this wonderful news with. Just a few weeks ago, it would have been a cause for celebration, a private triumph for her and Tom in the slightly ludicrous ongoing competition involving most parents of their acquaintance, whereby you were encouraged to boast about any instance when you had been cunning enough to escape the tyranny of your children's demands: who could snatch the longest lie-in on a Sunday morning, or who had managed to farm them off most successfully for a weekend with Granny.

You won't believe it, Hector slept from eleven till eight last night . . . These days, however, she and Tom were no longer players on the same team; they limited themselves to exchanging all but the most terse information about Maro and Hector: who was collecting Maro from nursery or whether Hector was maintaining the right centile on his growth chart.

Sappho pulled herself up, making room for Maro beside her. Her entire body ached; she felt as stiff as an old woman. Maro must loathe watching her mother going to seed like that; she remembered spending her own childhood trying to keep Celia looking more or less presentable. Now her palms were so rough with eczema, she could sense Maro flinch as she slipped her hand in hers. Loyally, though, she said nothing.

'Did you sleep on the sofa last night, Mummy?'

'Of course I didn't sleep here, darling,' she lied. 'I only came down a few minutes ago.'

'Is Daddy asleep?'

'He's in the shed. Shall I get you some breakfast before Pesty Boy wakes up?' Somehow, she would force herself to go into the kitchen and find something for her daughter to eat. . .

'Can I just sit here on the sofa with you?'

Maro didn't say it; she didn't need to. *I never see you any more* . . .

'D'you think she's pretty, Mummy?'

Sappho looked up at the television; the two young TV

presenters were interviewing a blonde, round-faced girl on the sofa who looked vaguely familiar. Like Martha Stewart, only younger.

'Yes, my love. Do you?'

Not as pretty as you, Mummy . . . That was what Maro used to say to her all the time: *You're even prettier than Eden, and Eden's mummy* . . .

'I think she's VERY pretty,' replied Maro firmly. 'What's her name?'

'I don't know, darling; let's see if the presenters tell us.'

The girl interviewer, dressed in a stripy one-shouldered top, jeans and spiky boots, was leaning back on the sofa, one leg crossed tomboyishly over her knee. She was wearing far too much make-up for eight o'clock in the morning.

'So, are you going to tell us if the lyrics of your new song are based on your own experiences?' She spoke in an annoyingly chirpy mockney, with hissing, sibilant s's. 'I bet our viewers are dying to find out . . . I know I certainly am!'

'Well, not specifically . . . in that all my songs are based on my life . . .'

'So it *is* autobiographical, then?'

'Well, I don't ever really explain what a song is about . . .'

'Come on, mate, give Dido a break, it's too early for a third degree . . .' interrupted the boy presenter, shifting uncomfortably in his seat.

'Dido, her name's Dido, my darling.' Somewhere that name had registered; she remembered now, she'd seen a flier of her new album posted on the railway bridge on Golborne Road.

'But that's a boy's name!'

'No, it's a Greek girls' name that ends in . . .'

'O, like my name!' said Maro delightedly.

'Dido was the queen of a country called Carthage in the olden days.'

'Where's Carthage, Mummy?'

'Where's Carthage . . .? I'm not sure. I think it's in Africa somewhere. Listen, she's going to sing her song for us now.'

'. . . So, let's give it up for Dido, and . . . "White Flag".'

She looked awkward as she sang, the microphone clutched tightly in both hands, her voice a haunting, nasal falsetto. There was something strangely affecting about the contrast between the lyrics (you could hear her catching her breath, gasping almost, between phrases, as though the pain they described was still raw) and the dreamy, slightly druggy electronic background music: all tinkling chimes, synthesised percussion beats together with the occasional bleep which sounded like a heart monitor.

It must have been tiredness, that and the shock of hearing about Lorna, but for an eerie moment Sappho had the absolute certainty that this rather commonplace-looking young woman in a BBC studio in White City was singing directly to her, in the language of her own heart; it was uncanny, every single word resonated, a nightmare world of total correspondence. Firstly *The Rugrats* with their Mirrorland, now this . . . Before long, she'd start believing the weather forecast was a coded message . . .

The sitting-room curtains were still drawn; outside on her street, people were walking down to the newsagent's to pick up the Saturday papers, a latte and croissant from the Starbucks on Salusbury Road. Families were beginning to stir, negotiating the day's itinerary over breakfast, dividing it up into equitable chunks: ballet lessons, park, shopping, a snatched visit to the hairdresser. That's what their Saturdays used to be like . . . It was dark in the room, but not dark enough.

Theirs felt like a house in mourning, a place where some terrible catastrophe had just taken place, where all the comforting routines had been abandoned. Mary Lennox of *The Secret Garden* awaking to an empty house in India which had been decimated by cholera . . . What if Tom never emerged from the shed, or if Laleh decided to spend the day up in her flat? Would she find it in herself to open the curtains, dress Maro, try and impose some order to her day?

She looked down at her daughter, the Baby Annabel doll on her lap; even in the grainy half-light, you could see the tangles in her long hair. She couldn't remember the last time she had brushed it, let alone washed it. The trim little Filipino lady in John Lewis had suggested blackout lining for the curtains, but Sappho had refused: 'You need all the light you can get in this country.' She wished now she hadn't been so facetious; it was darkness she needed now, to cover her shame . . .

'Are you sad, Mummy? Tell me.' Maro held Sappho's face between her hands, twisting it round to hers.

'Mummy's not sad, my darling.' She closed her eyes, unable to meet the urgency of her daughter's gaze.

'So why are you crying?'

'Mummy's not crying . . . She's just remembering.'

Greece, 1997

Twenty-nine

One afternoon, he walked into the gallery.

Sappho looked up from the rings she was displaying in a cabinet; some she had slid on to elongated pebbles from the beach on Patmos, others she arranged around an old leather-covered box of watercolours from the flea market at Monastiraki. She was just wondering how best to prop open the yellowing pages of a volume of Cavafy's poems when she heard the old-fashioned bell trill above the door.

'Hello, Sappho.'

She looked up; there in the doorway stood Alexander, dressed in a pair of torn work trousers, with a dark-blue paint-spattered shirt buttoned up to the neck. His cropped hair was covered in building dust; and for a split second Sappho thought he had gone prematurely grey.

'Alexander.' She felt herself blush violently, mostly with shock; she loathed being wrongfooted by unexpected en-counters. To hide her discomfort, she picked up a pair of earrings, gold doves carrying tiny pearls in their beaks, and replaced them inside their velvet-lined box.

'I'm sorry about Theo, Saff. Lorna told me.'

'So you're back in Athens? I thought the two of you were living in Larissa.' How long had it been? Five, six years since the last time she had seen either of them? His voice certainly hadn't broken yet, that much she remembered.

'We left Larissa two years ago. Lorna's job in the old people's home never worked out . . . We spent that first winter on Samos, you remember, the American we always used to house-sit for, then we were in Hastings for a while, then I came here to look for work.'

'Where are you working?'

'On a building site. You know, the new Olympic Velodrome? We're laying down the wooden indoor track.' He held out his hands above the open cabinet; his square palms were criss-crossed with cuts and splinters, and the thumb of his left hand was black.

'Aren't you supposed to be still at school or something?' How old *was* Alexander anyway? Seventeen? Eighteen? Could he already be twenty?

'School . . . what's school?'

Sappho felt a sudden breathtaking spasm of joy; in all the sorrow at Theo's death, here was a part of her childhood restored to her, intact. *Will you be my sister, Sappho . . .?* She wanted to talk about so many things with him, relive those boring winter afternoons in Athens, darkness falling early over the Acropolis, the purr of the charcoal stove in the hall, Alexander lying on the floor of her room, playing endless games of Jenga against himself while she did her homework at the desk, and the adults sat drinking ouzo and listening to records in the kitchen . . .

'So they never did find a way of keeping you in school?'

'Not really . . . Lorna taught me some stuff at home, maths mostly, a bit of history and geography . . . I might go back one day, who knows.'

Lorna . . . of course, they came as a pair. Two for the price of one. At once, Sappho felt her joy at seeing Alexander evaporate, and a kind of black dread settled in the pit of her stomach.

'How *is* Lorna?'

'She has her good days. And her bad. At the moment she's just pleased to be back in Athens; you know, she always hated it in Hastings.'

Alexander had filled out since the last time she'd seen him; he was broader, working on building sites must have toughened him up. He was still quite short, though, probably no more than five foot six or seven, just a couple of inches taller than she was. He looked nothing like Lorna; he never had. His father, whoever he was, must have had strong genes.

In Greece, no one had ever taken him for a foreigner; he had Mediterranean colouring with ruddy cheeks, dark eyes and thick, painted-looking eyebrows, like those you saw in pre-war tinted photographs of Greek men. With his blunt, shaved head and small ears, he looked like an otter; when he was little, Theo's nickname for him was 'Tarka'.

'How did Theo die, Saff?'

Sappho picked up a pair of lapis lazuli drop earrings and threaded their stems through the padded velvet display board. She had been dreading the question; she seemed to be able to cope with people asking who hadn't known Theo intimately: the owner of the *periptero* next to the gallery, the Canadian woman who all those years ago had rented him the flat for Lorna's ill-fated dance studio, Kyrios Melis, the photographer down on Veikou Street. *Silipitiria*, my condolences . . . *silipitiria* . . . She could keep her head above water with those people; it was the ones who had been close to him that squeezed her heart like a claw.

'He had . . . he had an accident in the house in London . . .' In an effort to steady her voice, Sappho picked up a small wooden box from a shelf and ran her fingers over the xylophone slats which formed its lid. She turned a handle on the side, and slowly the slats began to undulate, buffeting the painted sailing boat which was perched in the middle as though in a storm. She forced herself to stare at the twisted underside of the slats, until the pain in her heart subsided.

'He fell down the steps to the attic in the middle of the night. He was looking for some papers or something . . . His wife . . . Ghisela, you met her once or twice, here in Athens, remember? . . . Anyway, she didn't call the ambulance till the following morning.'

'What do you mean?' There were tears in Alexander's eyes, and suddenly Sappho remembered he had loved Theo.

'You know what Theo was like. He absolutely forbade her from ringing the emergency services, and when in the end she disobeyed him and called an ambulance, it was too late. A broken rib had punctured his lungs; they rushed him to St Thomas's to operate, but during the operation he had a heart attack, then he went into a coma . . .'

Just then, the shop door trilled open and two middle-aged foreign women walked inside. They looked like sisters, northern European, German or Scandinavian, with short, well-cut flaxen hair. One of them was wearing an amethyst brooch on her drill linen jacket in the shape of a dragonfly which Sappho recognised as one of theirs. A young designer from Samos, Fivos, whose stuff Celia was crazy about; they were expecting a new consignment of rings from him any day.

'There is no Celia?'

'No, she's away for a couple of weeks. She'll be back at the end of August.'

The woman looked disappointed. She touched the brooch on her lapel: 'Every summer I buy something from this gallery, my favourite in all Athens.'

Sappho smiled distractedly at her; she was aware, out of the corner of her eye, of Alexander picking up his rucksack which he had left on the floor near the till. There was so much she had to say to him still; what if he vanished, and that was the last she saw of him? Slinging the bag over his shoulder, he walked towards the door.

'I'll come and see you again tomorrow, Saff. If I can't make it, maybe the day after.'

He didn't come on that day, or the next, and on the Sunday, when three days had passed, and there was still no sign of him, Sappho rang her mother in Patmos on the pretext of talking about the gallery. She wanted to find out, in the most roundabout way possible, if she knew where Alexander and Lorna were staying. Celia must be in touch with them; how else could they have found out about Theo's death? She couldn't explain, not even to herself, why she was loath to mention Alexander's name to Celia. It was irrational, but she felt the moment she discussed him with her mother, this new, clean Alexander would vanish like a chimera.

'Did Fivos courier over the rings from Samos?' asked Celia. At the sound of her mother's voice, a firework of irritation exploded in Sappho's breast; nothing in the world could make Celia understand how viscerally annoying the sound of blunt-toothed masticating was down the telephone.

'He did in the end, just as I was about to close, but I checked the invoice, and there were two rings missing.' Sappho took a *silent, silent* sip of her water; she was naked, the shutters were closed, and she was lying on the carved wooden daybed of Theo's old study, the ceiling fan whirring above her head.

'No, no . . . it's all sorted, Saff . . . sorry, *chomp, chomp,* I forgot to tell you, Fivos isn't happy with the detail on the Byzantine pair, he wants to work on them a bit longer.' More snaffling, then the sound of paper being scrunched up; it must have been one of her favourite spinach pies from

257

the baker's down in Skala. Hopefully, that was the end of it now.

'Oh, and these two Danish women came in the other day looking for you . . . said they bought something every year from the gallery.'

'I know who you mean . . . Inge and Margarethe, they're sisters . . . did they buy anything?'

'Well, they were a bit put out at not seeing you, but once they'd got over the disappointment of me serving them, the one who got the brooch last year bought one of those engraved silver page markers with the tassels.' If only they'd come in just a few minutes later, she could have said goodbye properly to Alexander, found out where he and Lorna were living.

'Are you sure you wouldn't rather come here, Saff? Any time you change your mind, all you have to do is ring Vanessa and ask her to open the shop . . . she's a student, apart from anything else she could do with the money . . . I told her you were staying at the house . . . she'll be coming round at some point to collect the spare keys . . . She knows the ropes, she covered for me when I was in London for the funeral . . . To tell the truth, I'm not very happy about you being in Athens on your own, so soon after . . .'

'I'm OK, the gallery keeps me busy. The last thing I need right now is to mope around on a beach. We'll see, I might join you for the last week of August.'

She needed to grieve alone. Celia had her own history as far as Theo was concerned; that affectionate, cynical friendship of theirs – no point calling it a marriage, it had never been that – had its roots elsewhere, long before she was born. Celia had been devastated on learning of his death, even Sappho was shocked at how upset her mother had been, and she had flown to London for the funeral (there were no bad feelings between her and Ghisela, just as there had been no hard feelings between her and Theo), but he was her ex-husband, not her father, and their pain could not be the same. *If only you hadn't been too proud to go back for your A levels, you would have had two more years with him* . . .

'Have you seen anyone in Athens?'

'No one, just Eftichia . . . I wanted to give her the icon. Ghisela said I could have it.' The lie surprised her, coming as easily as it did; only then did she realise, finally, that she was not going to mention anything about Alexander coming into the gallery.

'Did Eftichia make it all the way to Filoppapou on her own?'

'Her niece brought her in a taxi . . . you know the one that's married to the baker in Nea Smyrni?'

'Yes . . . Irini, I think her name is. And what did Eftichia have to say for herself?'

'The usual; she made coffee, did her *xematiasma*, then fell asleep in the kitchen.'

'Honestly, Saff, she's such an old fraud! I don't know why you indulge her. Anyway, are you looking after yourself properly? Have you got any food in?'

'I'm fine . . . it's too hot to eat.' Sappho lifted her legs and pushed both feet against the wall in a half shoulder stand, the receiver resting on the pillow beside her head. She'd lost weight since Theo's death; you could see all the bones of her knees clearly defined, and her hip bones stuck out like blades. Theo was the one who first gave her a complex about her weight: he used to call her Fatty, *Hondroula* . . . Hopefully he'd be glad to know that his death had finally turned his daughter into a size ten.

Theo was such an aesthete, all his life he'd tormented his wife and daughter with the tyranny of his good taste; he insisted on having the last word on both their wardrobes, the decoration of the house, even the clothes pegs on the terrace had to be the spliced wooden ones with the ball on

259

top, *nothing uglier than a rusty spring*, and then out of the blue he went off and married someone like Ghisela.

Ghisela! Whose idea of an elegant home was a set of embroidered cross-stitch shepherdesses framed above the mantelpiece, or a Christmas tablecloth with matching centrepiece and napkins . . . Who, when she wasn't wearing her red Lufthansa flight attendant's uniform, was a walking, talking advertisement for Jacques Vert and Marks and Spencer's elasticated slacks . . . Even after all these years, it still seemed completely barmy. Because it *was* barmy . . .

'Maybe she's a goddess in bed,' Celia used to joke, but Sappho doubted it.

No, she was almost certain that sex hardly featured in his marriage to Ghisela. It was almost as though from one day to the next Theo had simply tired of being a bohemian.

The first holiday Sappho spent with them in London, she remembered being shocked at her father's infantilism. They had recently installed a satellite dish, and instead of spending hours locked away in his study, he would lie on his new La-Z-Boy recliner in the sitting room watching payview TV – films and sports matches mostly, though he wasn't averse to tacky foreign gameshows – while Ghisela plied him with Malaga sticks and florentines and endless cups of coffee and whipped cream.

Sappho's old room in East Sheen remained like a shrine to that one year she had spent at St Cecilia's; a pink rosette from a netball tournament hung above the bed, together with merit certificates, a lifesaving badge, and her collection of Roald Dahl books mounted on a small shelf. The rest of the house, too, was covered with framed photographs of her and Theo in Greece, almost as though Ghisela wanted her to know that it had never been her intention to distance Theo from his family. And she hadn't taken him away; even at the time, Sappho understood that Theo hadn't needed anybody's help in cutting free.

Slipping on a robe, Sappho walked out barefoot on to the balcony to water the plants. Uncoiling the hosepipe from its hook on the wall, she turned on the tap and lay the tube in the earthenware urn containing the lemon tree. Pulling back a chair, she sat down on the balcony with her hands clasped around her knees.

It was cooler this evening; the weather forecast said the heatwave could be over by the end of the week. Apparently, they were in for a period of thunderstorms. A steady line of tourists snaked up the Acropolis towards the Parthenon; even with the scaffolding on, they continued to visit the temple in their thousands. The entire city had turned into one gigantic building site; God only knows what it would be like when the Olympics finally began.

A great-niece had brought Eftichia, Theo's old wet nurse, by taxi from the flat in Patission which Theo had made over to her before the family's move to London; Sappho had wanted to give her a small icon which had hung over her father's bed since he was a boy.

She must have been ninety years old by then; yet her eyesight wasn't bad, and a few crazy stumps of teeth were still embedded in her gums. Some of them appeared to be hanging on by a mere thread; they would twist about when she talked, and Sappho could have sworn the occasional one ended up back to front. They sat together at the kitchen table, smoking, the shutters tightly sealed against the afternoon heat. When Sappho was a little girl, she had always pictured Eftichia breastfeeding her father in a nicotine haze, clay pipe clenched between her teeth; Theo said she taught him to smoke Amphora cigarettes when he was still a schoolboy at Athens College.

Eftichia shuffled over to the stove and boiled up coffee – she didn't trust Sappho to let the foam rise three times, to make it so *glikó* that you could stand a spoon up in the treacly undertow. Beneath the envelope neck of her overall,

Sappho could make out the coarse undyed wool of her vest; while, as always, on her legs she wore those thick flesh-coloured stockings that made them look like prosthetic limbs.

It was so hot that the only thing Sappho could bear to have close to her skin was a white cotton shift, handwoven by nuns between the wars, which had been part of her grandmother Maro's wedding trousseau, the initials 'M.M.' cross-stitched in tiny cursive letters above the breast. Alone in the flat, she mostly walked about naked.

Eftichia wept, they both did, when Sappho handed over the icon in its chamois bag; her crying sounded raw, virginal, like that of a young girl.

For years, the icon had hung in the nursery of the house in Kiffissia above the light green metal Army and Navy cot her father slept in when he was a baby. Then, after the move to London, she remembered it propped up on the canework table beside the high, narrow bed her parents had briefly shared . . . It was of a long-nosed, rather sulky-looking Mary, with thin lips and a determined cast to her chin. Her eyes were ringed with shadows, deep, livery smudges, which made her look as though her baby kept her up all night. The infant Christ had one arm around her neck, possessively cupping her sallow face with his hand, his round cheek pressed to hers.

When Sappho was a little girl, she liked to imagine that the infant Jesus was really her father; he looked like Theo in his tinted baby pictures, with the same side parting and row of bronze curls above his ears. Now, as she held the icon, the little gold face glowed eerily between her hands, as though some part of him, unbroken by that terrible accident, was still with them, hovering between them in the darkened kitchen.

After a while, Eftichia looked at Sappho through her tears, and said: 'What else is it, *mana mou?*'

Here we go, thought Sappho. Like evil foretold, she felt herself slump forward in her chair. The air around her grew charged, her lips and eyes burned, while a hollow dent of pain throbbed in each temple. She watched Eftichia pour a glass of water from the copper jug on the table; and without waiting to be asked, Sappho fetched the bottle of olive oil from the cupboard, together with a teaspoon, which she placed before her. I don't need this, Sappho thought to herself; I really, really don't need it. At five, she was due in Plaka to open the gallery. Yet there was no stopping her now. Besides, the relief, later, would be exquisite . . .

First Eftichia poured oil into the spoon, then three slow drops in the glass. They fell, magically arranging themselves into an ordered line – large, medium, small – then floated around the surface like a set of amber celluloid discs. Eftichia hooked a crooked finger into the glass and stirred; Sappho watched as the water grew opaque: the beads would rise now in a slick, *yes, they would,* and that would be the end of it, proof that no one had wished her ill. She would lie down on her bed until the headache lifted, then that afternoon she would process the pile of orders Celia had left on the desk –

Instead, what she saw before her was the impossible: a glass of pale lemonade, greasy and flat, the hard little granules of oil broken up into fleck-like bubbles which buzzed listlessly around the glass without breaking through the surface. Not even one.

Eftichia licked her middle finger – *because Christ was licked in the manger by the animals* – and, closing her eyes, made the sign of the cross on Sappho's face – forehead, both cheeks, chin – muttering hoarsely to herself under her breath. Her saliva smelled of gravy and camphor. Twice, she yawned, shaking her head sideways and chucking out loud like a mangy old lion; then clasping her hands over the dome of her apron, she settled back into the chair and fell into a deep sleep, only waking when the niece returned to collect her.

Down on Tsami Karatasou Street, Sappho could see the gypsy melon seller crawling along the road in his three-wheeled truck (which was really just a 50cc moped concealed inside a tin carapace), the square microphone of his loudspeaker pressed lasciviously against his lips – 'Kar-pouzia, pe-ponia, Kar-pouzia . . .' – that suggestive, nasal whine of his luring the housewives down on to the street to buy his wares.

She looked down at the watermelons piled up in the back of the truck, a pair of old-fashioned weighing scales dangling precariously above them. She felt thirsty; for a moment she could actually taste the watermelon in her mouth, imagine herself biting through the raspberry-coloured flesh with its texture like fibreglass to the plump cells of juice within. But it was too fresh, too healthy; these days all she wanted was dried foods – rusks, breadsticks, the occasional factory-baked croissant tasting of some obscure vegetable fat that coated her tongue and palate.

For weeks, ever since her return from London, she had been at war with her body, subjecting it to an ordeal by junk: endless glasses of iced *frappé* from pavement cafés (shaken-up Nescafé, topped by fat, salty-tasting evaporated milk), which jangled the nerves then settled in the gut like rust. To tamp up the acidity, and steady her trembling hands, she would buy food from the streets: *koulouria*, flat, stale-tasting bread rings from the stand outside the National Gardens, or little packets of roasted chickpeas from the cart in Plaka which dissolved to a gritty hummous in the mouth. The skin on her forehead grew dry, lustreless, rutted with tiny, subcutaneous bumps, and the corners of her mouth split then crusted over; licking the new blood became a compulsion. She absolutely resented the demands her body made on her those days, mocking her grief with its babyish clamouring for food and water; even the bright stain of her period was an offence.

In the flat across the street, the shutters were open, and she could see her neighbour's son, Socrates, sitting on his parents' bed in his vest and pants. His grandmother, dressed in black, was combing his sleek dark hair in preparation for the evening church service at the cathedral in Mitropoleos Street. She would only dress him in his Sunday best when they were about to leave the house; the heatwave had made clothes unbearable to most people in the city. Sappho picked up the hosepipe and, burying it deep into the container of gardenias, settled back on her seat. The scent of the flowers was overpowering, waxy and fatty, like those tins of solid perfume you could buy in the souvenir shops in Adrianou Street.

Sappho picked up the box of green mosquito coils from the table; she was about to light one, when she heard the buzzer ring from inside the house. Who could it be on a Sunday evening? Then she realised, of course, it must be the Vanessa woman coming for the keys to the gallery. Knowing Celia, she'd probably rung her the minute she got off the phone, hoping that if she sent Vanessa over right away, Sappho would be tempted into handing her the keys and catching the next ferry to Patmos.

For a moment, she was inclined to ignore the buzzer; but for all she knew, Vanessa had seen her sitting out on the terrace as she walked down the hill from the Acropolis. She thought rapidly: if she gave her the keys now, she would get it over and done with without having her visit hanging over her head for the rest of the month. She looked down at the cotton shift she was wearing; the question was, how transparent actually was it? Providing she kept the rest of the shutters in the house closed, and didn't turn the light on in the hallway, she should just about get away with it.

'Hang on, I'm coming,' she called out over the balcony

railings, then she walked through Theo's study into the house. Barefoot, she ran down the marble staircase, pausing to pick up the gallery keys from the table in the hall; and without opening the glass behind the ornate ironwork shutters, she unlocked the door.

There on the pavement stood Alexander. He was carrying a watermelon in one hand, and a bottle of cherry cordial in the other.

'I brought you *karpouzi* . . . I thought we could share it.'

Thirty

One morning, two weeks later, Sappho walked down Parthenonos Street, past the Divani Palace Hotel.

It had been raining since early that morning. She had awoken in the middle of the night to the crack of thunder, and when she opened the shutters, the Acropolis was illuminated in a ghostly flare of lightning.

The air was hot and damp, and the pavements steamed with the odour of cats, mingled with the piles of rubbish lying uncollected beside the municipal bins: an old fridge, covered with stickers from a judo federation, bulging black sacks, smaller carrier bags bearing the name of the local HellaSpar supermarket, even an abandoned car covered in hessian and brown tape.

Turning into Makriyanni Street, she heard the sound of a TV coming from a shuttered basement on the corner; she recognised the programme: it was *The Bold and the Beautiful*, the same soap she used to watch all those years ago in the kitchen with Kemal.

The ground was littered with little greeny-brown oranges which had fallen unripe from the trees. The door of the butcher's on Mitseon Street was open, but the shop was empty; it was too hot to keep any meat out in this weather, it must all be in the safe out the back. Through the curtain of plastic strips, she caught sight of a woman with her shopping trolley sitting companionably in the bare tiled shop. Outside the *periptero* in the square, an old man in a satchel and cap was selling lottery tickets spiked on to a tall stick; he had been there for as long as she remembered. Theo always used to buy a ticket from him on the day of his birthday. For a moment, she considered approaching him, telling him that her father was dead, overcome by a sudden desire to make her loss official. *Why should he remember or care? Theo left years ago . . .* Her eyes filled with tears; her father's life had left no trace on the neighbourhood, he had been gone too long.

An old tramp was shuffling down Makriyanni Street, gaping boots dragging along the puddles, past the tavernas and souvenir shops opposite the entrance to the Plaka. Bundles and plastic bags were looped through the belt around his waist, which puffed and hissed as he walked.

She watched a small boy outside a taverna sweep the rainwater along the pavement into the gutter, tucking his face inside his shirt to protect him from the rank, gamey smell the tramp left in his wake. Sappho looked at her watch: it was ten o'clock, Vanessa should have opened up by now. In the end, after all her protestations to Celia, she had been the one to hunt Vanessa down to give her the keys; Sappho hadn't worked in the gallery for ten days now, yet nor was she any closer to joining Celia on Patmos. Too many things had changed, might, *God willing*, still change . . .

Crossing the lights on Amalias Avenue, Sappho walked towards Zappeion, past Hadrian's Arch and the statue of Byron cradled by Hellas, to the row of buses waiting along the side of the National Gardens. She needed to get out of the city for a few hours; her days alone in the house had become unbearable. She bought a *carnet* of tickets from a vendor who had set up a card table outside the railings of the National Gardens, sheltering from the rain beneath a large golfing umbrella inscribed with the Citibank logo. She watched him select the tickets from the row of tidy little piles weighted down with coins, ignoring the hissing sounds emanating from the direction of the bushes. She knew better than to look towards where the sound was coming from; the National Gardens were a magnet for flashers. Unless you were careful, you could find yourself eye to eye with an erect penis, seemingly divorced from the rest of its owner's body. Celia said the gardens had always been full of voyeurs and exhibitionists, even when she and Lorna first arrived in the seventies.

Boarding a bus to Glyfada, Sappho punched her ticket and settled back into one of the wooden seats. The bus was almost empty; most Athenians who could afford it avoided the city in the month of August. The only time Sappho herself had ever been in Athens during the summer was when she flew back one weekend from Kos to collect her A level results from Hellenic College. Most summers, they stayed in the house on Patmos from the end of June until the first week of September.

Alexander was working at the Olympic Sailing Centre at Agios Kosmos; for a moment she considered texting him to say that she was going to be at Lake Vouliagmeni for the day; it wasn't far, she could meet him after his shift. Or perhaps they wouldn't be working today because of the rain; for all she knew, he could be back in the hotel making breakfast for Lorna.

Filled with a kind of fury, Sappho took out her phone and laboriously began to punch out a message: 'Am close by; shall we meet for a drink later?' She stared down at the tiny screen; the moment she pressed 'Send' the day would no longer be her own; surely wasn't that the whole point, to cut loose from everything for a few hours . . .? Besides, knowing Alexander, he wouldn't go anywhere after work without first checking up on Lorna in the hotel in Omonia.

She snapped the phone shut; the message would be stored in Drafts. If her resolve faltered, she could always send it later from the lake.

She was stalking Alexander; some tiny part of her brain was still able to see that. She needed to know where he was, every minute of the day. She hadn't done it yet, turned up at one of the building sites where he worked in the midday sun together with all the other foreign labourers, but if things carried on like this, it was just a matter of time. The tables had been turned; she felt he owed it to her now to be there in her moment of sorrow, luxuriating in the special status her father's death conferred upon her . . . *For what, though . . . what is it exactly you need Alexander for?*

Sappho stared out of the window at the giant billboards lining Syngrou Avenue: Dimitris Bassis, Anna Vissi, Despina Vandi, bouzouki singers advertising their summer spectaculars in the clubs along the coast. The posters were rain-streaked, veined with wrinkles like badly hung wallpaper. She needed to sleep with Alexander; there was no other way of putting it. Her body literally throbbed with desire, subsuming even her grief about Theo. She had never felt like that about a man before; no love affair had begun with so much hunger.

As the bus turned into Leoforos Vouliagmenis, Sappho shut her eyes. It was obscene; she had no right to feel like that about someone whom she had always thought of as her unlucky little brother. Part of it was the shock of seeing Alexander grown up after that five-year gap; if she'd watched it happen, witnessed with her own eyes the gawky transition from boy to man, she might have remained immune to his charms.

And anyway, was Alexander charming? Or even good-looking? Yes, she supposed he was, in a kind of Levi's 501 way. Not that that had ever been her type; until now, she had tended to go for effete, artistic men: Phillip, the half-

Greek boy she had gone out with for the last two years of Hellenic College, looked like Jarvis Cocker's younger brother, while Geert, the Dutch news photographer she had been having an on/off affair with ever since, resembled his older brother. She thought of Alexander's squat figure, his shaved head, those massive shoulders which seemed made to bear the burdens of a far older man.

And therein lay the root of his attractiveness, or at least one deviant element of it. In truth, the whole thing was so deviant that Sappho could scarcely bear to dwell on it. She wanted to sleep with Alexander for a number of reasons, one more unwholesome than the next.

First, because he continued to care for Lorna in spite of the misery, humiliation and unhappiness she had caused him (and everyone else, come to that) over the years.

Second, because he never discussed it.

Third, because she needed to see what his adult penis had evolved into. (The bulge beneath his trousers looked promising.)

Fourth, because she also needed to know how it would feel to lie on his back, arms around his shoulders, face in his hair, stomach resting in the hollow of his spine.

Fifth, because Lorna couldn't always expect to have things her way.

Sixth, because her father's death had had an unexpected aphrodisiac effect. (Lately, she would orgasm in her sleep, awaking a second before she came, her face wet with tears.)

Seventh, and perhaps most unwholesome of all, she had invested so much in Alexander's childhood, groomed him, so to speak, to be the delicious man he had grown up into, that if anyone deserved to sleep with him now, it was her. A kind of *droit de seigneur*, recognition of his and Lorna's leech-like dependence on them for all those years.

Picking up her rucksack from the seat, Sappho got off the bus at Limni Vouliagmeni. She crossed the highway, careful

271

to avoid the lorries splashing through the river-like puddles eddying along the road, and walked up the slope towards the entrance to the lake. She gazed down below at the monolith of cratered, rusty-looking rock erupting from the water, the dark slit of the cave which as a child had frightened her so much.

Before the move to London, Theo used to take her to Vouliagmeni, mostly in early spring and late autumn, when the temperature of the sea was too cold to swim in. Sometimes Celia would come, but mostly it was just she and her father, who, after changing into his dark green swimming trunks, would perform a series of excruciatingly embarrassing callisthenics exercises at the edge of the water. '*Mens sana in corpore sano*,' he would utter serenely, barrel chest thrust out. Once, his penis slipped out of his shorts while he was doing a lunge; without saying a word, he calmly tucked it back inside the net gusset of his trunks. All afternoon, the thought that he might know she had glimpsed it made Sappho frantic with shame.

White ropes threaded with buoys delineated the swimming area; rain had broken up the surface of the lake into the texture of rhinestone. The man in the ticket kiosk glanced up from his newspaper. '*Tha kanies banio?*'

He looked surprised that she was planning to swim. The air had grown chill, and her wet clothes clung to her.

'*Tha thoume*,' *we'll see*, replied Sappho as she took her ticket. Perhaps a cup of tea at the cafeteria would warm her up. It began to rain again as she walked down the path towards the white plastic tables, chairs tipped forlornly around the edges. Sitting down beneath the bamboo-covered tin roof, she waited for someone to emerge from the kitchen.

Vines planted in gigantic amphora-shaped pots grew thickly up the walls, little bunches of unripe velvety grapes dangling in clusters from the branches. She and Theo would always order hot chocolate after their swim, to which he would add a shot of brandy from Grandfather Charles's battered RAF hip flask he carried in the pocket of his leather postman's bag.

Ghisela was now the custodian of all her father's possessions, including no doubt both the flask and the satchel. To be fair to Ghisela, she had invited Sappho to take anything she wished from the house before her return to Athens: '*I only shared ten years with Theo . . . for you, these objects are your life.*'

But out of pride – no, pride was the wrong word, it was more a desire to be out of that fussy, bowdlerised house – she had refused all but the little icon for Eftichia. One day, perhaps, she would find the courage to go up into the attic and look through the boxes filled with her father's papers, all those thousands of hours of work come to nothing.

The beige Wilton carpet on the landing was stained with a pool of his blood; neither she nor Ghisela mentioned it, but the night after the funeral, Sappho came out of her old room to use the bathroom, and found Ghisela in her dressing-gown and a pair of Marigolds, sobbing as she knelt on the floor, attacking the stain with an array of vicious-looking German cleaning agents.

Sappho forgave Ghisela everything, even the fact that she had not called an ambulance until the morning after the accident; she knew what a tyrant Theo could be, and right from the start she had understood the dazed, helpless quality of Ghisela's love for her father. She'd been a fifty-year-old spinster with buck teeth when they married: 'Never I thought a man will choose me, and surely never such a man as Theo . . .' she had apparently confided to Celia whilst helping her pack up her belongings in the weeks before the move back to Athens.

'She'll find out soon enough what she's let herself in for,' Celia had remarked drily, yet she remained fond of Ghisela, who in some respects had paved the way for her return to Greece. Theo, generous to a fault, made out the house in Athens in Celia's name; and, in lieu of a divorce settlement, sold the last two remaining apartments in his family's once extensive property portfolio to enable her to set up the gallery in Plaka.

A kindly-looking woman in a sleeveless housecoat came out on to the terrace to take her order. She had beautiful, heavy-lidded grey eyes, and the kind of serene, aloof manner which appeared to have its origins buried deep within her psyche. How had her soul arrived at such a garden of peace? thought Sappho wonderingly.

'*Oriste*,' smiled the woman, holding up her notepad and pencil.

Sappho ordered a pot of tea; she felt like hot chocolate, but couldn't trust herself not to weep at the memory of Theo doctoring the heavy little pewter jug with his brandy.

'*Stin yassou*,' he would announce gravely, holding out the steaming cup. His wet hair hung in a slick over his forehead, and beads of moisture clung to the lenses of his glasses.

'*Stin yammas*,' she would reply, cradling her cup between the sleeves of her jumper. In truth, she would have preferred her hot chocolate without the brandy; ever since she was tiny, she'd loathed rum babas, trifle, Christmas pudding, all liqueur-based desserts, but she didn't dare disappoint Theo by refusing. She always imagined the sweet, slightly rotting smell of brandy mixed with chocolate to resemble the drink that the White Witch in *The Lion, the Witch and the Wardrobe* conjured up hissing from the snow for Edmund during his first visit to Narnia.

What was it that really made Theo tick? wondered Sappho as she waited for the woman to bring her tea. Her father was such a mass of contradictions; the amateur sportsman who was equally at home watching a bare-fist wrestling match in some gypsy dive in Platia Klathmonos, or playing squash with his Syntagma set at the club in Kiffissia. He loved sport so much that he was planning to return to Athens for the first time in seven years in order to be part of the 2004 Olympiad; they would have spent his seventieth birthday together at the house.

Her eyes filled with tears; Ghisela told her that he had even acquired, and learned to use, a computer, so that he could keep up with the city's preparations for the Games via the internet. They had been about to install Broadband when the accident happened.

She always used to think that as a father Theo was miserly with his time when she was growing up, but in truth they had done many things together. Not only the swimming, which had been more or less a constant throughout her childhood, but endless lunches in restaurants and trips to archaeological sites of interest: Delphi, Knossos, Mycenae, Ancient Corinth. The things that he enjoyed, private pleasures he felt able to transmit to her. At the end of the day, Theo's only real failing as a father was that he couldn't bear monotony; routine, above all the routine of parenthood, was anathema to him. If only she'd made peace earlier with this truism, she could have saved herself years of low-level resentment, gained hours of his time . . .

'Efharistó,' said Sappho as the woman placed a pot of tea down on the table, sliding the folded bill beneath the sugar bowl.

Sappho was about to pour herself a cup when she heard her mobile phone ring. Rooting around in her rucksack, beneath her swimming costume, her towel and her white Havaiana flip-flops, she pulled it out and stared at the illuminated blue screen; it was Alexander.

At the sight of his name, she felt desire flood through her like a kind of radioactive ink; once more she was a sexual predator, high on testosterone. She stared down at her thumb hovering over the 'Yes' button with its picture of a tiny green telephone receiver; she could ignore the call, wait for the rain to stop, and have a peaceful, restorative swim to the caves –

'Alexander.'

'Where are you, Saff?'

'I'm at Limni Vouliagmeni . . . where are you?'

'At Aghios Kosmos . . . they sent us home early, there's been an accident. A beam swung off a crane. One of the pulleys snapped.'

Sappho's heart shrivelled.

'Are you OK?'

'I'm OK . . . I just got hit on the ear by some other guys carrying a metal door . . . they were trying to dodge the beam.'

For the first time, she heard a tremor in his voice. The building sites of the new Olympic venues were turning into Athens's graveyard; some sources estimated the loss of life as one worker per day.

'Did the beam hit anyone?'

'I don't know, Saff, they sent us all out and locked the site. The ambulance crews are in there now.'

'Where are you?'

'I'm at the bus stop outside. I'm waiting for a bus back into town.'

'Why don't you come here instead?' Sappho looked at her watch: it was nearly midday; knowing Lorna, she'd still be in bed, sleeping off her hangover. The air in that little roof hut of theirs would be poisonous.

'I'm filthy, Saff, I need to wash.'

'You can shower here at the lake.' *I'll wash you, if you like, inch by sweet inch . . .*

Alexander hesitated, and Sappho felt her desire corrode into hard little granules of rage.

'I'll be there in around half an hour . . . sooner if I find a taxi.'

Sappho placed the phone on the table and looked out towards the lake. He'd come looking for her, not Lorna. Her heart flipped with triumph; *now* at last they were getting somewhere . . .

Association with his mother was the one thing that tainted Alexander in Sappho's eyes. Otherwise, he was perfect, at least within the consciously narrow remit of her desire. She literally could not see one instant into the future beyond sleeping with him; apart from his sex there was nothing new to discover about Alexander. Even a relationship wasn't really what she was looking for; try as she might, she could not seriously imagine them as a couple: the idea was almost comical. As for what he might stand to gain out of an affair, well, that was his business, he wasn't a baby any more . . .

He'd been a quiet, kind-hearted little boy, who had grown into a quiet, kind-hearted man, that was more or less it. They'd never talked much, even when they were children, and now, in his visits to the house, they would sit in companionable silence on the roof terrace while Sappho waited for him to declare himself. She knew he adored her, she could see the love and admiration shining in his beautiful brown eyes; the fact that he kept his distance merely made her desire him more. Yet, for now, at least, she was damned if she was going to make the first move.

To her chagrin, it turned out that he was by no means a sexual innocent. On Samos, he had had a two-year affair with the teenage daughter of friends of the American he and Lorna had been house-sitting for.

'So how come it ended?' she'd asked him lightly. She squeezed the thick stem of her glass of cherry cordial in an effort to keep her voice steady.

277

'She had to go back to college in the States. It would probably have ended anyway.'

'Did you love her?'

In the darkness, he'd turned his face away. Enjoying his discomfort, Sappho stared across at the red-tiled roofs of her neighbours. When she was a child, from the terrace, you used to be able to see as far as the port of Piraeus, right the way across the Saronic Gulf; now it was a jumble of satellite dishes and rickety little illegal *garconieras* built atop the blocks of flats. Just feet away from her, an elderly Dutch painter stood hunched over a canvas behind the sliding glass windows of her studio; she heard a car bump over the pothole in Tsami Karatasou Street, and the sound of bouzouki music drifting up from the new club on Filoppapou.

'So . . . did you love her?'

He never answered her question; not then, or later. Even when he was a boy, it was impossible to get Alexander to do anything he didn't want to. He was generally so sweet-natured that people, adults especially, would mistake this sweet nature for docility. And yet discipline of any kind – school, timetables, restrictive clothing – was a kind of violence to his soul; he was literally incapable of bending his will to that of others.

Sappho looked down at her watch; any minute now he should be arriving at Vouliagmeni. She took a sip of her tea; the rain seemed to have let up, at least for now, and a man in a light blue bath robe was walking towards the edge of the lake. A lifeguard had climbed up the ladder to his little open-fronted cabin, and salsa music was drifting out from a transistor radio perched on the roof. Should she change into her swimming costume now, or wait until Alexander arrived?

'Saff?'

She spun around. 'You gave me a fright!'

278

'I was lucky, I managed to pick up a taxi in Glyfada.'

Alexander's face looked ashy beneath his tan, and beads of sweat stood up around his hairline.

'Sit down, you look as though you're about to pass out.'

Dropping his rucksack to the ground, he sank into one of the white plastic chairs; it was then that she noticed the deep gash along the side of his ear.

He touched the wound with his finger. 'It was the corner of an aluminium door – I was lucky it didn't take my ear off. Luckily the plastic wrap was still on.'

Sappho peered closer at the cut, at the crescent of beautiful pink flesh, pale as veal; his wound made him even more desirable to her. She had to force herself not to take his hand in hers and hold it to her cheek.

'Did you get it cleaned up?'

'The foreman on site disinfected it. A swim in the lake should kill off any germs. Either that, or else I'll get blood poisoning. What was it Theo used to say? If it doesn't kill you . . .'

'. . . it makes you stronger,' Sappho finished off. She smiled. 'Did you bring your trunks?'

'I've got shorts on under my trousers. They'll do.'

Yes, quite, thought Sappho as she entered the café to settle the bill, I'll say they'll do . . .

Shyly, they walked towards the wooden changing booths at the edge of the lake. She was wearing the black Speedo swimming costume under her clothes that she and Theo had bought together on her last visit to London. Theo had always loved going to Lillywhites, even though he no longer played any sports. After years of Ghisela's Mittel-European cooking, he had developed a comical little paunch, though his limbs remained long and rangy. In time, his arteries would probably have packed up; he wasn't used to eating all those saturated fats.

279

She glanced down at her thighs; she hadn't been to the beach at all this year, and her skin was shockingly white. Luckily her body felt wiry and spare after weeks of missed meals; she placed her hands around her ribs, each one clearly visible. In her grief about Theo, she had tricked her body into feeding off itself . . . A faded bikini top, together with a fluorescent yellow *pareo*, hung on a nail above the door. The cabin smelled of mildew, mingled with suntan oil, and omelette drifting over from the café kitchen. Maybe after a swim they could have some lunch; food would do Alexander good after the shock of the accident.

He was waiting for her by the lake. She walked across the spongy AstroTurf to the steps at the edge of the water; it had begun to rain again, and a hot wind whipped the drops sideways into their faces. On the other side of the lake, an elderly couple dressed in bath robes were dancing to the salsa music beneath a canopy of overhanging vines, their movements circumscribed yet joyous, elbows crooked, hands clasped together at waist height. Their happiness seemed like an omen; she smiled at Alexander, and together they walked down the wet carpeted steps into the water.

She knew then that by the end of the day they would be lying in each other's arms; and that Alexander knew it too. It was just a question of time; all the hours of the day were theirs to play with, the moment would reveal itself without their having to search for it. A burden had been lifted from her shoulders; the fact that he came to look for her after the accident signified a shift in their relationship: she was no longer navigating in the delirium and self-doubt of fantasy.

Small black fish darted beneath the shallows, while buds of papery bougainvillaea, their edges browned and faded by the sun, blew along the surface of the water. He walked ahead of her towards the centre of the lake; the skin on his back was the glorious hot bronze it had always been, stretched tight as a sheath over the muscles and sinews beneath, but he had acquired a new, darker builders' tan on his forearms and neck from working on the sites.

Alexander turned to face her, blunt cheek tilted upwards to the rain. The water was up to his chest now, a bobbing rim of dark silver brushing against his nipples. Aching with desire, Sappho ducked under the surface and began swimming towards the caves.

'Are you coming?'

She watched as Alexander lowered himself gingerly into the water, waiting for that exquisite moment as the salt penetrated the raw flesh by his ear. He flinched, and his brown eyes swam with tears, and again Sappho had to stop herself from taking him into her arms. *Wait, no need to rush, you have all day . . .*

Together, they swam around the rock towards the white-faced clock mounted on a green metal stand; each time he raised his arm in his powerful crawl, she saw the tendrils of wet hairs sprouting from the deep cave of his armpit, and it was as though she already knew, from some barely re-membered past, what it would be like to bury her face in that hollow.

After their swim, they got dressed without rinsing the lake water from their bodies. Theo had always been a believer in Vouliagmeni's restorative properties; his mother, Maro, swore it cured Grandfather Charles's rheumatism, while, more prosaically, Theo proclaimed it was the perfect hangover destination. *Mens sana in corpore sano . . .*

As she stood in the wooden changing booth, Sappho held her hand to her face; her skin smelled sulphurous and felt surprisingly soft to the touch. She licked her arm; it numbed her tongue, but the taste wasn't unpleasant.

Alexander was waiting for her outside the booth in his paint-stained jeans. On his feet, he wore the same dark brown monks' sandals Theo used to buy them both every summer from the poet-sandalmaker on Pondrossou Street. 'You live in the country that invented the sandal, and you expect me to buy you cheap Italian imports from Ermou Street?' Theo would say to her when she begged for something less austere.

At Hellenic College, they looked down on anything made in Greece; the trick was to appear as foreign, that is, American, as possible. Theo would have been touched that Alexander had carried on the sandal tradition on his own.

'Don't tell me they let you on to the site without boots?' she said, looking down at his brown feet.

'This is nothing; some of the Asian and Eastern European workers show up in flip-flops and shorts. They're not into safety here like they are on sites in the UK . . .' His face clouded, and he turned pale beneath his tan. 'The guy the beam fell on . . . Abu . . . he was a really good bloke . . . he was saving up to buy a tourist bus back home in Bangladesh.'

'He might be OK, you know. Try not to think about it now.' Sappho looked at her watch. It was almost three o'clock. 'D'you want something to eat?'

Alexander frowned, and she watched the thoughts traipse openly across his countenance. Lorna. Lorna. Lorna . . .

'Let me go back to the hotel and change. I can come and pick you up later on from the house.'

Gathering their belongings, they walked out of the gates and down the path towards the main road. At the bus stop, Sappho flagged down a taxi driving slowly past with the window rolled down.

'*Pou pate?*' asked the driver, flicking his wrist upwards interrogatively.

'Omonia, then Filoppapou,' replied Sappho, getting in before he had a chance to refuse. Taxi drivers were being sent to charm school in preparation for the Olympics, but so far it hardly showed. They would still only pick up the passengers whose destination was on their route.

They settled back in the seats, the red vinyl sticky beneath her bare thighs. Strictly speaking, Filoppapou came before Omonia, but she didn't want to leave Alexander to pay the driver, nor to humiliate him by leaving him the fare. They hadn't discussed money, but she guessed Alexander was supporting Lorna with his work on the building sites.

On Singrou Avenue, they passed the Fixx brewery where he and Lorna had squatted for almost a year towards the end of the eighties. Recently, the brewery had hosted an exhibition of the naif Greek painter Yannis Tsarouchis which Sappho had visited shortly before Theo's accident. Theo had been slightly acquainted with Tsarouchis; he had visited him at his studio in Maroussi, and one of his paintings hung in the house on Patmos. His naive homoerotic portraits of sturdy-limbed, narrow-waisted Greek boys, oversized hands resting on their laps, reminded her now of Alexander – or of her peculiarly two-dimensional perception of him. *Sailor with Coffee Cup*, *Sailor Dreaming of Love*, *Young Man Posing as Olympic Statue*, all of them gazing out of the canvas with their haunted brown eyes.

There was something equally fetishistic about her desire for Alexander; like Tsarouchis's urban peasant boys, he had become a blank canvas for her fantasies. She remembered lingering over one untitled watercolour of a young man emerging naked from a grey sea, long thick arms dangling by his sides like a monkey, his slender, almost girlish waist in contrast to the massive articulated thighs – a black star anise of pubic hair above his club-like penis.

Sappho felt her clitoris pulse, and a slow swoon spread upwards through her body. Shutting her eyes, she leaned back in her seat and placed her palm on her belly. Now, the object of her desire was sitting beside her in this airless cab, close enough for them to kiss without even shifting in their seats.

Turning away from Alexander, she looked out of the taxi window at a family of four on a beat-up scooter by some traffic lights: father, two children in the middle, mother at the back. Recently she had come across a photograph of Theo, Celia and Lorna riding as a threesome on Theo's Vespa outside her Grandmother Maro's villa in Kiffissia. It was Lorna in the middle who looked like the real girlfriend, not Celia . . . Did those two young English girls, one dark, one fair, *one pretty, one less so*, ever imagine that their two, as yet unborn, children would one day be sitting in a taxi, planning later on that day to make love?

'First left, then second right after the cinema,' said Alexander, directing the driver towards the hotel. The taxi stopped and, picking up his rucksack, Alexander turned towards her.

'So?'

'So?'

Too shy to kiss, they smiled at each other. His cheeks were flushed, and his beautiful brown eyes were brimming with joy. All around them, the traffic of Omonia swirled and eddied, and finally receded into silence. Their surroundings had shrunk and contracted into nothing; had the driver too entered the erotic, airless cave of their desire?

'I'll be about an hour,' said Alexander; then crouching down on the pavement before the rolled-up window, he placed two fingers on his lips and tipped them upwards towards her in a kiss. Picking up his rucksack, he stood up, and she watched him walk towards the shabby lobby of the hotel.

'Alexander, wait.'

He turned around and walked back to the pavement, while the driver shifted impatiently in his seat. The backrest was covered in a wooden bead massager, threaded on to monofilament and edged with black velour. She wondered whether by the end of each day the skin of his body was pixellated like a Chris Ofili painting with the imprint of those beads.

'Here, take these.' Reaching out through the open window, she handed him the spare set of keys she had collected the day before from Kyria Soula, the cleaning lady; for a moment, Alexander hesitated, then modestly lowering his head, he took them and tucked them into the back pocket of his jeans.

Back at the house, Sappho let herself in and walked up the staircase towards the sitting room. The shutters were closed, and striped shadows criss-crossed the parquet floor. The rain had finally ceased, and a bright evening sun was pouring in through the windows. Yesterday's copy of the *Athens News* lay unopened on the low coffee table; was there a time when she might really have been interested in reading a newspaper?

She looked at her watch; it was almost five. In less than an hour Alexander would be back. She stood by the window, watching needles of sunlight burn through the narrow linen curtains. She had never really looked at them properly, noticed the button-hole stitching down the edges, the embroidered design, white on white, of overhanging grapes.

She wandered through the house, past Celia's room with its woven blue and white Cretan bedspread, her British Council library books piled up crookedly on the canework bedside table. The latest Ishiguro, and Patrick Leigh Fermor's *Roumeli: Travels in Northern Greece.* Guiltily, Sappho remembered that she had promised Celia to renew the books before she left for Patmos; as soon as she was back in the real world, she would do it.

In the kitchen, she stood at the shallow marble sink and poured herself a glass of water. On the draining board stood a miniature red dustpan and brush to sweep up food scraps; all Greek kitchens had them, but she had never seen them anywhere else. The plastic bristles were long and wiry with a faint kink towards the tip which she had never noticed. She opened the fridge and looked inside; it was empty, apart from a bowl of cherries she had bought earlier that week from the market, and a jar of last year's olives from Patmos. The air in the fridge felt cool, freeze-drying the sweat from the taxi ride on to her face.

Perhaps there was time for a shower before Alexander returned; she had a new bottle of bitter almond shower milk she wanted to try from the Korres homeopathic pharmacy on Ivikou Street.

Still in a kind of dream, she walked barefoot along the corridor to the bathroom, removing her clothes as she stepped through the door. The bathroom had not been touched since the 1920s when the house was built. The walls were lined with pale green narrow tiles, and the double basins rested on a large free-standing mahogany cabinet, beneath Grandfather Charles's medicine chest with the mirror doors, which he used to stock up each time he visited the UK: Galloway's Cough Syrup, Vicks VapoRub, Milk of Magnesia, TCP, Germolene, Andrews Liver Salts, all of them long past their sell-by date, the austere 1970s packaging primitive yet familiar.

In the corner of the bathroom, on the black and white mosaic floor tiles, stood a gigantic indoor palm from Yia-Yia's house in Kiffissia, whose long, strip-like leaves overhung the clawfoot bath. Stuffing her clothes into the wicker laundry basket, Sappho stepped into the bath and switched on the heavy copper shower.

At some point she was going to have to do some washing; Kyria Soula was not coming in until the first week of September, and the sheets she had washed last week were still hanging on the roof terrace, begrimed by days of *nephos* and rain. Reaching for her straw glove, she filled her palm with the body milk and began to scrub her arms. To her surprise, she realised that in spite of the clouds and rain, she had caught some colour at Vouliagmeni; the blurred stripes of her swimming costume were visible on her shoulders. She rinsed her body, then filling up the enamel mug on the edge of the bath, she watered the potted palm, pressing her fingers down on to the dry spongy earth.

She was just drying herself on the mat when she heard Alexander let himself into the house. She paused, waiting to hear where he was heading. For a moment she considered walking out naked into the hallway – why postpone the inevitable? – but again she felt herself swept up by the delicious certainty that together they would recognise, and obey, the moment whenever it arrived.

Slipping on Theo's old paisley silk dressing-gown, Sappho walked out of the bathroom. Alexander was sitting on one of the low sofas in the hallway, dressed in a collarless shirt made of some kind of thin linen material, and a pair of faded khaki trousers. He too must have had a shower; his dark, otter's head glinted in the half light, and he looked as though he had shaved.

'How's the cut?'

'Stings a bit . . . but it's fine.'

'Give me a minute to get dressed, and we'll go out for something to eat.'

What time was it anyway? wondered Sappho as she stood before her wardrobe, trying to decide what to wear. It must be at least six, if not later. Alexander looked so clean and fresh in his white cotton shirt that she didn't want to ruin it by choosing something too tricksy or sophisticated; in her mind's eye, she could already see them walking through the Plaka together. In spite of everything, a couple . . . In the end she settled for a brown sleeveless T-shirt over the turquoise embroidered silk skirt she had bought before

Theo's accident from the new Zara on Stadiou Street, which she had not yet had the chance to wear.

As she looked in the mirror, she felt a pang of guilt at the sight of her flushed, hectic face; was she done with mourning Theo? Already? And yet in some ways, being with Alexander meant that her father was more alive to her than he had ever been.

Slipping on a pair of flat gold leather thong sandals, she walked out into the hallway where Alexander was standing by the bureau looking at the photograph she had found the other day of Theo, Lorna and Celia on the Vespa. He turned to her, and again he lowered his eyes, as though unable to contain his emotions.

'She was a stunner, your mum,' said Sappho lightly, as she stood behind him, near enough to rest her cheek against the thin cotton of his shoulder. The material was so fine, you could make out the outline of the nipples beneath. He smelled of unperfumed olive oil soap, mingled with something like creosote. Then she remembered: the roof of the hotel in Omonia was coated with it; all their possessions had always had that tarry smell, even the sugary pink kaftan Lorna had worn all the summer on Patmos.

She *was* stunning; she looked a bit like Kate Moss, with her slanting eyes and fair, Asiatic face. Sappho could afford to be magnanimous now about her beauty, seeing as she was about to sleep with her son . . . Alexander had inherited nothing of her looks or build, apart, perhaps, from a kind of bluntness about the cheekbones. He had beautiful smooth skin, with the invisible pores you usually only found on children.

'Does she ever talk to you about your father?' asked Sappho impulsively.

'Not really . . . to be honest, I don't think she's that clear about things in her own mind. I'm not that bothered, so it's never really been an issue between us.'

Covertly, Sappho studied his expression for signs of resentment; on top of all the chaos of his childhood, how could Alexander not hold it against his mother that she was unable to tell him the identity of his father? Not even a name? . . . Surely no one could be that noble. Yet his face remained impassive; from a very early age, there'd always been a kind of steely equilibrium at his core . . . no, steely was the wrong word . . . it was a centredness about him, an inviolable sense of self, that meant that in spite of his clothes, Lorna, his obvious air of poverty, he was never teased or picked on by other children, not even the pampered ex-pat kids at Hellenic College, which he had attended briefly for a couple of terms, or the rougher gypsy children he would hang around with in the Plaka.

Together, they walked out of the shuttered house and up Propilleon Street towards the Acropolis. The muggy skies of the last few days had been swept clean by the rain, and a brilliant evening sunshine illuminated the glistening cobblestones on the pedestrianised boulevard which led down to Thisseon. Dionisiou Aeropagitou, together with the new métro, was one of the things Theo had most been looking forward to seeing. 'About time Athenians got to enjoy their own city,' he had said to her one of the last times they spoke on the phone.

They climbed up the smooth marble flagstones towards the tiny Cycladic village of Anafiotika, a cluster of whitewashed house clinging to the north wall of the Acropolis, built right into the bedrock by stonemasons from the island of Anafi, who had been brought to Athens after the war of independence to build the new king's palace. Geraniums and marigolds grew in pots and rusting oil drums piled haphazardly in the doorways, washing strung between the narrow alleyways. The village was inhabited, but always deserted; the occasional plume of woodsmoke, the sound of a radio, a strip of lace curtain at a window the only signs of its occupants.

Athens was the city of their childhood, his as much as hers, yet she had no memory of ever having walked these streets with Alexander; he had become utterly new in her eyes. Where did he go to in the evenings? she wondered. Did he hang around Omonia Square with all the other foreign workers? A picture came into her mind of Alexander and Lorna hunched over a table in one of those miserable neon-lit tavernas around Platia Klathmonos, a plate of oily *pastitsio*, a copper quart jug of retsina, a hunk of bread on the paper table mat between them. She shuddered; this was the last thing she wanted to think about now.

Climbing down the worn steps towards Pritaniou Street on her thin-soled leather sandals, she lost her footing, and Alexander reached out to take her hand. As their palms touched, Sappho felt the blood sing in her veins. His fingers were dry and rough; she could have held on to them for ever, the bones of his hand sturdy as the handle of a bentwood walking stick, but she couldn't bear to let the waiting end so abruptly . . . She was pacing herself like a marathon runner, amazed at her own restraint . . . Smiling to herself as she let go of his hand, they walked past the Tower of the Winds towards Adrianou Street.

'Shall we have a drink at Brettos?' suggested Alexander as they turned into Kydatheneon Street. This was the oldest distillery in Athens, where Theo would buy metal canisters of ouzo and brandy to store in the cellar. They entered the dark, cave-like shop, illuminated only by a wall of backlit bottles of liqueur: shelf upon shelf of grenadine, cassis, Fernet Branca, absinthe, Chartreuse, maraschino, Campari, curaçao, glowing like brightly coloured jewels all the way up to the panelled ceiling. They sat on stools at one of the scrubbed refectory tables, flanked by giant barrels of ouzo, each with its own red-handled tap.

The owner brought them a jar of ouzo and a jug of iced water. Alexander poured it out, and briefly they clinked glasses.

'*Stin yammas.*'

'*Stin yammas.*'

As the ouzo smouldered through her veins, Sappho felt a kind of soul-weariness overcome her. She had eaten nothing since the slice of bread and honey that morning before catching the bus to Vouliagmeni. She was tired of waiting, tired of holding aloft that quivering burden of desire which at that moment seemed hers alone to bear. *Are you a lover or an orphan?* . . . Who was she kidding, with her gold sandals and silk skirt? All that preening before the mirror . . . and for what? A good daughter would be dressed in black, her arms modestly covered . . . at least until her father was cold in his grave. He had been laid to rest in the cemetery at Mortlake . . . he would never return to the country of his birth.

'Are you OK, Saff?' Across the table, Alexander took her hand, and this time she let it remain. She nodded, and pressed his fingers to her lips to hide their trembling. Reaching across the table, he stroked her face, wiping the tears from her cheek with the rough pad of his thumb.

'It's time to go home,' he said.

They stood up together, and Alexander slipped his arm easily around her shoulder, holding her close, as though their bodies, weary of all the feints, the day's endless dance, had finally taken matters into their own hands. They turned out to be a perfect fit. As they walked back through the Plaka down Vironos Street, past the sunken monument to Lysicrates with its green painted railings, she could feel their hips rolling in their sockets at some infinitesimally precise rhythm, each step allowing for the difference in their height and the length of their stride so that the distance between them never widened. You could have placed an apple in the hollow between their waists, polished it to a high shine, without it ever falling to the ground.

Down Makriyanni Street, they retraced the route she had taken early that morning, several lifetimes ago, it seemed now, to catch the bus to Vouliagmeni.

'Did you plan on calling me at the lake today?' asked Sappho, looking up at him as they cut through Drakou Street, past the Italian *gelateria* with its outdoor tables filled with people lingering over their sundaes and cocktails.

'I wasn't sure . . .'

'Wasn't sure of what?' she teased.

She felt his chest tighten against her cheek beneath the thin cotton of his shirt as he breathed in deeply.

'Of . . . lots of things . . .'

'Like what?'

'Like . . . whether you'd want to see me . . .'

In the dark, she felt her eyes gleam with triumph. Had she been so cunning? Could he really have never guessed?

Back at the house, they stood on the marble step as he searched his pocket for the keys. She wanted him to be the one to open the door; had she already foreseen the eroticism of the moment when she handed him the keys in the taxi?

They entered the hallway, and Sappho pushed the door shut behind her. Hand in hand, they climbed the staircase, and on the first landing he stopped and took her into his arms. They kissed, and she felt his heart knocking violently beneath his shirt. His saliva tasted sweet, as though he had been eating green apples. The entire front panel of her body was alive to his touch. Without turning on the lights, she led him through the shuttered house towards her room, their sandalled feet clicking lightly on the parquet. At the doorway, they paused to kiss again, and she felt his erection stir beneath his trousers. He stroked her hair off her face, and smiled.

'Pleased to meet you, Saff.' In the semi-darkness, the pure whites of his eyes shone like duck eggs.

Together, they sat down on her single bed, and she watched him slip his thin cotton shirt over his head without opening the buttons, the massive arc of his ribcage bent forwards like the skeleton of some Viking ship. There was no shame in his body; naked, he was all of a piece, just as when he was a little boy who refused to wear clothes. Even his penis appeared to spring from his thighs with the same joyous thrust as the limbs from his torso, or the dark hair on the nape of his neck, the skin on his body the exact texture and sheen as that on his face.

He knelt before her on the white sheets and he hooked his fingers through the waistband of her skirt, feeling for the button. Slipping it off her legs, he rolled down her pants, and parted her thighs with his hands. As he leaned forward and the tip of his tongue touched her clitoris, she felt herself shudder, and a low moan escaped her.

He looked up and smiled. 'I've been wanting to do that for a long time, Saff.'

Sappho stroked the crown of his shaved head, cupping her hand around the sweet velvet roundness of his skull. His breath was hot on her belly as he spoke.

'For how long?'

'Oh . . . since I was about five years old.'

'*Five?* What could you know about sex when you were five?'

'Not very much . . . but I just knew you'd taste nice.'

'And do I taste nice?'

'Very nice. Even nicer than I thought.'

She was so wet, she had left a silvery trail down one side of his neck.

'And what else did you know?'

He twisted around, pulling himself upwards along her body like a seal, until he was lying beside her, his penis resting heavily on the inside of her thigh. 'I knew that I'd get an erection every time I saw you in your swimming costume on the beach.'

'So *that's* why you always had your willy tucked between your legs when you were hiding inside your den.'

'Of course it is. Why d'you think I needed a den in the first place?'

Taking her wrist, he led her hand down to his crotch. She circled his penis in her fingers, marvelling at its weight, the babyish silkiness of the skin. Even the glans shone brand-new like something that had just been unwrapped. Covering her hand with his, he slid his penis between her closed legs, burrowing deeper into her thighs until he found her sex. Unable to wait any longer, Sappho opened her legs and guided him inside her.

She came almost at once, even before he began to move. Yet the moment her orgasm subsided, she was flung right back on to that dizzying ledge, each thrust bringing her closer and closer to a second, higher, peak. Streets began to flash before her eyes . . . the Upper Richmond Road . . . a little haberdasher's behind Eolou Street . . . a cobbled alleyway on Patmos. They kissed, and the instant she felt his tongue brush hers, she came again. She opened her eyes just as he withdrew, rearing back on to his heels, penis in his fist, gazing down almost in wonder at the dense flower of sperm spurting downwards on to her belly.

He kissed her and got up from the bed. 'I'll be back in a moment,' he said, walking naked towards the door; then as an afterthought he returned and kissed her once more.

She heard the hiss of ancient pipes from the bathroom as he flushed the chain, then he returned with a hand towel to wipe her belly. To her surprise, it felt hot and damp; the square of coarse linen steamed on her skin like one of those microwaved hand towels airline staff handed out with tongs at the end of an inflight meal. Alexander must have held it under the hot tap and wrung it dry; the sweetness of the gesture, all that care and attention, seemed typical of him.

Later, they slept, limbs entwined on her single bed. They'd left the balcony shutters open, and Sappho awoke to the beams from the *son et lumière* on the Acropolis illuminating the side of Alexander's head as he lay on the pillow. She let her gaze travel over his face; the ear where the steel door had hit him had already turned black; and the edge of the crescent-shaped wound was frilled with a dark red crust.

It must be between nine and ten in the evening if the *son et lumière* was still on. She placed one hand on her stomach; most satisfyingly, her hip bones jutted out like blades. They had never made it to a taverna that evening; perhaps when Alexander awoke they could go to Strofí on the corner of Roberto Galli Street, hoping it would still be open. She was suddenly ravenous; in her mind's eye she could already see them sitting on the roof terrace with its views of the Acropolis sharing a plate of grilled octopus. Then after they had eaten, they could return to the house and make love again.

And again.

He'd been lucky to escape from that building site with his life. It was ridiculous for him day after day to keep putting himself in such danger . . . He'd got away with it once; there was no guarantee he'd be so lucky next time. They needed to escape from the madness of the city, go somewhere alone together for a few days. Patmos! They could sail that night to Patmos! There was a ferry leaving from Piraeus at midnight . . . no need for him to even go back to the hotel for his things. He could pick up the basics in one of the shops in Skala . . . the impetuousness of the journey seemed like the perfect end to the accumulated follies of that day . . . They would return to all the places where they had played as children, make love in every single one of them.

As she sat up, she felt Alexander's arm tighten instinctively around her waist in his sleep. He opened his eyes, and she bent forward and kissed him on the lips.

'What time is it?'

'Around ten, maybe a bit earlier . . . Why?'

He passed his hand over his eyes. 'I've got to go, Saff. I never realised it was so late.'

'Go?' she repeated stupidly. 'Where?'

'Back to the hotel.'

Sappho felt a slow burn of fury. 'Alexander, Lorna's a big girl now.'

'You don't understand, Saff . . .' He sat up, scanning the room for his clothes.

'What don't I understand?'

'Lorna's got no one else.'

He got up and walked across the floor to pick up his trousers. Numbly, she watched him button up the flies with one hand, his face anxious and absorbed. In his mind, he was already elsewhere. When he had slipped his shirt over his head, he came down to sit beside her on the bed to fasten his sandals.

'Please, Saff, try and understand.'

'What's there to understand? Two hours after making love, you're already out of the door.' She sounded bitter, shrewish, a whiny little girl. How could it already have come to this?

He placed one hand on her leg, squeezing her knee beneath the sheet.

'I'll come back later . . . I just need to check that she's got water – it gets like a furnace up on that roof.'

He made it sound like he kept a dog up in the *garconiera*. She stared towards the wall, refusing to meet his gaze. She would catch that ferry at midnight, with or without him.

'Saff?' Gently, he turned her face towards him until their eyes met. 'I love you . . . you know that.'

'If you loved me, you'd put someone else first for a change.' She twisted her neck away, feeling the tears pricking behind her eyes.

'I promise, I'll come back tomorrow.'

'Don't. You needn't bother. I won't be here.'

Thirty-one

Kyria Vasso's niece was hosing down the kitchen steps as the taxi drew up outside the house. Sappho stepped out and reached inside her rucksack for her wallet.

'*Ochi*,' said Kyrios Sotiris, the driver, firmly pressing his calloused hand over hers. It was useless arguing; he'd spent the entire journey from the port reminiscing brokenly about Theo, who had been his summer playmate when they were boys. 'We always said we'd play backgammon in the *kafenion* together when we were old men,' he said, shaking his head in sorrow.

Shading her eyes against the sun, Sappho watched the taxi coasting slowly in neutral down the steep gravel driveway towards the road. She raised one hand in salute, then picking up her rucksack, she walked towards the house.

Kyria Vasso's niece looked up as Sappho approached the kitchen steps; she was barefoot, and her jeans were rolled around her knees. Sappho felt a stab of irritation at the sight of her stubby calves planted on the wet stone; she was tired after the journey, she hadn't been able to get a cabin, she'd spent the crossing curled up uncomfortably in an armchair which smelled of vomit and feet, and the last thing she felt like was more small talk. She tried to recall the niece's name: Daphne, Demi . . . no, Despo, that was it. She had a dim, sly face, with pale eyes and lardy skin; as long as she wasn't planning on mentioning Theo's death: she couldn't face another round of condolences. Not before a strong coffee, at any rate.

'*Yassou*, Despo. Is my mother still asleep?'

'You didn't know? Kyria Celia caught Monday morning's Dolphin to Samos. To visit her friend Carole.' Despo looked delighted at being in the know. Or maybe it was just lack of sleep making Sappho paranoid.

'That's right, I remember now,' she said dully.

Had Celia mentioned she was going away the last time they talked on the phone? Maybe she had, who knows, all she'd been interested in was winkling out Alexander from his hiding place. So now she was going to be stuck alone on Patmos with Kyria Vasso and her niece. Great. Already Sappho was regretting the impulsiveness of her journey. *He would have come back to you last night, you know he would have* . . . She had behaved like a spoilt little girl over Lorna, blown it, and now she was paying the consequences.

'When will my mother be back?' she asked sharply.

'*Then xero*,' replied Despo, self-righteously, as though keeping track of Celia's movements were not part of her job description.

What was the point of Celia pressing her to come to Patmos if she wasn't even planning on being here herself? thought Sappho. Unreasonably, tears stung her eyes; her father had just died, and she'd travelled all this way to find an empty house. Fumbling in her rucksack for her sunglasses, she slipped them on to hide her tears. Lack of sleep invariably made her weepy.

'Where's Kyria Vasso?' she said.

Despo looked knowing, as though the sunglasses had not fooled her for a moment. 'My Aunt Vasso couldn't make it this morning. She will be here in the afternoon to finish the washing and ironing,' she intoned in a lying singsong.

No doubt she was moonlighting as a chambermaid for one of the hotels in Hora, as she'd been doing for years, even though she was paid by Celia to work full time over the summer.

Sappho climbed the rough wooden staircase to the top of the house, aware all the while of Despo's pale blue eyes watching her from the hallway. Her bed was made up with her Grandmother Maro's monogrammed linen sheets; it was true, Celia really had been expecting her. It looked so inviting that Sappho considered skipping the shower and lying down for a nap. She walked towards the window and opened the shutters: a hot *meltemi* wind was blowing, and the sea was ruffled with tiny even waves. The stony crescent of beach was empty, apart from a woman lying topless beneath the overhanging branches of Alexander's lair. He had said he loved her, *I love you Saff, you know that . . .* though he had nothing to gain, and perhaps everything to lose, by declaring himself so soon. Just a few hours earlier they had been lying asleep on her single bed, after probably the best sex of her life.

She closed her eyes and groaned as desire for him thrilled through her. She hadn't even given him a chance to explain, or to say when he'd be back that night. Fool, fool, fool. She owed him an apology, at the very least. Sitting down on the bed, she took out her mobile from her rucksack and checked the screen: Messages 0. Then again, why should he text her first? She was the one in the wrong, not him. She looked at her watch: it was almost midday. Who knows if he had gone back to work at the building site after the accident. He had been extraordinarily affected by the accident to the guy from Bangladesh. *My sweet, kind-hearted boy . . .*

Then she began to type out a text: 'Patmos, miserable. Shall I come back? S xx.' Quickly Sappho pressed 'Send', before she had the chance to reconsider, then placing the mobile on the desk beneath the window, where the reception was better, she took off her clothes and walked into the bathroom.

Instantly, the hot water from the shower restored her. She looked down at the curves and planes of her body, which she loved now because he loved it . . . *I've been wanting to do that for a long time, Saff,* his tongue flicking inside her . . . As she soaped her breasts, she felt desire for him quicken in her; if she touched herself she would come at once. No, she would hold back, wait to feel his fingers sliding inside her.

She washed her hair, and hunted in the medicine cabinet for one of the unused toothbrushes which were kept there for unexpected visitors. She cleaned her teeth with Celia's homeopathic fennel toothpaste, and after rubbing herself dry with one of the towels folded up on the straw-covered chair, she walked naked across the stone floor towards her room. The radio was on in the kitchen, and she could hear Despo banging cupboard doors open and shut, like someone trying to sound busy. She was just crossing the threshold of her room, when she heard the chime of her mobile: a message! She picked it up, feeling the phone vibrate excitedly in her palm; then, heart shuddering drily, she pressed 'Read'.

'I'll be waiting for the ferry in Piraeus. I love you, A x.'

Sappho felt her heart sing. She felt like running naked down in triumph to the beach, and throwing herself into the sea. There was no need to even unpack: she would lie down for an hour or so on the bed, just enough to recharge her batteries, then hitch a lift back down to Skala to find if there was any chance of getting a cabin this time. She would leave an ironic note for Celia: 'Hello (and goodbye!)' then ring her later from Athens.

Picking out one of Grandmother Maro's cotton shifts from the marble-topped chest of drawers, she slipped it over her head, breathing in deeply the tang of laundry soap mingled with thyme and wild lavender. I love this place, she thought as she closed the shutters and lay down on the bed. He should have been there on the sheets beside her, listening to the distant sounds of tourists on the beach. Never mind, these things happened for a reason; perhaps it would teach her in future not to take Alexander for granted. They would catch a taxi from Piraeus and go straight back to the house and make love. No need to mention her childish outburst; it wasn't going to be that kind of angsty, analytical relationship, anyway. Maybe not even a relationship at all, come to that; they would be lovers because . . . well, because it was written in the stars, the corollary of her grief . . . And if Alexander wanted more, *he might, you know, you realise this isn't a game for him* . . . well, she would deal with that once the desire subsided enough to permit rational thought.

She heard the front door slam, and the sound of a scooter's engine coming to life. Good, Despo had gone, she had the house to herself. Shutting her eyes, Sappho felt herself sliding instantly downwards into sleep.

In her dream, Alexander was leaving her again; they were at the airport, waiting in line at the check-in desk where he was about to board a flight to Bangladesh. His face was set, and everything about him suggested purpose and flight. Once again, she was begging him not to go.

'I have to, Saff, I promised to tell Abu's wife about the accident,' he insisted, shuffling doggedly along the queue.

'But who will look after Lorna if you go?' argued Sappho craftily; and at this, Alexander appeared to hesitate. Then, reaching inside his pocket, he pulled out a key with a blue glass charm hanging from a leather thong.

'I want you to go to the *garconiera* and bring her some water,' he said, handing it to her.

A slow fury burned through her at the sight of the key, and in a fit of rage she threw it to the ground, watching the glass cyc shatter into pieces. Then, inexplicably, she found herself back at St Cecilia's with her friend Gail; they were running down the forbidden corridor which led to the High School when they came to a door. She pushed it open, and there in a corner crouched a skinny dog chained to the wall, the saddest dog in the world . . . its coat was dry and matted, the coarse pelt stretched tight over the bones of its ribcage. The dog was Lorna, she recognised it at once, though she pretended not to.

'Don't worry, Theo will see she's looked after,' said Gail in Greek; and Sappho stared at her in surprise.

I didn't know you spoke Greek, she thought, as she opened her eyes, forcing herself to slough away the layers of sleep into wakefulness.

The shutters were banging, and the narrow linen curtains were billowing and curling upwards against the window-panes like sails. It was a dream; she was back in her room in Patmos! The dog wasn't real, it wasn't Lorna . . . Sappho stared ahead at the washstand, with its cracked china jug, her mobile twinkling on the desk beneath the window. Of course, Alexander's message! *I'll be waiting for the ferry in Piraeus. I love you* . . . Joy rippled through her like oxygen – he wasn't going anywhere! Soon she would be in Athens, back in his arms.

'Kyrios Theo will look after them, what d'you expect?' said the same voice from her dream. How strange, it had been Vasso talking, not Gail – she must have let herself into the house while Sappho was asleep. In fact probably that was what had woken her up.

Sappho looked at her watch. It was almost five o'clock; could she really have been asleep for all that time? She got up and fastened the catch of the shutters. There was time for a quick swim before going down to Skala to find out about the ferries, a way of expending that surge of endorphins. Groggily, she knelt down on the floor and unzipped her rucksack. Her swimming costume was at the bottom in a HellaSpar plastic bag, still damp from her swim at the lake. Shuddering slightly, she eased the rubbery Lycra upwards along her body.

'Oh, she was a *ponirouli* one all right; right from the start she knew which way her bread was buttered.'

That was Despo's voice; the two of them were sitting in the kitchen, discussing Theo's death, like a pair of market women! For a moment, Sappho considered walking into the room and surprising them, *how dare they!*, but she was loath to let their prurience stain her joy. It was obvious it was Lorna they were talking about. It was incredible, even after all these years, Vasso still considered her worthy of gossip. Who knows, maybe Theo *had* left her a legacy, though as far as she knew they hadn't been in touch since his marriage to Ghisela. Alexander certainly hadn't mentioned it. A familiar feeling of unease overcame her, tamping down her joy like a fire blanket engulfing a flame: *left pocket, right pocket, it comes to the same thing* . . . Even in death it seemed Theo hadn't managed to escape Lorna.

Picking up her towel and flip-flops from the chair, Sappho tiptoed through the door and out on to the dark landing. The front door was ajar, propped open with a boulder from the beach, and she could see the two mopeds parked side by side on the gravel path. She heard the scrape of the kitchen table being dragged across the flagstones; and taking advantage of the noise, she shut the door and walked towards the top of the stairs. She was halfway down when she realised she had forgotten the keys. Damn! She couldn't risk it; if they happened to leave while she was still down on the beach, she'd be locked out of the house in a wet swimming costume – and she'd miss the ferry back to Athens.

She crept back up to her room and unzipped the front pocket of her rucksack: her keys were right at the bottom, tangled up with her sunglasses. Back on the stairs, she heard the spin cycle of the washing machine down in the outhouse; even better, they'd be out at the back hanging up the clothes on the terrace overlooking the garden. Her subterfuge was ridiculous, on some level Sappho knew it was, but at that moment her happiness seemed so fragile, hanging on such a slender thread, that she couldn't risk destroying it.

'. . . of course he'll have made provisions for the boy.' They were money-mad those women, didn't they have anything better to gossip about than Theo's will? thought Sappho angrily as she paused on the stairs to listen. 'Don't talk about my lover like that,' she whispered, loath for them to smear him with the slurry of the past.

The chink of plates being dropped into the shallow marble sink, a gush of water, then the niece's voice again: 'D'you think it's true what they say, you know . . . about –'

'*Ella*, Despo-*mou*, you know how people will talk . . .' Vasso's tone was sly, inviting.

'But what do *you* think, *thia* Vasso . . . after all, you knew them all when they were young?' wheedled Despo flatteringly.

True about what? Shivering beneath her damp swimsuit, Sappho gathered the folds of the towel tighter around her shoulders, until the edges cut into her skin.

'Let's just say, Kyria Celia is a sainted woman.'

'Because of . . .?'

'Because of what she's put up with over the years . . .'

They were lovers, of course they were. Celia had never stood a chance . . . no wonder Lorna looked like the real girlfriend in that picture on the Vespa! They must have been fucking for years. Sappho's heart cracked with pity for her mother, remembering her hopeful face that summer's evening in the house in East Sheen, the day her marriage ended.

'And the boy . . .?'

'Well, it's the oldest trick in the book, isn't it . . . she got an allowance out of him, school fees, rent . . . the lot . . .'

'But is Theo really . . .?'

He was a cunt. Her father was a cunt. So was Celia. And Lorna. No wonder none of it had made sense when she was a child. Theo didn't give a shit about anyone, but he cared about Alexander, enough at any rate to go looking for him when he ran away that time to Aegina . . . Her bowels turned to water; *his son*, Alexander was his son.

She hardly knew what she was doing any more – down the stairs she ran, not caring if the two women heard her; she had to get out of the house, away from that shame. Out on the road she paused for a moment; the wind was stronger now, and the last few tourists were straggling up the dirt path from the beach towards their cars. Her teeth were chattering; her tongue felt thick against her palate, and her mouth was flooded with saliva as though she were about to be sick. She looked down at her bare arm; at the goose-bumps standing up like cactus hairs on her skin. To think that she had loved her body just because he had loved it . . . It was vile, everything about her now was.

Will you be my sister, Sappho, when I'm a man . . .?

Without thinking, she turned towards the path down to the beach. The ground was littered with broken glass, while scraps of yellowing newspaper blew up against the purple spear thistles which grew in clumps alongside the path. She stepped aside to allow a Jeep to pass; Italians, she thought dully, you could tell by their mahogany tans, the matching red bandanas knotted around their throats.

Who else knew about Alexander? Ghisela, perhaps? *Of course he'd have told her, what d'you expect after ten years of marriage* . . . They all did, everyone knew except for her. How could Theo die without telling her Alexander was her brother? *Because he didn't care, that's how* . . .

306

The beach was deserted, apart from a figure down at the far end by the lumpy concrete jetty; it was too windy to sit outside for long when the *meltemi* blew, even for tourists. As a picture came into her mind of Alexander's swollen penis lying inside her thigh, without warning Sappho felt the sickness rise up inside her; leaning forward, she vomited a jet of liquid on to the stones.

Panting, she watched it trickling thinly down the cracks between the rocks, then she walked away from her mess and crouched down at the edge of the sea with the towel wrapped around her. Cupping her hands, Sappho splashed the salty water on to her face, snorting up her nose until her nostrils burned. Where could she go now? Where could she run to? *Where can I go, where can I go?* One thing was certain: it was finished with Celia, she was on her own now. And a picture came into her mind of her mother leaving the spare room that morning in Athens, while her husband and Lorna lay fucking in her bed.

And as for Alexander . . . she could never see him again. She had crashed through the flimsiest of paper screens into the squalor she'd always known to lie there . . . all the shadows of her childhood made flesh.

I fucked my brother . . . It was beyond the pale, it really was. Something in her life had been lost for ever, she had joined the ranks of the deviant. *Incest. Murder. Rape.* At the end of the day, what was there to choose between them? She'd have to live with what she'd done for the rest of her life, she could never be limpid again.

'With that guilty face, you'll be the very Pied Piper of school inspectors!' Theo had mocked her open countenance, made sport of it . . . And yet . . . and yet . . . perhaps she was not such an innocent after all. Hadn't she been toying with Alexander, even though she knew he loved her? Used his body, his ardour, for her pleasure?

Letting her towel fall on to the stones, Sappho walked

into the water, watching the tiny, ribbon-like waves ruffling the surface. The wind whipped her hair into her face, and she shivered. Ahead of her lay the coast of Turkey, a blue smudge of hills in the distance. A different country, where nobody knew her story; she and Celia had been planning to visit Istanbul in the autumn . . . With sickening certainty, she understood that what she had just done would travel with her, follow her like an albatross to the ends of the earth; she had become her story, nothing else about her counted any more.

If only she hadn't gone back for her keys, she would never have overheard the two women talking. Or else if she'd made some noise on the stairs, they would have realised she was awake, made a sign to each other to remain silent until she had left. Cravenly, she thought: what the eye doesn't see, the heart doesn't grieve . . . they could have fucked, she and Alexander, at least one more time.

As much as anything, she grieved for his body, remembering piteously his beautiful broad shoulders, the tapering girlish waist . . . Minutes ago, just minutes, she'd been lying on her bed, planning to meet her lover, imagining his penis stirring inside her. *My brother, my lover* . . .

Or maybe it wasn't true – a sudden burst of hope. Where was the proof? Who's to say Vasso wasn't making it up? She wouldn't put it past her, Vasso had always had a vile tongue. But of course it was true, thought Sappho, diving down angrily into the cold water, every one of those words had sprouted in her heart like something that had been planted years before.

Holding her breath, Sappho began to swim underwater, feeling the current dragging her towards the first finger of rock. She could go on for ever, all the way to Turkey, like one of those wind-up mechanical bath toys, the bones in their sockets ground down to powder before she was done. *I am finished*, she thought, treading water as she looked

across the bay towards Kampos. My life here is finished . . .
The sun had disappeared, and down on the deserted beach,
the rows of umbrellas were flapping starkly in the wind.
There was nothing for her here, her life in Athens was over.
But the pain of that was unbearable; and as a great sob
overcame her, she heard herself wailing out loud like an
animal. The sea was empty, there was no one to hear her.
Diving back under the water, she swam further out towards
the horizon.

'What am I going to do, what am I going to do?' she
groaned under her breath, each circular stroke of her arm
powered, seemingly effortlessly, by the sticky black fuel of
her grief.

She had never swum this far out before; the current must
have dragged her further than she thought. Turning
around, she looked back towards the beach. The expanse
of water surrounding her, the swollen glassy emptiness of it,
made her feel nauseous. Not a single person knew she was
out here; if she drowned, nobody would come to save her.
At the thought of her death, a voluptuous wave of pleasure
overcame her: she could end it now, her shame would die
today, with her . . .

No, she thought, treading water, somewhere she would
have to find the strength to reinvent herself, start again; you
couldn't throw away a life just like that. Look at Theo; one
minute he was at home, watching his films and being
babied on the sofa by Ghisela, the next, he was lying on
the attic stairs with one of his own ribs pierced through his
lung. It was as random as that. If she drowned now, her
father's line would end – if not to him, at least she owed it to
her Grandmother Maro to survive. *Not two of us in the
same month, it's too much* . . . Besides, she was too cow-
ardly to die, she knew that now; her despair and shame
were not fierce enough. Resolutely, she turned around and
began to swim back towards the shore.

At first, the waves seemed harmless enough, tidy frills of water slapping into her face as she swam; the unexpected reverse side of the current. Besides, she wasn't all that far from the beach; she could clearly make out the figure standing on the jetty she had noticed earlier on her way down the path. But soon she found herself having to tilt back her head as she swam to stop the water going up her nose, and she didn't like what happened if she let her neck drop forward.

Sappho knew she wasn't a particularly stylish swimmer, but she had stamina, that was the one thing she did have, and she'd learned to swim in those seas. *If anyone can make it, it's you* . . . Turning around, she tried to gauge how far she had swum; no – it wasn't possible! Not only had she not made any progress, but she actually seemed to be further away from the shore than before.

OK, the trick is to stay calm . . . She was a wind-up toy, *you're a wind-up toy*, she would get there in the end. But, inexplicably, her swimming mechanism seemed to have jammed, her limbs ached, and something about the rhythm of the waves was confusing her, cutting into her strokes. 'You never swim in a *meltemi*,' her Grandmother Maro always used to say. But the sea hadn't looked that rough, thought Sappho, you wouldn't have even known they were waves.

Nothing in her body worked properly any more, she had lost the will to keep moving, and the *slap, slap* of the water in her face was making a mockery of her efforts to keep her head above the surface. Bad adrenalin crackled through her, her heart a juddering machine. How was it possible? She was using every ounce of strength she possessed merely to remain on the spot. She would tire in the end, it was inevitable; soon she would stop fighting the current and let it carry her away. She was one person, while the enemy was all around her, mysterious, implacable; there was nothing in it she could appeal to. 'Help me,' she cried, 'help me, someone,' her mouth gurgling with brine like a person who was already drowning. Coughing and gulping, she looked towards the beach; the figure on the jetty down by the fishing boats had gone. So this was it; she was going to die alone.

I'll do anything to live, anything it takes . . . her life had blossomed before her eyes into a thing of beauty; how could she never have seen it? She still had to do an art course, visit Istanbul, look through her father's papers in the attic. She couldn't die now, she wasn't even through with mourning Theo . . . It didn't matter about Lorna and Alexander, she forgave her father everything, *you can't knock a man when he's dead* . . .

Treading water again, she resolved to make one last effort to swim towards the shore; she owed it to this new sense of wonder at least to try. Closing her eyes, she gathered her forces inwards in an attempt to still her heart; but it was hopeless, in her bones she knew she was done for – she might as well give in now, die in peace.

Then she opened her eyes, and found herself staring at a miracle.

A rowing boat was approaching from the direction of Vagia. There was no mistaking it – it was definitely coming towards her! Sappho hesitated for a moment, suddenly shy about going public with her predicament – *like at this point it really matters* – then called out: 'Help! Help!' Her voice sounded reedy, pathetic, as though she was acting a part. *Is this what you do when you're drowning . . .?* In the distance, she saw the rower raise one arm in salute to show that he had heard her: the nightmare was over, she was safe.

All at once, the fog in her mind cleared, and a great lassitude overcame Sappho; she understood now she should stop fighting the waves, as she should have done from the start, let the current drag her to a place of rest; someone would have seen her in the end from the road. Lying down on her back, she succumbed to the current, allowing the water to carry her out further, towards the second finger of rock. The boat was getting nearer, she was close enough to make out the name painted in Greek letters down the side: it was *Moira*, which meant destiny, but the significance of that would only come to her later.

'Here, grab on to this,' said a man's voice. Sappho turned around, and looked up. A chunky light-haired man in a brown Fred Perry tracksuit top was holding out an oar in the water. She stared up at him; he was pale and sweaty, panting, as though he were part of an entirely different crisis. Everything about her had become hyper-real; who *was* this man, how could he have just appeared like that in his boat?

'Are you OK?'

She nodded, resting her elbows on the side of the boat, as though she had just stopped for a chat.

'Can you pull yourself up?' he said slowly, enunciating every word. Then it came to Sappho: *Oh I see – he thinks I'm foreign.*

Somewhere, deep inside, lay buried a voice – her voice – but she couldn't appear to locate it. It suddenly seemed important to consider her words before she spoke . . .

Cradle-snatcher. Brother-fucker . . .

The man hesitated for a moment; then resting the oar on the side of the boat, he leaned forward. 'Put your arm around my neck, and I'll pull you up,' he said.

Obediently, Sappho placed her wet arms around his shoulders, and the man dragged her up out of the water. Stumbling over the oars, she crouched down on the little wooden bench, hugging her knees to her chest.

'Here, take this,' said the man, unzipping his brown tracksuit top and placing it around her shoulders.

I didn't die, thought Sappho, as she watched him rowing

back to the jetty, I didn't die back then! And yet instead of triumph, she was filled with a kind of dreariness: so was that it then? *You still fucked your brother* –

'You gave me a fright, I thought I wouldn't get to you in time,' said the man with a sudden catch in his voice.

Sappho paused and looked up at him, vainly trying to connect with his drama. Was she still in shock, perhaps? I've been through rather a lot recently, she thought to herself in wonder.

How old was he? Thirty, thirty-five? He was very fair-skinned, with dense blond hairs covering his stocky limbs. She lowered her gaze before their eyes had a chance to meet. She didn't want anyone peering into her soul right now. On his feet he wore a pair of sensible-looking neoprene trekking sandals with Velcro straps. A picture came into her mind of Alexander's beautiful brown feet in his leather monks' sandals, and she felt her throat constrict with sorrow. Was it just yesterday they had swum together in the lake, that long, wilful swoon before they made love?

'Can I call anyone for you? Get someone to come and collect you? I left my mobile in my rucksack down by the jetty.'

Sappho shook her head, waiting for the lump in her throat to subside. She had never lain on his back with her stomach in the hollow of his spine, her pubis pressed against his buttocks, where she knew it would fit, she just *knew* it, and now she never would –

'Or is there anywhere I can take you?'

'My house is just there,' she enunciated slowly, turning around and pointing towards the edge of the cliff.

He paused, letting the oars drop to his side. 'You mean you live here? On Patmos?'

'Just sometimes. I'm visiting.' Her teeth were beginning to chatter, and she felt a tremor run through her thighs. She clasped her hands around her ankles to keep them still, pressing her jaw hard against the bones of her kneecaps.

'Not long to go now,' he said, easing the boat skilfully back up towards the jetty. Looping the rope through one of the rings sunk into the concrete, he pulled the knot a couple of times to test it, then stood up and held out his hand. Wordlessly, Sappho took it and stepped out of the rocking boat on to the jetty.

Removing the tracksuit top from her shoulders, she handed it back to him. He took it, and stuffed it into a small rucksack he had left on a rusty oil drum. 'Lucky no one nicked this – my passport's in here, and my wallet, and my mobile,' he grinned, picking it up and peering briefly inside. 'Nope, looks like it's all here!'

He seemed like a kind man, thought Sappho, sensible and kind, but her silence was making him uncomfortable, she could tell.

'I'd better go and get changed,' she said, looking up towards the house. The women had gone, the driveway was empty, but they had left the door of the kitchen terrace ajar. Not that it mattered any more, in the way that nothing did now. In silence, they began to walk along the stony beach towards the path, listening to the pebbles crunching drily beneath their feet. Her legs felt shaky as though she had just got out of bed after a long illness. She would catch the ferry to Piraeus anyway that night, there was no way she would sit here waiting for Celia to return.

'So that's me then,' he said, as they reached the hired moped parked at the end of the path. Awkwardly, they looked at each other.

She would have drowned if he hadn't turned up, no doubt about it, she thought, staring at the peeling Australis Moto Rent sticker on the windshield. She ought to say something to him – anything – but her mind seemed incapable of coming up with the appropriate words.

'Are you sure you'll be OK?'

She nodded, aware of her nipples protruding obscenely under her wet costume. Self-consciously, she folded her arms across her chest.

'Really sure?'

She smiled, in spite of herself. He too had crossed his arms, mirroring her body language, which she remembered was a sign of sexual attraction. He likes me, she thought, and, obscurely, this knowledge pleased her. There was a split second's silence, where a faster man might have asked her for her telephone number, but the stranger didn't, which, more puzzlingly, also pleased her.

'What's your name?' she said suddenly.

Unexpectedly, the man flushed. So she was right, he did like her. 'Tom. My name is Tom. And what about yours?'

Sappho paused, instantly regretting her words. She couldn't deal with intimacy, not now.

'It doesn't really matter . . . not now, but it was nice meeting you, anyway. And thanks,' she mumbled, deliberately turning towards the gate, so that her words remained unheard.

Thirty-two

He'd been dazzled by Sappho from the moment he laid eyes on her on Patmos, *the evening I pulled my darling out of the sea* . . .

He never expected to run into her again on the island; he was leaving that night on the midnight ferry to Piraeus; and besides, apart from the actual rescuing, which he supposed had been ultimately successful (in that she didn't drown), he'd managed to bungle almost every single other aspect of their first encounter.

'*Jerk! Prick! Loser!*' he howled to the wind, as he drove back down to the port on his hired moped. He hadn't even got her name, let alone a telephone number. Back in the hotel, after returning the moped to the garage and picking up his deposit, he sat on the unmade bed and looked at his rucksack. The ferry to Athens was leaving in two hours. He had time for a coffee and a last wander around the harbour.

A name. Since when was it such a big deal to give someone your name? It's not like he was coming on heavy to her; you'd think it was the least she could do in return for him having saved her life. *Ding-dong – hello? She was in shock maybe?* Locking the hotel door behind him, Tom walked out into the cobbled alleyway towards the port.

He'd tried to string out the walk back from the beach to her house as long as possible, but by the time they reached the gate, he still hadn't managed to tip himself over the edge enough to ask to see her again.

Her house! Tom stopped outside a stall in the harbour selling sponges. Of course – he knew where she lived! Why hadn't it occurred to him before?

OK, this is what you do: you catch a taxi back up to Vagia – fuck the ferry – and go and knock on her door. And . . . And then what? Charm her with a bit more of his dazzling repartee? She'd been crying, when he pulled her out of the water, he was almost certain of that. She had beautiful eyes, light green with flecks of gold, her long lashes gummed into spikes by her tears.

Come to think of it, there'd been something strange about the whole business; from the jetty, he'd watched her crouched over the stones, hugging her sides, almost as though she was feeling ill; then, without warning, she'd got up and walked straight into the sea. She must have known about the *meltemi*; down at the hotel, both the concierge and the receptionist had warned him not to swim. And she wasn't even a tourist: she had to have been aware of the danger. Maybe she had walked into the sea deliberately, changed her mind at the last minute.

Tom paused outside the taxi rank. A cruise liner had disgorged its evening cargo of tourists, ready for dinner at a taverna and a whistlestop tour of the monastery up at Chora. The drivers, who had been leaning lazily over the roofs of their cabs, suddenly grew animated, sidling down into their seats and switching on their engines, ready for the onslaught.

Anyway, she probably had a boyfriend; they must have had a barney and she'd stormed off into the sea to teach him a lesson. No wonder she didn't exactly invite him in for a coffee when they reached the house. One, two, three, four, five, six, seven . . . The taxis were all taken, and the last bus had left long before; he couldn't even get up to the house if he wanted to. *Forget it, man, this kind of thing's not your style, anyway . . .*

Slowly, Tom walked back towards the harbour. Sitting down on a bench, he watched a woman on a scooter leaning over the handlebars holding a round loaf of village bread in her arms. By the end of the week, he would be back in London, ready to sort out the last flat in Ladbroke Grove. The holiday on Patmos had been an impulsive treat; he needed to get the smell of building dust out of his nostrils, at least for a few days. A holiday fling had never been on the cards, or at least not consciously. Who knows – if it had, he might have been a little more on the ball with that girl. So, he had saved her life . . . and then what?

Fallen in love with her?

No. Yes. No.

Picking up his rucksack off the bench, Tom walked towards the church on the harbour. Somewhere inside him, above his stomach, wrapped in layers of damp newspaper, lay his heart. Without which he was capable of nothing.

Was nothing.

(Would always be nothing . . .)

Turning around, he looked back towards the taxi rank: one of the cabs was already back from Chora; the neon cube light on its roof glimmered palely in the evening air.

Pressing his hand against his chest, at the very place where the damp bundle uselessly squatted, he closed his eyes, willing himself not to notice the vacant taxis behind him, a long line of them now, mocking him with their availability. '*Kalispera . . . Vagia, parakaló.*' Not so hard, really. But it was hopeless, he didn't have it in him: as simple as that. *At least you know you're not a player.*

On an impulse, Tom pushed open the heavy wooden door of the church and stepped inside. He would hide in there until it was time to board the ferry.

An old woman dressed in black was sitting on a wooden chair in the vestibule, crocheting a foamy piece of lace which gleamed on her lap like a thin little disc of moonlight. She was so tiny that her mottled stick-like legs barely reached the floor. She stared at Tom as he entered; then, not unkindly, she motioned for him to leave his rucksack on the floor beside another holdall.

The church was in semi-darkness, illuminated only by a circle of tall yellow candles on a beaten metal stand, crammed tightly together, like stalks of burning corn. The acrid smell of incense filled the air.

That's when he saw her, the girl from the beach. She was standing with her back to him, beneath an icon, burying one of those thin candles into a bed of sand.

Her wet hair was tied in a ponytail off her face; and she was wearing jeans and a dark blue jumper zipped up to the neck. Out in the harbour a ship's horn sounded, reverberating through his body like a heartbeat.

She looked up at him, her face flaring like an angel's in the circle of light.

'I leave for Athens tonight. I'm lighting a candle for my journey.'

Even now, he couldn't swear it had happened.

Dazed by love, he'd stood at dawn on the deck of the ferry, watching the stained concrete apartment blocks of Piraeus drift into view. The air was so polluted that in the smog everything shimmered in the distance like a sepia photograph. She stood beside him, *Sappho! Her name was Sappho!*, sipping the tea in a polystyrene cup he had bought her from the cafeteria.

She was quiet, but he'd been expecting that; the important thing was that she was still there, beside him. All night long, he had watched her as she lay, fully dressed, on the bunk beneath him. Once, she called out in her sleep; and when he looked down, he saw in the glow of the nightlight that her lips were pulled back in a kind of sneer, her cheeks wet with tears. They hadn't so much as held hands, yet she was already his.

Oh no, he wasn't taking any chances this time! It wasn't every day you got a second chance like that. No more Mr Nice Guy; from now on, they were doing things properly. Freed of its involucrum of damp newspapers, his heart careened and battered against his ribcage like a wild animal.

As the ship drew into the port, Tom could make out smudged figures standing on the quayside in the hazy yellow light: tourists, port officials in short sleeves, an old man with crates of chickens, a couple standing beside a motorbike, a woman holding a baby, a group of gypsy women in brightly coloured shawls.

So, did he or didn't he see him? *I don't know, you tell me* . . . A young dark man in an open-necked white shirt, one arm raised in salute. He was waving to her. To Sappho. His girl. (Or more likely to one of the hundreds of other people on that crowded deck.) Who knows? *You tell me.*

Tom just remembered turning to her, questioningly, but with a stab of panic, *not again, please*; and then, without warning, Sappho lifting her face to his, and kissing him full on the lips.

Even now, it had to rank as one of the most thrilling moments of his life; he'd been poleaxed by that kiss, literally. Standing amongst all those people on the deck, the thrumming of the ship's engine, the sound of car horns mingling with the *trac-trac-trac* of the anchor chain being pulled in, all that bustle and confusion, and at its centre, a great stillness and joy.

So this is what it means to live . . .

Thirty-three

When Sappho awoke, it had grown dark.

From the bathroom, she heard lusty hawking and spitting; the unfamiliar sounds of an Anglo-Saxon man cleaning his teeth. Then the metallic swoosh of the shower curtain along the rail, and water drumming like pebbles on to the tiled floor.

Sappho looked at her jeans folded over a chair. *Off with the clothes. Into the bed. Change your partners, one two three.*

Another temple defiled. Two men in forty-eight hours, though they hadn't made love. Until now, she had never had so much as a one-night stand. *Lost my father, fucked my brother, all in a day's work.* Her body seemed literally capable of anything now, she didn't trust it any more; it frightened her.

Drawing back the sheet, Sappho got up from the bed and reached for her underwear. Quickly, she dressed before Tom re-emerged from the bathroom. She didn't want to wash yet; the smell of his body on her skin was like a talisman, swimmers' grease, protecting her against the harsher elements which lay beyond this room.

At some point, she was going to have to go back to the house in Filoppapou, decide what to do. Tomorrow Tom was leaving for London, his aeroplane ticket was on the bedside table. One day, she thought, he would look back on this as the strangest holiday fling that never happened.

She would have drowned on Patmos; she had stared death in its mean, implacable face. One second more and it would have been too late. Her heart lurched as she remembered the salty water gurgling down her throat, the sea pulling her down to itself like it already owned her. But she didn't drown, because from out of nowhere, it seemed, Tom had appeared with that boat . . . *Moira*: destiny. She shuddered: it seemed her destiny had been written long before, in that photograph of her parents and Lorna on the Vespa.

He had the kindest face she'd ever seen; as they lay on the bed, he held her in his arms, demanding nothing from her, as though he understood she had nothing to give. They had taken off their clothes before they lay down, but chastely, like children. Maybe after that kiss on the deck – *I had to, though! I had no choice!* – he'd expected more, who knows; yet, modestly, no matter how close they lay, his sex never touched her. A great sadness lay over the room. She would take his address in London, write to him, and maybe even one day go in person to thank him properly.

Sappho got up from the bed and walked towards the window. Long linen curtains hung to the ground, the hems rimmed with grey like a pencil line. She heard the whine of the hotel lift; then the sound of the bathroom door opening.

'So you're awake?' He smiled at her uncertainly. He had washed his hair, and he was wearing a grey T-shirt, with long, khaki-coloured shorts. There were shadows under his eyes, as though he hadn't slept enough.

Sappho nodded, aware of the sleeping sand in her eyes, the dryness in the corner of her lips.

'So?'

She smiled thinly. 'So, what?'

'So what happens now?'

'I thought I'd go back home, let you enjoy your last night in Athens in peace.' It was better this way, no point dragging things out.

'And where's home?'

'Not far from here . . . the other side of the Acropolis.'

That bed, with rumpled sheets, waiting for me . . . a fist of black horror clenched her heart. It was Alexander on the quayside, she was almost certain it was.

'I leave tomorrow morning, Sappho . . . my flight is at seven.'

'I know. I saw your ticket.'

From the next-door room came the muffled sound of a TV, followed by a thumping on the wall.

'Why don't you come with me?'

'Come where?'

'To London.'

He looked like someone who'd jumped over a cliff, his face whipped bare of its defences. Unexpectedly, she felt her heart quicken with tenderness.

'You're mad, Tom. You hardly know me.'

His eyes gleamed, completely transforming his face. 'I don't care. Plenty of time for that.'

He walked towards the window and, grimacing slightly, ran his thumb along the gaping crack between the wall and the sill.

'That's Greek builders for you,' she smiled. Everything about this man was a blank slate; she knew nothing about him, nor he about her. *Remember, all he knows is what he sees . . .*

'Look, come and stay with me as my guest . . . simple as that.'

'Simple as what?' teased Sappho. Everything was hurtling into place, all the broken pieces magically reconfiguring. Who knows, maybe she was the one who was mad.

'No strings . . . you know what I mean.'

'I'm not sure if I do, Tom . . . and anyway,' she took a deep breath, 'maybe strings are what I need now.'

For the second time that day they kissed, only this time properly.

She was sober when Sappho came to collect the keys.

'I thought you'd turn up. Alexander left these for you.' Reaching inside the dark *garconiera*, Lorna picked up a pair of keys on a ring and dropped them carelessly into Sappho's hand.

Washing was strung up on the roof; a tie-dye smock, shorts, socks, vests, Alexander's paint-stained work trousers. And everywhere, a profusion of plants in rusting oil containers.

Lorna had changed surprisingly little; her skin was more lined, in the way of most Northern Europeans after years of the harsh Greek sun, and the veins around her nose and cheeks were more pronounced, but her hooded, sea-glass eyes were clear. And she had kept that amazing figure.

At the sight of her, Sappho felt the words shrivel up inside her. All the things she had been meaning to say, the bitter little speech she had rehearsed in her mind as she walked through the covered market from Tom's hotel to the *garconiera* in Omonia – *you destroyed our family, you were the cancer of my childhood, I hope you're satisfied now* – vanished at Lorna's eerie composure.

And she was literally overwhelmed by memories of the past, so many of them: her parents and Lorna weeping with laughter around the kitchen table on a winter's afternoon in Athens, the purr of the charcoal stove; the rectory in Hastings, Lorna wiping her tears on her sleeve as she watched their taxi pull up in the driveway – *the night she turned up drunk in the house in East Sheen, and you looked her in the eye as she stood on the doorstep in her tatty man's jacket, and you betrayed her like a Judas.*

'I'm not sure what games you've been playing with Alexander, Saff . . . but leave him alone now. Please.'

So it *was* him on the quayside in Piraeus; he had seen her kiss Tom on the ferry: a stunning bull's-eye. *It was the only way, remember you had no choice . . .*

'That's a bit rich, coming from you,' mumbled Sappho weakly, trying to gather her wits.

Lorna crossed her arms over the bib of her overalls, and wound a strand of her greying, blonde hair behind one ear. The half-glimpsed *garconiera* behind her looked surprisingly neat; two single beds, side by side, a table and two chairs in one corner, with a cooking area in the other: a sink, fridge and portable hotplate attached to a gas bottle. *Is this what you were so scared of?*

'You're right, Saff, I haven't been a good mother to my son. I fucked everything up in my life. But I did my best with Alexander, he's a kind-hearted boy . . . you know he doesn't deserve this.'

By tomorrow morning, she would be gone, none of this would matter any more. For the second time, she would be flying to London, leaving Lorna and her mess behind. She must cauterise this pain in her heart. *He doesn't deserve this*: of course he didn't, Alexander had done nothing wrong.

Sappho felt the words popping out of her mouth, singly, like breaking ampoules of poison.

'Alexander's been hassling me, Lorna. And it has to stop.'

Lorna flinched, but only for a second. 'You were such a cold child, Sappho . . . I don't really think love is your bag.'

325

London, 2003

Thirty-four

Tom picked up the baby and wrapped it in a shawl; it was cold out in the corridor. He climbed the two flights of stairs to the top of the house and pushed open the door. The curtains were drawn, but he knew Laleh was awake; she would have heard the baby's cries over the monitor.

Pecking blindly at his neck, the baby flexed its strong little legs, digging his toes rhythmically into the shelf of his stomach; it was nearly three hours since his last feed. 'You're a hungry man,' whispered Tom, sliding a bent finger into the baby's mouth. He felt the shard of a tooth, the first, breaking through the bottom gum.

For a moment, he stood in the doorway, hesitating.

'Come in,' said Laleh, switching on the lamp beside the bed. She sat up and passed the back of one hand across her eyes. Her hair hung in two glistening plaits over her shoulders; she must have washed it before going down for her nap. A towel lay spread out over the pillow, a darker patch in the middle like the shadow of her head. Tom entered the room and, kneeling beside the bed, placed the baby in her outstretched arms. He watched as Laleh drew the shawl tighter, subduing the writhing body in its folds; then unbuttoning her shirt, she held the baby to her breast.

Tom exhaled as relief flooded through him; only now did he realise he had been holding his breath. He stood up and looked about him; her clothes were folded tidily over a chair and the room smelt pleasantly musty. Of Laleh, he thought. A book lay open on the desk, beside a jug of water and a glass. He walked across the wooden floor towards the window. In a corner of the ledge, a pair of wasps were locked in an ambiguous, polyphonic embrace, conjoined thoraxes flicking against the glass. Through a gap in the curtains he peered down on to the street. Two builders sat eating their sandwiches on some scaffolding which had gone up just that morning: looked like a roofing job. One of them had taken off his shirt, his long weaselly torso stretched out in the pale sunshine. Someone had left the garden gate open and drifts of leaves had settled over the path. Later he would bag them up for the binmen to collect.

He turned towards the bed. Glassy-eyed, the baby lay slumped over Laleh's arm as she caressed his back in long upward strokes. His mouth was half-open, cheeks flushed and engorged; with his head lolling forward, he looked drunk on milk. A pair of silver bangles on her wrist tinkled with the rhythmic movement of her arm. A blue vein snaked from her collarbone down one breast; the skin on her body was a sallow, brilliant white, paler than her face. You could tell she'd never sunbathed, thought Tom. He shut his eyes, resting his cheek on the cool glass of the windowpane.

Downstairs, a door slammed and there was the sound of footsteps in the hallway. Laleh gave a start, gathering up the collar of her shirt around her throat. For a moment, they stared at each other without speaking. Then Tom got up from beside the window and took the baby from her arms.

'Mummy's home,' he said.

Thirty-five

Enzo arrived fifteen minutes early for their appointment in the park.

Somehow, he knew she'd be the punctual type, she had that severe look about her, and he didn't want to risk getting things off on the wrong footing by being late. It was a miracle that she'd even agreed to meet him; so much so that a part of him was resigned to her blowing him out. Not that he'd have been the slightest bit daunted if she had; anticipating it could take weeks, even months, to get Laleh to go out with him, he'd managed to rearrange all his shifts with Sayyan and Claire, so that now he'd always be on lifeguard duty when she brought the little girl to her lesson. One way or another, he would just browbeat her into another date.

Then, just like that, after weeks of giving him the cold shoulder, she'd said yes. 'I come.' The astonishment must have been evident on his face, because she smiled. Which had the effect of making her even more beautiful, assuming such a thing were possible.

'Where . . . where you like we meet?'

'You know café in Queen's Park? I come here at Saturday morning, nine a.m.'

So there he was, at eight forty-five, prudently early, sitting on a bench, watching a park keeper in orange headphones hoovering up leaves with one of those noisy fuel-powered blowers. Enzo felt sleepy; Margherita, one of the girls he shared with, had friends staying from Udine, and they'd had a noisy *spaghettata* in the kitchen when they got back from clubbing in King's Cross. As he left for the park, he had to step over sleeping bags and wine bottles to get to the door, noticing on the way that Stefano and Paola seemed to have got their shit together at last – Margherita said they'd liked each other for years, ever since *liceo* . . .

Enzo drew his padded bodywarmer closer around him, sliding his fingers into the pockets; it was cold, hopefully the café would have opened its doors by the time she arrived. Then across the park, towards the bandstand, he became aware of a figure with a pram walking across the grass. It was her; he recognised her ugly maroon jacket. Thank God he'd come early; she might have left if she'd found no one there. Unable to sit still, Enzo stood up, debating whether to walk towards her. Of course there would be those corny few seconds of slow motion as they approached each other, eyes lowered, but he didn't care; it seemed too dishonest to turn away and simply pretend he hadn't seen her.

He was relieved to see she had only the single buggy with her; she was always so attentive towards the children she looked after that she would have scarcely said a word to him if they had been present. And yet it was also one of the things that made her so attractive to him.

'Hello, Laleh.' Sensing that any attempt to kiss her would be absolutely the wrong move, Enzo held out his hand to shake hers. 'You come,' he added unnecessarily. Her fingers were icy and the tip of her nose was becomingly pink.

'You like drink coffee? Tea?'

'I like.'

Together they walked across the grass to the café. Enzo felt extraordinarily elated, as though he'd managed to inveigle a teacher out on a date. And yet they were probably the same age; he would be thirty next birthday, though most people still took him for twenty-five. He dressed and behaved like a far younger man, while Laleh . . . Laleh gave out the vibes of an old soul, someone who had lived through several lifetimes.

'Your baby sleep?' He peered into the pram; Reza stared back solemnly through a curtain of thick lashes.

'Later sleep. Only finish breakfast now.'

What did you have for breakfast, young man? Enzo nearly said it, but again he held his tongue. An image flashed into his mind of her beautiful heavy breast, a single drop of milk hanging from the tip of the nipple. *Respect*, he told himself sternly; she was a goddess and a mother.

The café had opened now, and the gardener he had noticed earlier was already in line at the counter.

'You like sit inside or out?'

'Outside. Cold is good for make Reza sleep.'

A caffè latte would warm him up, though no doubt it would be weak as dishwater, as coffee invariably was in this country.

'What I get for you?'

'I like tea. Please.'

Was that a smile that came with the 'please'? Enzo wondered as he waited in the queue to be served. She had a sense of humour, he could have sworn she had, though he had precious little proof of it until now. Something teasing about her manner, like she knew he adored her, but was too stern with herself to flirt back.

Through the window, he watched Laleh rock the handles of the pushchair; her hair was as dark as the Sicilian girls' back home, glossy and clean-looking, hanging over her shoulder in a heavy plait. Yet no Italian girl, not even the most wretched *figlia di mamma*, would be seen dead in such middle-aged clothes. With legs like that, she should be in a

333

miniskirt, thought Enzo indignantly, or at the very least a pair of spray-on jeans.

Carrying the drinks on a tray, he walked out into the courtyard. To his satisfaction, he saw that Reza had fallen asleep; for a while, at least, he could pretend they were on a real date.

Enzo sat down opposite her at the table. He took the lid off his cup and blew the anaemic-looking foam into peaks. Far too much milk, as usual; he should have asked them to only half fill it.

'Today you not at pool?'

'I no work weekends. You?'

Laleh paused, while stirring her tea. 'Sometimes I take children to park.'

'Is work? Or no work?'

'Is . . . help,' she said guardedly. She frowned, as though uncertain whether to continue. 'Children's mother tired with new baby.'

'And you no tired? You have baby also.'

'Reza sleep good now. Not so difficult for me.'

'How long you been in London?'

'One year . . . almost.'

'So Reza born in this country?' He was seven months old – twelve minus seven was five, nine minus five was four – she'd been four months pregnant when she'd left her country. What could have forced her to leave in those circumstances?

He was sailing dangerously close to the wind with his questions, he knew it, but he wanted to get as many answers as possible before she gathered her wits enough to rebuff him. Not having the children with her, being off-duty, so to speak, seemed to have made her relax her guard.

'Which country you from?'

'From Iran.'

'Your husband there?' *Too soon, coglione – you've blown it.*

'I have no husband.'

'And father of Reza?'

'Reza . . . he have no father.'

Enzo's heart cracked with joy. There was no other man in her life . . . his boldness had paid off! One day she would tell him her story, but for now he didn't need to know; the field was clear, that was all that mattered.

He looked down at the child asleep in the pram, and his heart flooded with tenderness. He would love the boy, be his protector, cherish this sweet nascent family.

'For have Reza you must to leave your country?' he enquired recklessly.

'For this . . . and other things.'

'You are refugee?'

'Not refugee. Asylum seeker. Is different.'

At once her face grew hard and closed, as though she were withdrawing into the private darkness of her past. He felt desperately sorry for her, ached to communicate solidarity with her situation. But he had to get her out of that tunnel before she retreated into herself.

'I know many refugee in my country. Come from Liberia.'

'Which your country?'

'My country Sicily. You know Italy map? Is shape boot? Sicily is island on toe, like football. Many refugees – we call *extracomunitari*, because from country outside Europe community – is come to us because Sicily first country after Africa.'

'Is not only Sicily come refugee in Italy. Also Lichy arrive many . . . like me.'

'Lichy? Where is Lichy?' Frantically, Enzo racked his brains; the important thing was to keep the conversation moving, the flame ardent.

'Is other side, in front Albanie.'

'Ah, you mean Lecce?'

'Is what I say, no?'

'You right, I no hear good. Too much swimming-pool water in my ear. You say you arrive Lecce?'

'I say that. But now I finish talk about me. How long you are in England?'

'I come two years in May.'

'Why you leave your country? Italy is good place.'

'My town very small. See same faces every day. I boring.'

'No boring, must say bored.'

'Again you right. I bored in my town.'

'Italy have many beautiful cities.'

'Is true. One day I take you. You like? We visit Roma, Venezia, Napoli?'

'Is impossible. I cannot to travel. I have no document.'

'Where is your passport? Everybody must have passport. Or maybe *carta d'identita* like my one.' He pulled out his ID card from the back pocket of his jeans. Wordlessly, she took it from him and glanced down at the creased photograph. Idiot, his hair was too long, he looked like a pot head in that picture. Hurriedly, he slipped it back into his pocket.

'My passport is bottom of river in Istanbul. The fishes eat now, I think.'

'You lose, or thief is take?'

'No thief want passport from my country,' she said scornfully. 'Is useless for all persons. I throw away.'

'You throw away your passport?'

'When begin my journey. All smuggler tell is better arrive UK with no papers.'

'Is correct, I forget this. In my town, is name "Realmonte" – *Re-al-mon-te* – many times we find passport wash up on beach. When arrive *profughi* – is how we call refugee in Italian – they never has no passport. Only dollar in trainers, for this they is never separate from shoes.'

'You wait permission now to stay in UK?'

'I wait,' she repeated simply.

'How is called the permit you need?'

'Is name "Indefinite Leave to Remain". From Home Office. Every day I wait this letter, but no letter come.'

'And if no have permission?'

'If no give permit . . . I must . . . I must to return to my country.'

She couldn't leave him, not now that he loved her. *Stai calmo, stronzo, non ti agitare* . . . He would marry her and adopt Reza, they would have another child of their own, his life would finally acquire purpose and beauty.

'Now I must to go home. Have plenty things do before Reza is wake.'

'Is too early to go, look is ten o'clock – all of London is still sleep!'

'I must do homeworks. Houseworks. Too many things.'

There was no point hassling her. Far wiser to capitalise on the new bright understanding that had grown between them by tying her down to another date.

'When I can see you again?'

'I come pool for lesson. Friday afternoon, like always,' she said mischievously.

'Outside pool. You, me, Reza – like this.'

'You want I cook you? Food from my country?'

'Where?' he said stupidly. She had a habit of wrongfooting him with these sudden bursts of intimacy.

'In my flat. You come Thursday evening. Is across park, you see house with green door?'

'Hmmm, Laleh . . . I not sure . . . maybe I too busy that day . . . maybe I am boring to come . . .'

He lowered his eyes, concentrating on subduing the grin that was threatening to split his face in two. She had offered to cook for him; there could be no better sign that she liked him. He even had her address, what more could he ask for? She would never elude him again!

'Goodbye, Enzo, I see you Thursday.'

She got up and held out her hand. Without thinking, he kissed it, breathing in the smell of her skin. Her fingers smelled of soap, with a faint undertone of onion. The smell of a real woman who cooked real food, not like the English girls he had met until now, who seemed to subsist on crisps and convenience foods, and those abominable pots of rehydrated noodles that Claire at the pool had every day for lunch.

Settling back in his seat, Enzo watched her walk across the park. There was nothing in the world he liked more than a woman cooking for him, unless of course it was him cooking for a woman. There was no greater joy to be had in life . . . food, love and sex, preferably all combined into the one occasion, though he flushed with shame, and something like panic, at the thought of importuning Laleh too soon. He would wait as long as it took, years if necessary, before even attempting to kiss her.

The next thing to arrange would be her coming over to the flat in Mozart Street for Sunday lunch. He would beg Margherita, Carlo and Stefano to go out for the afternoon, then he would move Carlo's things from the sitting room where he slept and bring in the dressing table from Margherita's room.

Pasta or risotto, that was the question. Of course! He would make Sicily's national dish, *spaghetti alle sarde*. Fresh sardines from the fishmonger on Golborne Road, fennel from the market, and he would go down to the Italian on College Road to see if he could pick up pine nuts and sultanas, and some real perciatelli. A light salad of rocket from Margherita's pots on the balcony, followed by homemade cannoli stuffed with ricotta for dessert.

He watched her stop outside the house with the green painted door and let herself in with the key. The people she worked for must be well-off to live in such an area. And yet they employed an asylum seeker with no papers to look after their children . . . The ways of the rich were a mystery sometimes.

A few minutes later, he caught sight of a stocky fair-haired man pushing a pram, a little girl beside him, walking up the driveway of the same house. She was a sweet child . . . Mary . . . Maria . . . no, Maro, that was it. The father looked familiar too; several times he'd seen him go upstairs to the gym when he was doing late-night sessions at the pool. Drove a great big Volvo estate, which was now parked in the driveway.

He looked at his watch: ten thirty. He ached to share his happiness with somebody; if he didn't, he might have to do a few backflips across the grass to let off steam, get rid of some of that pent-up joy welling inside him.

He would go back to the flat, fry up some eggs for the others, then once Margherita was properly awake, he would tell her about Laleh.

Thirty-six

He was a leaky barrel of radioactive waste that had been dumped in their house. Everything about the man disgusted her – and she was not the one sharing his bed.

With the elongated scoop of his little finger nail, he would pick his teeth and dig out the wax from his ears; and when he thought no one was looking he rearranged his privates, then sniffed his fingers like someone in love with his own smell. In the evenings, as he sat on the couch watching his western video cassettes, and drinking his contraband Scotch, he would slip his hand under the high waistband of his trousers, watching the girls all the while out of the corner of his eye.

She would look at Ladan, as she lay on her bed in their old room for her nap, filled with despair and disgust at the thought of the man's DNA clinging to her sister's skin, transferring itself on to her own pillow as she slept. Ashamed, she would change the sheets before getting into her bed that night, wiping the tears with her sleeve as she carried them into the bathroom to wash. She, who had always loved her sister's flesh more than her own . . . She wanted to say to Ladan: *tell me, talk about it if it makes you feel better*, but a kind of shame prevented her. She was a foolish virgin who would never be able to comprehend the horror of her sister's nights.

Marriage to the man had brutalised Ladan; when she wasn't sleeping, all she wanted to do was watch Jordanian soap operas on the television, refusing to pick up her books from the university, or even go for a walk.

Then, today at the bath house, Laleh saw the bruises. Ten dirty fingers on her sister's thighs. In that instant, murder became her destiny; if he had been standing there before her, she would not have been responsible for her actions. So this is why I was put on this earth, she recalled thinking with a rolling flash of surprise.

At that moment, nothing but his death could have satisfied her. Whatever it took, she would have done it: crammed a poisoned *koofteh* into his mouth as they did to those poor street dogs who wandered the neighbourhood in packs; or if there had been a gun in her possession, she would have known how to fire it, without being shown, aiming straight between those cunning, close-set eyes. And even with no weapon to hand, she would have used her own body as a weapon, throwing herself on to his face and bludgeoning him to death with her skull. But murdering the man would only have left her sister more alone than ever; and she had come to realise that Ladan was slowly losing her mind.

Laleh got up and, pulling aside the curtain, peered out on to the dark street. It was raining and water was rushing along the open drains. She had to act before it was too late; her sister, once so mercurial and light-hearted, was crumpling into her unhappiness like a balled-up sheet of silver foil that would never again regain its lustre. Only the other day, Ladan claimed to have forgotten the trip they had taken with their parents to the Caspian Sea.

'You remember, *jan*, how wet our manteaus became . . .'

'I *think* I remember . . .'

'. . . and then you got told off by that *komiteh* woman when you swam past the barriers into the men's section?'

Ladan smiled at her sadly, apologetically, her neck sinking like a tortoise's right down into her thin shoulders, until they were level with her ears. She had begun biting her nails again, as she used to do when she was a little girl, and the skin around the cuticles was puffy and inflamed. Madar used to dip her fingers in chilli pepper, to make her stop.

'You'll never find a husband if you chew your nails,' she would scold. So Ladan did stop, never imagining this trophy of a husband was to be her reward.

She wanted to shake Ladan, force her back into the reality of their shared past. This life they were leading now was no life; sometimes she wished they had perished with her parents in the earthquake, at least they would all be together. Drawing the curtain behind her, Laleh returned to the settle and pulled her shawl closer about her shoulders.

She must do what she should have done from the beginning: be her sister's shield. *My body is my only weapon.* Underneath his shifty manner, she knew the man desired her; unfortunately most men did.

'Why did God punish me with a beautiful daughter?' her father used to humorously complain when men in the street turned around to boldly stare, and anonymous declarations of love would be slipped under the door.

Because her beauty had never signified anything within her family, Laleh had never allowed it to be a part of who she was; if anything, her behaviour outside the home had always been that of a plain girl; and she had never met a man who had excited even the mildest interest in her.

What was she saving herself for? Another man? It was either that, or else kill their relative. She could not go on another day knowing that he was harming Ladan, beyond the daily abuse that must constitute their conjugal life. Besides which, her own unhappiness was such that initiating sexual relations with the man could add little to its sum.

If anything, self-disgust would lighten the unbearable guilt she felt about having permitted the wedding to go ahead.

Laleh heard a car door slamming, and the sound of the man's key in the lock. He entered the hallway, tunelessly humming an old Googoosh song; he must have been drinking again. This should make her task easier.

As soon as he appeared in the doorway, she could smell the Scotch on his breath. The lapels of his cheap grey jacket were stained; he must have stopped off on the way home for street food. Swaying slightly, he looked down at her crouched on the settle.

'You're not in bed?'

'I waited up for you.'

She watched the uncertainty flicker across those coarse features.

'My fair sister-in-law waited up for me. To what do I owe this honour?'

'I wish to talk to you.'

Her relative pulled out a chair from beneath the table and sat down heavily. He had removed his shoes in the hallway, and she could smell his feet in their nylon socks. Never before had she been so physically aware of his presence; it was like staring into an open sewer, trying to pluck up the courage to wade into it . . . *It's either you or Ladan, one of you has to do it* . . . Her heart was beating furiously, yet at the same time she felt curiously detached. After months of suffering in silence, finally the release of action.

'Is there anything in particular we need to discuss?' he asked sarcastically.

'We need to talk about my sister.'

An expression of low cunning crossed his face. He knew that she had seen the bruises, and he was preparing to play dumb.

'What is there to say? Your sister is not what she seemed

'. . . Sometimes I think she might have tricked me into marriage.'

God give her strength to drive the anger back down her gorge. Briefly, Laleh shut her eyes, waiting for the hot wires of rage to irradiate away from her heart and through her limbs.

'My sister is sick . . . and I believe over time she can only get worse.'

'Sick . . . how do you mean sick?'

'It is an illness more of the mind. She is not happy. Perhaps she is not suited to certain aspects of married life . . . in the way that . . . in the way that other women are.'

'Other women . . .?'

'Other women.'

His features grew suffused and she watched understanding, followed by a spasm of lust, dawning on his face. Already, he was undressing her with his eyes. Puffed up by desire, he was staring at her as though he owned her, as though the keys to the house were already in his hand. She watched his fingers travel down to his crotch, then slide automatically back up to his nostrils.

'On one condition.'

'It is yours to name.'

Laleh stood up and let her shawl fall away from her shoulders. 'The marriage is over . . . my sister is no longer your wife.'

Thirty-seven

Laleh picked up the dark-green recycling boxes from the pavement and dragged them inside the front garden, careful to place them behind the hedge, where they were not visible from the street. These were new, better ones, with lids, after the other boxes had been stolen, and she did not wish to put temptation in anyone's way.

Tom's car was in the driveway, but the house was dark; he must have walked over to the Lofts in Kensal Green. Better this way; while the babies slept, she could complete the finishing touches to her supper for Enzo. The supermarket in Kilburn stocked everything; the herbs were not as fresh as at home, the yoghurt was of an inferior brand, and disgracefully expensive, but at least she had managed to obtain all the ingredients necessary for the meal. She was shocked, and a little ashamed, at how desperately she longed for her first evening with Enzo to be a success.

Easing the buggy up the step, she slid her key inside the lock; and opening the front door, they entered the hallway. As she bent down to remove her bags from the shopping tray, she saw an envelope lying on the black and white floor tiles, half-hidden beneath a pizza delivery leaflet. At once she knew the letter was addressed to her, it was not even necessary to read the name. 'If undelivered, please return to Lunar House, 40 Wellesley Road, Croydon.'

Picking it up, she held the letter in her hand, steadying herself against the polished wooden pineapple on the banister rail. *Why today of all days?* Ever since the coffee with Enzo in the park, her heart had been singing and fluttering like that of a young girl – *because you are still a young girl, in years at least* – then in one stroke the crushing grip of reality. Her future, both of theirs, hers and Ladan's, lay spelled out inside that envelope. No point in delaying; it was better to know her fate now. Pulling off her gloves, she stuffed them into her jacket pocket and ran her finger beneath the flap of the envelope. Her hand was shaking so much she could scarcely get the letter out.

'Dear Ms Motie, We regret to inform you that your claim for asylum in the UK has been unsuccessful . . .'

Letting the paper fall to the ground, Laleh sat down on the bottom step. Her first thought was: why? Why now, when the Turkish contact in Kilburn had received most of the advance payment? Eight thousand dollars, almost all the money she had earned since she had been in this country. All he needed was a further thousand for Ladan to begin her journey. Today, she and the man had even discussed dates: sometime before the first snows of winter caused the mountains on the border to become impassable. Was this to be the pattern of her life from now on? Hope, purpose, love – *so you admit it, you do love him!* – only for the whole lot of it to be snatched away?

Glancing down in the buggy, she looked at the sleeping children. She shouldn't have been so reserved during her interview at the Home Office, it was her fault: her lawyer had told her she must make her story sound dramatic – 'lay it on thick' were the words he used. But when the lady in the interview suite asked about the man, her relative, Laleh felt the words turn to stone in her mouth. How could she describe the horrors of those evenings, when she waited for him to return from the café, his sexual organ already dangling out of his trousers, like that of a dog's, before he'd even made it through the living-room door? The hair around his privates matted and crusty with the emissions of the previous night, grinding his organ into her face as she lay on the couch, whispering shameful words, terrible names that no woman should ever hear, *bitch, whore, dog*, pulling her hair, flicking and biting her nipples like a spiteful girl, while upstairs Ladan lay sleeping. It was this image, and this alone, of her sister's face in repose, the tranquillity she had bought with her body, that each night kept her from spitting in his face.

Afterwards, she would sit on the edge of the toilet and wash her privates with undiluted vinegar; never once flinching as it burned through the lacerations from his unwashed nails, the humping and rubbing which caused the skin between her thighs to crack and peel like chilblains.

Picking herself up from the step, Laleh stuffed the letter into her pocket. Dear, sweet Enzo; soon he would be arriving. Lucky she had done most of the cooking the night before. She had earned this evening with him, she deserved some happiness after all the terrible things she had been through, and nothing was going to ruin it for her. Not even this letter. Tomorrow, when it was over, she would telephone her lawyer and ask what she must do next. Before Sappho got sick, she had been helping her with her case; but now she could ask her nothing, not even advice. A cancer, some savage unhappiness, appeared to be destroying Sappho's marriage, consuming the family along with it, and there was nothing Laleh could do to help. *All I can do is let her know her children are being looked after . . .* Though recently, with Tom, this too had become complicated.

Hector was awake; eyes still closed, he was snaffling and gnawing at his fist. Gently, careful not to disturb Reza, Laleh unzipped his sleeping bag and pulled him up out of the pram. Just then, she heard a noise coming from the

347

direction of the sitting room. She pushed open the door and peered inside. At first the room appeared to be empty, but then she saw Tom sitting in the dark by the unlit fire.

'I'm sorry to disturb, I think no one is here.'

Tom looked up and, to her shock, Laleh saw tears were glistening on his cheeks.

'Is something happen? Maro?'

'I've dropped her off at Bridget's. She's spending the night there.' Tom got up heavily and, rubbing the back of his hand across his eyes, switched on the table lamp beside him.

'And Sappho?'

'She's gone.'

'When she will return?'

Angrily, Tom held out the telephone in his hand. 'You don't understand, Laleh. I've been trying to call her all afternoon. Her mobile's switched off. If she's not back soon, I'm going to have to . . . I don't know what I'll have to do. Here, let me take the baby.'

His face softened as he held his son in his arms.

'I think he's hungry, Laleh.'

Please, no. Not again. 'I have prepared bottle for Hector in fridge. I heat, if you like.'

Tom stared at her above the baby's head. 'We've talked about this before, Laleh. Formula milk is not what Hector needs. His mother is sick, and by the time she's better – assuming she *is* going to get better – it'll be too late for Hector. This is a window in his life which will never come up again.'

'I understand this, but –'

'Allergies, eczema, diabetes – even cot death. Breastfeeding protects against all of them. As if it wasn't enough that his mother is sick, and has now disappeared off the face of the earth,' he added bitterly.

As though he understood his father's words, Hector began to cry, piteously nuzzling against Tom's neck. Her milk was going to waste, anyway; Reza preferred solid food now, and had become impatient each time she tried to put him to the breast. Besides, it wouldn't be the first time she had fed Hector; even before Tom had suggested it, she had already nursed him in secret up in her flat when Sappho had first started disappearing. She couldn't help herself; he had smelled the milk from her breast, it was too cruel to deny him. And if it was wrong to nourish another woman's child . . . well, so was everything else in her life wrong. By this time next month, she might be on an aeroplane headed for home, back into the welcoming arms of their relative. In her letters, Ladan said he had told the neighbours she was working as a prostitute on the streets of the capital. He knew nothing about Reza, no one back home did apart from Ladan. She brushed her hand against her pocket, feeling the hard edge of the envelope crackle. It was finished with Enzo, she thought sadly, their love story was over even before it had the chance to begin.

'Please give to me Hector, I will feed him now.'

She sat down in the armchair beside the lamp, unzipped her jacket, and held out her arms. Smoothing his cheek, she opened the buttons of her blouse, and pulled out one breast from her bra.

As his gums clamped around the nipple, she was aware of Tom, dimly, standing beside the fireplace, of the streetlights shining in through the window. The whole world could see her breasts: she didn't care; she understood now that association with the man had destroyed all sense of shame, to care now was nothing but false modesty.

No matter she had only initiated relations with the man for the sake of Ladan, it was still her fault for having allowed the wedding in the first place. She was marked by him; her life would never regain beauty. He was her curse; the bad luck he had brought on her family would follow her to the ends of the earth.

349

A picture came into her mind of Enzo smiling at her as he brought her tea from the café. He looked so young beside her, with that crazy hair of his, his laughing green eyes; it was difficult to believe they were the same age. If she had been born in this country, if they had met at college like a pair of ordinary European sweethearts . . . who knows what could have happened. I would have married him, she thought, unexpectedly, and the idea of it made her smile.

'Are you happy, Laleh?'

She looked up; Tom was kneeling beside the fireplace, sweeping up the ashes which had fallen from the grate.

'I think maybe happy is not possible for me now. When I am child in my country, with my parents and my sister, yes I am happy . . .'

'I was happy, you know, Laleh. For six years I thought I was the luckiest man on the planet. Until the day I discovered my wife didn't love me.'

Laleh paused to consider her words. 'I think, Tom, Sappho is only sick, she must see doctor. I believe all problems is come from illness.'

'You're right, I should have made her see a doctor when all this started, before it got out of hand. But actually, I think it's too late now, I really do. There's only so much you can do to make a person love you.'

She'd never liked Tom, right from the start, she understood that he and his mother were suspicious of her, and he had a habit of treating her as though somehow she had tricked her way into their house. When in fact the very opposite was true; it was Sappho who had begged her to stay the afternoon after they met in the park. She must fight this instinct to distrust Tom; now they must work together as a team until Sappho was better. Until it was time for her to leave . . .

'I think doctor will make Sappho better. Some womans have problem after baby. Is because of changes . . . in how you say?'

'Hormones.'

'I think that is right. Is hormones. Perhaps she must take one woman's medicine to correct this.' They were two desperate people; all decorum had fallen away. Never before did she think it would be possible to feed another man's child whilst discussing the most intimate aspects of female health issues. The curtains were open; the room was lit from within like a stage. As though in a dream, she watched a woman in a bicycle helmet walking down the street, beneath the bare, swaying branches of the trees, waiting in vain for a sense of shame to preserve her.

'It's not as simple as that, Laleh . . . It's not just a physical thing with Sappho. She doesn't love me . . . that's what this is really about.'

Laleh paused, letting the nipple fall from Hector's mouth. Propping his chest up against her hand, she rubbed his back until he gave a delicate little burp, then lay him down to the other breast. Enzo would be arriving soon; they had not established a specific time for supper, although she was almost certain he had said he was working at the pool. Without disturbing Hector, Laleh glanced down at her watch; another forty minutes until the pool closed, time to bathe both babies and give Reza his supper. It would take Enzo at least another fifteen minutes to get to the house on his bicycle. Whatever happened, she was not going to mention the letter from the Home Office. In spite of everything, this latest crisis with Sappho, the thought of their evening continued to pierce her with joy; for a few hours, at least, they would be together. She lowered her eyes, ashamed of her hunger for him.

'What am I going to do, Laleh?' Tom's face had turned white and he was crouching beside the unlit grate as though someone had plunged a knife into his heart.

'Perhaps Sappho will come later . . .' she murmured. 'Perhaps mobile is no work because battery dead.'

'I put it to charge myself, last night, when she was asleep. And she had it switched on when she left the house this morning, I checked. She's never done this before . . . she's left me, Laleh, and I don't know how I'm going to tell Maro.'

'We must wait. Tonight, perhaps, you can look where she may be . . . telephone some friends before –'

'Before I call the police?'

Laleh remained silent; Tom knew without being told what he must do.

'Hold me, Laleh.'

Startled, she looked up.

'Just for a moment. Before I go out.'

Out on the street a car door slammed, and she heard the sound of children running through the leaves. Everything was finished, anyway; this moment would have no consequences. Besides, her body could never bring her happiness; it was not made to serve her or her needs. She had used it to shield her sister, to bear one man's child, feed another's. She understood now, finally, that she would never lie in Enzo's arms; tonight she would tell him she could not see him again. Why pull him into this mess? She was too tired to keep fighting; she could not repeat her story to the authorities, there was no point. They had heard too many such tales at the Home Office, some true, some made up; she did not have it in her to turn her own horror into theatre.

She and Reza would just have to go into hiding; if they did not leave the country, the police would come looking for her, here, at the house. She must find the Turkish man in Kilburn, see if she could get back some of the eight thousand dollars – use it to live on until she had sorted out false papers. The man once said he knew someone who could arrange this.

Thoughts flipped through her mind one after another, like someone shuffling a deck of cards. Tom had crawled across the carpet and was now sitting on the floor at her feet. Holding Hector over her shoulder, she allowed Tom to rest his head on her lap, his hands clasped inside her jacket around her waist. She was aware of her naked breasts hanging over his head; some part of her brain registered the ridiculous strangeness of the contrast – his fair hair and her dark nipples, outdoor clothes and bare skin – but it was not enough to break the spell. She was too tired to stop him, too tired to work out whether this was the wrong sort of comfort.

She heard the ring of a metal gate striking against the post, then more footsteps crunching through the leaves. Life on the street carrying on as usual; no one knew, or cared, what was happening in this house. Tom's lips closed around her nipple, and she closed her eyes. Then, opening them, Laleh looked up towards the window. A man was standing in the front garden and peering into the room.

It was Enzo.

Thirty-eight

This time, even the sleeping bag was gone. The site was empty, and the area where Alexander had been sleeping was fenced off with bollards.

Sappho paused amidst the sea of commuters walking along the bridge towards Waterloo. She had known he wouldn't be there, she had known it sitting on the Bakerloo line from Queen's Park, but there was nowhere else to go.

'Sappho, *hi!*'

She froze, staring at the coffee shop inside the Festival Hall. Perhaps she could slip inside, pretend she hadn't heard.

'It's me, Arlette.'

Slowly, Sappho turned around, forcing herself to face the woman.

'D'you remember, we met at Paddington Rec – the fancy-dress party? My little boy Jacob is at school with Freddie?'

It was the beautiful black woman with the shaved head. Sappho drew her cardigan closer about her chest, aware of her unwashed hair, the rotten softness about her waist and hips.

Everything about the woman radiated health, equilibrium – bohemian good taste. She was wearing tweed trousers and a grey wool jacket with large mother-of-pearl buttons, a red scarf knotted about her throat.

Sappho stared at her, casting her mind back to the day of the party. She had liked her instantly; there'd been a definite connection between them. Once or twice, they had smiled across the crowded hall; they would have chatted, perhaps even exchanged numbers, if there hadn't been all that carry-on about Eden not turning up, Bridget lumbering around trying to organise everyone, those feral little girls coming in and stealing her purse. *In the days when you considered those to be problems . . .*

'Hi, yes . . . I remember now . . . Maro's birthday.'

'You were pregnant, I think. I take it you've had the baby?'

'He's with his father,' said Sappho sharply.

A puzzled frown crossed the woman's features; but then she rapidly collected herself and smiled. 'So you had a boy?'

'Yes.'

Her radiance was a kind of aggression, it had to be; Sappho could feel her thin sense of self withering in its light. *Know your place: you are black, I am white . . .*

'Congratulations. And how have you been keeping?'

She was a single mother, an illustrator, she lived in a housing association flat in the middle of a council estate. *I am rich, you are poor, I have a husband, you don't . . .* How strange, she was literally unable to talk to her; even people she didn't know had now become too dangerous. *I have crossed the Rubicon . . .*

There was a silence, while a siren wailed and inside the café a child knelt by the window and began banging the plate glass with a toy.

'Anyway, it was nice seeing you again, Sappho.' Arlette held out her hand, as though to shake hers.

Instinctively, Sappho slid her fingers into the pockets of her cardigan. Her palms were too rough to be touched by anyone but Maro; and it was a sign of her daughter's new devastating maturity that she no longer even flinched.

The sleeve of Arlette's dove-grey jacket flopped down over her outstretched arm; fascinated, Sappho stared down at the slender wrist, the bone gleaming like a burnished hazel nut. 'A fine wrist is a sign of breeding,' her Grandmother Maro used to say. Still, there was no way she was up to shaking anybody's hand. She had left that person behind.

Drawing the jacket about her neck, Arlette swiftly converted the handshake into a wave, and attempted one last smile. Then, unexpectedly, she reached into her battered leather satchel and took out a card.

'My numbers are here – mobile and landline. I live just behind Kilburn High Road, in West Hampstead. If you ever feel like a coffee, give me a call.'

Sappho removed her hand from her pocket just long enough to take the card, then quickly slipped it back in. She watched the elegant figure weave through the crowds towards the river, then stared down at the card, with its hip, flock-wallpaper design of blowsy pink flowers on a brown background. Childishly, she crumpled it in her hand and dropped it on to the ground. There – she had never seen Arlette.

The fever was emanating from her hand, she was almost certain of this; in the sodium glare of the streetlights, the skin of her palm was pitted and marked like a close-up of the moon; even in the last few hours, the pustules appeared to have multiplied. Wires of pain irradiated around her body; she had no idea it was possible to feel pain in so many places. And her breasts were aching with unexpressed milk.

She must take something to bring the fever down, clean up her hand, then . . . Then she would decide. Letting herself be carried along by the crowd, she walked past the Shell Building, along the covered walkway, back towards Waterloo.

The bright lights and confusion of the station unsettled her; so many trains, so many destinations, all those competing announcements echoing beneath the glass roof of the terminus; the clack and whirr of the boards, growing blank and black, with the departure of each train, the fatty smells of buttered croissants, McDonald's, Millie's Cookies, Délices de France, cauldrons of soup from a little wooden cart. You could lose yourself in a place like this; though if you looked carefully, you could spot the ones like her, the ones who were only pretending, the ones with nowhere to go.

A few days, perhaps that was all she needed; she couldn't go home in this state. She'd think of somewhere to stay, maybe even a hotel, until her hand was better, and she'd got rid of the fever. Stepping inside a dirty recess beside Smith's, she reached into her pocket, pulled out her mobile and scrolled down the recent calls until she came to 'Home'.

One ring, two rings, *let no one be in, please let no one be in*, three rings, four, five. It would be easier if she could just leave a message to tell them she was OK. *A bit late in the day for that, wouldn't you say?* She stared down at the cigarette butts littering the floor, one of them still smouldering, with a smear of lipstick on the white filter. At last, the click of the answerphone: then the terrible, piercing intimacy of her daughter's voice.

'Please. Leave a . . . a . . . *messhage* . . . after the BEEP!'

When had Tom recorded this? Instinctively, Sappho pressed the mobile towards her chest, as though to muffle the sound, then held her finger down on the 'Off' button until the screen grew dark, and the connection to her daughter dissolved before her eyes.

She walked towards the direction of Boots, past a man in a suit wheeling a bicycle with double panniers, a pretty blonde girl texting, and a group of noisy French school children heading for the Eurostar terminal. She had stumbled on to a stage, a complicit fake, where everyone except her knew their part. Before entering the chemist's, she took a ten-pound note out of her purse and held it in her good hand. At the prescriptions counter, she stood behind a woman buying vitamins and looked at the rows of medicines. Stomach and Digestive. Cough and Cold. First Aid. Eye, Ear and Mouth Care. Fever and Pain Relief. Well, she had a fever, and she certainly needed relief from pain. All kinds of different pain. But there were too many products to choose from; how would she know which was the right one for her? She must decide quickly, before the young Asian pharmacist started asking too many questions. Nurofen, Panadol, Migraleve, Solpadeine, Anadin.

'Can I help you?'

'I'd like a box of Nurofen, please.' Her voice sounded croaky, apologetic.

'Nurofen Plus, liquid capsules, gel or meltlets?'

'I'm sorry . . . .?' whispered Sappho. She should have chosen Anadin, surely they didn't come in so many varieties.

'What are you taking them for?'

'Taking what?'

'The Nurofen.' He looked too young to be a pharmacist; black adolescent down grew over his upper lip, and beneath the starched cuff of his shirt a woven thread was tied around his wrist. Away from his job, he must have another life filled with festivals, tradition – perhaps a little sister who tied that thread around his wrist during Diwali celebrations. 'May I ask what are your symptoms?'

'Oh. Fever. And pain.'

'Do you have a fever now?'

'Maybe . . . I'm not sure,' she lied.

'Well, the meltlets are a new line, they're very popular. They dissolve on the tongue, so you don't need water.'

'I'll have those, please, and some bandage. For a burn,' she added quickly.

Handing over the ten-pound note, she took her medicines and her change and walked towards the ladies' toilets. The Albanian attendant was not here this time; but the photograph of the little girl in the party dress was still up on the wall of her kiosk. Like her, she had abandoned her child for a better life . . . Dropping twenty pence into the slot, she pushed her way through the turnstile and walked towards the furthest cubicle. She locked the door behind her and pushed two pills out of the blister pack then placed them in her mouth. They foamed briefly on her tongue, leaving a synthetic lemon taste. Then she looked at her hand; she should have bought some disinfectant spray to clean it up before dressing it; later, the bandage would stick to the pustules when she tried to remove it. But there were too many people out there, she couldn't risk washing it at a basin. Then she remembered: breast milk was sterile; once she had seen a woman in a village in Greece disinfect an older child's cut whilst feeding her baby. Unbuttoning her jacket, she took out one breast and squeezed the nipple between her fingers. She wept as her son's milk ebbed away, splashing through her fingers down into the toilet.

Thirty-nine

Later that night, Laleh heard knocking on the door. Tom was out in the car, looking for Sappho, and the two babies were sleeping head to toe in Reza's cot.

'Who is it?' called Laleh through the letterbox. It was almost midnight; in a fury, she had been cleaning the kitchen cupboards for hours. Every now and then, she would take down the letter from the dresser and read it again to stoke up her despair.

'Is me. Enzo.'

Joy and shame flooded her heart. She never imagined he would return. Drawing back the chain, she opened the door.

He was standing on the doorstep, his hands in his jacket pockets. He looked pale and tired, and much older, all the sparkle and fun emptied from his features. She realised she loved his face even more like this.

'I come to learn why, only this. Then I leave.'

Laleh felt her cheeks burn; she could scarcely bring herself to look him in the eye. *My breast was in Tom's mouth – he saw everything . . .*

'Is not so easy for me to explain, Enzo. Perhaps you come in.'

Enzo appeared to hesitate; then shrugging, as though nothing she could tell him would change a thing, he followed her into the hallway. For a moment, they stood

360

beside the pram, while Laleh deliberated where they should go. She didn't want to risk Tom returning and finding her in the sitting room with a strange man, yet to take him up to her flat seemed too intimate. In the end, she decided on the kitchen; under the circumstances it seemed like the most neutral option.

'Is late for clean, no?' said Enzo, looking at the basin of soapy water on the floor beside the dresser.

Laleh smiled wanly. 'I cannot sleep, busy is better. Please sit,' she said, pulling back one of the kitchen chairs. 'You like drink tea or coffee?'

'Only water. Thank you,' he added with exaggerated politeness.

Pouring him a glass of mineral water from the bottle in the fridge, Laleh placed it on the table, then pulled up a chair opposite him.

'Why you do this thing, Laleh?'

She felt her face grow hard and closed, just as when the woman at Immigration asked her about her relative.

'You are lovers with this man, is the father of Maro, I think?'

Explain to him, explain how it happened.

'I cannot give you reason. Everything . . . everything in this house is strange today.'

'I see – is only strange? To make love with the husband of your family?'

'Is not what you think,' she protested weakly.

'I think nothing, Laleh – is enough what I see with my eyes. You invite me to your house to eat dinner, for one week I am thinking only of this, and when I arrive, I find . . . no matter, you know what I find.'

'I know, yes.'

'You like this man?'

Laleh lowered her gaze. It was unbearable; he must not leave here thinking this thing of her.

'I do not like this man, I am only sorry for him.'

'Now sorry mean you —'

'His wife, children's mother, have gone. Disappeared. The baby is hungry, I am feeding —'

'You feed this man's child?'

'I feed this man's child, yes. And when I am feeding ... what ... what you see from the window ... is happen.'

Enzo stared towards the darkened french windows. 'And you let this to happen?'

'Enzo ... I am confuse to stop to him. I learn just one hour before I must leave —'

'Leave? Where are you going?'

'Maybe to my country, maybe somewhere else in UK.'

'Why?'

Wordlessly, she took down the letter from the dresser and placed it before him on the table. He read it in silence, then looked up at her. His expression had softened.

'Why you never tell me this? Maybe I can help you.'

'I didn't know before. Only today ... I mean yesterday evening, the letter arrive.'

'What you will do?'

'Tonight is too hard for me to think what is best thing for me and Reza now.'

'I am your friend, Laleh. One friend must to help another friend. Otherwise for what we are here in the world?'

Love for him welled up inside her; her father used to talk like that, he too was a human being before he was a man. Until her relative ... the journey, Reza, she would have known instinctively how to respond to the kindness in Enzo, but now ...

'You feel nothing for me, Laleh?'

She could see the rest of her life stretching out before her: arid, empty, barren, like the plains of her country.

'I . . . I love you, Enzo.' Never before had she uttered those words to someone who was not of her flesh and blood.

'And I love you too, Laleh. But I think you already know this.'

It was not possible to feel so much happiness; she was raw with it.

'I did not want to tell you, Enzo, this I promise to myself I will not say my feelings. But my promise is not a good one.'

'It is a very good promise, it helps me a lot. Tonight I come to this house a very angry man, and I leave the happiest man in the world.'

'But you don't understand, Enzo . . . my life now is only make of problems. Police – hiding, is nothing good for you.'

'Why you must to hide? If you marry me, you do not need to hide.'

She had let herself dream of this; if she was honest, they had already been married several times over in her head, sometimes in London, sometimes in his village in Sicily, but now . . . not with this hateful letter lying between them.

'I cannot marry you . . . just for this. Too many foreign womans is marry only for stay in this country, I cannot do this. Not with you. I . . . I love you, Enzo.' She said the words again, just for the little shock of hearing herself say them. 'And I am not free to marry, I have Reza.'

'You think I want to marry you only for passport, Laleh?' he said scornfully, striking the letter with the back of his palm. 'I love you when I see you sitting in my swimming pool with the pram – same day I love you, and I promise myself one day you will be my wife, Reza my son.'

Outside in the garden, the sky was beginning to lighten. A blackbird shrilled in the tree, a high, pure note. Enzo looked at his watch. 'I have Dawn Dippers, is early swimming session at pool. If nobody is drown, I will have plenty of time to think. Many things to plan.' He got up and zipped up his khaki jacket. As though in a dream, Laleh followed him through the hallway to the door. Again, they stood opposite each other by the empty pram. He stroked her cheek.

'Sleep, *cara mia*, you look tired. I will return this afternoon, when my work is finished. We will talk again.'

It was unbearable to see him go, even for a few hours. She would die before the afternoon came. Is this what it meant to love somebody? Was the rest of her life going to be like that?

'How I will know you come back? Maybe in this day you change your mind?'

Enzo looked down at his hand; he was still carrying the letter from the Home Office. He paused and frowned. 'Like this you will know,' he said, methodically ripping the paper into shreds. Then, stuffing the pieces into his pocket, he touched his fingers to his lips and let himself out of the door.

'I will see you this afternoon. Sleep now.'

Forty

The level crossing was closed when Sappho got off the train at Mortlake. She climbed over the footbridge, walked down the steps and out of the station on to Sheen Lane.

The timber merchant's was still there, and so was the vintage-car showroom, but the little bijou emporium Theo used to call the Guilty Husbands' Shop, *he'd know all about that, wouldn't he?*, had become a Chinese alternative-health centre, while Mr Higgins, the newsagent's, who would order in his two-day-old *Kathemerini*, was now a florist's.

She could stay with Ghisela for tonight at least, get her to phone Tom and say she was safe. After that . . . one day at a time, as they say. As for Maro and Hector, well, out of sight, out of mind, as they also say.

She stared into the window of Dr Barnardo's charity shop at a gigantic, moth-eaten teddy bear. What she really wanted to know was this: what had become of her love for her children? For Tom? Where had it gone to? Why did the bruise no longer ache when she made herself picture them, together, in the house without her? Had she cut loose already? Until all this started, she had been morbidly attached to Maro; even those three hours a day at nursery had sometimes seemed too long to be parted from her daughter. Who knows, maybe Lorna had been right, love was not really her thing – at least not the kind of love that endured . . .

But what about/When we're dead and gone?/Would you love me then?/ Does love go on?

Sappho crossed the Upper Richmond Road and continued down Sheen Lane towards Vicarage Road. The sky was a deep enchanted purple, and the air was filled with the smell of fallen leaves gathered in glossy drifts by the side of the kerb. As she passed the doctor's surgery she looked at her watch; it was gone seven o'clock, after all this she hoped Ghisela would be in. And, if not, well, she'd walk back to the station, make another plan.

At the house, she saw a light was on in an upstairs bedroom; but she knew from experience that didn't mean anything – Ghisela could have left it on a timer switch to confuse burglars. Almost every house in the street had a security alarm and a Neighbourhood Watch sticker in the window – legalised voyeurs, Theo used to call them.

Memories of her father were everywhere; subsumed by years of motherhood, the move to London, she had scarcely mourned him, making sure to keep all contact with Ghisela on neutral territory. And now, back here in his world, it was all returning.

She opened the gate and walked down the path. At once, a security light came on above the door; startled, Sappho paused before pressing the polished brass bell. The sitting-room curtains were drawn, but the lining was so thick you couldn't tell if anyone was in. Sappho slipped her bandaged hand in her pocket; it had stopped throbbing, and for now the fever appeared to have subsided. She was about to ring again when from inside she heard the sound of footsteps in the hall. Behind the stained glass panel, a light clicked on, and the door opened.

Alexander.

In Ghisela's house.

'You?'

Alexander had turned pale, while she could feel her own face burning with the awful knowledge of how she must look in his eyes: unwashed hair, no make-up, a cushion of baby fat around her middle. *Lorna, only fatter . . .*

'I'm staying at Ghisela's. She's gone to Waitrose, she'll be back in a minute.'

He'd never even been to this house before, how could he possibly be staying at Ghisela's? And Waitrose? What did Alexander know about Waitrose? Shock made her temperature soar; she could feel the fever punching through the Nurofen barrier, while everything became unreal again.

'You can wait for her, if you like, she shouldn't be long.'

Alexander looked pale, but composed; surely he couldn't have been expecting her? In silence, they trudged through the house into the sitting room. The lights had been on all along, she noticed: two fringed lamps on each side of the fireplace.

They sat down opposite each other in silky, overstuffed armchairs. She looked down at her shoes, a pair of tatty green Converse which she had bought on a trip to Barcelona just before Maro was born. She had dragged some mud in with her on the powder-blue carpet; too late, she remembered slippers were the rule in Ghisela's house.

Alexander was wearing socks.

'I'm sorry about Lorna,' she blurted out.

'How did you know?'

'By chance I saw the documentary on TV.'

He looked older, sadder, like a newly bereaved widower, whereas she . . . she was just a scruffy middle-aged woman on the edge. *But he knows all about those . . .*

'Where are your children, Saff?'

My children? 'They're at home,' she stammered. 'I left them with their father.'

'Tom?'

She blushed. 'So you know about Tom. Did Ghisela tell you?'

'Bits and pieces. And Celia filled me in. Also, I saw him once, remember, on the ferry?' The expression in his dark eyes was unreadable.

Before she had a chance to absorb this dreadful image, ask him, too, why he was still in touch with Celia, they heard the front door slam and the sound of footsteps in the hallway.

The rustle of shopping bags, and Ghisela's voice: 'They were out of venison at Waitrose, but I got us a nice bit of pork shoulder –'

She froze as she walked into the sitting room. 'Sappho! Thank goodness you are here! Tom has been so worried!'

Sappho stood up to kiss her, breathing in the familiar smell of 4711 cologne and napthalene. Ghisela peered at her anxiously through her glasses. 'You are not feeling so good? Your face is burning.' Then she turned to Alexander. 'Have you offered our guest a drink? Tsk, I thought not! This is typical of men,' she said, winking conspiratorially at Sappho. 'What can I bring you? Tea, coffee, some hot Ribena perhaps?'

'Ribena would be nice,' murmured Sappho weakly.

'You stay here, I will bring it to you.'

Sappho looked around her; Theo's La-Z-Boy Aspen chair, upholstered in hideous light green leather, was still in its place opposite the widescreen TV. Theo had delighted in the ugliness of the armchair. 'A true couch potato needs a recliner,' he would say, pressing the control panel to make the footstool rise, and the backrest fall, until he was almost horizontal.

So Alexander was staying at Ghisela's! All those times she had gone looking for him at the South Bank, convinced he was sleeping rough, he had been comfortably ensconced in this fussy, overheated house –

'How long have you been staying here?'

'A few weeks . . .'

'How many weeks?'

Before he had a chance to reply, Ghisela returned carrying a tray with three glasses of hot Ribena in stainless-steel holders. Resting the tray on a sideboard, she pulled out a nest of tables and placed one beside each of them, with a cork-backed laminated coaster depicting a photograph of a rural scene.

'Sappho, before you drink I wish to take your temperature. Please put this under your tongue.'

Obediently, she put the thermometer in her mouth, listening to the droning electronic pulse. Briefly, her eyes closed, and a great tiredness overcame her, limbs flopping like sandbags over the edges of the chair. A volley of staccato beeps, and Ghisela removed the thermometer.

'Hmm, just as I thought! You have thirty-eight and seven. You have a pain somewhere? A sore throat, perhaps? What is this on your hand?' she said, noticing the bandage.

Sappho clenched her hand. The last thing she felt like doing was unwrapping the bandage in front of Alexander. Though, frankly, she still had to entirely convince herself of the reality of what was happening.

'It's an infection . . .' she murmured.

'We will go to the bathroom. I will take a look at this hand of yours, *liebe*, and after that it is bed for you. Doctor's orders. I bring you up your Ribena later. You can talk in the morning,' she said, frowning meaningfully at Alexander. 'Come now, I will help you up.'

Sappho allowed herself to be led up the stairs and they entered the bathroom on the first floor. Pulling down the toilet lid, with its stringy, violet cape, Ghisela motioned for Sappho to sit down, then took her bandaged hand in hers. As Ghisela unwrapped the dressing, Sappho stared towards the mock-Edwardian sink, the rim scalloped like a shell, with its gleaming golden taps. Dimly, she was aware of Ghisela hunting in the medicine cupboard by the door, and she felt the burn of disinfectant on the sores, but even the pain seemed to belong to somebody else.

'Now to finish we will put some antibiotic powder I brought with me from Germany,' said Ghisela, shaking the canister over Sappho's hand; then, tossing the old bandage in the waste bin beneath the sink, she put on a new dressing, fixing it in place with tiny metal clips.

'Come now to your old room, the bed is already made up, and the nightshirt you left from last time is in the dresser.'

In silence, Sappho followed her across the landing to her old room. A fringed bedside lamp was on, bathing the room in a womb-like orange glow.

'Do you need help to undress?'

Sappho shook her head and sank down on the edge of the bed; her legs suddenly felt weak.

'I go down to fetch your hot drink, and some Panadol for the fever. I will be back in one moment.'

After the door had closed behind her, Sappho bent forwards to unlace her plimsolls. She had never known tiredness like this, not even after the children were born. She folded her clothes over the edge of the chair, and hunted in the drawer for her nightshirt. Little muslin envelopes of lavender were placed between the clothes; everything ironed in tidy piles. Buttoning up the striped flannel nightshirt with her good hand, she padded barefoot across the carpet and climbed up on to the bed.

Two fat feather bolsters were propped up against the headboard, the stripy ticking material bursting out of the linen pillowcases. It was comfort beyond her wildest dreams; the quilt hovering, weightless as a downy cloud, above her limbs. I've done nothing to deserve this, she thought, sinking down into the bed.

There was a knock on the door, and Ghisela entered carrying the glass of Ribena, which she placed on the bedside table.

'Have you taken paracetamol today?' she asked, sitting down at the foot of the bed.

Sappho nodded, trying to block out of her mind the memory of the cruelly lit station, the young pharmacist with his downy moustache.

'What time, more or less?'

'Three or four hours ago, I think. Maybe more.'

'Take some more now. It will help you sleep,' she said, handing Sappho two tablets.

Sappho sat up and reached for the glass on the bedside table; washing the tablets down with the now luke-warm Ribena, she settled back on to the bolsters.

'Ghisela?'

'What is it, *liebe*?'

'Why did Alexander . . . Why did he come here?'

'Sleep now. We will talk in the morning,' said Ghisela, switching off the bedside lamp with a click. Then, after kissing Sappho on the forehead, she tiptoed out of the room.

In the middle of the night, Sappho heard a noise in the garden. Turning on the lamp, she got out of bed and, drawing back the curtain, peered through the window. A fox was standing in the middle of the garden, gazing calmly across the lawn. It could have been a dog, were it not for the unnaturally pointed ears, the pinched muzzle, the luxuriant brush of white-tipped tail crooked obscenely towards the ground. She gazed in horror and fascination into its bright, sly eyes.

And then she saw Alexander, sitting cross-legged on the loveseat beneath the canvas roof of a wrought-iron ornamental gazebo. Quickly closing the curtain behind her,

Sappho slipped on her cardigan which was folded over the chair and, picking up her Converse trainers, tiptoed down the stairs, through Ghisela's spotless kitchen towards the garden door. The digital clock on the cooker showed the time: 3:17 a.m. Sliding her feet into her plimsolls, without doing up the laces, she drew the cardigan closer about her body, and walked out into the garden.

Alexander looked up, watching her inscrutably as she crossed the lawn.

'Shouldn't you still be in bed?'

'I'm feeling better now. What happened to the fox?'

'It went towards the alleyway to forage in the dustbins.'

'Can I sit down?'

'You'll be in trouble if Ghisela catches you out here.'

'I'll take the risk. Anyway, shouldn't you be in bed yourself?'

It was delightful teasing him; a freakish backwards hurtle through time. Enough, for a moment at least, to make herself forget everything: her hand, the fever, Tom and the children waiting for her on the other side of the river. Lorna. That dreadful kiss on the ferry . . .

Without answering, he slid along to make room for her, and Sappho sat down beside him on the bench.

They sat in the darkness in not uncompanionable silence, until Sappho was the first to speak.

'I didn't even realise you knew Ghisela.'

'I didn't. At least not really.'

'So what made you decide to come here?'

'Lots of things. Way too complicated to go into now.'

'OK, can I ask you something? You can refuse to answer if you like.'

'Something tells me I probably will then,' he said sombrely.

'It's nothing . . . personal. I just wanted to know . . . whether you ever . . . I mean, where you were staying when you first came to London.'

'Nowhere.'

'As in?'

'As in nowhere.'

'So it *was* you.'

'Was me, where?'

'Sleeping rough. On the South Bank.'

'I wasn't actually sleeping there.'

'But you *were* hanging out on that building site? At least some of the time?'

'Only during the day. We weren't allowed back in the hostel until six.'

'What hostel?'

'A St Mungo's shelter in New Cross.'

'How did you end up there?'

'An old Scottish geezer I met on Waterloo station told me about the hostel. He used to work on tugboats in the Persian Gulf, then he got sick and ended up homeless in London. He took me to St Mungo's, and they sorted me out with a temporary bed. Only, like I said, you had to be out and about during the day. And you weren't allowed to leave your stuff there.'

'But surely couldn't you have . . .?'

'Called you? I thought it could make things awkward,' he murmured delicately.

'So how did you end up at Ghisela's?' she asked, quickly changing the subject.

'She saw me once. There was a lunchtime concert in the foyer of the Festival Hall, an Austrian string quartet or something, and I'd gone in to use the toilets and warm up a bit. There was a guy from Thessaloniki I was friendly with in Costa Coffee who sometimes used to slip me a cappuccino and a sandwich, but his boss was on duty that day, so I was just hanging around, waiting for him to leave.'

'And Ghisela recognised you?'

'Actually, I recognised her first. Remember we all went out to that taverna in Kiffissia, the last time she and Theo were in Athens? I didn't get the chance to talk to her much that time, but I remembered her face, and I was pretty sure it was her. Anyway, I went over and said hello, and she asked me what I was doing in London. Turns out she'd been trying to contact me in Athens when she first heard about Lorna.'

'How did *she* know about Lorna?'

'I don't know. I guess Celia must have told her.'

'So turns out everyone knew apart from me?' murmured Sappho wonderingly.

'Pretty much. Not that it really matters now.' His voice was steady, neutral. 'Anyway, we got talking, and when she found out about St Mungo's, she wouldn't hear of me going back, and she asked me back to her place.'

'And you went?'

'It was only meant to be for a while, until I got myself sorted. I was a bit of a headcase . . . and I had some health problems too.'

'What kind of health problems?'

'The usual stuff all homeless people get. A chronic bronchial thing I couldn't shake, ringworm, headlice, that kind of attractive complaint. Nothing Ghisela's GP couldn't sort out with a course of antibiotics.'

Sappho shivered. Her teeth were chattering, and the effects of the Panadol were beginning to wear off.

'I think you should go back in the house now, Saff. You'll catch your death out here.'

Standing up, he held out his hand to help her up from the bench. For a moment, they looked at each other, and Sappho hesitated. Then she held out her good hand, and slipped it easily into his. Together, they walked across the wet grass towards the house. Halfway across the lawn, a security light came on above the garden door and, startled, they looked at each other. In its glare, Sappho noticed for the first time that his hair had begun to go white around the temples. Her heart smarted with tenderness; could Alexander have grown old before he'd had a chance to live?

They slipped off their shoes and left them on a sheet of newspaper by the kitchen door; then, giggling, they tiptoed up the stairs to the landing. Outside her bedroom door, Sappho paused with her hand on the polished brass doorknob.

'Come in for a bit. Until I get to sleep.'

Impassively, Alexander stared at her; then, without answering, he followed her into the room.

Sappho placed her hand on her forehead; the fever had returned, though not as fiercely. Popping two Panadol out of the box Ghisela had left on the dresser, she gulped them down with some water and, shivering, she slipped under the covers, pulling them up around her ears.

'You look like a little mole,' he said, sitting down on the end of the bed.

'R-r-remember when Theo used to call you Tarka?' she said, teeth chattering.

In the light of the fringed lamp, Alexander's face grew sombre. 'I loved Theo, you know. He was like a father to me.'

He didn't know. It was unbelievable, but he really didn't know.

'Did you ever ask yourself why?' she asked slowly.

'Why what?'

'Why Theo felt like a father to you?' She hadn't looked for this moment in the end; after all these years it had come looking for her.

'No.'

'Come on, Alexander. Surely you must have wondered. Or perhaps you knew all along.'

'Knew what?'

'I'm not going to spell it out for you.'

'All right then, if you won't, I'll say it. You think Theo is my father.' His face was unreadable, and Sappho felt a sudden stab of anger at the secret she had been forced to carry alone all this time.

'I happen to *know* Theo is your father.'

'Oh, and how is that?'

'On Patmos . . . that time I went off after our argument, I overheard that cow Vasso talking about it to her niece down in the kitchen. The moment I heard it, I knew it was true. And not only that, I can't believe we were so naive that we didn't think of it before. Come on, Alexander, it's obvious.'

'What's obvious?' He picked up the edge of the counterpane, running the fringe along his finger.

'That Lorna and Theo had something going.'

'They did, years ago, but not when we were kids,' he replied steadily.

'What makes you so sure?'

'Because Lorna already had a lover.'

'Oh, and who was that then?'

'My father.'

'Your father?'

'Yes, my father.'

'Hang on, when . . . you know, when we had our . . . our *thing*,' in spite of herself, Sappho felt herself blush, 'I remember we talked about your father, and you said you didn't know who he was. In fact your very words were "Lorna's not that clear about it in her own mind", or something along those lines. So you were lying?'

'I wasn't lying. When you asked me I really didn't know.'

'But you do now.'

'Yes.'

'And?'

'His name is Roy Strong, he lives in a nursing home in Eastbourne.'

'You're joking! Not that old guy on the documentary – sorry, I mean Tatiana's . . .'

'That's the one.'

'Hang on. In that interview . . . I distinctly remember him saying it was all over between him and Lorna when she gave away Tatiana for adoption.'

'It *was* over. He chose to stay with his wife, tried to brush it all under the carpet. But Lorna kept up with him when she was staying with her parents in Hastings, and I guess during one of those visits –'

'So Tatiana's your full sister, not even a half?' Jealousy pierced her heart; Tatiana had taken her place, she was nothing to him now.

'My full sister.'

'And when did you find out?'

'My grandfather told me before he died. He showed me a photograph of Lorna and Roy on the pier in Brighton, when she was still at boarding school. I actually look a bit like him; he had Welsh blood, he was quite dark when he was a young man. His name is on my original birth certificate. Lorna only changed it when we came to live in Greece.'

'But on the documentary, Roy said nothing about having a son. Surely he would have mentioned it – if nothing else, to smoke Tatiana out?'

'He didn't know either, at this stage.'

'What, Lorna never told him?'

'I guess she thought there was no point. He didn't leave his wife first time round when she was pregnant with Tatiana, so she knew she couldn't exactly count on him in a crisis.' For the first time, a note of bitterness had crept into his voice.

'And she never let it out about Tatiana? Not even to you, when she was . . .?'

'Drunk? No, not once. Lorna was like that. If something hurt her, she could push it to the back of her mind, kid herself that it never happened. The drink was to cork it all in.'

'Do you mind talking about this, Alexander?' There was a kind of austere beauty in his self-control; it was disgusting, she was actually getting off on his pain.

'Mind what?'

'That, you know . . . that she could leave you like that. After all, she still had another child in the world. You don't have to answer if it's too painful,' she added hurriedly, suddenly ashamed of her prurience.

'I thought I was losing it, Saff,' whispered Alexander, rubbing his knuckles into his eyes. 'I kept having these dreams, where she was drowning, and there was nothing I could do to save her. But I can't hold it against Lorna that she chose to take her own life. There's only so much unhappiness a person can take; beyond that, life just becomes pointless. Lorna reached that point; she literally had nothing left to live for – or at least she thought she did . . .' he trailed off, impassively.

'So does Roy know about you now?'

'I wrote to him. We've spoken on the phone.'

'But you've never been to see him?'

'I will at some point. Maybe. I've talked to Carole a couple of times, too –'

'Carole?'

'Tatiana. My sister. Her name is Carole now.'

'What – so she got in touch?' asked Sappho falteringly.

'She finally wrote to Roy after the documentary was broadcast. She's been to visit him at the Home.'

'What's she like?'

'Scottish. Nice. She lives in Aberdeen. She's a GP, married, with two little boys. Which makes me an uncle.'

'So you're sorted then, Alexander,' she said lightly. 'New father, sister, nephews . . .'

'If you say so. Now can I ask you something?'

378

Sappho nodded, licking her fever-scorched lips.

'Do you love your husband, Saff?'

Therein lay the border, the line in the sand. The demarcation between two selves, two entirely different kinds of life.

'I thought I did . . .' she said, slowly, treacherously.

'Until?'

'Until I saw you that time on the South Bank.' Her heart beat faster, and she lowered her eyes, remembering their first kiss on the stairs of the Athens house. Her unlucky little brother. *Except of course now he isn't . . .*

'I don't understand, Saff. What's seeing me got to do with your feelings for Tom? Either you love someone, or you don't,' he said stubbornly.

'When I saw you sitting there with your sleeping bag under the Royal Festival Hall, it was like opening a cupboard and having a ghoul lash out at you. Once I saw you there, it seemed my life in London just wasn't possible any more.'

'What about if you hadn't overheard Vasso on Patmos that time. Would we have still –'

'Stop – please don't say it . . .'

'Can I lie next to you? Just for a bit?'

'I'm a married woman now, Alexander, remember?'

In spite of herself, Sappho felt her heart quicken. Shifting further down the bed, she lifted up the quilt and, fully dressed, Alexander settled down beside her. They lay together, face to face on the pillow. He stroked her cheek then tilted her chin up with his forefinger and she felt his lips close around hers.

As his hand slid up her nightshirt, caressing the belly which until recently had held her baby son, an exquisite pang of loss pierced her at the memory of the lithe young girl lying naked on the bed in Athens, the shock of his tongue on her clitoris, her gold sandals tossed on to the floor. In just six years she had grown old, mumsy, her flesh lumpen and set in its ways; Tom, the children, had claimed her body as theirs.

He parted her thighs and unbuttoned his jeans with one hand. She felt his penis sliding inside her. He groaned, and lay there perfectly still, as though holding back from the gateway of pleasure, his face buried in her neck, while she felt his heart hammering through his breastbone. Beneath the quilt, his hand found hers, and their fingers locked.

'How can I go back to my life now that I've found you again?' She was crying now, the tears sliding unheeded down her cheek.

Rolling her nightshirt all the way up, he kissed one breast. The tip of her nipple was wet with milk.

'I feel like a thief,' he groaned.

'I mean it, Alexander. What can we do?'

She felt him shudder as his penis withdrew, flopping heavily, still erect, inside her thigh.

'Listen to me, Saff.' His eyes were serious. 'We'll manage like we managed when we were little. Remember it would never have worked between us –'

'But –'

'Shh.' His finger was on her lips. 'You know what I mean. You were always trying to get away from us. From me and Lorna.'

She must have told him about that night she turned up at the house in East Sheen.

'Forgive me, Alexander,' she whispered. 'I'm sorry.'

'You're too hard on yourself, Saff. Just because a long time ago our parents were friends, and we slept together once, it doesn't mean you owe me anything. You've made your own life now –'

'So you don't love me any more?'

'I'll always love you, you should know that. Even if we never see each other again.' *Love, like starlight, never dies*

. . . He smiled, and wiped the tears from her cheek. 'Who knows, maybe one day we'll even find a way to be friends.'

Then he took her in his arms, and she lay her head on his breast, while he stroked her hair until she slept.

Ghisela found them like that, slumbering like babes, when she came in next morning with Sappho's breakfast. Wordlessly, she left the tray on the dressing table and shut the door behind her.

Forty-one

Maro was eating fishfingers in Bridget's kitchen.

She looked up, accusingly, as Sappho entered the room.

'Bridget said we were going to feed the ducks.' She stared at her mother. 'She *said* we could, when Freddie and Martha come back from school.'

'Daddy's waiting outside, *moró mou*. He's in the car with your brother. I . . . I can take you to feed the ducks later, if you like.'

Discreetly, Bridget melted out of the room, through the french windows into the garden, where she began unpinning the washing from the line. A bright harsh light poured in through the glass, which seared Sappho's eyeballs, making her dizzy. She held on to the back of a chair to steady herself.

'What happened to your hand?'

'Mummy hurt it. It's getting better now.' Her daughter's hostility was frightening; she ached to take her in her arms, but she was terrified of being rebuffed.

'Did you have a nice time with Freddie and Martha?' Sappho swallowed in an effort to keep her voice steady.

'Freddie kept coming into our room in the night and annoying me. He wouldn't let me sleep. He said something mean to me . . .'

'What did he say, my darling?'

382

'He said a *big* lie. About you.'

'About me?' Sappho flushed hotly.

'He said . . . I'm not telling you what he said.'

'Tell me, my sweet. That way we'll know if he made a mistake or not.'

Hesitantly, Maro got up from her chair and walked slowly across the kitchen. She was wearing slipper socks over red and green striped tights, and one of Andrea's hand-knitted cardigans over her pinafore. Her hair had been brushed, and neatly braided, with a Hello Kitty clip on each side of the parting. Sappho stood perfectly still, willing her to come towards her, as though her daughter had been transformed into some timid, woodland creature. She tried to relax the muscles on her face, wishing she had sat down earlier so she would not now be towering, monstrously, above Maro.

Out in the garden, Bridget was killing time, slowly gathering up the clothes pegs from the table, and dropping them one by one into a cloth bag. A ginger cat slunk across the top of the fence. *If it carries on walking through over to the next garden, my daughter will return to me –*

'He said you weren't coming back!' howled Maro, head-butting Sappho's stomach with her skull. Her arms were round her mother's waist, rubbing her eyes against the waistband of her jeans, as though to wipe away some private horror only she could see. 'He said you'd gone away from us, Mummy . . . he said you weren't *ever* coming back!'

You did this to her . . . Five years old, and her daughter's childhood was over. There would always be shadows now, a sunless quality to her life, a question mark about love. She'd had her chance to break the pattern, to set her children free; instead, she'd crassly reverted to type. Gently, Sappho unlocked Maro's hands from behind her back, and knelt down before her on the kitchen floor.

'Look at me, Maro,' she said, tilting up the little bowed face. 'Look up at your mummy.' All that history swimming about in those grey eyes; she ached for the days when her daughter's face had been a mask of childish self-absorption. Or maybe that was how she chose to remember it – her way of plunging the knife deeper into her own heart. 'Listen to me, just for a moment.'

Sitting down on one of the chairs, she picked Maro up with her good hand, and settled her on her lap. She felt lighter than she remembered, a wraith, a spirit child, the bones of her haunches digging heartbreakingly into her thighs. Whereas Hector, Hector seemed to have grown into a little bullock since they'd started him on the formula. She touched her breasts; her milk was still there . . . if he wanted it.

'Mummy hasn't been very well, Maro. You know that, don't you?'

Maro nodded, gnawing distractedly on the cuff of her sleeve.

'Well . . . well, I'm better now, and you'll see everything is going to be back to normal.'

Maro let her arm fall to her lap. 'Did you get ill because of Hector?'

'Of course not, my sweet! Why would you think that?'

'Because Daddy keeps saying "Mummy's tired, Mummy's tired, let Mummy rest" – all the time! It's *boring*! You weren't tired before we had Hector.'

'You're right, my sweet. It *is* boring. How about we go to the chemist and get some special energy vitamins. Shall we do that right now? Some for me, and some for you?'

'And what about Daddy? Will you get some special vitamins for him?'

'We'll get some for Daddy, too. Just a minute, my darling, let me open the door for Bridget.'

Loath to let Maro out of her arms, even for a moment,

she picked her up and, settling her on her hip with her good hand, walked towards the french windows. Beneath her hair, Maro's hot neck smelled musky and sweet; the joy of it made Sappho faint. As she turned the handle, Bridget gazed down enquiringly at the bandaged hand.

'I'm taking antibiotics for it. It's fine. Listen, Bridget, I just wanted to say –'

'Say nothing, I don't want to hear a word.' Placing the basket of folded washing down on the floor, she turned to Maro. 'Listen, poppet, why don't you find your shoes and run and get your Topsy doll from Martha's room while I make your mummy and me a nice cup of tea.'

Maro hesitated for a moment, then slid out of her mother's arms and hopped in her slipper socks along the wooden floor. At the kitchen doorway, she paused and peered back into the room.

'You'll wait for me here, Mummy?' Her expression was comical, gallant, but the flicker of fear in her eyes pierced Sappho's heart.

'I'd better pass on the tea, Bridget. Thanks, anyway, but Tom's waiting in the car with Hector,' she said, swallowing hard, to make the lump in her throat subside. She looked around Bridget's tidy kitchen, at the recipe books lined up on a shelf above the fridge, Freddie's Key Stage One flashcards helpfully pinned up on the doors of the cupboard – 'the', 'with', 'that', 'dad' – the family weekly planner on the wall.

'I should take a leaf out of your book, Bridget, maybe go to one of your Positive Parenting classes,' said Sappho wryly, listening to the door of Martha's room banging upstairs.

Bridget was silent, then a kind of low cunning crossed her features and, unexpectedly, her face crumpled.

'Nick's been having an affair. A woman from the gym. But we're working through it,' she said hurriedly, as Maro's footsteps were heard on the stairs.

Guiltily, Sappho felt a stab of delight at this news – *so, we're partners in failure* – instantly followed by a wave of remorse. Poor Bridget; she worked so hard to get it right, harder than anyone else she knew. And yet at the end of the day, everybody's marriage was a patch job; hers was probably no worse than anyone else's.

She didn't have a template, that was the problem. There had to be a middle ground out there which lay somewhere between Theo and Celia's non-marriage, and Bridget's high-maintenance fantasy. What she didn't know, of course, is whether she and Tom would find that middle ground – whether it had been too churned up for them ever to build their house on it.

'You're too *hard* on yourself, Saff . . .' Alexander had already gone when Tom came to collect her; he left Ghisela's house when she was in the bath, before she had a chance to say goodbye. It was better that way, she wouldn't have known what to say to him. *One day, I hope you'll find a woman who loves you as much as I loved you, as much as I'll always love you.* Forcing herself to imprint that desire on to her brain until it started to feel like the truth. Almost.

'Come, my darling,' she said, taking Maro's hand. 'Daddy's waiting in the car.'

Forty-two

'I wondered where you'd gone,' said Tom, suppressing the hysteria in his voice.

Resisting the temptation to switch on the Anglepoise lamp, he sat down opposite Sappho at the desk, gazing out across the dark lawn until his heartbeat returned to normal. Every single light in the house blazed as though to mock his frantic search. She'd only been missing for a few minutes, and yet already he'd allowed himself to imagine the worst.

'Sorry, I should have said I was going into the shed,' murmured Sappho politely.

They could go on like this for ever, thought Tom bleakly, two strangers circling around the elephant in the room. The thought of years and years of this filled him with anguish. *Though if you'd had the courage to talk to her, she might never have left in the first place.*

'You still love him, don't you?'

Sappho started. 'How did you know?' she stammered.

'Celia told me some; I rang her in the end. And Ghisela. The rest I pieced together.' His voice, even to himself, sounded eerily composed. 'You didn't answer my question, Saff. Do you still love him?'

'I can't talk about it, Tom . . . not now.'

'So it's business as usual, then,' he burst out savagely.

'You have your secrets, and I just have to learn to live with them!'

'You're right to be angry. It's just that I can hardly make sense of it in my own mind. It's been six years. I never thought I'd see Alexander again –'

'And now you have, you wonder why on earth you married me.' Clean, righteous anger surged through his veins. *Though pity you never showed some of that fire before, Tom.*

'I don't, Tom. I love you, and I never regretted marrying you, no matter how bad things have been recently. You might not believe it, but it's the truth. It's just that back then, I mean when I left Greece, everything was unresolved, and now it's all come back, I hardly know what I feel about anything.'

Tom felt a hot wind fanning about his face, as the angel of fury beat its gigantic wings.

'I don't know what will happen to us, Saff; maybe we won't get through this, maybe we will.'

Astonishingly, his marriage seemed to have become a thing of probabilities, a fragile construct to be tossed about to discover how deep the fault lines lay.

In the dark, he heard a sudden intake of breath, and what sounded like Maro's pencils clattering from the desk on to the plywood floor. Sappho wasn't used to hearing him speak his mind, but she would have to learn. And then a strange thought came to him: One way or the other, this will be the making of you, Tom.

'If we do try, and make a go of it, I mean, then things have got to change. I'm tired of living with someone who has nothing to share. In the end, the children aren't enough to keep us together.'

There was silence, and he heard the hollow musical chime of wood on wood as she laid the pencils out on his desk.

'But don't you see, that's the tragedy of it, Tom?' she burst out. 'I can't allow myself to have a past if we're to carry on. I have to forget about . . . about all this. Which leaves us precisely where we started. With secrets.'

'You're wrong. We can never go back there, Saff, even at the expense of our marriage. I just can't do it any more,' he said slowly. 'I'd rather get a divorce.'

'I can't either, Tom,' she whispered. 'So what do we do?'

'We wait and see, I suppose. Play things by ear, while I learn to know and love your past.' He tried to prevent a note of bitterness from creeping into his voice.

'Even if that past has ghosts?' In the dark, Sappho's voice sounded thin, ethereal.

Tom sighed. 'At least the ghosts have faces now.'

Greece and England, 2004

Forty-three

Tom awoke early and lifted back the cabin curtain. The sky was getting light, and the low brown hump of an island was visible in the distance. Just a bare rock, with a small white church perched on its furthest promontory. He glanced at his watch; it was half-past five. Another hour before the ferry was due to dock.

He'd booked a family cabin this time: three single beds and a travel cot for the baby. Their suitcases stood lined up at the door beside the folded-up pushchair; the rest of their stuff was going as freight. For a moment, Tom closed his eyes, listening to the thrumming of the ship's engine, the slap of waves against the hull, hoping the sound would lull him back to sleep. But it was hopeless; he felt too alert to stay in bed a second longer.

He switched on the reading light above his bed, picked up his clothes from the chair and hurriedly dressed, careful not to make any sound. Both children were in the bed with Sappho; Maro must have climbed in during the night, one arm flung around her mother's neck as though to pin her down to the pillow. While Hector . . . Hector, sensibly, was rediscovering the joys of the breast.

Picking up his wallet off the metal side table, Tom slipped on his shoes and tiptoed towards the door. The key was hanging in the lock, with the cabin number engraved on to a perspex fob. Seventeen. A lucky omen – he and Sappho met on Patmos on the seventeenth of August, the address of the house in Ladbroke Grove where they had been so happy was 117 Bassett Road, Hector was born on the seventeenth of October. Though in truth, it was an engineered sort of coincidence; he had selected this cabin himself when he booked the tickets online.

Gently, Tom turned the key in the lock, and was about to step out into the corridor when he heard a voice.

'Where are you going, Daddy?'

In the dark, he saw Maro's eyes were wide open.

'Go back to sleep, darling. Daddy's just going for a walk around the ship.'

'Can I come with you?'

Tom hesitated, and looked at his watch. Less than an hour before they docked, but she could always have a siesta in the afternoon.

Siesta . . . just the word made him feel happy. *Long afternoons to get reacquainted with my wife* . . . A knuckle of anxiety clenched around his heart. The shadows were still there, but he forced himself to push them to the back of his mind. *Don't even go there* . . . What did that funny old bird Ghisela say: 'Dark thoughts lead to dark places . . .' Well, no more dark places; they were travelling south, now, towards the sun.

'Come on then, Mousie. Try not to wake your brother.'

Releasing Sappho's neck, Maro slipped out of the bed and stood in the middle of the cabin floor in her pyjamas.

'Are we there?' asked Sappho sleepily from the bed.

'Not long now. Maro and I are going exploring. They'll announce it when you need to get up. D'you want me to bring you anything from the café?'

'Yes, please. A *metrio*.'

'What's that again?'

'A Greek coffee. Medium sweet.'

'Where are my clothes, Daddy?'

'Don't worry about getting dressed, you can go as you are.'

'In my pyjamas?' Maro's voice was outraged. 'Everyone will *laugh*.'

Tom sighed; at this rate it was hardly worth bothering. *Here we go again, knee deep in the old domestic blob*; yet in truth he couldn't get enough of it. The keys of paradise had been restored to him. All night long he kept waking up, listening to the sounds of his family slumbering, the four of them together in the cosy little cabin, the sighs and the breathing, the intermingled dreams; Maro calling out once or twice in her sleep, the lusty clicking of Hector at his mother's breast.

'How about we put your Maisie jumper over your pyjamas, and your plimsolls underneath? It'll look like you're wearing a very smart tracksuit.'

'All right, Daddy.'

'Come on then.'

Shutting the cabin door behind them, they walked down the carpeted corridor towards the upper deck. People were already lining up with their suitcases in the smoky lounge; a wall-mounted television set showed a studio panel arguing noisily in Greek: a blowsy middle-aged woman with dyed red hair, a busty blonde, sipping from a tumbler of water, and a clownish old man wearing a Zorba-style fisherman's cap. The first thing to sort out was going to be language lessons. Then a nursery school for Maro.

'D'you want anything to eat, Mousie?'

'You mean breakfast?'

'I'm not sure if the restaurant's open yet. Let's see what they sell over at that kiosk.'

He picked her up and walked across the floor towards the bar; the sun was up now, casting brilliant shafts of light on the royal-blue diamond-patterned carpet. Sappho was right, Maro had lost a ridiculous amount of weight. Hope-fully, she would put it all back on with a bit of sea air.

'What did Mummy ask for again?'

'A *metrio* coffee. Remember?'

'Clever Mousie. You'll see, you'll be yacking away in no time. D'you want a juice and a bag of those mini crois-sants?'

'Yes, please. Peach juice. Can we go outside to drink it?'

'Just for a sec. Otherwise Mummy's coffee will go cold. And I'm not sure we're supposed to be taking the china cups outside, but let's hope no one sees us.'

After paying for the food, they carried it out of the door on to the deck. Placing the coffee between them on the green painted bench, they sat down. The wind blew through Maro's hair, whipping her curls over her eyes.

'Is that Patmos over there?' she asked, pointing to a distant land mass as she swept her hair off her face.

Tom looked at his watch. 'I'm not sure – it's either Leros or Patmos, depends if the boat's on time or not. Why don't you try one of those croissants?'

He took one out of the foil bag and handed it to Maro. Contemplatively, she held it in her palm, then took a delicate little bite from one corner.

'Daddy?'

'Yes, Mousie.'

'Did the packers put my sailor in the boxes?'

'I'm almost certain they did –'

'And my Felicity Wishes calendar? And my sea shells from Sardinia? And my Geomag set, *and* –'

'I'm pretty sure it's all there, but if anything's missing, we can get Laleh to send it out to us.'

'But how will she know our address in Patmos?'

'Well, we left it for her, of course.'

'But Laleh can't write very well, Daddy.'

'Who told you that?'

'Granny Andrea said so one time when Laleh signed my reading record book . . . when Mummy, you know, that time when Mummy wasn't there . . .'

'Well, Granny Andrea probably wasn't wearing her glasses that day,' interrupted Tom. There were advantages, he was coming to see, to being a rich property developer with no job. The miracle, of course, was that Sappho agreed to Patmos without a fuss.

'I *know* what we can do . . .'

'What's that, Mousie?'

'We can ask *Enzo* to write the address on the parcel,' said Maro triumphantly.

'Of course we can. I'm sure Enzo's got beautiful handwriting. Now why don't you finish your croissant.'

Frowning, Maro took an even smaller bite out of the opposite corner, while Tom pulled his BlackBerry out of his pocket, and idly scrolled down the screen for emails. *You're a lucky man, Tom.* If Laleh had been a different woman (*go on, admit it, the woman you and your mother believed her to be*), if Enzo hadn't come along when he had . . . if he hadn't found Sappho at Ghisela's, who knows what madness might have taken place that night . . . He shivered; his whole life had been balanced on the slenderest of knife-edges. Somehow he had managed to pull back from the abyss. *Though that doesn't mean the abyss isn't still there waiting to gobble you up . . .*

The first thing he would do when he got to Patmos was light a candle in that church down by the port. One email from his accountant, that could wait, another from an investment company flogging a plot of land up towards College Road. Deliberately, he switched off the screen and stuffed the BlackBerry back into his pocket. He'd had enough of properties, building them, selling them, speculating on other people's lives . . . He shut his eyes and stretched out his legs, basking in the warm sun. It was surprisingly hot when you were out of the wind.

'I was wondering what happened to my coffee.'

'So you're up?'

'Hector decided he wanted to go exploring, too.'

'Quite right, little man,' said Tom, taking the baby from Sappho and holding him upright on his lap. He had solid, footballers' legs, with wide, square feet. A gull shrieked above them, landing clumsily on the white-painted rail. Hector stared at it intently, then began bouncing up and down excitedly on his toes.

Maro laughed, then slid her face under Hector's fist, swaying her head from side to side, teasing him, until he grabbed a handful of her hair.

'I miss Reza,' she said wistfully, untangling a lock from his fingers. 'Why couldn't Laleh come with us to Greece?'

'You know why, darling. She's got to stay in London to practise her English. And she promised to feed Tibby and look after the house for us until we come back.'

'Enzo can feed Tibby, and Laleh can come and stay with us in Patmos,' she said stubbornly.

'I'm not sure Enzo would think that was such a good plan,' said Tom, glancing sidelong at Sappho drinking her coffee. She hadn't uttered a word since handing him over the baby. 'Anyway, what's wrong with us being together for once as a family?'

He couldn't help it; it still made him nervous when Sappho went quiet.

'How's the *metro*?'

'Not *metro*! It's *metrio*, Daddy!'

'Fine. Actually it's quite good. D'you want to try it?'

Tom took a sip. 'Yuk! I forgot about the grounds! Why on earth can't they sieve it?' he said, wiping the corner of his lips with his thumb.

'The grounds are the most important bit. They use them to read the future.'

Tom peered into the cup. Any mention of the future made him uneasy. They were still living day to day, locked into a ruthless present.

'Sorry, but it looks like a load of old mud to me,' he declared firmly.

'Well, of course it would. Look, you're meant to turn it upside down.'

They watched as Sappho placed the saucer over the cup, and in one neat movement inverted it.

'Can I see what's underneath?' asked Maro.

'Go on then, lift up the cup. What can you see?'

'It *still* looks like mud! What about you, Mummy, what can you see?' asked Maro anxiously.

Sappho's eyes were clear, the irises speckled with gold.

'I see nothing,' she said. 'I like that.'

Forty-four

Laleh sat in the sauna, warming her bones.

She was naked – or at least as good as. The red Arena swimming costume Enzo had chosen from Debenhams was cut high in the leg and low in the breast, but he assured her the design with its crossed straps was ideally suited for swimming. The black one she wanted to try on in Bhs he said was too old-fashioned – 'is for my grandmother!' was his appalled comment as he dragged her out of the store.

A Sainsbury's bag was wrapped unbecomingly around her head, fixed into place with a clothes peg. Her hair was shorter now, but even so she wished to protect it from the extreme heat of the sauna.

Picking up the sports bottle of Evian which stood beside her on the bench, she unscrewed the top and, leaning forward, squeezed a thin jet of water over the coals. A screech of steam burnt her cheeks, instantly drying the whites of her eyes; then leaning back on the bench, Laleh shut her eyes, letting the heat settle deep into her bones.

She looked down at her thighs and smiled: so there she was, baring her body for all to see in a public place; it seemed marriage to Enzo had suddenly made this possible. Admittedly, for now, the pool was quiet and she had the sauna to herself, while her robe was hanging on a peg outside, ready to slip on should her nerve suddenly fail.

After a few minutes, the glass door clicked open, and a young black man entered the sauna. Nodding briefly, he sat down on the lower step, and stretched out his legs.

'Do you mind if I put some of this on the coals?'

Laleh started, resisting the urge to cross her arms over her breasts. 'I'm sorry?'

He held out a small bottle. 'Olbas Oil. D'you mind if I put some on? Clears the sinuses, and all.'

'Please. Is good for me, I have cold.'

A delicious cloud of eucalyptus and mint rose up from the coals; Laleh inhaled deeply, letting the steam penetrate deep into her lungs. The smell was like the herbal poultices their mother would place on their chests when they were children. *Olbas Oil.* She must remember to buy some, send a bottle to Ladan. *No, she can buy it herself when she comes over.* Quickly, Laleh forced herself to think of something else; she must not make a single plan for her sister's visit until the tourist visa was actually in her hands.

She looked at her watch; almost an hour before she had to meet Reza and Enzo in the park, time for a quick dip in the pool. Climbing down the steps of the slatted bench, aware – but not *that* aware – of how exposed her rear must look from this angle, she picked up her bottle of water and, nodding politely to the man, opened the sauna door and stepped outside.

After showering briefly, she took her robe and walked down towards the shallow end of the pool. The young girl lifeguard with the creole hoops was on duty; she knew her name now, Claire. They smiled at each other, and Laleh suddenly remembered she was still wearing the Sainsbury's bag on her head. Once this would have been enough to make her flee the swimming pool in shame, but now she merely smiled, imagining how ridiculous she must look. Reaching up, she calmly pulled the bag off and stuffed it into the waste-paper basket beside the lifeguard's chair.

'Enzo not workin' here no more?' asked Claire casually. A sharp spot of pink had appeared on each cheek.

Of course – Laleh remembered now, Claire had always been a little bit in love with Enzo. How mad it made her to see them talking when she used to take Maro for her swimming lessons!

'No, he has left the Centre.'

'Ze still lifesavin', then?'

'For now, no. He is caretaker for flats. And he studies Westminster College in the night.'

Out of the blue, Tom offered him the job of managing the Iskander Lofts before the family left for Greece; Enzo accepted immediately, as it meant he could afford to begin his degree in sports psychology. And, as if that were not enough, Sappho had asked them to look after the house in their absence, so they could put money aside each month for a flat of their own. So much good fortune made Laleh uneasy, but she was learning to push such darkness to the edges of her thoughts.

'Well, anyways, say hi to him from me,' mumbled Claire, gnawing the inside of her cheek.

'I will,' promised Laleh as she walked towards the steps of the pool.

The shallow end was empty, apart from a pair of plump Arabic ladies gossiping at the edge. Laleh smiled briefly at them, then entered the water, gasping for an instant as a dark stain rimmed the red fabric of her swimming costume. When the water was up to her breasts, she leaned forward and let her body slump. Her face was beneath the surface now; she could feel the delicious coolness of the water penetrate deep into her ears and her open eyes, sweeping her hair back off her forehead.

Left arm, right arm – breathe; left arm, right arm – breathe . . . His voice was in her ear; she could hear him as clearly as though he were standing in the pool beside her, coaxing her along with his words, as he had done so many times before. *Trust the water, Laleh, she is your friend* . . . Buoyant with love, Laleh kicked up her heels until her body became horizontal, feeling her legs bob up, one by one, to the surface.

The stone in her heart had gone. She was swimming.

ACKNOWLEDGEMENTS

My thanks to Sarah Ballard, Alex Canneti, Romana Canneti, John Bicknell, Dick Davis, Jude Drake, Sarah-Jane Forder, Rose Gaete, Brian Gannon, Pat Kavanagh, Mary Morris, Sarah Morris, Alexandra Pringle, Avi Riechenbach, 'Azad' Sharif, Christiano Sossi, Mary Tomlinson and Michaela Wenkert.

A NOTE ON THE AUTHOR

Simonetta Wenkert was born in London and has lived in Athens, Rome and Jerusalem. She has worked as a teacher and as a translator of film scripts. She currently lives in West London, where she owns and runs the Italian restaurant Ida with her husband. They have three children. This is Simonetta's second novel.

A NOTE ON THE TYPE

The text of this book is set in Linotype Sabon, named after the type founder, Jacques Sabon. It was designed by Jan Tschichold and jointly developed by Linotype, Monotype and Stempel, in response to a need for a typeface to be available in identical form for mechanical hot metal composition and hand composition using foundry type.

Tschichold based his design for Sabon roman on a font engraved by Garamond, and Sabon italic on a font by Granjon. It was first used in 1966 and has proved an enduring modern classic.